The Star Catcher

Morgan True Blum

First Printing, 2023

ISBN 978-0-9980429-3-0

www.MorganTrueBlum.com

To my husband and childhood sweetheart, Michael. Every day I am humbled by your gentleness, kindness, and Christ-like patience. Your presence in my life is a constant reminder of God's unfailing goodness and love. This book is for you. Happy Anniversary, Peter Parker.

To Nonnie. I once asked you if you'd ever felt like you'd never be happy again. Your response now lives on in this book, in the words Aunt Poppy tells Faina.

To every child or teenager who has felt pressured to grow up too fast. To every child or teenager who has been mocked for their innocence. I hope this makes you feel seen.

Suggested Reading Order of The Breadwinner Series
The Breadwinner
The Glassblower
The Dream Chaser (Prequel)
The Star Catcher (Prequel)

Trigger Warning
The prologue of this book deals briefly with suicide.

Prologue
A Feast of Omens
1924

The greatest threat to a marriage after death is lack of communication. Plain and simple. You can't simply cease all conversation just because one of you is dead. The Law of the Dead needn't put an end to your correspondence with your spouse, one need only apply a little creativity.

This was the first chapter of Povelia Sterling's *Loving Your Spouse in the Afterlife*, a book Staccato's mother had gifted him shortly after the death of his wife Evangeline. He'd quailed over her purchase at the time. After all, no one was supposed to know he and Evangeline had been married, lest it be discovered that their daughter was likely a Nimbus and not a Northstar. And yet, the book had proved useful. Even now, thirty-one years later, he could often discern the purpose of his wife's visits to his dreams by way of her expression, without her having to say anything at all.

Tonight she greeted him with a relaxed and open countenance. There was none of that tension that normally seasoned her features when she was anticipating a difficult discussion, or game of charades, as Staccato often referred to it. No stiff smiles. No fidgeting. The Law of the Dead, better known as "Dead Men Tell No Tales," meant there was some information Evangeline was physically incapable of directly disclosing in a Widow's Dream. Rather, she could only help guide Staccato towards a conclusion. Prophetic dreams, thankfully, were another matter entirely. And it was clear, as she stood there with that devilish little smirk of hers, measuring his every movement with an enthusiastic glance, that Evangeline had come with a prophecy.

"I take it there shall be no guessing games tonight?" he said, with an arched simper of his own.

They were standing in a dark hall with vaulted ceilings and a checkered floor. An enormous wooden door faced them on the opposite side of the room.

"I can't promise to be entirely forthcoming," Evangeline crossed her arms, looking him up and down. "Where would be the fun in that?"

Staccato's nerves buckled beneath the thrill of her flirtations, despite his best efforts to resist. She had aged a mere three or four years following her death, as was custom for those who had died before their prime. Evangeline's demise had come just short of her peak. But she would age no more than this, appearing somewhere between the ages of twenty-five and thirty, her hair forever gold and thick, her tanned skin firm. Staccato at fifty-four, albeit a handsome fifty-four, looked it. Wavy hair of dark blonde had faded to gray, which he had shorn clean so that he was now completely bald. Even his beard had lost most of its brownish color. His face, which had been chiseled to begin with, had only sharpened with time, and his blue eyes with the long, gold lashes had grown tired and heavily-lidded. Povelia Sterling had mentioned nothing of this in her book, nor was it to be found in any book.

In Widows' Dreams, a grown miraculous always appeared at the age of their prime, but for some reason, over the years, when Staccato met Evangeline in his reveries, he continued to age. And Staccato, being the sort of man he was, was beginning to grow uncomfortable by the physical differences between them.

Evangeline crossed the hall and kissed him, paying little mind to his graying beard. Caution and joy warred inside him, neutralizing his expression into one of unreadable emptiness.

"You're late," she chided, taking his arm.

Staccato cleared his throat. "I wasn't aware I was on a schedule."

"You're not. But I expected you to fall asleep much earlier."

"Blame it on the coffee."

"I do."

Staccato rolled his eyes and smiled. "And where are we this evening, dearest?"

"A hallway."

"Well, yes, dear, I can see that," he teased.

She giggled. "I can always count on your skills of observation."

He could not help smirking at her. "Just as I can always count on your cheek."

As they approached the threshold the doors peeled back of their own accord, revealing a grand dining room. Before them were two long tables, each set with a variety of familiar foods. At the head of the table to Staccato's right sat a version of their grandson Pasha bedecked in an evergreen uniform. A coronet of silver shone against his thick, dark hair. Staccato's eyes widened.

"Is that—"

"Pasha as the King of Ursa."

Staccato's breath was stolen away. He neared his grandson, taking in his confident gaze, an expression Staccato had never seen him wear before. This version of Pasha was healthier, and more robust looking. There was self-assuredness in the way he carried himself, and yet his eyes remained as large and as gentle as ever.

At the table to his left sat a version of Pasha not quite different from his current state. This boy was thinner, weaker, and yet somehow appeared older than the Pasha sitting at the right. Dark purple lines were smeared beneath his eyes like smoke. Without speaking a word he managed to express an attitude of bitterness and defeat.

Staccato was accustomed to this arrangement. The many feasts were a fairly common setup in prophetic dreams and simple to read. Each table represented the potential outcome of a decision. The more potential outcomes, the more tables. Here there were only two.

Evangeline clung to his elbow. "A time is coming when you will have to decide whether or not to return Pasha to Voiler or leave him in New York. The table on the right will show you what could happen if Pasha takes back the throne of Ursa. The one on the left will show you what could happen if he stays where he is now. I think you know the rest." She let go and stepped back.

Staccato began with the table to the right. He reached first for the ear of corn in the golden bowl. Carefully, Staccato peeled back the husk. A strand of silver hair sprouted from amongst the pale silk. Staccato plucked it from the ear.

"One."

As he continued to peel back the husks, more and more silver hairs began to sprout from the corn.

"Two … three … five … twelve …" They were growing exponentially. Weary of counting, he pulled back the leftover husk to discover all the remaining strands of silk were silver, and too numerous to count. Staccato's mouth hinged open as he stared up at his grandson in awe.

"A long, and prosperous reign."

Pasha made no sign that he could hear or see Staccato, but went on sitting regally at the head of the table. Staccato moved on to the chalice sitting on Pasha's right. As he lifted it to the light, wine as red as a sunset sloshed over the side, spilling onto the table. Staccato raised his eyebrows, impressed.

"Marriage," he explained to Evangeline. She may have known the general meaning of the prophecy, but she wasn't always acquainted with the finer points. He appraised Pasha with a proud smile. "A passionate one."

Had the cup been empty it would've signified a single life. That it was spilling over illustrated a heart overflowing with passion for his bride.

Careful to keep the wine from spilling any further, he held the cup to his lips and drank.

Evangeline took a step closer. "How does it taste?"

Staccato offered her the cup and watched her take a tentative sip. Her eyes crinkled with delight.

"It's sweet."

By now, Staccato was beaming with pride. "A bitter taste would have signified a bitter marriage. But in this scenario, Pasha's is as sweet as cake."

He eagerly reached for the pomegranate sitting before him. Glittering, red seeds like rubies fell from the open wedge and scattered across the table.

"Fertility." He split the fruit open. There, embedded in the pale flesh, were four golden seeds. Staccato tenderly cradled the pomegranate in his palm, his words soft. "Four children."

Gently, he coaxed the seeds from their hull with his finger. Two of the seeds stuck together. Staccato chuckled and held them out for Evangeline to see.

"Twins."

When he had managed to successfully remove the four seeds without changing color, he sighed in relief. Had any of the germs traded their golden hue for black it would have foretold of a miscarriage. A seed that turned green and then marbled with mold indicated a child that would die before it reached maturity.

Staccato returned the pomegranate with the four seeds to the plate. "A secure and healthy dynasty indeed!"

At the center of the table was the heart of a pig. Staccato frowned and scratched at his beard.

"War."

Evangeline put a comforting hand upon his shoulder. "Well, you can hardly be surprised. If Pasha were to take back the throne and drive the C.O.N. out of Ursa, then war is inevitable."

Staccato gave a vague and distant nod. He supposed she was right. Still, what would it mean for their grandson?

As he moved further down the table, he happened upon some items with multiple interpretations: a salmon, a basket of yeast rolls, and an unripened peach. Staccato eyed these dishes warily. A miraculous's prophecy was not always set in stone. The future was a malleable thing that could easily be altered by choices and false steps.

On a small plate lay a single black spotted mushroom. Staccato plucked the fungus from the dish and held it to the light. His brow furrowed.

"What is it?"

Staccato glanced hesitantly towards his wife, wondering if it best to share the omen's true meaning. Under ordinary circumstances, the dead were at peace and could not be shaken by earthly fears and woes. However, for reasons Staccato could not explain, this was not the case with Evangeline. She was as she had been in life: easily affected by strong emotions, and prone to fits of despair. But she'd sense if he were lying.

"Before he has outlived his youth, Pasha will lose someone very close to him."

Color drained from Evangeline's complexion like water from a sink. "Lydia?"

"No. Not Lydie," he hastily explained. "The loss of a mother has its own symbolism."

Evangeline fingered her collar, regaining some of her stability. "He's already lost his father. Could that be what it's referring to?"

Staccato shook his head. He studied it for some time, but could not conclude who the person might be. He sighed. "Well, there's no use dwelling on it."

As he was returning the mushroom to its plate, his eyes snagged on a symbol he had often heard of, but never seen for himself in his fifty-four years of prophetic dreams. Nestled in the bottom of a basket were two golden eggs. For a moment he had convinced himself it was a trick of the light, and that the eggs were brown rather than gold. But as he picked one up and held it, there was no mistaking the glittering metallic sheen.

"It can't be …"

Curious to the point of distraction, Evangeline was peering around his elbow within seconds.

"What? What does it mean?"

"I was taught to identify such omens as a boy during my miraculous studies at school, but I never dreamed I'd actually see one! Let alone two!"

"A golden egg?" She plucked the spare from the basket and turned it over in her hand.

"They're rare to the point of legendary."

"What do they mean?"

"Resurrection … In this case, two!"

They each stared down at the eggs in their hands.

"Perhaps it's metaphorical," Evangeline suggested. "Such as the resurrection of an idea or system."

"It's possible. But if the omen was meant to convey the resurrection of an idea as opposed to a person, why would it be so rare?"

They had come to the end of the first table. He stared at the feast laid out on the left but could not bring himself to move. The boy at the head of the table looked like his grandson, but there was something ominous about him that Staccato could not quite place. Swallowing, he forced himself towards the chalice. He lifted the cup and drank.

"Just as sweet."

With some difficulty, Evangeline managed to overpower her anxious expression with a weak smile. "Good to know."

Staccato ran his tongue over his teeth, the saccharine flavor still lingering. "Yes, whatever hardships our grandson would face in this reality, there is at least some joy to be found."

Staccato moved on to the pomegranate. A modest number of seeds spilled onto the floor. He split open the flesh. This time there was only one golden seed, and the second Staccato freed it from the hull, the germ turned green and then mottled with black. Staccato set down the pomegranate, unable to form the words. Evangeline asked no more questions but trailed away towards the window, her attention on the wall.

There was pork: a desire for a normal life; vinegar: hardship; wild mushrooms: doubt; a lone pear: isolation; and a plate of raw meat signifying discouragement. It was a feast of bad omens. At the end of the table was a turned over pitcher. Half the tablecloth was soaked in milk. A loss of faith.

Only one item remained on the table: a black teacup near Pasha's elbow. A teacup could mean any number of things depending on what was inside, and yet the sight of it frightened Staccato. Steeling his jaw, he made his way around the table. A bitter odor stung his nose. The leaves were potent, whatever it was. Carefully, he lifted the cup and peered over the edge. Inside, the string of the teabag had been tied into a knot, and the sachet torn. It was the symbol for suicide. A cry of horror leapt from Staccato's throat as he stumbled backwards. The cup fell from Staccato's grip, hitting the floor and smashing to pieces.

"No!"

Evangeline peeled herself away from the wall. Before Staccato could think of what to say, she bent over and gathered the broken pieces into her hand. Her eyebrows were drawn together but she remained calm overall.

"I know what you saw."

Staccato shook his head. "It can't be … I … surely I'm misinterpreting something."

Evangeline rose to her full height. "If Pasha doesn't leave New York, this is what will happen: as he continues to serve the Breadwinners, Pasha's mental and physical health will decline. When he is twenty-one, his wife and child will get caught in the crosshairs of a shootout with a rival gang. The grief and self-blame will be more than Pasha can handle, and he will take his own life."

Staccato braced the table to steady himself. Would this really be his grandson's fate if he remained in New York City? All this time Staccato had been trying to protect him, but in reality he had endangered Pasha's very life.

***

Staccato awoke with a gasp as his subconscious was ripped unceremoniously from the dream.

"Pasha …" Cold sweat dampened his neck. "I have to get Pasha!"

He passed a hand over his brow, struggling to catch his breath, when someone pounded on the door of his hotel room.

"Now what?" he grumbled, looking back at the clock. It was four in the morning. He ripped back the covers. "Who is it?"

"It's me," squeaked Sonata. "And Melodious, and Pyro, and Skelter."

Staccato hastily slipped on his robe and shuffled irritably to the door.

"What could the four of you possibly want at this hour?"

"Melodious had a premonition, and you need to turn on your radio now!"

Staccato groaned, turned on the light, and ushered them inside. "And you decided it required four of you to deliver this message?"

Pyro took one look around Staccato's room and tangled his arms across his broad chest. "What? How'd you get a room with a double bed?"

"Because I requested one."

"What do you need a double bed for?"

"What do *you* need one for?"

Sonata began opening up the cabinets. Her hurricane of cola-colored curls was tied into a braid, and instead of using her wheelchair, she had put on a silver pair of enchanted prosthetic legs. "Where's your radio?"

Staccato sighed and sat back down on the bed. "It's over in the corner." The mattress bounced, and Staccato was jostled unexpectedly up and down as Pyro face-planted onto the pillow next to him, musing his wild, red hair.

"Oh, yeah. This is much nicer than what I got."

Staccato's mouth hinged open in outrage. "There is a chair over there!"

There was another bouncing motion on the opposite side of the mattress as tall, lanky Skelter plunked down and squeezed one of the pillows, signing about how soft it was.

Staccato snatched the pillow out of his grasp. "Do you mind?" But by then, Melodious, who was an impressive seven feet tall with a solid frame, was already settling on the edge of the bed. Lastly, Cello, Sonata's cat, leapt atop the mattress and settled in Staccato's lap. Staccato threw his arms over his chest and gave vent to an exasperated growl.

"Alright, Melodious. Explain this premonition of yours."

"I was sleeping in my bed. I'd had a mostly dreamless sleep up to that point but—"

"Faster, Reverend, faster." Staccato knew he was being surlier than usual, but the hour made him particularly crabby.

"I had a premonition of a bird—a *phönix*—who would appoint two competitors to pursue and catch her in exchange for one wish. The first competitor she chose was Cobra Samael. And the dream ended there."

Sonata released the dial just as a voice was breaking through the static. "…*We're just getting word now that the Firebird has been spotted flying over Alnasl, making it the fifth city to have witnessed the Firebird this morning. News stations across Voiler have received hundreds of calls as more and more Fay begin prophesying the meaning of such a phenomenon. The reports generally assert that this legendary creature will challenge two people to compete to catch her. Whomever succeeds first will be granted one wish. Many are asserting that the first competitor to be appointed will be Cobra Samael.*"

"Well, why are they bloody telling everyone?" said Pyro, lifting his freckled face from the pillow. "We don't want him to find out!"

Staccato clutched the neck of his robe. "A wish would be a dangerous thing in Samael's hands." He wasn't quite sure if it was the early hour or the over-abundance of dire information he had just received, but his head was spinning.

"But what kinda wish are we talking here?" Pyro rolled onto his back.

"Yes, good question." Sonata laid out on her stomach at the end of the bed, the only addition Staccato did not object to. "There are rules about such kinds of magic, aren't there?"

It took Staccato a moment to process the question, but at length he nodded. "There are, though I'm a bit rusty as to the specifics. What I do know of the Firebird is from a card game that was popular when I was coming up. Hand of Miracles. It incorporated Voilerian myths and legends, including the Argentum.”

“What is the Argentum?” asked Melodious.

“Seven magical birds that serve as omens. I can’t remember all seven but the Firebird was one of them. It was said that the Firebird represented passion and miracles, and would one day appear at a time of great division in Voiler. She would choose two people, one from each opposing side, and have them compete to catch her. Whomever reached her first would be granted one wish, though I can’t recall what kind. It’s been so long, I’m afraid I’ve forgotten.”

They were all silent for some time, equal parts fatigued and shocked. Staccato passed a hand over his face.

“Well, you might as well all go back to your rooms. There’s nothing we can do at present but get some rest. We can discuss everything in the morning when our heads are clear.”

But not a single one of them budged. Staccato threw up his arm, utterly exhausted at this point.

“What? What is it?”

Sonata tucked her hands under her chin, the dim light casting shadows on her tawny skin. “It’s just that … we’re a little afraid to return to our rooms.”

Staccato pinched the space between his eyebrows, feeling as though he were dealing with four children.

“And why is that?”

“We think there’s a man on our floor keeping tabs on us. Pyro noticed him last night. He doesn’t look like he’s from around here—”

“It’s a hotel! Nobody is from around here!”

Sonata ignored this remark, her eyes skittering off to the side. “We all get an uneasy feeling around him, like we do with ophidians.

Especially Melodious. And he's a Moira. Not to mention, the man is unsettlingly beautiful."

Pyro lifted his head sleepily to flash her a look, but Sonata ignored him.

Staccato massaged his temples. "So a handsome stranger has you all spooked because he's been pacing the halls?"

Skelter waved and gesticulated with his free hand, which was long-fingered and rather bony. He had snatched up the pillow again and was hugging it close to his body.

"Yes," agreed Sonata. "And because he gives us a bad feeling. We're certain he's an ophidian."

"And so what if he is? We run into them now and again! It doesn't mean every single one is hunting us down!"

"Staccato, we've been attacked in three different hotels now!" argued Pyro.

"I nearly lost my arm at our last stop." Melodious cradled his elbow protectively.

"And I had half my beard blown off!" Pyro fingered the bristle. "Never did grow back quite as thick."

Sonata sat up and faced her godfather. "Can you blame us for being a little cautious?"

"Well, for goodness' sake! You can't all sleep in here!"

"Why not?" yawned Pyro, yanking the blanket over his shoulder. "We all sleep in the same room in the caravan."

Staccato stripped the blanket off. "Then go sleep there! The only one of you allowed to stay is Sonata … and the cat."

Pyro rose and stretched his arms over his head. "Alright then, fine! Come on, fellas! Let's go!"

Melodious, Pyro, and Skelter made their way to the exit. Sitting up, Sonata stared after Pyro and cleared her throat. Pyro froze with his hand on the doorknob. His eyes darted towards Sonata. When she held his gaze, Pyro glanced back at the others, his eyes bouncing around like a pinball.

"Oh, for the love of stars!" Staccato exclaimed. "Will you two quit flicking your eyes at each other? You're not fooling anyone, you know! Even Melodious here can see that there's something going on between you two, and he's blind! You may be hiding your relationship from the rest of the world, but it's no secret to us!"

"Don't look at me," sniffed Sonata. "It's not how I would have it, keeping our romance a secret."

Pyro hunched his shoulders and shuffled his way toward Sonata. "Alright, alright! I'm sorry! Forgive me if I don't want the C.O.N. targeting you to get to me!" He lowered his lips to Sonata's upturned face.

"Take one step closer, Pyro," began Staccato, clearing his throat, "and that stranger wandering the halls will be the least of your worries!"

Pyro threw up his hands and growled. "Ugh! Fine!" He jerked his thumb towards the door. "Let's move out, fellas."

The three of them headed for the door, Skelter still holding Staccato's pillow.

"Skelter!" Staccato held out his hand.

Skelter's shoulders sagged in disappointment as he tossed the pillow at Staccato.

"Thank you!" Staccato used his powers to lock the door behind them.

Sonata laid back down on her stomach, and propped her chin up with her fist. "We really didn't mean to disturb you."

"Oh?" Staccato gave her a teasing glance and leaned back against the headboard.

"I didn't realize you would be coming off a prophetic dream. It must have been really important."

"How did you know I'd been having a prophetic dream?"

Sonata shrugged. "I'm an empath. And I have lived with you for ten years now. Something is weighing on your mind. If it weren't you'd realize that we have a good reason to be concerned."

Staccato sighed and shut his eyes. "I am a little overwhelmed at the moment."

"Why don't you tell me what happened?"

Staccato took his time explaining everything to Sonata. By the time he was done, she was staring at him, horrified.

"Well, you're going to go back and get him in that case, aren't you?"

"Of course I am!" He placed a hand over his lips. "But it will require some planning." The moment Sonata began to frown, Staccato held his hand up. "Now, don't look at me like that. As Pyro mentioned earlier, we've been attacked in three different hotels. We need a safe place to stay. Not only that, but we're going to have to convince him to come with us."

"Why don't you just tell Lydia you're alive?"

"I'm not involving her. It's too risky."

Sonata rolled her eyes, too weary to argue with him just now, and laid her head back down. "What will you tell the others? Pyro and I know the truth about your relationship to Pasha, but Skelter and Melodious don't."

"I'll say we've discovered an heir to the throne of Ursa we hadn't known existed before." Staccato stretched his arms over his head until he felt his back pop. "Thayer will certainly be pleased."

As head of the rebel network, Thayer had known of Pasha's existence for some time, as well as the truth about Staccato and Evangeline. For years he had been urging Staccato to try and restore Pasha to the throne, and now he was finally about to get his wish. Staccato looked back at Sonata.

"I suppose the others are safe if they're staying in the caravan. You're welcome to stay here if you like."

Sonata poked at a wrinkle in the sheets. "It would be nice to not have to listen to Pyro fighting in his sleep all night."

Staccato yawned and stretched his arms over his head again. "Very well, dearest." He grabbed one of the pillows and kissed the crown of her head. "I'll take the sofa."

Chapter 1:

I Do Not Have a Crush on Faina Spichkin

If you were to find yourself standing on the corner while a police officer threatened to drag you all the way down to the precinct by your hair, you'd more than likely have the sense to pay attention, or at the very least nod your head every now and then. Pasha Chevalsky was, by all accounts, a sensible person. But he was sixteen and in love with his best friend, despite his best efforts to deny it. Kissing Faina Spichkin should have been the last thing on his mind as Officer Lynch jabbed his nightstick at Pasha's chest, but it was difficult not to fantasize with her looking the way she did that bitter February evening, standing a block away in front of the Foxhole, her thick, black hair dripping about her shoulders in shining coils, and that ever-present look of joy sewn into her freckles.

I do not have a crush on Faina Spichkin, he told himself again and again. But the longer he stared at her the more he could feel his resolve softening and crumbling away like a cracker inside a bowl of hot soup.

"Chevalsky!" barked Lynch, realizing Pasha wasn't paying attention.

Pasha returned his gaze to the aging officer's surly glower. "Yes, sir?"

"A sixteen-year-old like you walking up and down the Bowery by yourself on a Saturday night can only mean one thing: trouble."

Pasha waited patiently until Lynch had finished before explaining in the calmest voice he could manage.

"Actually, sir, I'm just on my way to a dance competition." He held open his coat, showing off his fine evening attire. "You're not gonna catch me scaling any fences tonight. Not in this getup. Besides, I don't have any warrants, not since my last arrest, and I haven't broken the law."

After four years of working for the Breadwinners, the thought of being arrested no longer frightened Pasha. It was bound to happen now and then, and Klokov was almost always able to get them off the hook.

"A dance competition, huh?" Lynch snorted. "No doubt in some speakeasy. Isn't that right?" He spat.

Pasha refused to appear fazed. He would not give Lynch the satisfaction. "I understand why you're suspicious, but with all due respect, sir, I think you have bigger fish to fry than me."

He gestured to the missing poster of Pearl Sulzbach hanging in the laundromat window, one of hundreds plastered all over the neighborhood.

Have You Seen This Girl?

Name: Pearl Sulzbach
Age: 16
Last seen inside her tenement on Hester Street,
January 25, 1924, getting ready for bed. Believed to
have been kidnapped when her family's home was
broken into.

If you have any information please notify the N.Y.P.D. or Irving and
Laurel Sulzbach.

She was not the only person to have gone missing either. Several homes and businesses in the Lower East Side had been broken into lately, sometimes with the whole family disappearing altogether. Though police had investigated several times, no one could determine a motive, as there were never any valuables stolen, and the families had little in common outside of being immigrants. As a result, there had been an increase in police presence in the neighborhood, something the Breadwinners complained about constantly.

Lynch hitched up his pants and drew a long inhale. "You're right about one thing." He waved him on with his nightstick. "Alright, be on your way then! And be quick about it!"

Pasha retrained his eyes on Faina, who, by the looks of it, had witnessed the whole thing from the sidewalk.

"I thought for sure he was gonna search you," she said when Pasha was within earshot.

"He wouldn't have found anything if he did. What are you doing out here? It's freezing."

Faina took his arm and led him towards the staircase. "You're my dance partner, you can't expect me to make an entrance without you!"

"I doubt anyone would notice." He could hear the music growing louder as they neared the top floor.

"That's where you're wrong! It's all psychological. We've won three dance contests so far. We're the ones to beat, and the competition knows it! Think how intimidating a dramatic entrance would be!"

Pasha smiled and rolled his eyes. She'd lost none of her flair for theatrics over the years.

"You're the expert, I suppose."

Faina paused and reached out to cup his face with her hand, causing Pasha's eyes to dilate.

I do not have a crush on Faina.

"That bruise is healing up nicely." She stroked her thumb over a faded blue cloud at the corner of his mouth. "I'm surprised you've managed to keep your face so clean this week. No one will recognize you!"

I do not have a crush on Faina.

She kept her hand in place, continuing to caress the corner of his lip.

I have a crush on Faina. Pasha opened and closed his mouth several times before he managed to make the words come out. "Well, you know what they say: looks count for everything."

She pulled her hand away and latched onto his arm once more. "In that case, with you as my partner we've got this in the bag."

Pasha made no remark but cast his eyes towards the floor with a shy smile.

"Come on, Huncamunca. We better get a move on."

The building seemed to physically sigh as the door opened and a gust of warm air breathed across their faces. The restaurant was rather full as it often was when there was a dance competition, with the majority of the patrons being under twenty-three. Sergei and Yuri waved from across the room, beckoning for the two to join them.

"Back for your fourth win?" teased Sergei as they approached.

Pasha was impressed to find Maimie Kessler hanging on Sergei's arm, but then, being a top-ranking street fighter had its perks. At seventeen, Sergei was one of the largest street fighters currently serving the Breadwinners, and it had been this way for quite some time. In fact, he was regularly mistaken for a grown man, not just because of his size, but the boy could grow a full beard faster than most adults. Some jealous street fighters were even so bold as to complain that Sergei's thick five o'clock shadow gave him an unfair advantage, protecting his face from the full force of their blows, and demanded that he be made to shave regularly. No such regulation was ever implemented, but he shaved regardless to keep in style.

"With any luck," said Pasha, scanning the room for their competition.

"The way you two dance?" Yuri scoffed and lit a cigarette. "Luck ain't got nothing to do with it."

Yuri was solo, which did not surprise Pasha. A year ago, Yuri had surprised everyone when he entered into a serious relationship with a girl who worked in the meatpacking district. Yuri had never struck anyone as the committed type, but after six months of dating, the girl told Yuri she was pregnant.

Street fighters were required to marry their girlfriends if they ended up in the family way, and Pasha had fully expected Yuri to drag his feet. However, that wasn't the case at all. He readily stepped up to the plate, and would've asked regardless. It turned out to be a false alarm so they didn't go through with it in the end, but they'd been together ever since. But Yuri never brought her around the Foxhole.

Yuri had remained small and slight over the years, and even at seventeen his adenoidal voice had only dropped an octave or two. Age and time spent with the Breadwinners had kept his manners coarse, and he swore frequently.

Pasha reached for Faina's collar. "Your coat, Madam?"

Faina allowed him to peel the outer layer from her arms. Pasha's eyes flicked from shoulder to shoulder, from hip to foot, struggling to find a place to land. Attention pooled around her as though she were the center of a downhill stream. The dress was sleeveless and a startling shade of scarlet that flattered her dark eyes and hair.

Though she was generally liked, Faina had never been popular and had few close friends outside of her cousin and Pasha. She may be sweet, funny, and compassionate, but she could also be intense, emotional, overbearing, and impulsive. Her interests were so varied that no one ever seemed to know what she was talking about, and she had a hard time paying attention to things she had no interest in. But despite all that, Faina had managed to keep a steady string of boyfriends circulating ever since she was fourteen.

"I don't understand what anyone sees in her," Pasha once overheard Marjorie Schwartz say to Reyna Herzl. "She looks just like a witch with that long black hair, thick eyebrows, and big nose of hers. Not to mention she's got more freckles than an old banana."

"And how! She'll never be able to wear the latest fashions. Not with that figure. Ten years ago she might have been a doll. But she's too curvy to sport a modern look."

"It all comes down to charm, I suppose. They say Cleopatra was the same way."

While Pasha adored her nose and freckles, worshipped her hair, and drooled over her figure, her looks were neither here nor there. The truth was Faina was flirtatious, persistent, and knew how to dress to her advantage. And that was more than half the game.

Now she cycled through boyfriends like they were cans of soup. It started with a paper boy from across the street, then progressed to the butcher's apprentice, then Gregory Sochinsky's little brother. The next thing Pasha knew, she was dating Breadwinners. And though Faina constantly flirted with him, the last thing Pasha wanted was to confess his feelings only to be thrown aside when she grew bored—that is, if she would even be interested in the first place.

"Faina!" exclaimed Maimie, her jaw stretching open in awe. "That dress is to die for!"

You look gorgeous, was the phrase poised to leap off the tip of Pasha's tongue, but he quickly caught himself and toned down his compliment.

"Nice dress … as usual."

"You think so?" Faina's eyes flicked nervously towards the ground. "Ethel Kovak says I'm a gangster's moll." She pinned a hair behind her ear, examining Pasha's reaction from beneath her lashes.

At first, Pasha said nothing and began to pull out a chair, but when he saw the downcast look in her eye, he quickly thought up a remark.

"Gangster's moll, eh? And just who have you been seeing this time? Arnold Rothstein?"

Faina wrinkled her nose and giggled. "Rothstein?"

Pasha waved his hand in a dramatically self-deprecating gesture. "No, you're right. It's probably someone young, someone good looking, like Lucky Luciano! Tall, dark, and handsome. Sounds like your type."

Faina shrugged with an exceptionally mischievous smile. "I'd be willing to accept just tall and handsome."

Pasha pulled out her chair for her, and the two sat. Yuri eyed them with a comical expression before turning to Faina and asking, "So, how are things between you and that delivery boy from the coffee shop in Little Italy?"

"You mean Nario?" Faina turned down the corners of her mouth and shrugged. "He's history."

Yuri turned to Pasha with a significant look. "Really?"

Pasha gave a discreet signal for Yuri to cut it out, but Yuri ignored him. "So it's back to the single life once again."

"Not for long," ribbed Maimie with a sly wink. "From what I hear, Faina is one hot commodity these days."

Faina appeared to receive this remark with mixed feelings, and could only manage a shy smile. "I don't know about that."

Maimie leaned forward with her elbows on the table. "Embrace it, honey. You can have any man you want."

Faina scoffed and lowered her gaze. "If only that were true." But only Pasha seemed to have heard her.

Pasha was just asking Faina if she would like something to drink when a fellow street fighter, Vlad Gershkovich, better known as Steed, practically threw himself onto their table, propping himself up on his elbows, and staring directly at Faina.

"Hi."

Faina raked him over with an amused smirk. "Uh, hi."

Steed said no more but remained staring at her and biting his own smug grin. Pasha was not a fan of Steed, for, on top of being arrogant and rough, he was a friend of Anastas's and enjoyed tormenting Pasha, though to a much lesser degree. When Steed continued to gawk insolently, Pasha sneered and drummed his fingers on the table.

"Can we help you, Steed?"

"Huh?" He feigned oblivion. "Oh, uh, yeah, yeah! I just wanted to see if I can borrow the salt."

Pasha shoved the shaker towards him. "Here. Is that all?"

Steed ignored the shaker for the most part and continued grinning at Faina. "Yeah. That's it."

When he still didn't move, Pasha raised his eyebrows and pinched his lips together. "Bye, Steed!"

Steed took his time getting up and tearing his gaze away from Faina. When he finally began to leave, Pasha gave a sigh of relief.

"As I was saying—"

"You guys wouldn't happen to have any pepper, would you?" Steed twirled one of the chairs around and sat down in it backwards.

He can't be serious, thought Pasha, trying to suppress a groan. Yuri flung the pepper shaker in his direction.

"Now will you beat it?"

But Steed was having too much fun putting on his little show. "What about ketchup?"

Yuri rolled his eyes. "Look around you! Do you see any table with ketchup? Does this look like a joint that would have ketchup on the table?"

Faina lowered her head and giggled behind her hand, encouraging Steed further. Pasha snatched up the half-empty caddy with the napkins and the place where the salt and pepper had been and pushed it at Steed.

"Here! Just take it! Take all of it!"

But Steed looked right past Pasha and made eyes at Faina. "Your boyfriend seems pretty eager to get rid of me."

Faina's smile dropped. "Oh, he's not … he's not my boyfriend." The way she looked at Pasha could almost have been taken as an invitation to dispute her.

Steed's grin grew wilier by the second. "Ah, so you're single then?"

Before any of them could counter, Maimie smirked and gave Faina a playful nudge. "She certainly is. Completely unattached!"

Sergei signaled for Maimie to hush but either she didn't notice or was ignoring him.

"Swell!" Steed rocked the chair forward on two legs. "In that case, what would you say to me and you getting better acquainted?"

No! No! No! Pasha was screaming inside his head. Faina painted her lips with a coy smile and drew back her shoulders, letting the strap of her dress slide a measure or two down her arm.

"I'd say I'm free next Saturday."

Pasha was aghast. His eyes narrowed and sharpened on Steed. "Do you even know her name?"

"Well, sure! Everyone's heard of Faina!" Though his expression did not change there was something nasty in his gaze as he looked at Pasha. "You talk about her enough!"

Pasha's chin bowed towards his chest while his face grew hot and red. Just then, the music ended and the bandleader called the contestants to the dance floor. Faina rose from her seat and pulled Pasha up by the elbow.

"We can discuss the details afterwards." She turned her back on him with a coquettish flourish. "Right now we have a trophy to win."

"Faina, you can't seriously be considering walking out with Steed!" said Pasha the moment they were out of earshot.

"Why not?"

"You don't even know him!"

Faina shrugged. "Isn't that what dates are for? Getting to know someone?"

They took their place on the dance floor. "Allow me to save you the trouble: he's a *pridurok*." A jerk. "He's no good!"

Faina turned and faced him. "Don't they say that about all thugs?"

"Would you say that about me?"

"*Nyet*, but I'm sure someone who didn't know you would."

Pasha knit his eyebrows together, surprised to find her so resistant. "Faina, I know Steed. Trust me, you wouldn't like him."

"Okay, then I won't see him again." She took his hand and placed the other on his shoulder. "After this date."

Pasha's tongue tripped over his own teeth. "After this—?!" The opening notes of *I Wish I Could Shimmy Like My Sister Kate* cut him short. He pulled Faina towards him and lowered his voice. "After this date?"

"I already said yes. I don't wanna be rude."

"Why not? He's rude all the time! It's the only language he understands!"

He stepped back, leading Faina towards him and twisting his foot as he went. Faina mirrored his step with her opposite foot.

"Do we have to talk about this right now?"

"When else are we gonna get the chance? Just look at him!" He inclined his head towards Steed. "I bet you as soon as the number's over he's gonna march right over here and drag you off the dance floor." He turned her around and allowed her to fall back into his arms. "I'm not trying to tell you what to do or anything, but trust me when I say you don't wanna get mixed up with this guy!" He pushed her back up and they faced each other once again. "He's bad news!"

"I'm not getting mixed up with anyone! I'm just going on one date, and if it's as bad as you say it is then it's over."

Pasha's eyebrows rose to his hairline, and he actually stumbled over his own feet.

"Pasha, pay attention!"

But Pasha wasn't listening. "What do you mean if it's as bad as I say?"

Faina rolled her eyes and pivoted to stand beside him facing the crowd. "Don't start that."

"Don't you trust my judgement?" Pasha's movements were getting less sharp.

"This has nothing to do with your judgment!" She twirled towards him, wrapping herself in his arms. Her voice was barbed. "Why do you care so much?"

"Because I care about you!" Pasha felt the back of his neck grow hot. Again he repeated the phrase inside his head, *I do not have a crush on Faina Spichkin.* "I would do the same thing for Katya."

The energy drained from Faina's steps. "Just because Leo's dead doesn't mean I need you to be my older brother, Pasha!"

The music wound to a dramatic finish. Pasha and Faina dragged themselves back to their table while the judges deliberated. Seeing Sergei's strained smile, Pasha scoffed.

"Not our best, huh?"

"Well—"

"What happened?" interrupted Yuri. "That was terrible!"

Faina hinged away from Pasha, her irritation palpable. "I think it's safe to say our winning streak is broken. We can kiss the finals goodbye!"

Pasha's hand jumped to his ear as feedback squealed through the speakers. Heads wrenched towards the stage to see the bandleader toying with the microphone.

"Alright ladies and gents, the scores are in. In first place we have Jacob 'Overland' Warszauer and Ida Blonski!" The crowd roared while Pasha and Faina applauded halfheartedly. "In second place, Tessie Vass and Davy 'Irons' Loeser!"

Pasha went ahead and took his seat, only half listening as the bandleader continued to read off the finalists. Steed was floating nearby, pretending to mingle as he continued to size up Faina. Pasha wondered what the attraction was. There were certainly better-looking street fighters. Steed had a wily face with steep arched brows and a sarcastic-looking simper. But he was well built and healthy. Pasha glanced down at his own massive hands and feet, which looked out of proportion with his skinny frame. While Yuri remained boyish, and Sergei looked like a man, Pasha was lost in between. He may have been toweringly tall, but he was lank as ever with a skinny neck and huge doe eyes. There were times when he could've sworn his eyebrows were thicker than his neck. Still, Steed was nothing special. He supposed it all came down to charm.

Pasha balked as he found himself echoing Marjorie and Reyna.

"And in fifth place, Pasha Chevalsky and Faina Spichkin!"

Pasha and Faina gaped at each other in total shock.

"Boy," Yuri shook his head and applauded. "You two must have gotten in by the skin of your teeth!"

"The competition will resume in two weeks," continued the bandleader. "And then we'll see which of our five talented finalists will take home the prize!"

Faina took one look at Pasha and huffed. "Hopefully, next time Pasha will save the chatter for after our routine."

Pasha passed a hand through his hair. "I'm sorry, it's just—"

At that moment, Steed returned. "So, how's about those details?" He offered his arm, and Faina allowed him to lead her off to somewhere more private.

***

When the evening was over, Maimie and Faina walked home together while Pasha headed downstairs with Yuri and Sergei to meet briefly with Klokov, who had asked to speak to him. Street fights were still going on at the center of the room despite the late hour, and none of the boys seemed eager to leave.

Unfortunately, when Pasha reported to Klokov's office, he was temporarily occupied with an associate from the West Side, forcing Pasha to delay his trip home. He took his place beside Yuri and Sergei at a table near the bar. Steed too had decided to drop in, and had started a game of pool with Anastas nearby. Pasha hadn't planned on saying anything to either of them, but Yuri could always be counted on to run his mouth.

"That was a lousy thing you did, Steed. You know Pasha is crazy about Faina."

Pasha could only surmise Yuri was itching for a confrontation, as it was obvious Steed didn't care one way or the other. Steed didn't bother to turn around but aimed his cue at the ball.

"If he likes her so much then he should have done something about it."

He struck the ball with an audible clicking noise.

"I do not like Faina that way," Pasha muttered unconvincingly. Steed and Anastas looked at each other, then threw their heads back with derisive laughter.

"You ain't even interested in Faina," asserted Yuri. "You just did it to be a jerk."

Steed stepped back from the pool table with his hands up. "Woah, woah, who says I ain't interested?" He stood the cue on its end and puffed out his chest. "You've, uh, seen Faina's … assets, haven't you?" He gestured to different places on his body.

Pasha's neck contracted into his collar. His fists clenched.

Sergei leaned forward and put a hand on his shoulder. "Don't listen to him. He's just trying to bait you."

"Chevalsky can have her when I'm done."

Pasha pivoted around in his seat. "Done with what?"

Steed exchanged an amused simper with Anastas before leaning in patronizingly with his hands on his knees. "What they don't teach you about the birds and the bees in Sunday School?" It wasn't the first time a fellow Breadwinner had made fun of him for attending church, but he was hardly the only one. Steed returned to the table and aimed at another ball. "I'm a modern man and your friend is a modern woman."

Pasha's voice wavered uncertainly. "You don't know anything about her."

Steed turned and raised an eyebrow. "I don't?" He gestured to the room at large with his cue. "I know she's kissed half the fellas in this room." He narrowed his gaze on Sergei and Yuri with a wicked smile. "What kinda kisser is she, Sergei?" He leaned on his cue, enjoying

Sergei's discomfort. He faced Yuri. "What about you, Mishkin? Was she any good?"

Pasha fought for composure of his features. He often forgot that Faina had kissed both Yuri and Sergei during her stint as the Kissing Cat Burglar. Yuri did not so much as bat an eye, instead he squinted at Steed as though he were the biggest idiot he'd ever laid eyes on.

"I was ten, you moron."

"Why don't you ask Roan then?" suggested Anastas as Alexander "the Red Roan" Karp was passing by. Roan and Faina had dated a month ago and, after a fairly brief courtship, had parted amicably. "Hey, Roan! How far'd you get with Spichkin?"

Roan didn't even bother to look at them. "Shove it, Sippenhaft." And he went on his way.

Pasha turned his back on the pair and leaned his head into his palm.

"Don't get yourself worked up." Sergei spoke with a lowered voice. "Steed is all talk. He ain't gonna do anything. He just wants to get you mad."

Pasha flicked a stray ash from Yuri's cigarette off the table and eyed Anastas. "You'd think Anastas would be a little more upset that Steed is flirting with Faina, seeing as he's always been so jealous of me."

As children, Anastas had carried a torch for Faina and had been rather possessive of her, getting angry any time she mentioned Pasha. They had ceased their friendship after Anastas tried to force a cigarette on Faina and kiss her. But Anastas continued to harass and catcall her over the years, even flirting with her just to get a rise out of her. And yet he never seemed to mind whenever she dated anyone else, though he continued to resent Pasha.

"That's because he knows Steed doesn't stand a chance with her, unlike you." Sergei offered him an amiable smile. "There's still hope."

Pasha forced his face into what felt like a neutral expression. "Hope for what? I'm not interested in dating Faina. I just don't want her to get hurt."

Yuri casually examined his cigarette. "And you're lying to us because …?"

"Chevalsky!" Klokov poked his shining bald head around the corner of the hallway. The smoky light of the bar glinted off the kopeck in his right eye as he beckoned Pasha forward. It was the first time Pasha had ever sighed in relief at the sight of his crime lord boss.

"I gotta go, fellas."

In four years, Klokov had altered little, but then he had little to no hair to gray; he hardly had eyebrows, and his rounded face and stubby neck were not given to gauntness. Instead, he remained just as severe looking and bad tempered as before. Pasha followed him into his office, relieved to hear the clamorous racket of the bar fade as the door was shut behind him. Klokov indicated to the armchair before his desk with a snappy gesture.

"Sit."

Pasha did as told without expression or comment, and watched his boss settle into the chair across from him and light a cigar. He examined Pasha from the corner of his good eye.

"Why you always gotta look so dejected every time you come in here? You're not smiling, you're not angry, what are you?"

Inwardly, Pasha groaned. Surely, he was not going to be expected to give some kind of performance every time he entered Klokov's office now.

"I'm tired, sir."

Klokov checked his pocket watch. "It is getting late."

Eager to get home, Pasha tried to muster some life into his voice. "What is it you wanted to see me about?"

"You've been doing good lately, Stallion. Real good. We're coming up on what? Four years now since you joined the Breadwinners?"

"Four years last week."

Klokov's lips unraveled in a greedy smile. "You've come far in all that time. Tell me, how's your ma?"

"Still working at the factory job you landed her."

"And your sister? How's her health?"

Pasha drew in a deep breath. "She's well. Doctor has her sticking to a low copper diet." It may have seemed foolish, but there was a part of Pasha that was afraid to tell Klokov the truth: that Katya was stable if anything, still talked out of her head, and had a brown ring around her blue eyes from excess copper in her tissues, a ring that should have diminished as long as she avoided certain foods.

Klokov examined the rings on his fingers. "Not much longer, and you'll be able to leave the Lower East Side if you want."

It was true. Pasha had made a lot of money bootlegging alcohol. They all had. And Pasha had the benefit of a smaller family to care for. As a result, Pasha was one of the wealthiest amongst the street fighters.

"That's what I'm hoping for, sir."

"The reason I asked you to come down was because I need you to clear your evening for the twenty-sixth." Klokov shuffled the papers on his desk until he had unearthed a leather planner.

"You mean Tuesday?"

Klokov ran his stubby finger along the page. "Of June."

"June? That's four months away!"

Klokov impaled him with a sarcastic sneer. "Really? I thought this was May. Write it down." He waved his hand towards the door. "You're dismissed."

But Pasha remained sitting there, his brain too caught up in processing his confusion to obey. Klokov slammed the book shut.

"Chevalsky! Didn't you hear me? I said you can go!"

"Yes, sir, but first may I ask what it is I'll be doing that day?"

"No, you may not." He pointed at the door again. "Now go home."

Pasha got up, shoved his hands inside his pockets and pivoted in the direction of Klokov's finger.

Okay then.

Pasha shut the door behind him and made for the exit of the Foxhole. A group of street fighters had gathered at the bar. One had a straw in a glass of whiskey. The others giggled uncontrollably as he placed the straw up his left nostril and snorted. A wave of deafening cackles rippled down the bar. Pasha paused with his hand on the knob and stared dully at the display of idiocy unfolding before him, wondering how on earth he had let himself end up in such a place.

Chapter 2:
Cigarettes

The tenement was completely dark when Faina returned home, with no signs of dinner having been consumed and put away.

"Uncle Matvei?" Faina called, but there was no answer.

Faina looked questioningly at the clock. It may have been late but it was still too early to find everyone asleep on a Friday night, especially her uncle. Removing her gloves, she made her way down the hall towards her cousin's room. The crack beneath the threshold remained dark. Careful not to make any noise lest Anya be sleeping, Faina gently poked her head in. Anya's room smelled of fresh linens and lavender soap. Even in the dark, Faina could see it was as neat as a hospital. But the bed remained empty.

Faina headed down the stairs to *Opa!* The shop was closed for the night, but Uncle Matvei slept in the back room. Lately, it felt as though he rarely came upstairs. Business kept him busy, though it was far from booming since they had been forced to convert from a liquor store to a grocery store.

"Uncle Matvei?"

She slipped down the back hall and opened the door. Uncle Matvei was asleep at his desk, his head resting on his open account book.

"Uncle Matvei?"

Uncle Matvei winced and rubbed his eyes. "Faina?" He rose and stretched his lanky arms over his head. "Was I asleep?"

"I can't imagine why else you would have your face plastered against the account books."

He sighed and shook his head, smoothing his rumpled mustache. "It gets tedious after a while."

He turned to the oil lamp at his elbow and turned up the dial, but the flame remained dim. Faina's eyes flitted curiously towards the light switch.

"What's with the oil lamp?"

"There's a problem with the electricity. The Shuckwits and the Malkins have made similar complaints, and this room appears to be on the same circuit." He shuffled through a stack of papers. "We're on a waitlist for the electrician. With any luck he'll show up tomorrow."

"You could do what Borsuk does on her side of the building and use kerosene lamps in the hallway."

Uncle Matvei shook his head. "Vile woman."

She shifted her weight and shoved her hands down in her pockets. "Hey, you wouldn't have happened to have finally graded my book report, would you?"

Uncle Matvei winced. His mustache appeared to droop. "Sweetheart, I'm so sorry. I still haven't gotten to it."

Faina wilted against the doorframe. "It's been two weeks! Why have me write it if you're not even gonna grade it?"

"It's a book report, my bookworm. I already know without looking at it that you did an outstanding job."

"Okay. Well, what about my geometry? Have you gotten around to that yet?"

Uncle Matvei opened his mouth to say something only to smile apologetically instead. When Faina continued to stare irritably at him, he raked a hand through his coarse hair and rubbed at his lower back.

"I don't see why you're so upset. You're a clever girl. You learn more from those books you read than you do me anymore. In a month you'll be sixteen years old. Most children your age have discontinued their education by now."

"Not Anya."

"Sweetheart, I don't understand. You hated school."

"But not school with you!"

"Faina, it may be time for you to accept that the pupil has surpassed the teacher." He picked up his pen and returned his attention to the account book.

Faina shuffled awkwardly in the doorway. She wanted to shout, "You don't really mean that! You're just saying that to get rid of me!" But she was too tired to fight just now. Weary of standing, she seated herself on the edge of the desk.

"But there's still so much you can teach me—"

What followed seemed unexplainable. The flame inside the lantern ballooned suddenly until it was taller than the glass, and reached for Faina with its long yellow fingers, burning in a bright, blazing stream. Faina screeched and jumped back, terrified. As quickly as it had swelled it shrank back to normal leaving the air tinged with the odor of burning fibers. When Faina looked up at Uncle Matvei again he was patting a flame out from the end of his hair.

"*Chort voz mi!*" Devil take me! "What is it with you and fire?"

"I didn't mean to! I—I guess I just sat down too hard. I'm sorry!" Faina was trembling. In the past four years, Faina had fallen prey to what many of the old babas of the neighborhood considered a curse; Faina had developed an unexplainable knack for starting fires, accidentally of course. Matches exploded in her fingers. Candles seemed to topple over when she looked at them. It became such a problem that Faina grew to fear fire, and Mrs. Borsuk was terrified of having her come near her side of the building due to the kerosene lamps.

Uncle Matvei met Faina's gaze with tight lips as the ends of his hair crumbled away into ash, dusting his large, aquiline nose.

"Faina, why don't you head on upstairs and get ready for bed?"

"But Uncle Matvei, I didn't—"

"I know," he conceded. "I know you didn't mean to, *Faishka*. Everything is fine."

Faina twisted the ball of her foot into the floor. "But you're mad."

"I'm not mad."

"But … you look mad."

Uncle Matvei forced a smile to his wide mouth, looking very much like a dog baring his teeth. "I'm not mad, darling." He set his large hands on her shoulders and turned her around, nudging her back towards the shop. "Now, go get ready for bed. It's getting late."

Before Faina could protest, he had shut the door behind her, the cold handle jabbing her arm. Faina's chin fell to her chest. She could hear him muttering to himself on the other side of the wall. In her mind she envisioned a curse hanging about her shoulders like a black shroud. Or worse, maybe *she* was the curse, and it was Uncle Matvei who had been doomed to suffer her nuisance.

She left the shop and headed for the main stairwell in search of Anya. If she wasn't in her room, perhaps she was on the roof getting her pajamas off the laundry line. The wind struggled against Faina as she thrust her head out the door.

"Anya?"

Anya's diminutive silhouette with the drawn-in shoulders filled in the scattered bits of moonlight near the ledge. Her sweater hung heavily from her shoulders and she shivered in the open air.

"There you are!" Faina hurried towards her, relieved to have someone to spill her burdens to. "You'll never guess what happened tonight! I went to the dance competition with Pasha, and while we were there this boy comes up to the table and—" But Anya did not turn around. "Anya?" She placed her hand on her cousin's shoulder and tugged. "Are you listening?"

Anya turned with one hand pasted over her lips as though she'd accidentally uttered some swear word, and a cigarette wedged in the other. Faina's eyes flickered from the cigarette to Anya's horrified countenance and back again. It was rather a stupid thing to say, but Faina was in such a state of surprise, it was the first thing that flew out of her mouth.

"Anya, are you smoking?"

Anya finally released the billow of smoke she'd been retaining inside her mouth and let her hand flop lifelessly to her side.

"Don't tell Papa!" She opened her mouth to say more but stopped and snuffed out the cigarette on the ledge.

"But … I don't understand."

Anya was the last person Faina would have ever expected to be caught with a cigarette. Proper and well behaved, Anya was a model child, the one who never caused any trouble, and a godsend to Faina's overwhelmed uncle. While Faina had been forced to continue her education at home after being kicked out of school by the age of ten, Anya was a straight-A student who served with the Junior Red Cross, and who had never had a boyfriend, let alone kissed a boy.

Anya crossed her arms and shuddered against the wind. "Look, I have this big test tomorrow, okay? And everyone says smoking calms your nerves."

Faina eyed the cigarette once more. Anya appeared to know what she was doing.

"This isn't your first cigarette, is it?"

Anya rubbed the back of her neck and turned to face the city. "No. But is it really that bad? The legal age is eighteen, only two years older than I am."

Faina stepped back, continuing to think things over.

"Please don't tell Papa!" Anya begged again, her eyes widening with desperation.

Faina paused, then nodded. Anya was under a lot of pressure with her studies lately. It would do her good to let off a little steam.

"I won't tell."

"Thank you!" She paused and raked her eyes over Faina's tense posture. "I'm sorry. Cigarettes still bother you, don't they?"

Faina shoved her mouth into a stiff smile and tried to appear relaxed as memories of Anastas trying to force a cigarette between her lips floated to the surface of her mind.

"It's fine."

"No." She stored the unfinished cigarette in her pocket. "I'll try to remember not to do it around you." She leaned against the wall. "How did the competition go?"

"Awful!" She tossed her hands in the air and began pacing. "This street fighter named Steed asked me out on a date, and Pasha nearly cast a kitten! We managed to get into the finals though."

Anya wagged her eyebrows. "Sounds like somebody's jealous."

Faina thrust out her lower lip and groaned. "Don't bet on it. Apparently all Pasha sees when he looks at me is a sister. He basically said as much."

"Just because he said it doesn't mean he meant it."

Faina rose and headed for the door. "Face it, Anya. If Pasha had any interest in me he would've done something about it by now."

Chapter 3:
Eggs and Omens

Staccato shuffled through the cramped hallway of the tenement building towards Aunt Poppy's apartment, weary and travel-worn. There was snow collected in the brim of his hat, and he'd nearly lost his suitcase on the subway ride over. A fragrant cloud of garlic and herbs was already leaking out from under the door, prompting Staccato's stomach to growl. He was just about to rap on the door with the head of his staff, which had now been disguised as a walking stick, when the door of the Chevalskys' apartment opened. Without a second thought, Staccato made himself transparent.

"I doubt Uncle Matvei even noticed I was out," came the voice of Matvei's niece.

"I'm sure that's not true," said Pasha.

They rounded the corner and began making their way down the narrow hallway. Staccato cursed his instincts. It made little difference whether Pasha spotted him or not, for he would have no idea who Staccato was. Now he was stuck in the passage, blending in with the wallpaper. The hall was so constricted, it would be nearly impossible for the pair to brush past without bumping into him.

"I'm nothing but trouble to my uncle," continued Faina. "The other night he told me he doesn't want to teach me anymore."

Staccato pressed himself against the wall, sucking in his non-existent gut, as though that would make a difference.

"Woah, woah!" Pasha stopped and faced her. "Doesn't want to, or doesn't have time to?"

"He says I don't need it anymore!"

Staccato glanced in the opposite direction of the hall. The way was clear, but he feared if he moved they might notice the wallpaper rippling. After all, he wasn't so much invisible as he was expertly camouflaged.

45

Pasha shrugged. "Because you've outgrown him. Didn't you say he never had a formal education? He probably thinks you're too smart for him now."

"Or too annoying! Whenever I try to help out, he just gets frustrated and treats me like a big, dumb klutz who only gets in the way."

They resumed walking down the passage. Staccato tried turning out his feet in an attempt to clear the way.

"Your uncle just has a lot on his plate right now. He loves you, Faina. You're like his daughter."

Faina gave a harsh scoff. "More like a nuisance he got saddled with."

And then it happened. Pasha's toe struck the side of Staccato's foot, forcing him to stumble forward. Faina whirled around to stare at Pasha.

"Stems tangled, Stilts?"

Just as Pasha was looking back, Staccato struck them both with a vision of a broken floor tile. Pasha sighed.

"At least it's not on Borsuk's side of the building. It would never get fixed."

"I'll tell Uncle Matvei about it." Faina covered her face with her elbow as she was overcome with a hacking cough. "Come on. I think I need a cup of tea."

Staccato waited and listened for the door of the Dalkas' apartment to open and shut before fading back into existence with a sigh of relief. His ordeal finally at an end, he turned and knocked on Aunt Poppy's door.

"Aunt?"

"It's open, dear!"

Staccato swept into the apartment and found Aunt Poppy hard at work in front of the stove.

"Sorry it took so long. Were it not for the circumstances, I would have been here as soon as I woke up from the dream."

Aunt Poppy turned to look at him and let her arms drop by her side. "You look terrible!"

Staccato flashed her a wry smile. "And you look as lovely as ever!"

"Ordinarily, I'd say you couldn't spare five pounds. Now you look as though you've lost ten!"

"I'm afraid it's slim pickings when you're on the run. Though we're currently staying in Xifāng, so there are more opportunities for heartier meals."

When Staccato and the others had managed to steal the Jar of Elijah right from under Cobra Samael's nose, the company had moved further up on the C.O.N.'s Most Wanted list. The more power Samael amassed, the more mercilessly they were hunted, until finally, as of last year, they had been forced to go on the run.

"Xifāng?" Aunt Poppy sniffed. "I'm surprised you made it here at all. How far away is the nearest gateway station?"

"Only an hour … but I had to go through China and then enter a portal in Jishui to get to a portal to Flushing, and then take the train to Manhattan."

"Great Northern Star!" Aunt Poppy reached for a broom and gave it a flourish. A thick slice of cake flew from a tin and landed on one of the empty plates lined up on the tea tray. "I can't promise you'll gain ten pounds while you're here, but I can at least get you five." The plate drifted towards the table. "Have a seat. I'll be just a minute longer."

Staccato pulled out a chair and dug his fork into the soft confection. "What are you making?"

"Smoke soup, for the Feurstelles. Their eldest boy is going through the change."

"What change?"

Aunt Poppy clicked her tongue impatiently. "Growing his ignition glands! They're igneous!"

Staccato raised his eyebrows. "Ah."

"Child has all the symptoms: starting fires, snoring, night sweats, coughing up ash in his sleep. Of course, the doctor wants to remove his tonsils but we know better!" She slipped on an oven mitt and removed the lid from the pot. "Fortunately, they grow back! The ignition glands, that is, though I suppose tonsils grow back as well."

"His throat is sore?"

She reached for the pepper grinder and nodded. "Poor thing. And he has the reflux as well! I hear reflux in an igneous can be quite awful."

"I imagine so." He eyed her warily. "Should you be putting all that pepper in like that?"

"It's to satisfy the cravings. Nothing stirs up an appetite for spice like growing ignition glands! And it clears the sinuses. Sinus trouble is another symptom."

"Matvei mentioned his niece has been suffering from sinusitis lately. I ran into him at the door." He took another bite of the cake and swallowed. "I wonder if it'd do her any good. Treatment seems to be no different than a remedy for the common cold. What's in it, anyhow?" He added with a sidelong glance, "Aside from copious amounts of pepper?"

"Briarkell pork, cottage foil, some pascadillos, tomatoes, and onion."

Staccato's eyes dilated. "Briarkell pork? How much did that set you back?" Ten years ago, Briarkell pork had been rather commonplace, but after the Land Lock had shut down the Subaquatic Rail, shipping prices had grown astronomical, and the Briarkells were all the way in Aries.

Aunt Poppy shrugged. "I don't know what you mean! It was the same as what I pay at the butchers."

"And pascadillo peppers? The Jar of Elijah may have been returned to Virgo, but last I checked the city of Pascadillo was still under Draconian occupation." A thought struck him. "Are you … are you buying from the black market?"

Aunt Poppy narrowed her eyes. "If you must know, my friend from the Home Sweet Home Society, Mrs. Fósforo hails from Pascadillo, and happens to keep some in her garden."

"And the pork? Briarkell boars are wild. It's game meat. Don't tell me you've a friend raising pigs on the roof."

"Alright! So I shopped at the Salt Cellar for the sake of a sick young man! Tell me, is that really so bad?"

"The fine for black market trade is a hundred dollars. You tell me."

Aunt Poppy grumbled once under her breath, then said no more. She gave the soup a final stir before closing the lid and joining him at the table.

"Now," she adjusted her owlish glasses, sliding them up her aquiline nose with one aged finger, "tell me about this dream of yours."

Staccato went on to explain all the details of his prophetic dream, taking care to describe each and every omen. By the time he was finished, Aunt Poppy had polished off two cups of tea.

"So, Pasha is to return to Voiler then?"

Staccato sighed and shrugged. "What choice do I have? If he stays here he'll die."

Aunt Poppy leaned excitedly forward. "When is this to take place? Will you tell him today?"

"Accommodations will have to be made for his safety before I can do anything. As of now, we're constantly on the run. We need someplace quiet, safe from the C.O.N., where the boy can be kept secret. If he wishes to take back the throne he'll need training."

"What did you have in mind?"

He sighed and scratched under his collar. "I'm thinking of settling back on my old property in the Floodgates."

Staccato was referring to the property he had inherited in Aquarius that he rented out to a veterinarian. He had never actually stayed there but he did receive free medical care for the pegasi as part of the deal.

"They say Aquarius is one of the safest regions for the time being. And Harpagos's wing doesn't seem to be healing properly since our last run-in with the C.O.N. He can convalesce, and Pasha will be safe from Samael."

"How will you get there? You can't possibly take Sonata on a boat, not with the Land Lock, and most of the gateway stations near Aquarius have been closed. And flying is out of the question. It's too dangerous!"

Staccato passed a hand over his face and sighed. "Aries won't tolerate the C.O.N. advancing any closer. They may very well push them back within a month or two, and then we can fly."

Aunt Poppy nodded approvingly. "And then you will get Pasha?"

"That depends. For Pasha to enter Voiler legally I'll need the approval of the Voilerian Immigrant Protection Agency."

Aunt Poppy looked as though she might hurl her teacup at him. "The V.I.P.A.? Your grandson's life may be at stake! You really think it wise to trifle with bureaucratic nonsense? Must you do everything by the book?"

"Now, hear me out for a minute!" Staccato put a hand to his temple, her volume threatening to summon a headache. "I've a good reason for involving the V.I.P.A. If I'm to present Pasha to the Ecliptic Council as the legal heir of Ursa, he mustn't break the law by entering illegally. Otherwise, we could both face criminal charges."

The fire dulled in Aunt Poppy's eyes. "True. And they're not likely to consider him if he's there illegally." The saucer rattled as she set down her teacup with an impatient huff. "Well, how long will that take?"

"It will be difficult … I'll first have to prove Lydia's heritage, which would be a great deal easier if Theo, Javaid, and Estella were available to testify, and not trapped beneath the water. It'll have to be done by correspondence."

"Why can't you just speak with Queen Calliope? Or King Ignitus? You've got friends in high places, and I doubt any of them would object to welcoming the true heir of Ursa back into Voiler."

"With the C.O.N. hunting us down we need to be able to travel anywhere in Voiler. And for that I'll need the Ecliptic Council's approval." Staccato closed his eyes and pinched the bridge of his nose. "Let's hope they're cooperative. There's no telling how much time we have."

"Now, now, let's think about this logically." Aunt Poppy jammed a finger at the tablecloth, as though pointing to a date on an invisible calendar. "According to Evangeline's timeline, Pasha considers suicide only after the death of his wife and child. The boy is only sixteen years old, and has no sweethearts to speak of."

"True." Staccato paused and made a face. "Not even one?"

Aunt Poppy cast a sly glance towards the window. "He's carried a torch for Matvei's niece ever since they were small children." She chuckled. "Talking with Pasha one might be fooled into believing no other girl exists. There is only Faina."

An amused smile edged its way up one side of Staccato's mouth. It did not surprise him to hear that his grandson was a romantic. His amusement was short-lived, however, as he recalled how Pasha and Faina were practically joined at the hip.

"Now, wait just a minute—they are together an awful lot!"

Aunt Poppy shook her head. "Faina has a new suitor every month. Poor *Patulya* can hardly get his foot in the door. Besides, Pasha is a good boy. You have nothing to worry about."

"*I* was a good boy!"

Aunt Poppy gave him a clever nod. "Yes, too good! People who strive never to break the rules always end up breaking the biggest rules. I daresay Pasha has had his fill of rule breaking."

"Very well. But keep an eye on them for me." He cast a final wary glance at the window before setting his cup aside and scooting close to the table. "Now, what can you tell me about the golden eggs in the dream?"

Aunt Poppy clicked her tongue and stared thoughtfully at the wall. "A rare portent indeed. Two is unheard of! Only three occasions recorded in history."

"And it definitely signifies resurrection?"

Aunt Poppy shrugged. "Well, as Evangeline suggested, it doesn't have to be literal. After all, such omens rarely unfold in the way we expect. It could be alluding to the resurrection of a system or regime."

"That seems rather anticlimactic for an omen so rare."

"It could even be referring to a ghost."

Staccato bit his lip. A ghost? Could such a thing be possible? He'd never come across an omen foretelling of a ghost before, at least not that he was aware of. After a moment or two of contemplation, he shook his head and reclined back in the chair.

"I'm beginning to think I may have to write it off as undecipherable."

Aunt Poppy lifted her cup from her saucer. "Not even miraculous can solve every mystery. Just more than most." She leaned on the arm of her chair with a shake of her head, looking rather wearied. "It's just as well that you are taking him back with you. New York has become just as dangerous for Voilerians these days. At least in this neighborhood." She removed her glasses and inspected the lens.

"What are you talking about?"

"The disappearances of course!" She produced a handkerchief from her pocket and buffed away at a smear. "Fay are vanishing left and right. You've seen the missing posters for the Sulzbach girl, haven't you? She was a mermaid. Her mother is a chairman for the Home Sweet Home Society, you know. Poor thing. They say she was taken right out of her bed! And she's not the only one. Entire families of Fay are disappearing in the night!"

"How do you know they're not running off?"

"They're leaving everything behind. If they were running off then they would be taking at least some of their belongings with them. And worse, there have been sightings of haig beasts."

Staccato drew back in surprise. True, haig sightings had grown more common in Voiler as the C.O.N. employed the dog-like creatures to hunt down Fay, but to see one in such a crowded metropolis like Manhattan was unheard of. The foulest of creatures were haigs, who stalked at night, infecting Fay with nightmares so that they cried out in their sleep, thus disclosing their locations to their predators.

"How close?"

"The last reported sighting was on Allen, near where the girl disappeared."

Staccato passed a hand over his face, feeling rather dizzy all of a sudden. Fearing that his emotions might cause a surge in his powers, he reached for his staff.

Aunt Poppy placed a comforting hand on his knee. "Don't add me to your troubles. You know me. I'm tough. I can take care of myself."

"You're my aunt. I can't help but worry about you. And what about Katya and Lydia? They don't even realize they're Fay! They're in danger and they don't even know it!"

"Hush now. I'll keep an eye on them, you know that. You have Pasha to think of, and now this business with the Firebird."

Staccato pressed his lips together and glanced uneasily at the copy of *The Daily Compass* on the table. At this point he didn't even want to think about the Firebird, no one did. But the headlines were impossible to ignore.

"No word on who the second competitor is, I suppose?"

She waved her hand. "None that I've heard. What are King Thayer's thoughts about the bird?"

"We've yet to hear anything. I suppose he's waiting to learn more. I'd like to do some research of my own but with the C.O.N. on our heels I haven't had an opportunity. You wouldn't happen to know anything about wishes, would you?"

Aunt Poppy rose from her chair and waddled towards the bedroom. "As a matter of fact I do." After a moment, she returned with a particularly ancient-looking volume; particles of the spine were flaking off in a trail behind her. "There are three types of wishes: novelty, organic, and chimeric." She sat down and opened to the first chapter.

"*Novelty wishes are not very powerful and are, for the most part, pure amusement. They possess no permanence, and are typically manufactured by Fay. Rarely are they found in nature. These sorts of wishes can often be found as prizes in carnival games, or in children's stockings at Christmastime.*

"*If seeking a more effective wish with long-lasting capabilities, one must turn to nature. Organic wishes cannot be manufactured, and will require some foraging. But be warned, wishes of this variety will cost you something. You may be required to sacrifice material possessions, or promises. You may even discover that your wish was fulfilled in a way you did not expect. Though far less limited than your common wish, these wishes are still restricted to the basic principles of wish making. Note: While novelty wishes are harmless, these wishes can at times be dangerous. Proceed with caution.*

"Finally, there are chimeric wishes. Chimeric wishes are purely theoretical. They may not exist at all. Typically associated with mythical creatures and prophecies, chimeric wishes, if real, would likely not fall within the limits of the basic wish-making principles, making them not only powerful, but dangerous in the wrong hands."

"The basic wish-making principles being …?"

Aunt Poppy's hand flew to her chest as though she had been stung by a bee. "You can't remember any of them?"

Staccato narrowed his eyes as he tried to recall. "You cannot wish for love or death, though either may occur as a consequence of a wish being fulfilled."

Aunt Poppy waved her hand with urgent impatience. "Yes, go on."

"You can't resurrect the dead, or wish for more wishes." He was certain there were more, but it had been so long ago, and with everything going on he was lucky to have remembered any at all.

She nodded. "Very good."

"Is that all?"

"There may be a few minor stipulations here and there, but these are the *basic* principles." Aunt Poppy shut the book and the cover disintegrated into a pile of dust. She summoned the dustpan to her side. "In the case of the Firebird I'd wager we are dealing with a chimeric wish."

Staccato could feel his gut tightening as he imagined what Samael would do if granted such power. What would such tyranny look like unbound by the conventional laws of magic, and unrestrained by sanity?

55

"I was afraid of that." He placed a hand to his temple. "Now I understand why so many Fay are advocating the execution of the Firebird."

Aunt Poppy emptied the pan into the wastebasket beneath the window. "Don't get worked up just yet. It's only a theory after all. What do you know about the Firebird?"

Staccato rose and crossed to the window. "Besides what I read in the paper? I seem to recall it was a part of that fortune telling game Evangeline and her friends were so fond of. Until recently I had no idea the myth appeared in a multitude of Voilerian cultures, making it somewhat more likely to be true, at least by Fay standards. The oldest version of the legend originates with the ancient cetacean mermaids of the Phoenix Islands. They predicted a phoenix would appear in a time of great divide, and grant a wish to the person able to catch her. They built her a nest deep within the volcano of Fornax so that she might drink the Ichor running through the mountain and grow strong. The variations from other cultures are more or less the same, though without the volcano."

"You know the Slavs have legends of the Firebird as well."

He turned and faced her, curiosity reflected in his eyes. "Do they really?"

"Many different versions. Some tales claim she was once a woman, and was transformed into the Firebird by magic."

Staccato arched an eyebrow and scoffed. "Well, I think we can safely rule out that edition." He turned back to the window, watching the snow drift silently down through the courtyard. "Until the second competitor is appointed I suppose the best thing we can do is try to prevent Samael from catching the Firebird himself."

Outside, a man and a woman somewhere near his age were walking down the sidewalk arm in arm, looking wholly in love and quite content. Staccato edged away from the glass, not wishing to be reminded of Evangeline just now, not with everything at stake. It was these sorts of predicaments that stirred such longing for her, made him yearn to crawl into the shelter of sleep and find her there amongst his dreams.

"Staccato!" Aunt Poppy suddenly snapped. "Are you listening?"

Staccato swerved round in shock, as though hearing her for the first time. "I'm so sorry. I'm afraid I missed what you said."

Aunt Poppy lowered her spectacles and examined him with a wise and penetrating eye.

"There's more on your mind that you haven't told me."

Staccato lowered his head between his shoulders and stared down at the windowsill, too embarrassed to come out with it. And yet, who else could he turn to? Aunt Poppy joined him at the window. Her eyes fell on the couple.

"Something to do with Evangeline?"

Staccato sighed and rubbed at his forehead, covering his eyes slightly. "It's just … I've told you before that in my dreams with Evangeline I never age back."

Aunt Poppy's eyebrows stretched far above the rim of her glasses. They'd only ever talked about it once, and some time had passed since Staccato had brought it up. He had been thirty-eight then, and had just begun to notice.

"You still haven't aged back?" She flinched as her words bounced off the walls. Clearly, she hadn't meant to be so loud.

"No. And to be honest," he pulled at his collar, "it's starting to make me a little uncomfortable."

Aunt Poppy looked him over with a sympathetic frown. "Well, I can imagine. You are fifty-four after all."

"I want to show her … affection." He could feel his cheeks coloring. "But it feels a little … well, wrong."

Aunt Poppy did not quail over such matters, she rarely did, but crossed her arms and chewed thoughtfully on her lip for a moment before answering. "And how does she feel about your reaction?"

"I can tell it upsets her. Even if she doesn't always say so. She will if it goes on much longer." He massaged his fingers in an anxious motion. "And that's another thing, aren't the dead most often at peace?"

"I should say so, yes."

"Well, Evangeline … sometimes it seems as though she's just as distressed now as when she was alive. In fact, were it not for her youth, I'd say she's changed little overall. Sometimes I think, if I didn't know any better, I'd say she's still alive. Not because I'm in a dream state, and partly asleep, mind you. It's just, my dreams with her seem so … tangible. More so than with *Maman,* or anyone else I've encountered."

Aunt Poppy stared at him for a long while, her eyes narrowed in thought. "That is rather odd."

"You've never heard of such a thing happening?"

"I don't believe I have."

She looked sad, sorry even. Staccato crossed back to the chair and sank down with a heavy sigh, feeling utterly helpless.

"If I were you, I'd let it go."

Staccato's eyebrows rose. "Let it go?"

She shrugged, her countenance still distant with contemplation. "The fact of the matter is, you *are* the same age, whether she looks it or not. And it's not as though you're out in public; you're in the privacy of your dream." She paused. "You said it doesn't bother her that you're aging, correct?"

"She insists I look quite handsome."

"So what's the problem?"

"It bothers me!"

Aunt Poppy rolled her eyes. "Of course it bothers you, you over-complicate everything! You make yourself miserable!"

"I'm not over-complicating, you're over-simplifying!"

Aunt Poppy steadied herself against the back of a chair and held up her hand. "Perhaps I'm not the person to ask. After all, I myself have never had a desire for such relationships. If it bothers you that much you can always consult the Miraculous Council."

Staccato cringed and made a face. "I don't want them knowing my personal business! And besides, no one can know Evangeline and I were married, remember?"

"Then let it go." She pointed a finger at him. "Do you know how many would kill to be in your position? To be able to speak with a loved one from beyond the grave? We are privileged, Staccato. Remember that. Don't spurn your gift."

Staccato lowered his head. "I suppose you're right. It's just …" He bit his lip. "Something doesn't feel right. Deep down, I just know something is wrong. It has been from the very beginning."

"Sometimes our feelings are just that. Feelings. And there isn't any truth to them. That's why the heart is so deceitful."

Chapter 4:
Pearl Sulzbach

Billiards clicked noisily in Pasha's ear as Yuri dovetailed the cards and dealt them out for the seventh time that evening. Again and again Pasha told himself that the best way to survive the night of Faina's date with Steed was distraction, something the Foxhole was never short on. But after swimming in a cloud of cheap cigarette smoke on the second floor all evening, and listening to a crowd of sweaty men sing *Dos Bisele Mashke* five times in a row, the overstimulation of his environment was beginning to make him rather agitated.

Yuri snapped his fingers at Pasha. "Hey, *Pavlushka*!"

Pasha sat up straight and blinked several times. Yuri had finished dealing the cards.

"Pay attention!"

Pasha sighed and dully examined his hand.

"If you're gonna be such a wet blanket," said Yuri, his cigarette clamped between his teeth, "you might as well go home." Behind him, one of the younger boys sped past, knocking his chair. Yuri clenched his fists and exhaled a stream of smoke. "I swear, one of these days the foals are gonna push me too hard." Foals being any street fighter under the age of fourteen. Boys Pasha's age were referred to as colts, and any boy above eighteen was a stud.

All at once a deafening roar rose up amongst the other street fighters, drowning out their conversation, and causing their ears to ring. Yuri threw down his cards and swore as everyone clustered near their table.

"Ro-de-o! Ro-de-o!" they chanted over and over. A few of the boys shifted and at last the object of their excitement appeared; Bug Boy, a bespectacled young foal, was standing on a table crowded together with Stayer Sochinsky's little sister, Ruby.

Pasha rolled his eyes. "Not this again."

Around the time Pasha was fourteen, the other street fighters began a custom for whenever a boy got his first girlfriend. They'd chase and corner the couple into a space where everyone could see, standing on a chair, or a balcony, or a stoop, and would force them to kiss. They called it a rodeo. One time they even pushed Ethel Kovak and Hersh onto a pool table.

The floor pounded and pulsed as the boys stamped their feet and clapped their hands. "Kiss! Kiss! Kiss!"

Bug Boy's cheeks looked like fat red beetles as he turned towards Ruby and removed his glasses. Some girls were shy when it came to rodeos, like Tessie Vass who had cried and run out of the Foxhole. Fortunately for Bug Boy, Ruby Sochinsky was more outgoing. She threw her arms around her beau and gave him several sweet pecks. Satisfied, the others cheered and tossed their hats in the air.

When the crowd finally began to disperse, Yuri picked up his cards and resumed his cigarette.

"At least it wasn't a sloppy one." He exhaled, fogging the air with a cloud of cheap nicotine.

Sergei coughed and waved his cards. "Yuri, as much as you make in street fights, can't you afford to smoke something a little less … awful?"

Yuri leaned back in his chair and purposely breathed his smoke in Sergei's direction. "It's called being economical. Didn't your old man ever teach you the value of a dollar?" He dabbed his cigarette in the ashtray. "Talk to me when you got six little brothers and sisters and another one on the way." He bent over his cards with a hard stare. "Things get any worse, and Fedya's gonna have to join up next. And he ain't cut out to be a Breadwinner."

"I didn't think your old man could still father children." Sergei was referring to the fact that Yuri's father had lost the use of his legs while fighting in the War.

"Neither did I!" Yuri blurted, throwing his cards down on the table in exasperation.

Anastas brushed past with a nasty simper he'd sharpened especially for Yuri. "My guess is he still can't."

Yuri slammed his fist down on the table, rose, and lunged for Anastas's throat. Sergei grabbed Yuri from behind and picked him up off the ground.

"Let it go, Yuri! He ain't worth it!" He forced Yuri back into his chair.

"Save it for the ring," advised Pasha as Anastas walked away. "You go up against him in a couple of days anyway."

Yuri cracked his knuckles and cursed under his breath. "Boy, just wait until Monday."

Several other street fighters were eagerly gathering at a table nearby, clamoring over some unseen object with whistles and hoots. Pasha rolled his eyes.

"What are they doing now?"

Scarcely had he breathed the question than Victor "Furlong" Sirotovsky shoved a photograph in his face. The minute Pasha's eyes adjusted to the image, his cheeks burned, and he pushed the photograph away. The crowd that had gathered around the table roared with laughter.

"What'd I tell ya," cackled Furlong. "I told you he'd blush!"

"What's the matter, Chevalsky?" teased Clyde "Dark Horse" Husik. "Ain't ya ever seen a naked girl before?"

The girl in the photograph wasn't actually naked but she was dressed down to her underwear and looked to be about Pasha's age.

"I knew he was a virgin!" declared Furlong.

Anastas threw back his head and snorted. "Of course he's a virgin! Who would he being doing it with?"

Pasha got up from the table and turned away. Furlong pursued him. "What are you so afraid of, Chevalsky?"

"Leave Pasha alone," called a well-meaning Moneyrider from the billiard table. "He's just trying to be chivalrous."

When Pasha first joined the Breadwinners he had avoided Moneyrider, who talked rough and enjoyed a high winning average, but he seemed to have taken a liking to Pasha, and regularly defended him to the other boys. He wasn't particularly tall, but he had an athletic build with thick arms. His wavy brown hair parted in the middle, and his eyebrows were so heavy and thick they nearly touched at the center.

"What?" Furlong threw out his hands as though nothing were amiss. "It ain't like stealing a peep through a window. If she didn't want anyone to see anything she wouldn't have posed!"

"You can tell all that from a picture, can you?" bit Pasha over his shoulder. "How do you know someone wasn't holding a gun to her head?"

"If you know so much about it, why don't you tell us then?" Furlong shoved the picture in his face a second time. "Did she do it willingly?"

Pasha was about to turn away again when the girl's face stirred up a memory.

"Wait a second." He took the photograph. Several of the street fighters exchanged surprised glances. "I've seen this girl before."

"Oh, you have, have you?" ribbed Clyde.

Pasha sneered and shook his head. "This is that girl they're looking for! Pearl Sulzbach! The one that went missing!"

The others gathered around Pasha, clamoring for a better look. Yuri leaned in and squinted his eyes.

"It *is* her!"

Sergei pointed to the inside of her wrist and bicep. "What happened to her arm?" Several cuts and marks had been dug into her skin.

"Must be a junkie," said Franklin "Sticker" Horrowitz. "Those are needle marks."

"Yeah, but what about the cuts?" countered Blinkers, Bug Boy's twin.

The cuts looked almost surgical in precision. They weren't pell-mell and slanted as though made by a wild animal, but were neatly lined in rows and columns.

Sergei pointed again. "They're on her neck too."

Moneyrider pivoted around to face Furlong. "Where'd you get this?"

Furlong tossed his shoulders. "Gorelik found them during a raid of Fazio's car."

"You mean a Breadwinner got it from a Butcher's car? The photograph was taken by the Butchers?"

"I guess so."

Pasha shook his head. "We should tell Klokov."

"Are you stupid?" Furlong lunged for the photograph, but Pasha drew it back. "If Klokov finds out we were breaking the rules, he'll flog us all!"

Moneyrider narrowed his eyes skeptically. "What rule?"

"You know! No slumming for whores!"

"It ain't against the rules to look at porn, dummy! You said it yourself just a minute ago!"

"Yeah, but … what if I was wrong?" Again he reached for the photo, but this time Moneyrider shoved him back.

"Will you relax? No one's gonna get flogged!"

"Well, I ain't gonna risk it!" Furlong and half the other boys threw themselves at Pasha, while the other half shielded him from their attack.

Before either could get very far, Trifecta waltzed past and plucked the photograph out of Pasha's hand.

"Money's right. It ain't against the rules. I'm taking it to Klokov. So you can all pipe down."

All fell silent at Trifecta's command. As the eldest street fighter in the set, Trifecta was the unspoken leader, and respected by almost all of them. He was an excellent brawler, and always made it into the top ten bracket. Indeed, if he wasn't in the top five he rarely ranked lower than seven. Furthermore, it was his final year as a street fighter. Boys could join up anytime after they turned fourteen, but after twenty-two they graduated to more serious roles within the hierarchy. Like many of the studs, Trifecta had joined at the earliest age possible, meaning he had been fighting for the Breadwinners for seven years, and it showed in the shadows of his perpetually tired eyes.

They followed him silently down the stairs, past the stage, and straight to the door of Klokov's office, holding their breath all the while. After what seemed like minutes, Klokov thrust his bald head out the door.

"Furlong says this was picked up from Fazio's car during a raid," said Trifecta without preamble. "It's the girl from the missing posters. Pearl Sulzbach."

Klokov furrowed his brow and snatched the photograph out of Trifecta's hand.

"Well, I'll be." He plucked the cigar from his mouth and held the photograph to the light.

"Looks like they've been treating her pretty bad, sir," added Sergei. "She's got cuts all over her and everything."

Klokov nodded and directed his attention to Franklin. "Sticker, get me Yakov." He slipped the photograph inside his jacket pocket. "I'll deal with this." He turned and addressed them all. "Those Butchers are no good, you hear? This just goes to show you boys how lucky you are to be part of a respectable brotherhood like the Breadwinners." He shut the door and the boys returned upstairs.

"What's he gonna do?" squeaked Elmer Malkin, better known as Stride. "Call the police?"

"He can't call the police, stupid," sniped Furlong. "He's a criminal!"

Trifecta kept his voice cool as he corrected Furlong yet again. "Also not true. The Breadwinners have several police officers working for them. Now quit running your mouths and get back to whatever it was you were doing before."

While the others continued to speculate in hushed tones, Pasha, Sergei, and Yuri resumed their card game. Heads turned as a figure emerged at the top of the steps, smothered in what appeared to be a strawberry milkshake. It was Steed, looking tired and irritable. When Pasha looked up to see him marching his way, he actually snorted trying to hold back his laughter.

"What happened to you?"

"Hey, Chevalsky, what gives? I thought your friend put out."

Pasha leaned back in his chair and pretended to examine his cards. "I said you knew nothing about her. Guess you were just too stupid to listen."

Without warning, Steed knocked Pasha across the face so hard his chair rocked to the side. Pasha did not retaliate. He did not rise up in indignation. He shut his eyes, took a deep breath, and popped his jaw. Then, he returned his attention to Steed, and said with an unmistakable air of superiority:

"Good. You got that out of your system." He grabbed his coat and headed down the stairs to leave.

Steed's eyes were wild. "Where do you think you're going?"

"You know Pasha's rule," said Irons, "he doesn't fight outside the ring."

"Doesn't fight outside the ring?" Steed thundered from the top of the steps. "Must be because he's chicken!"

But such tricks never worked on Pasha. He stopped on the landing and faced Steed. "Look, I got three fights scheduled this week with fellas a lot bigger than you. I'm not gonna waste my time just so you can feel like a big man. You got a problem with me, then I suggest you step it up so you can meet me in the ring."

The other boys oohed and aahed. This was an especially witty barb as Pasha was currently ranked several places above Steed, and as a result the two were rarely scheduled to fight each other. Steed's complexion simmered with the scarlet flush of impotent rage, the sort of fury one usually sees in little, yapping dogs.

"You come back here right now, Chevalsky, and fight me like a man!" he roared into the rafters. "Coward!"

Pasha regarded him with a bored and unimpressed air. "Call me whatever you want, Steed: fairy, nancy. I've heard it all before." He turned carelessly on his heel. "You're not worth it."

As Pasha walked away, a smile spread across his lips. Not only had Faina rejected Steed, but she had emphasized her feelings by pouring a milkshake on his head. The other street fighters gazed after him in solemn astonishment. From that day forward there wasn't a single Breadwinner who didn't have some measure of respect for Pasha, even if they didn't like him.

Chapter 5:

The Face

Faina awoke coughing and clutching her chest as a burning sensation traveled up her esophagus. Rolling over, she reached for the dyspepsia tablets she had left on the nightstand. It was the third night in a row she'd awoken from indigestion despite avoiding any triggers. Acid stung and scorched the delicate lining of her throat until she could have sworn her insides had been barbecued.

She leaned her elbow against the pillow. Dry, grainy dust brushed against her skin. Through the thin shroud of moonlight leaking through her curtains, she could just make out a layer of pale black dust ground into the sham. Faina ran her finger across the stain. It was dry. Brittle. Almost like ash. When she turned her fingers over, the tips were stained with black. How could ash have ended up on her pillowcase?

Footsteps reverberated on the rusty fire escape outside her window. Faina gave a start, her eyes darting towards the drapes. Was it Pasha trying to get her attention? She waited for a knock. When nothing happened, Faina rubbed her sleep-worn eyes and pulled back the curtains. The fire escape appeared empty. Across the courtyard, Pasha's blinds were open just enough that she could see his head resting on the pillow. He appeared to be in a deep sleep.

Faina lay back down. The iron groaned on the landing above. Something like pebbles skittered across the grate … no, not pebbles. More like claws. She opened her eyes again. It almost sounded as though a dog were walking up and down the fire escape.

Faina rolled over onto her knees and opened the window. The bitter air was such a shock to her sleepy skin that she instinctively recoiled as she stuck her head out. She forced her chin up, but the courtyard remained empty.

Faina shut the window and lay back down. Perhaps the noise was coming from one of the tenements above?

Faina lay completely still. Her jaw softened. Her eyes began to roll back. Consciousness drained from her mind in a slow-moving stream, gradually making room for dreams. An odd sensation stirred within her. Her eyes were closed. There had been no noise. And yet she was aware of someone watching her. A slow, heavy breath dragged through a wet mouth. Faina's eyes snapped open.

White, pupil-less eyes pierced the darkness. The silhouette was oddly lanky, with a long neck swathed in wiry black hair. It was poised the way one might hold a puppet, as though a long arm were sheathed inside. Atop the neck sat the bleached skull of … a deer? A cow? A deer or a cow wouldn't have had such teeth. It almost seemed to grin at her with curved fangs sticking out at odd angles, some even curling up over its snout. Black antlers branched from its crown, the points too many to number. Hot, moist breath fogged the window as it breathed in and out, watching her with its hard, soulless eyes.

Faina shrieked and writhed away in her sheets, tumbling out of the bed. Her cheek struck the cold wood floor.

"Uncle Matvei!" Her head collided with the underside of the bed as she tried to sit up, her hair tangling in the exposed springs. "Uncle Matvei!" She wrenched her head away, pulling bits of hair out as she did. She staggered to her feet, slipping on the sheet as she bolted for the door and dashed down the stairs.

"Uncle Matvei! There's something at my window!"

Shattered glass pierced the quiet. Faina froze on the stairs. Uncle Matvei tore out of the back room where he slept, his enormous hand clenched around a steel bat. A slender arm slithered through the broken pane of the door. Gloved fingers stretched for the knob.

"*Idti! Ubiraysya!*" Go! Get out! Uncle Matvei shouted. "Before I call the police!"

The hand withdrew, and Faina caught a glimpse of a shadow recoiling from the door before disappearing altogether. Uncle Matvei ran and wrenched open the door. He looked up and down the street. After what seemed like minutes, he turned, his tired eyes searching the shadows for Faina.

"Are you hurt?"

Faina shook her head and hugged her arms to her chest. "*Nyet*. But there was something at my window!"

"What?"

"Someone in a mask or—maybe a dog! I don't know! It had antlers!" Had she dreamed it? In truth, it happened so fast Faina wasn't quite sure she was awake. But then, what were the odds that she would've awoken just as someone was breaking into *Opa!*? Had they been wearing a mask too? Perhaps they were trying to hide their identity. Faina bent forward and clutched the railing with a terrified sob as missing posters of Pearl Sulzbach swirled around in her brain.

"They were coming to take me away!"

Uncle Matvei flew towards her, his arms outstretched. "Take you away?"

"They were coming to take me away just like the missing girl in the posters!"

Uncle Matvei wrapped his arms around her and held her to his chest as she cried.

"It's alright now, darling. It's over now."

When Faina was able to speak through her tears, she swiveled her head around.

"Where's Anya?"

Their eyes locked in a shared moment of panic, and then they were both tearing up the stairs, calling Anya's name. Uncle Matvei's long legs were the first to reach Anya's room. Faina thought he would break the knob as he threw open the door. The acid returned to Faina's throat, this time for a different reason. Anya's bed was completely empty. Uncle Matvei turned and marched back towards the stairs.

"Faina, go downstairs and call the police! I'll search the courtyard!"

The apartment door opened and shut softly behind them. Faina and Uncle Matvei jumped and turned. Anya stood with her hand frozen on the doorknob, the color draining from her face.

"Annabelle Dalka!" Uncle Matvei's voice came out in a hoarse, hollow bellow. He grabbed her by the shoulders with a breathless whimper and hugged her to his chest, unable to say any more.

Anya herself was looking as though she might faint in her father's arms.

"Where were you?" cried Faina, hugging her arms to her chest in the chilly night air.

Anya's mouth trembled as she struggled to confess. "I—I was on the roof."

Uncle Matvei squeezed her harder. "We thought they had taken you!"

Anya squirmed her way out of his embrace, desperate to make sense of what was going on. "Who? What are you talking about?"

"Someone tried to break into *Opa!* And Faina saw someone looking in at her bedroom window."

Faina took a step closer. "It wasn't you … was it? Wearing a mask with antlers?"

Anya seemed utterly lost at this point. "A mask? Of course not! Someone tried to break into *Opa!* wearing a mask with antlers?"

"Thank God you are safe!" Uncle Matvei smooshed his lips against her cheek. "You girls stay here in the sitting room while I call the police. Don't go back to your rooms! Not until we know it's safe!" He hurried back downstairs, clearly too harried to ask Anya why she had been on the roof.

The clock ticked on the wall behind them. Faina and Anya stared at each other in tense silence. Below, they could hear Uncle Matvei speaking with the operator.

"Went for a smoke break?" Faina finally asked.

Anya nodded her head. "Mhm."

Faina took note of the tartan dress peeking out from underneath her cousin's coat. Thick stockings covered her legs, the same ones she had worn earlier that day. Faina glanced back at the clock. It was two in the morning.

Chapter 6:

Shattered Bells

Staccato, Melodious, and Skelter sat in the empty conservatory of the Golden Bull Inn. Singed and bandaged, their wounds were still fresh from their most recent assassination attempt, which had occurred earlier that morning in Borego. Now they were three hundred miles away in Burra Kha, waiting for a room to open up. Rather than whimper over their misfortunes, the gathering had opted to play cards and snack.

"You suppose we'll have new accommodations by midnight?" joked Melodious.

"Seeing as it's their peak season, I'd be surprised." Staccato laid down a card. "We've arrived in the middle of the Luck Feast after all."

Outside, the boulevards banged with a boisterous clamor. Bright and bubbling was the Luck Feast with its blush and gold decor, and frolicking midnight parades boasting the fundamental token of the holiday: bells, the ultimate symbol of good fortune. For days the city throbbed with a constant knelling, and the wonder of brass bells rattling through the night. They covered the villages like snow. Chains of chimes were draped so heavily across storefronts and buildings that one could scarcely locate the doors. Handled bells wagged in the grasps of school children. They jingled from braids and belts. Even the Inn had decorated for the occasion, and bells filled the empty spaces of the conservatory.

"And I suppose all the other hotels will be full," Melodious added.

Skelter made a sign indicating that they might as well pack up and leave.

"And go where exactly? At least in a big city we're less conspicuous." Staccato eyed the abandoned newspaper sitting at a neighboring table. "Not to mention, it's easier to stay informed."

A photograph of the Firebird streaking over Apophis Manor crowned the headline. Samael's face was plastered on every popular journal north of the Eridanus, in addition to the ones no one ever read.

"Where are Pyro and Sonata?" inquired Melodious, dipping his crust of braided bread into a bowl of thick, scarlet sauce.

Staccato snorted. "Last I checked they were arguing in the caravan. You know how they get whenever there's been an attempt on our lives."

The conservatory door, which had been smothered in brass bells, burst open. A deafening clatter of ringing stung their ears. Pyro and Sonata stood in the doorway with a tension so tight it could've snapped in two.

"Torchin' bells," muttered Pyro. He took one look at the gathering sitting calmly at the table and threw up his arms. "How can you three sit there and eat like nothing happened?"

Staccato shrugged without looking up from his cards. "And pray tell, what should we be doing instead?"

"I dunno, panicking, pacing, engaging in some form of emotion that would indicate we just survived a ruitan attack!"

Large, flat, shapeshifting creatures, ruitans are often mistaken for shadows, an error they use to their advantage. Repelled by light, they are easily dispelled with a little illumination. That is, so long as the illumination isn't fire-related. Like igneous, ruitans are flame-resistant, and if given the chance will allow their bodies to catch fire and use it as a weapon against their prey. This is precisely what had happened back in Borego after the electricity had suddenly gone out in the hotel, leaving the company defenseless when one of the creatures made an appearance in Pyro's room.

Staccato continued to appear unfazed. "None of which sounds very useful."

With his free hand, Skelter signed something along the lines of "Another ordinary day in Staccato Nimbus's Singing Circus."

"We are reacting quite appropriately," commented Melodious. "We are happy to be alive, and now we are patiently awaiting a room."

Pyro's eyebrow twitched. "A room?" Steam seeped from between his teeth.

Staccato pushed the pitcher of water towards him. "Careful, Pyro, you're beginning to smoke."

But Pyro ignored him, bracing the table with both hands. "Staccato, why are we here? Enough with the hotels, and the motels, and the inns! We'd be better off just staying in a cabin in the woods at this point!"

"The further we are from civilization, the further we are from help if we need it."

"If we were out in the middle of nowhere maybe we *wouldn't* need it."

"Be reasonable, Pyro. Were it not for the staff at the last hotel, we never would have made it out of the wreckage. We would have been left to die."

Melodious waved his enormous hand. "Enough of this arguing. Come, Pyro. Sit down and eat. Then we can discuss these matters calmly."

But Pyro was inconsolable. "I'm not gonna sit down and eat!"

"Fine," conceded Staccato. "Then at least sit down and be quiet. Sonata, you too. Come sit down."

But Sonata merely pouted and sat down in a far-off armchair.

Staccato glanced from Pyro to Sonata. "Ah. You've split up again."

Scarlet splotches materialized on Pyro's and Sonata's cheeks. Staccato took a sip from his wine glass. "How many times does that make now, Skelter?"

Skelter pulled a notebook from his pocket and handed it to Staccato.

"Ah!" He raised his eyebrows. "Seven times in the past three years."

Pyro snatched the notebook out of his hands. "You've been keeping track?"

"That's our private business," insisted Sonata, her eyebrows lowered.

Staccato twisted around in his seat. "Well, you do a very poor job at keeping it to yourselves. Every single time we're targeted you two get in some sort of row, and half the time you call it quits. Either Pyro gets cold feet, or Sonata tires of keeping your relationship a secret."

Sonata scowled. "That is simply not true!"

"It isn't?"

Skelter snatched the notebook out of Pyro's hands and gave it back to Staccato.

"October twenty-third, 1920," read Staccato. "Sonata falls prey to a sleeping curse. Once the curse is broken, Pyro fears he is endangering Sonata by association, and breaks it off when we return to Feifior. Back together by December the first. April second, 1921. Attacked by a band of furies outside Girtab. Sonata sprains arm. Pyro breaks it off. Back together by April seventh. December eighth, 1922—"

"Give me that!" Pyro seized the notebook and crushed it with a flaming fist. The notebook crumbled to ash.

Staccato leaned back with his arms crossed, completely nonplussed. "And that's to say nothing of the countless times you got back together within twenty-four hours."

Pyro swore at them and stomped off towards the sofa, but not before the candle at the center of the table combusted. Staccato, Skelter, and Melodious ducked and shielded themselves from the debris.

"Get a hold of yourself," warned Staccato, shaking the hot wax from his sleeve, "or I'll see to it that you spend the rest of the evening hovering over the table in midair!"

Pyro merely snorted and crossed his arms.

"If you ask me," called Staccato over his shoulder, "I don't know why either of you bother with this ongoing drama. Why, if it were up to me you'd both retire from rebel work and get married already, then perhaps we'd finally have some peace around here."

At the mention of marriage, the tension in the room grew so thick it felt as though cement had been poured into the conservatory. Staccato bit the inside of his cheek. Apparently, he had touched upon a sensitive subject.

"Don't look at me!" Pyro stormed off in the direction of the exit. "I've only been asking her for the past year!" He slammed the door behind him, the bells punctuating his departure with tremendous volume.

"You did not have to share that with the world!" cried Sonata, jumping to her feet and running out behind him.

Staccato stared after them in shock. Had he known, he never would have teased them. He turned to Skelter.

"Did you know about this?"

Skelter's hand hovered off the table, suggesting he had some idea. Staccato wanted to ask if he knew why Sonata had turned Pyro down, but he didn't want to appear nosy.

"Perhaps you should talk to them," suggested Melodious. "Separately, that is."

"Yes. Yes, I suppose I should."

***

Staccato waited a good fifteen minutes or so before pursuing Pyro and Sonata. It wouldn't do to rush. Knowing their temperaments, it was better to allow them time to cool off before he meddled. Pyro was discovered first. Attached to the inn was an old pub, where Staccato found Pyro sitting before an abandoned fireplace, chain smoking.

"You said I could smoke as long as it was away from Sonata," Pyro hastily reminded Staccato as he took the seat adjacent.

"Have I ever confiscated your cigarettes?"

"No. Just reminding you."

Staccato leaned forward and lowered his voice. "I want to apologize for … what just happened."

Pyro shrugged as though it were no big deal, but a faint orange glow to his freckles suggested otherwise. When he gave no verbal reply, Staccato continued to push.

"I would like to have a conversation with you."

"About Sonata."

"I know it's none of my business but—you've proposed?"

"Three times." Pyro hunched his shoulders. "Suppose I should have asked your permission first, eh?"

Staccato threw up his shoulders. "It's not a requirement."

"Look, if you wanna know why Sonata won't marry me then why don't you talk to her about it? You didn't have to come chasing after me."

"I was concerned about you."

Pyro froze. His eyes darted towards him with surprised curiosity. Unprepared for such a reaction, Staccato rubbed his hands together and looked away.

"Come back to the conservatory and eat something. You shouldn't smoke on an empty stomach, you'll make yourself sick."

Pyro faced him with a hard, skeptical stare. "Did that caim check you for a head injury this morning? Is this one of those cases where someone gets hit in the head and their personality does a complete one-eighty? Because you are not acting like yourself."

Staccato drew back. "I beg your pardon! What do you mean I'm not acting like myself?"

"Well, for starters you apologized—"

"I've apologized before!"

"For stepping on my toe, maybe!"

Staccato gave an impatient huff. "I don't know what you're so surprised about! Sonata is my goddaughter and …" he trailed off, searching for the correct words. "You two have been together for a long time … you're a part of her, and Sonata is a part of—" Staccato didn't like the way Pyro was looking at him. All soft-eyed and expectant. "Look," he braced the arms of his chair, and took on a commanding tone, "you're going to have to work something out because you still have to ride in the caravan together! And I doubt we'll be here very long!"

He was just getting up to find Sonata, when a pygmy dragon the size of a hawk swooped through the open window and lighted on the arm of his chair. He was a stout little fellow, with a face and ears like a bat's, and shaggy fur about his collar. A leather tack was belted about his torso, and the words "Bi-Worldly Telegraph Company" were stamped into a gold plate fixed to his harness.

"Looks like you got a telegram," observed Pyro.

Staccato removed the correspondence from the slot in the tack. The envelope was addressed to L. Niles, the name he had been traveling under.

"Likely your aunt, don't you imagine?"

"Can't imagine who else." Staccato deposited a tip inside the pocket of the harness, and opened the telegram.

DEAR NEPHEW,

HAIG SPOTTED BY FAINA OUTSIDE HER BEDROOM WINDOW JUST BEFORE OPA! WAS BROKEN INTO—(STOP)— MATVEI WAS ABLE TO SCARE CULPRIT OFF WITH A STEEL

BAT—(STOP)—NO ONE WAS HARMED AND FAMILY IS SAFE—
(STOP)—POLICE HAVE NO LEADS
AUNT

Staccato's complexion turned white. He crumpled the telegram in his hand. Covering his eyes, he bowed his head and sighed.

"What is it?" Pyro sat up. "What's wrong?"

Staccato said nothing but handed him the telegram. Pyro screwed up his eyes and read quietly to himself.

"A haig? In Manhattan?"

"I haven't had a chance to tell you what's been going on in New York City. Fay are disappearing left and right. Someone is using haigs to hunt them down."

"Blazes." Pyro shook his head, his voice low. "Seems like nowhere is safe for our kind these days. Not even the Other. I've had my fair share of haig beasts working for the Saighdeoir. Nasty creatures. They'll gore you if they get the chance."

Staccato did not answer but stared absent-mindedly at the fire.

"Are you going back then?" pressed Pyro.

"I have to go back in a couple of days to see about getting Pasha to Voiler legally. I've an appointment with an immigration lawyer."

"Suppose that's the best thing you can do. Get them here as fast as you can."

Staccato bit at the side of his fingers. "I suppose so." At length, he sighed and rose from the chair. "See to it that you eat something. It's been a long day for everyone. I'll let you know if we get a room."

As Staccato was leaving to search for Sonata, the innkeeper informed him that a room had just opened. It would be tight quarters; at least one of them would have to sleep on the floor, but it was better than nothing.

It turned out, Sonata had been hiding in the caravan. She didn't seem at all surprised when Staccato entered through the door.

"I knew you would come find me." The doors of her berth were thrown open, and she was lounging on the bed with her pet cat Cello in her lap.

"A room opened up."

Her irritable expression softened. "Oh."

"But since you brought it up—"

Sonata groaned in protest, but Staccato ignored her.

"Pyro has proposed to you three times?"

Sonata sat bolt upright. "You talked to him?"

"Of course, I did! You can't just expect me to ignore it!" He took a seat on the end of the mattress. "Why on earth didn't you tell me?"

Sonata said nothing but cast her eyes off to the side.

"You didn't think I'd disapprove, did you?"

She fidgeted with a tassel on one of the pillows. "No. But perhaps I didn't feel like explaining myself when I told you I'd said no."

"I'm sorry. You're a grown woman, and it's none of my business." He bit his lip. "But I am surprised you—"

"You'd only laugh and say I was being ridiculous if I told you why." She shifted uncertainly, as though questioning her own motives. Staccato raised his eyebrows, irking Sonata further. "Really, I don't know why you're looking at me like that!" Her shoulders grew tense as she turned her back on him. "Weren't you just rolling your eyes and saying we'd be back together by the end of the week?"

"That was before I knew there was a marriage proposal involved." He edged towards her. "Sonata, I really think the two of you should talk about—"

"I'm going to get something to eat." She jerked up from the mattress and headed for the door.

Chapter 7:
Faina's Alarm Clock

At around half past noon, Pasha and Faina found themselves inside an unoccupied townhome on Park Avenue stuffing a bolster pillow with as much liquor as they could smuggle from a wine cabinet.

"Not that much!" Pasha insisted, as Faina took another bottle of wine and shoved it into the pillow.

"What? Don't you want as much as we can get?"

"We still gotta carry it, don't we?"

Faina put back the bottle with a sigh, which quickly evolved into a yawn.

"You didn't have to come with me today," said Pasha. "You're exhausted."

The truth was, she was more than exhausted, though Pasha didn't dare say more. She often had days like these, ever since Leo and his wife and child had died. Faina didn't know it but he secretly referred to them as her "alarm clock days." They began almost imperceptibly, with little to no obvious symptoms beyond a vague sense of discord, like a clock three seconds out of synchronization. Three seconds would grow to four. Four seconds would grow to one minute. And next thing he knew she would rattle and ring out in an uncontrollable clamor.

"I'd rather be out and about with you than lying in bed afraid to look out my window." She turned and coughed into her elbow, wincing in pain. Pasha took a step closer.

"Have you been to the doctor? You've had this sore throat for a month now!"

Faina buttoned up the bolster and waved him away. "It's allergies." She dropped her end of the pillow and surrendered to another fit of coughing.

Pasha stuck his lip out. "I'm worried about you."

Faina sized him up with a flirtatious smile. "That's because you're sweet." She reached up and flattened his lapels before bumping him with her hip and winking. "Don't sweat it, Stilts. You got nothing to worry about."

Pasha pushed back against the swell of excitement rising in his chest. His arms moved instinctively towards her waist, but he immediately forced them back down by his side. He waited as Faina began filling a second bolster.

"That's plenty for now," he said after she had taken a few. "We don't wanna be greedy." He reached for the heavier bolster. "You think you can help me carry this one down the steps? I should be fine once we're downstairs."

"Easy!" She leaned the lighter bolster against the wall and picked up the other side. They ambled in an awkward synchronization towards the landing. "Front or back?"

Pasha grunted as he lifted his end of the bolster higher. "You better let me in front. I can take the weight better."

"Uh-huh," retorted Faina sarcastically. "Then why do you need my help?"

"Just do it, please."

The upstairs hallway was rather narrow, and Pasha and Faina had to squeeze tightly together to keep from knocking any of the pictures off the walls. Pasha was careful to take small, measured steps so as not to miss a stair, but Faina was impatient to leave.

"What's the hold up, tiger?" She dared forward, forcing more weight onto Pasha's end.

"Hey, hey, hey! I'd rather not break my neck falling down these steps, thank you!"

"Hon, you spend half your days running with gangsters and jumping from rooftops. You really think this is how you're gonna go?"

Before Pasha could make a reply they were interrupted by the gentle turn of a door handle. Pasha and Faina froze. They were halfway down the staircase.

"I told you, Jane," said a posh, female voice. "Never order their meals if you can help it!"

Pasha wrenched around and began shoving the bolster back up the stairs. "Go, go, go!"

Unable to get her bearings in time, Faina slipped on the carpet and fell back on the landing. The pair froze. But no one seemed to have noticed anything. The two women went on talking.

"Have you had the lobster, Lucinda dear?"

Faina lifted her head off the ground and looked helplessly at Pasha. Pasha scooped up the bolster and dragged it quietly across the rug towards the bedroom.

"What do we do now?" hissed Faina, grabbing the lighter bolster.

"What do we do?" Pasha gaped at her in horror. "What do you mean 'what do we do?' You're the brains, remember? I thought you had a plan!" He shooed her back into the bedroom and gently shut the door, setting the bolster down by the window.

"Do I look like a planner to you? I'm just the one who gets things done!"

Pasha pointed a finger at her. "That's bull and you know it! How'd you come up with all that other stuff then?"

Faina screwed the tips of her fingers into her temples and paced in front of the door. "I make it up as I go along, okay?"

"Well, make up something now!"

The stairs creaked beneath a pair of hundred-dollar heels. Faina flattened her palms onto Pasha's chest and shoved him back into the closet.

"Stay quiet!" She dumped the bolster into his arms and slid the door shut.

"Wait until you see what Earl bought me the other day," said Lucinda as she opened the bedroom door. The light coming through the crack in the door was briefly eclipsed as a figure passed before Pasha. He had no way of knowing where Faina had hidden herself. His heart seemed to reach up and grope for his tongue as he realized the thing Earl had bought Lucinda might very likely be in the closet. He listened to a drawer slide open. Beads rattled and rolled together as they were lifted out of storage.

"Oh, my word!"

"Isn't it just darling?"

"You know what would go with that? That little blue number you wore to Meyer's New Year party!"

"Jane, you are so right!"

Pasha tensed as Lucinda's voice neared the door. She turned the handle. Faina's voice echoed across the room.

"Surprise, ladies!"

Pasha peered as best he could through the slats in the door. Faina burst out from behind the dressing screen, shocking Lucinda and Jane to such a degree they stumbled back against the vanity. While the women screamed, Faina jumped atop the bed, grabbed a bed pillow and socked Lucinda in the face with it. She took one flying leap over the footboard and ran out of the room.

"Help!" shrieked Lucinda. "Police!"

But Jane was much less passive. There was a clattering noise as she scrambled to her feet.

"I'll catch that little brat!" Her voice echoed as she passed out the door.

"Don't let her get away!" Lucinda followed after her.

Pasha listened as they raced down the stairs, then tentatively opened the door. His eyes darted from the window to the hall. He wasn't sure whether or not he should help Faina (for she rarely needed it) or try to escape with the goods. Worried for her safety, Pasha went with the former. The rush of adrenaline pulsing through his veins must have afforded him extra strength, for the bolster seemed lighter as he loaded it into his arms. Without a second thought he tore down the hallway.

An avalanche of banging notes pealed through the walls of the townhouse. Pasha skidded to a stop on the landing just in time to see the top of a baby grand piano collapsing as Jane dove under the bench like a cat after a mouse. Faina, meanwhile, had scrambled out from under the instrument and was climbing up the ladder of a bookshelf, soon to be cornered.

Pasha threw the bolster over his shoulder as noisily as he could and slid down the bannister.

"Hey!" Unlike Faina, Pasha was often too anxious and ashamed to shout witticisms at their victims.

Lucinda turned and jammed a heavily ringed finger at Pasha. "There's two of them!"

Pasha hopped off the newel post and tipped his cap in a pathetically hopeless attempt to appear cocky.

"That's right!" He pivoted towards the door. "So you better come and—"

Pasha ducked and slipped on the tile floor as an empty drinking glass went soaring past his head, shattering against the wall. Lucinda inched towards the telephone.

"I'm calling the police!"

"Hold it right there, toots!" Faina reached into her bootleg and pulled out a bottle of beer. "I wouldn't do that if I were you!" She tossed the bottle to Jane, who caught it like a seasoned pitcher. "You see my friend there?"

Lucinda and Jane turned to look at Pasha. It took him a moment before he registered what was happening. Blushing, he staggered to his feet and held up the bolster.

"Inside that bolster is thirty pounds of liquor he lifted from your cabinet!" Faina placed a hand on her hip, still clinging to the ladder. "You call the cops and we're all going to jail."

"It isn't illegal to own alcohol," Jane corrected her. "Only to purchase it. As far as anyone knows we've had our liquor since before Prohibition began!"

Faina flexed her lips downwards and made a clicking sound with her teeth. "Yeah, but four bottles of Canadian whiskey?" She made eye contact with Pasha. "Didn't they just do a raid in Jersey?"

"Raritan Bay."

Faina shrugged her shoulders. "But I mean, it's possible the police might buy your story."

Lucinda sat back against the upset piano and stared. Jane leaned against the wall.

Faina hopped down from the ladder. "Look, it's clear you broads have been through a lot today. So we'll make a deal with you."

She beckoned for Pasha to come closer. Pasha did as told.

"You don't call the police," Faina took the bolster from Pasha and dropped it on the coffee table, "And we give everything back."

Pasha threw her a questioning look, but Faina simply turned to him with a triumphant smile. Lucinda snatched up the bolster, her painted lips curling over her teeth.

"Listen, you little hussy! I let you go and I better not catch either one of you setting foot outside my doorstep again!" She got up from the couch and crept ominously closer, until she was standing eye to eye with

Faina. She grabbed her authoritatively by the chin. "If I were you, I'd spend a little less time running around in those trousers, and a little more time working on that face of yours. Who knows, maybe you'll find yourself a john who can pay to fix that nose up."

Faina swiveled her head away. "And if I were you I'd lay off the peroxide and get a real job so I could afford a wig."

Lucinda reared back to slap her, but Faina grabbed her by the wrist and shoved her back. Lucinda pointed at the door.

"Get out! Both of you!"

Faina hooked her arm through Pasha's and steered them towards the exit. "Pleasure doing business with you, ladies." And they swaggered out the front door with as much ease as if they had been visiting an old friend. The moment the door was closed, Pasha turned to face her.

"What'd you do that for? You had them with the whole Canadian whiskey thing! You didn't have to give it back."

Faina ignored the remark and climbed atop the cement bannister. Pasha arched an eyebrow as she reached for something on top of the broad, stone awning.

"Give me a hand, will you?" She screwed up her eyes as she pulled something heavy towards her. Pasha rushed to her aid, realizing for the first time that it was the first bolster full of liquor. They heaved it onto the landing. Pasha's head swiveled from the front parlor window to the sagging bolster at their feet.

"But … How did you …?"

"Grab the other end." She picked up one end of the bolster and dragged it towards the sidewalk. "You wanna stick around until they find out?"

Pasha picked up his side of the bolster, and they carried it down to the sidewalk.

"You had the lighter bolster, the one with less liquor." Faina hoisted it over her shoulder, leading the way.

Pasha thought back to their exchange in the bedroom. He'd set the full bolster down on the floor in front of the window. When Faina shoved him into the closet she must have handed him the other pillow, which was why it had felt so much lighter.

"But how'd you get the one with the alcohol onto the awning?"

"The bedroom window was right over the front door. All I had to do was open it and toss it out."

"But this thing weighs a ton! What, did you get superhuman strength all of a sudden?"

Faina shrugged, looking as though she herself wasn't entirely sure how she had managed it. "Uh, adrenaline rush, I guess."

Pasha stared at her in awe. "Faina, what would I do without you?"

Faina looked back at him over her shoulder and winked. "I told you. Go back to jail."

Pasha and Faina stashed their loot in the abandoned Heath-Coleman terminal with their other goods, and headed back to the Lower East Side with lunch on the brain.

"Are you ever gonna explain what happened to your face?" asked Faina as they crossed the street, referring to the bruise Steed had given Pasha the night before.

"I'm a Breadwinner, Faina. Do you need another explanation?" Pasha had avoided telling her about Steed, though she was bound to find out from someone sooner or later. "Hey, um, can I ask you a question?"

"Ask away."

"I, uh, heard things didn't go so well last night between you and Steed, and well, I just wanted to make sure you were okay."

Faina's eyes glazed over with a dull expression. "That's what happened to your face, isn't it?"

Pasha's nostrils flared as he sighed, but Faina cut him off before he could protest.

"I know you weren't scheduled to fight last night, and you didn't have it when I saw you yesterday afternoon."

"Fine. You wanna know what happened? After your date, Steed came barging into the Foxhole and slugged me in the face."

Faina ground to a halt. "What? Are you serious?"

"One hundred percent. Just—what happened?"

Faina raised her eyebrows. After standing silently for a moment, she resumed walking. "Now I feel like I have to tell you."

"It would be a nice payoff for getting unceremoniously punched in the face."

Faina took her hand out of her pocket to tuck a hair behind her ear. "Really, there's not much to tell. Steed was expecting something I wasn't willing to give. He got mad, called me a bunch of names, so I poured a milkshake on his head and left. But I don't see what that has to do with you."

Pasha furrowed his brow. "He called you names?"

Faina nodded and looked away.

"Gee, I'm sorry, Faina."

She lifted her chin, summoning up just enough strength to offer him a weak smile. "Guess I should have listened to you, huh?"

He gave her arm a playful bump. "Don't worry about it."

"But, I still don't understand why he punched you. You're saying he just walked up to you and hit you out of nowhere?"

Pasha slowed as he tried to think of a way to avoid telling her the whole story. "Well, I, uh—It may have been my response to something he said that set him off."

Faina stopped again. "What did he say?"

Pasha briefly met her eyes. He could see that she wasn't going to let it go, so he told her the whole story: how Steed had been expecting more out of her, how he had later confronted Pasha, and how Pasha had called him stupid.

"… And that's when he hit me."

Faina's head lowered. She looked like a candle whose light had just gone out.

Pasha's voice faltered. "I should have told you beforehand—"

"*Nyet*." Faina shook her head. "You tried to tell me what he was like. I didn't listen." The fire in her voice shrank and diminished, like a flame inside an oil lamp when the dial is turned down.

"Thanks for sticking up for me," she continued. "I'm sorry he punched you."

"Don't worry about it. Taking hits is how I earn a living."

He had hoped to see her smile, but it was evident Steed's words were still smarting. Inside, Pasha cringed. Why hadn't he just lied? It would have been worth it to spare her feelings. He eyed her, uneasy. Beneath the rhythm of her movements he could have sworn he heard a rapid *tick, tick, tick*.

A large, black speedster came barreling down the road and slammed on the brakes in front of them. There was nothing extraordinary about the incident. It was custom to jaywalk in the city, and on occasion a car might be forced to brake. It therefore came as a complete shock to Pasha when Faina lifted her hand and presented the driver with a gesture that would have prompted her uncle to glue an oven mitt over her hand.

Pasha hustled forward, pinning her arm down by her side and hurrying to the sidewalk. "What was that about?"

Pasha flinched as the roar of an engine ripped past them. The driver leaned out the window to yell something. Pasha could not make out the complete sentence, but he did manage to discern at least one nasty word unworthy of repetition, followed by a cacophony of cackling.

Faina tore off in a sprint down the sidewalk, waving her fist and screaming obscenities.

Pasha charged after her, his heart twisting in his chest. When he couldn't get a hold of her arm, he wrapped his arms around her waist and pulled her into his chest.

"What has gotten into you?" He grabbed her by the shoulders and wrenched her around to face him. "Calm down!"

Faina bent forward in a fit of coughing, struggling to get her words out. "He almost ran us down!"

"This is Manhattan! That's just how people drive! What you did was dangerous!"

Faina's mouth filled with a sneering sort of smile. "And what's so bad about that? Look at us, Pasha! Everything we do is dangerous!"

Something was very off. There was a push to her brass, and an edge to her daring. This wasn't Faina's everyday sort of cheek. This was the alarm clock.

"Let's go home."

"What?" Faina wrinkled her nose with an affronted twist. "You wanna go home because of some row with a driver?" She leapt atop the railing of a stoop. "Not a chance!"

"You hardly got any sleep last night, and you don't feel well. After our last heist we should probably lay low anyway."

She sat cross-legged on the post, her face pouty. "If you think I'm gonna go back to that apartment while the police question my uncle about the break-in—"

Pasha drew forward with a pleading look in his eye. "Come over to my place then."

Her scowl faded and was replaced by a smug, mischievous expression that under normal circumstances might have put Pasha more at ease.

"Well, ha-cha-cha!" She grabbed a hold of his shoulders and jumped down. "What'd you have in mind, tiger?"

Pasha hated it when she got like this. She was cycling through moods and expressions like props in a quick-change Vaudeville act, and he didn't know how to make her stop.

"Very funny." He cleared his throat and latched onto her arm, fearing she might decide to run off again. "What would you say to a game of Authors and chop suey?"

"I'd say swell!"

She shook off his hand and hooked her arm around his elbow. Pasha turned his head so she wouldn't see the cloudy sigh of relief rise from his lips.

Chapter 8:

Loyalty

On their way back to the tenement, Pasha and Faina passed the school just as it was letting out.

"What are you gonna order at *Fong's*?" asked Pasha, trying to keep Faina distracted. "Hot and sour soup might feel good on your throat."

But Faina wasn't listening. She was staring off into the schoolyard, her eyes narrowed. Fearing she was about to have another episode, Pasha nudged her shoulder.

"Faina?"

"Shhh!" Faina grabbed his shoulder and pulled him back behind the bushes.

"What? What is it?"

Faina peered over the hedge and pointed across the yard. "Am I seeing what I think I'm seeing?"

Pasha followed the direction of her finger to a couple holding hands and making their way out of the gate. The boy was a wide-set, sturdy fellow with tawny skin, full lips and cheeks, and hair in a slick side-part.

"Oh, hey! It's Leg! I fought him last week, remember? I told you about it."

Ted Kagan, or Leg Up as he liked to be called, was relatively new to the Breadwinners, having only been inducted as a street fighter six months ago when he left Brooklyn to live with his relatives after the death of his father. Leg Up was the only other Breadwinner besides Pasha who was considered a "white emigre," meaning someone who fled Russia to escape the Red Army. His father had been Buryat, a Mongolian indigenous group that lived in Siberia and sought national autonomy from Russia. Pasha knew Leg Up well, and he wasn't at all a bad sort. In fact, he had a great sense of humor and was known for keeping them all in stitches.

His real name was not actually Ted, but Tekhe Kharachachin. However, in an attempt to avoid discrimination, the family had changed their names. It was a common practice amongst immigrants coming through Ellis Island. Irving Berlin himself had been born Israel Beilin, and according to Faina, Uncle Matvei's surname had originally been Dyakina, but he didn't think anyone would be able to pronounce it.

"Yeah." Faina took his chin and turned it slightly. "And who's that with him?"

The girl was definitely familiar, being small and blondish with a distinctive pigeon-toed way of standing. Pasha's mouth fell open.

"Oh my gosh." He craned further around the hedge. "That's Anya!"

Faina jerked him back behind the shrub. "Shhh! Not so loud!"

"They're twenty feet away! It's not like they can hear us! Did you know she was dating anyone?"

"No!" She paused, biting her lip. "I did suspect something was going on though."

Pasha shook his head, continuing to stare as they traveled down the sidewalk. "Are we sure they're even going out? I mean, Anya? A filly?" Fillies were what everyone called a Breadwinner's girlfriend. "There's no way! They can't really be—"

But Pasha's thought was interrupted when he saw Anya throw her arms around Leg Up's neck and kiss him.

"Oh-ho!" Pasha could've sworn he saw little devil horns sprouting from Faina's head as she grinned. "They're dating alright!" She grabbed his hand and towed him towards the corner. "Come on, let's go!"

"Wait! We're gonna ambush them?"

"We certainly are!"

Pasha sighed and gave in. He supposed it would give Faina some leverage over her cousin. Overall Faina and Anya got along well, but Anya was often critical of Faina's deviant behavior, and she certainly didn't approve of Faina helping Pasha steal for the Breadwinners. But if Anya was dating a street fighter then she would be forced to cut Faina a break.

When Leg Up and Anya rounded the corner, there they were waiting for them. Faina saluted them with an exaggerated wave and an enthusiastic grin.

"*Annushka*, darling! How's tricks, babe?"

Pasha did a double-take, while Faina appeared especially pleased with her shocking turn of phrase. Anya stumbled back in horror, dropping Leg Up's hand and covering her mouth.

"No, no," urged Faina. "Too late for that. You lovebirds have been caught red-handed." She cocked her hands on her hips and examined Anya's beau from head to toe. "So, you gonna introduce us or what?"

Anya fumbled for some sort of explanation, but quickly surrendered and pulled Leg Up forward.

"Faina, this is Leg Up. Leg Up, this is my cousin Faina." Her eyes darted helplessly towards Pasha. "I believe you already know Pasha."

Pasha gave him an apologetic wave. "Hey, Leg."

Leg Up grinned as though it were all very amusing. "What's shaking, Pasha?"

Faina leaned against the chain-link fence and crossed her ankles one over the other. "So, if you're dating a Breadwinner, how come I haven't seen you together at the Foxhole?"

Anya gritted her teeth. "Well, we haven't exactly been public about our relationship."

"Well, the cat's outta the bag now!" Faina flipped her hair over her shoulder and examined her nails. "So, what do you say? Why don't you two join us for Tango Night? It's the finals you know, and Pasha and I could always use cheerleaders."

Weary of playing Faina's game, Anya took a step towards her cousin and stared up at her with pleading eyes.

"Look, you're not going to tell Papa, are you?"

Faina met her plea with a wicked grin. "Not if you come with us to Tango Night."

Anya looked back at Leg Up for assistance, but Leg merely shrugged.

"Sounds reasonable to me."

"Leg!" She whipped her head in Faina's direction. "You're only wanting us to go so they can pull one of those stupid Rodeo things! May told me all about it!"

"Relax! They only do that when it's a fella's first sweetheart. Come on! Let's have some fun for once! I'm tired of all this sneaking around, aren't you?"

Anya looked at Pasha, her arms crossed tightly over her chest. "Is that true? You promise they won't make me do a Rodeo?"

Pasha nodded his head. "You're safe."

"Fine." Anya tossed her hands up. "We'll go to Tango Night."

Faina jumped up and down with a cheer while Leg Up nudged Anya's shoulder.

"Don't look so blue. You could use a night out!"

Faina punched Leg Up's arm as though she had known him for months. "Listen to the man, toots! Meanwhile, Pasha and I here gotta split." She hooked her arm through Pasha's elbow and towed him in the opposite direction. "We got a date with a bowl of hot and sour soup!" She blew Anya a kiss. "*Tseluyu*, cousin!" Kisses.

***

Takeout bins crowded the kitchen table behind the sofa where Faina had fallen asleep. Pasha dozed in and out from the chair, every now and then looking over to make sure she was okay. Katya was still sitting at the table working on her stir fry. The Chevalskys were regulars at *Fong's* because the family who owned the restaurant had graciously helped them find a dish that worked with Katya's low-copper diet.

Amongst the clutter lay an empty milk bottle. Faina had been generous enough to let Pasha try some of her hot and sour soup, but the spice was so intense Pasha had had to drown himself in milk just to get rid of the burning sensation. He knew she had added pepper, but had no idea she had been so liberal with the grinder.

"They're peppercorns, Faina, not croutons!" he choked between gulps of milk.

But Faina didn't see what was wrong. "Tastes fine to me!"

Pasha was just drifting off again when a loud wheeze jolted him awake. He assumed he had made the noise, for he did sometimes snore, as was common amongst the street fighters. After getting punched in the nose so many times, they were bound to have breathing issues. But before he could close his eyes he heard it again.

He looked over at Faina. Pasha and Faina had fallen asleep at each other's apartments enough times for him to know Faina was not a snorer, but here she was with her mouth dropped open, snoring. She gave another little snuffle, this time so loud, her eyes snapped open and flitted about the room in a disoriented state.

"Was that me?"

Pasha and Katya both dissolved into snickers.

"Yeah," Pasha chortled, "that was you."

Faina bit back her own giggles and tossed the pillow at Pasha. "Well, don't laugh at me!"

"What? I'm not making fun of you!" He tossed the pillow back. "It's cute!" *Blin!* Crap, he inwardly scolded himself.

Katya opened her mouth, presumably to "ooh" and "aah," but Pasha silenced her with a look so severe she stuffed the open space with noodles instead.

Faina sat up, looking slightly bashful. "Cute, huh?"

Pasha fumbled for an answer. There was nothing he could do now but own it. "Yeah. Cute."

For a moment they stared at each other. Neither seemed sure of what to say. Thankfully, Katya interrupted them.

"Pasha, you told me to let you know when it was four, right?"

Pasha nodded and got up out of the chair. "We better start getting ready."

Pasha helped Faina gather her things and walked her to the door.

"I'll meet you on the top floor after I turn the goods in. *Khorosho?*" Sound good?

"Just peachy, tiger."

They bade each other goodbye, and Pasha shut the door. Katya was already working up a grin especially for him.

"Go ahead." He made his way towards the kitchen. "Get it out of your system."

"Pasha and Faina sitting in a tree! K-I-S-S-I"

"Agh!" Pasha grabbed hold of the edge of the sink as he tripped over Katya's stepstool for what felt like the billionth time that week. With clenched teeth, he recoiled against the wall and pulled his pant leg up over his injury. There was a bloodless cut where the corner had jabbed his skin.

"Katya, do you even still use this thing anymore?"

Katya stood in the doorway, her frame exceptionally small for eight-going-on-nine. "Yeah. Otherwise I can't reach the top of the stockpot."

Pasha waved her forward. "Show me."

Katya stood in front of the stove. Pasha placed the stockpot in front of her. Sure enough, it towered out of reach, though she would've been perfectly fine to monitor something like a frying pan. Pasha stood back and observed her with a hand over his mouth, trying to quell his mounting anxiety. How tall were eight-year-olds supposed to be anyway? When Pasha was her age he could have easily manned the stockpot, but then Pasha had always been rather tall.

"Let me see your eyes."

Katya groaned and arched her back in protest. "Again?"

"Just do it."

Katya craned her head back and stretched her eyes open in an exaggerated fashion. The Kayser-Fleischer ring, the brown ring lining her otherwise blue eyes, remained unchanged. It was said at the time of Katya's diagnosis that the ring would go away with treatment but Katya's never had. As far as Pasha knew, the disease was not known to stunt growth.

"They're fiiiiine," she insisted impatiently.

"Alright, alright." Pasha scuffled her hair.

"Do you ever stop worrying about me?"

"No, and I never will because I love you." He bent down and hugged her close, drowning in her thick, honey-colored waves. "Now, I better start getting ready."

Katya pulled away. "Your shirt is on the laundry line."

"Thanks, *Rybka*." Pasha grabbed his coat and left the apartment, headed for the stairs.

The roof was a veritable tapestry of clotheslines strung against the hostile breeze. Pasha weaved his way through a maze of shirts and sheets flapping like motley tents until he found his family's line. Pulling his sleeves over his chilled knuckles, he reached up and began plucking the clothespins from the linens. An odor like pool halls and stale playing cards drifted between the fresh sheets. Someone must have been smoking nearby. He dropped the laundry into the basket Katya had left behind.

A bold gust of wind broke across the rooftop, tearing a pillow sham from Pasha's grasp and carrying it several feet away. Pasha leapt over the laundry basket and ducked beneath the sheet of a neighboring line before pinning it to the ground.

"Got it!"

With the rogue laundry in hand, Pasha veered triumphantly around the line only to stagger back in surprise. There, hiding between two sets of clotheslines was Anya with a cigarette wedged between her fingers.

"Anya?"

Anya flinched and rocked back on her heels, dropping the hand that held the cigarette. "Pasha!"

Pasha took a step closer. "Anya, are you … are you smoking?"

"No. This is a Tootsie Roll I decided to light on fire." She threw her arms down at her sides, her hands curling into fists. "Of course I'm smoking! Why is it you and Faina can steal a truckload of liquor at the age of thirteen, but when I start smoking two years before it's legal you both gawk at me with that innocent doe-eyed, baby-faced expression?!"

Pasha pinched his lips together and waited to make sure she was finished before he spoke.

"I'm sensing you're a little angry."

Anya glared at him dully, looking as though she would like to put out the cigarette on his face.

"Alright, I get it! I'll quit stating the obvious!" He took a deep breath. "Why are you all the way over here? Why can't you smoke on your side of the building?"

Anya shrugged. "Less chance of my father seeing me over here."

"Well, as clever a hiding place as this is, you might be getting cigarette smell on our neighbors' laundry."

Anya huffed and ground out the cigarette. "You have a point."

"You said Faina knows?"

"Caught me red-handed." She sucked on her bottom lip and raised her eyebrows. "She's quite good at that lately."

Pasha popped his knuckles one by one. "Yeah, I guess you weren't too happy with her this afternoon." He sat down on the ground and crossed his legs. "I'm sorry that happened."

"It's alright. I know she didn't mean any harm. She just wants me to live a little."

Pasha glanced at the cigarette butt near her shoe. "Well, it seems to be working."

"So …" Anya lowered herself onto an overturned laundry basket. "What's 'hot and sour soup' code for? Necking behind some Chinese restaurant?"

Pasha's cheeks turned the color of smashed pomegranate seeds. "Necking behind … what?"

Anya rolled her eyes. "Oh, come on! You don't really expect me to believe you were taking a break from stealing to get Chinese takeout? What were you two really doing?"

"Getting Chinese takeout … Faina's throat was sore."

Her eyes clouded with confusion. "You two aren't secretly dating?"

Pasha rubbed his ankle, getting increasingly more uncomfortable by the second. "Why would you think that?"

"Well, you obviously like her!"

Pasha opened his mouth to protest but decided it was pointless.

"What are you waiting for?" she pressed. "Sweep her off her feet already!"

"In order for that to work I'm pretty sure she has to like me too."

Anya let out a bewildered scoff. "You think she doesn't? She flirts with you enough!"

"She flirts with everybody." Pasha looked down at his shoes. "Anya, I'm not interested in being someone's catch of the day only to be tossed out later."

Anya leaned back, examining him with narrowed eyes. "I'm surprised at you, Pasha."

"Why?"

"You don't think Faina's loyal."

"She's a loyal friend. I'm not so sure she'd be loyal in love."

"Who was it who begged her brother to let her stand by during your flogging? Who was it who cleaned your bandages and brought you laudanum? Who stole my father's van and drove halfway across town without a license to help you steal all that alcohol from the Yale Club so Klokov wouldn't kick you out of the Breadwinners? And let's not forget how she has spent every day risking her reputation to help you out for the past two-and-a-half years now. You don't think she'd show you that same kind of devotion in a relationship?" She shook her head. "Look, I like you, Pasha. You always try to make the best of the hand you've been dealt. You get into trouble sometimes, but in the end you always do what's right. And that's why I know you'd be perfect for Faina. But if anyone's being disloyal, it's you by not giving her the credit she deserves."

Pasha melted into the ground with a feeling of shame. Anya was right. Faina was supposed to be his best friend and yet he hadn't treated her with the trust she deserved. Anya slipped him an encouraging smile.

"Give her a chance for me tonight. I promise she won't disappoint you." She patted his arm and got up to leave. "And don't tell anyone about the cigarette!"

Pasha held up his hand with a wry smirk. "Thieves' Honor."

Pasha returned downstairs with the full laundry basket beneath his arm. The moment he set the hamper on the sofa, he sprang back in alarm as the sound of Mrs. Novak's shrieking echoed outside the hall. Pasha ran to the front of the tenement and flung open the apartment door. Katya wriggled her head around his hip. Mrs. Novak streamed past them, writhing and squealing.

"A rat! A rat!"

Katya and Pasha turned their heads in the opposite direction. An enormous black rat was galloping down the hall, its pale pink tail slapping the floor behind it with every hop. Pasha wrenched Katya back from the threshold as instinct forced him to slam the door and take several squirming steps backward. He looked down at Katya, who stared back at him innocently.

"Make sure you don't leave any food out the next couple of weeks."

He grabbed his shirt from the basket and plodded back to his bedroom. He hoped Klokov was right about his earnings. As far as Pasha was concerned, they couldn't leave the Lower East Side fast enough.

Chapter 9:
Knives

When Pasha finished turning in his goods at the Foxhole, a crowd of street fighters had formed around Yuri at the bar. Contrary to the usual brawls that would break out amongst the young men, several of the onlookers were laughing and smiling. Curious to see what all the fuss was about, Pasha made his way through the gathering.

As he neared the front he could just make out a whining, whimpering noise over the clamorous drone of patrons. He leaned over Stan's shoulder. Yuri was cradling what appeared to be an oversized, grayish-brown cotton ball with a chubby little face.

"Hey, Pasha!" Yuri stroked the top of the puppy's head. "My uncle's dog had puppies!"

Pasha was just as immune to the charms of the puppy as all the other young thugs, and instinctively let out an "Aww!"

"What kind of dog is it?" asked Sergei.

Yuri appeared insulted. "It's a Chow! Like the President's dog! Can't you tell?"

Pasha tilted his head, examining the dog's features. "I thought all Chows were red."

"Nah, they come in all sorts of colors!" He held him out to Pasha. "Wanna hold him?"

Pasha set down his empty bag and eagerly reached out his hands. The puppy's skin was warm, just like a newborn baby. He wriggled excitedly as Pasha propped him on his shoulder. He rubbed his head under Pasha's chin.

"What'd you bring him here for?"

"So's I could find someone to adopt one. She had five altogether, and one's already been adopted by a hunter upstate. I don't suppose you'd want one, would you?"

Pasha scratched the puppy behind the ears, marveling at the silky touch of his fur.

"I'd love one! But I can't see ol' Borsuk letting that happen anytime soon." A shame, for his mind instantly flashed to the rat. "Plus, Ma and I are gone all day, and I don't know if Katya's old enough to take the responsibilities of owning a pet seriously."

"Well, let me know if you can think of anyone who might want one. They make great guard dogs you know."

Jacob propped his chin on his fist and stared skeptically at Yuri. "Chows?"

"Yeah, Chows!" Yuri smacked the counter, his temper rising once more. "Why do you think they call them the 'lion dog'?"

When Pasha headed upstairs to meet Faina she had already snagged a table with Peggy Pensky, Leg Up, and May Frankowski. Anya was there too, as promised, and appeared to be enjoying herself despite her initial reservations. Behind Faina, Joe Cherney was grappling the back of her chair, grinning and laughing while Faina joked around and cracked peanuts in a napkin.

Not another one, he thought to himself.

She had changed into a dress that was obviously the most expensive in the room, and was clearly purchased with her bootlegging money. It was a daring gown of bright turquoise that popped against the golden undertones of her skin. Her shoulders were practically naked as the dress was held up by two skinny straps, and she had her hair piled off her neck with a big elaborate scarf tied around her forehead. Joe's fingers kept flexing on the back of the chair as though scheming for a way to climb up her nearly bare shoulders.

Pasha hovered uncertainly in the doorway, desperately trying to dig up a strategy to keep from drooling over Faina. His skin felt positively wired at the thought of tangoing with her in such a daring getup, a dance notorious for its close contact and pressing against one another. It was thrilling enough without the head-turning dress. Joe appeared to be having similar feelings.

Joe, a fellow street fighter, was only a year older than Pasha and had already made it into the top-ten bracket for the quarter. He was lean but heavily muscled, and was often mistaken for being much older than he really was. It was said he had inherited his good looks from his Italian mother, and Pasha did not question it. He had seen Joe turn the heads of women twice his age, and in the past year alone he had dated Danica Savik, Zelda Frumkin, and Reyna Herzl. It was rumored he and Reyna had been caught necking in the storeroom in their underwear, but that was just hearsay.

Pasha forced himself through the foyer and made his way over.

"Pasha! I saved you a seat!" Faina took her foot and pushed the opposite chair out from under the table. Pasha's gaze ran from her toes to her eyes. She knit her fingers beneath her chin, and smiled coquettishly.

"What, and you didn't save one for me?" exclaimed Joe in a mock-whiny voice.

Faina craned her head back to look at him. "What do you need saving for? You're already here!"

Pasha smiled and took the seat but did not really say anything.

"Faina took the liberty of ordering you a Coke." Anya slid the bottle towards him.

Pasha lifted the drink in a mock toast. "I can always count on you, can't I, Faina?"

She threw him a wink. "You know it, love."

Joe's eyes dashed from Pasha to Faina with a restless sort of glower. Pasha couldn't help but feel smug as he leaned back in his chair and took a long, satisfied swig from the bottle.

"Gee, Faina." Joe shifted his weight from one foot to the other. "You save him seats, you order his drink. What are you, his maid?"

Faina made an especially nasty face and rolled her eyes. "You still sore about the chair? Fine!" She got up from her seat and moved around to Pasha's side of the table. She looked back at Joe with a condescending grin. "Take mine." Pasha froze as she wrapped both arms around his neck and sat down in his lap. "Is everyone happy now?"

Without thinking, Pasha started to raise his hand, then dropped it with a rapid blush. Leg Up nudged Anya with his elbow.

"Maybe you should give up your seat too, eh, Anya?"

Anya bit down on a cigarette and struck a match, a smile leaking at the corner of her mouth. "Shut up, Leg."

"So, Leg," Faina crossed one ankle over the other, "you and Anya gonna tango tonight?"

Leg Up smacked the table. "You kidding? You should see the way she dips me!"

Anya rolled her eyes with a playful snicker.

"Dips you?" echoed Peggy. "Ain't it supposed to be the other way around?"

"Please!" Leg Up scooted his chair back with dramatic flair. "They don't call me Leg Up for nothing!" He pretended to faint backwards into Anya's lap, his leg extended daintily over his head. Everyone at the table roared with laughter. A surge of nervous energy seized Pasha's stomach as Faina tossed her head back, her hair brushing his cheek. His eyes were drawn to the long curve of her neck, and he felt a sudden urge to run his fingers along the skin under her jaw.

Joe inclined his head towards the doorway. "Hey, Chevalsky! Nadia Berkowitz just walked in."

The smile dropped from Faina's face. Pasha narrowed his eyes at Joe.

"So?"

"So, isn't that the girl you necked in the closet at Peggy's last party?"

Pasha gaped at him. "Is that what you think happened?"

"Well, you certainly weren't playing checkers in there."

"You and the other fellas locked us in a closet when we both refused to play Spin the Bottle."

"You're welcome by the way."

Pasha rolled his eyes. "Nothing happened, except a mild case of claustrophobia."

Joe raised his eyebrows and chuckled. "Yeah, right."

Faina's eyes sizzled with aggression. "He said he didn't like her, Joe. Nothing happened."

"I'm just curious. How do you get locked in a closet with a girl like Nadia Berkowitz and not take advantage of the situation?"

"Look," Pasha began again. "Nadia's a nice girl, alright? But I'm not interested!" Though, secretly, he did find her attractive, and had she wanted to kiss him while they were in that closet, Pasha probably wouldn't have turned her down. After all, he hadn't been getting anywhere with Faina at the time.

"I'm surprised you haven't taken a crack at her, Joe," said Peggy, trying to shift his attention for Faina's sake.

Joe paused, pressing his lips together, and looked off to the side. "To tell you the truth, I'm not sure she could handle someone like me." He leaned back in his chair, puffing his chest out. "I have a bit of a reputation, you know."

Faina propped her cheek in her hand with a lazy simper. "She turned you down, didn't she?"

"Who told you that?"

"No one."

"Hey, I turned her down alright?"

"Why would you do that? You were just saying what a knockout she is."

Joe's good humor was fading fast. "Yeah, well, she talks too much alright? I swear, every time I turned around her mouth was open!"

"As opposed to her legs, you mean."

Joe's face waxed crimson.

"Oh, come on, Joe," she went on. "Who do you think you're fooling? You gave yourself up after what you did to poor Kitty Perkins. You're lucky Klokov didn't come after you."

Pasha knew all about Joe and the Irish girl Kitty Perkins. After a one-night stand with Joe, Kitty had shown up at the Foxhole to inform him she was "late." Joe had reportedly thrown a fit. Thankfully, Kitty turned out to be wrong, releasing Joe of any marital obligations by Breadwinner standards. But unlike Yuri's girlfriend, whose pregnancy scare had been known only to those closest to them, Joe, in his temper, had kicked and screamed to anyone who would listen, until everyone in the Lower East Side knew Kitty had been compromised.

Afterwards, whenever anyone asked if he was concerned about Kitty's welfare, Joe was known to reply, "Haven't you heard? Cats always land on their feet."

"It was a false alarm!" Joe protested in indignation.

"But her reputation was ruined all the same." Faina examined her fingernails. "Poor Kitty's never gonna find another sweetheart in this town, and neither are you. You're gonna have to find a new pond to fish in now that every girl knows what kinda broad you're after."

Joe stared coolly at Faina. "Why do you think I'm talking to you?"

Anya gasped, while the other girls dropped their gaze to the table.

"I don't know. I've no doubt you heard what I told Steed."

"You may have turned Steed down but we all know it's just a matter of time before you hit the sheets. I know your type, Faina. I've seen it dozens of times before."

Pasha could feel Faina's skin turning hot. She reached for her drink to toss it in Joe's face but Pasha held her arm back. "That's enough."

"You'll fall in love with any guy who pays attention to you," Joe continued, "and you'll drop your drawers the minute he says 'I love you,' whether he means it or not."

Anya narrowed her eyes. "Shut your mouth!"

But Joe refused to quit. "You're easy! And everyone knows it!"

Leg Up rose to his feet. "I think it's time you found somewhere else to sit, pal."

Joe got up from the table and raised his hands in submission. "Hey, you don't gotta tell me twice! I know how emotional Faina can get. You know, it's pretty impressive when a girl's got so much baggage half the roster's afraid to take a crack at her!"

"Get lost!" interjected Pasha.

"You're welcome to her, Chevalsky. One man's basket case is another man's total package!"

"I said get lost!"

Joe hurried off and disappeared into the crowd. Pasha put his arm around Faina.

"You alright?"

"Don't listen to him, Faina." Leg Up dropped back in his chair. "Joe's a real scumbag."

Faina sniffed and jumped out of Pasha's lap. "I—I'm fine. I just have to go powder my nose real quick." She tore off in the direction of the bathroom.

"I better follow her," said Anya, getting up from the table.

The others didn't linger long. Peggy was soon asked to dance by Franklin, and May left to mingle at another table. Pasha was left with Leg Up feeling utterly useless.

"How long has Joe been a Breadwinner anyway?" asked Leg Up after tossing back a drink.

"About two years. After Joe's first six months Trifecta said Klokov would kill him before he turned sixteen; said boys like Joe never last long because they always end up popping their girlfriends, or forcing some girl into an alley on a dark night."

"And yet here he stands."

Pasha passed a hand over his eyes. "For the time being."

"Didn't he get in trouble for sleeping with that Kitty girl?"

"No, why would he get in trouble?" Sensing Leg Up's confusion, he quickly added, "It's not against the rules to fool around. You just have to be willing to marry the girl if she gets pregnant."

Leg Up looked awkwardly down at his lap. "Oh."

At first Pasha was surprised Leg Up didn't know this, but then it wasn't as though Klokov had pulled him off to the side right after his flogging and recited every little detailed rule. He usually picked up such things from the other boys.

"Has that ever happened?"

Pasha snickered. "You kidding? Blaze, Sochinsky, and Marathon are all married. And that's just out of the current street fighters."

Leg Up raised his eyebrows. "How old is Blaze?"

"Sixteen. Baby's due in May."

Soon Anya returned, tucking away a handkerchief and smoothing her hair.

"I think she just needs a few moments to herself."

"She gonna be okay?" asked Leg Up.

"Yeah, she wouldn't want to miss out on the competition, after all."

They sat and chatted for some time, but were eventually interrupted by a round of applause from the corner of the room where a large dartboard had been erected.

"I need a volunteer," a foal named Manny Caplan announced.

"I'll do it!" Faina, having just returned from the ladies' room, stepped out from the crowd and stood in front of the board.

Anya narrowed her eyes. "She'll do what?"

"A hand for my lovely assistant!" Manny took a knife from his pocket. It should have been obvious what was about to take place, but Pasha was so bewildered he could only watch them with suspicion, convinced there was no way they could be doing what it looked like they were doing.

Faina leaned up against the target and posed like a model. Manny hurled the blade at the board. It missed the cork and embedded into the wall six inches from Faina's arm. The crowd gasped. Anya jumped out of her seat. Pasha felt the air go out of his lungs.

Anya tugged on Leg Up's arm. "We have to stop her!"

Leg Up put his hand on her shoulder. "I'll get one of the fellas downstairs."

"Come on, Manny," Faina egged him on. "You can do better than that!"

While most of the onlookers were foals and too dumb to know any better, several of the older boys hung back, whispering amongst themselves. Pasha took several hurried strides towards the gathering, afraid to make any sudden movements lest Manny's hand slip.

"Faina," Pasha exclaimed while Manny got another knife from a table.

Faina didn't dare move but winked at Pasha and smiled. "What's cooking, Stilts? I'm a little busy at the moment."

Pasha waved her to come towards him. "Faina, can you come here for a moment please?" He didn't want to embarrass her by making a scene. This had all been Joe's fault.

"Unless you wanna see me shish-kebobbed it's gonna have to wait."

Manny hurled another. This time it stuck itself into the wood directly above Faina's skull. Pasha felt as though all the blood were draining out of him and onto the floor. Thank goodness for Anya who had the gumption to grab the next knife out of Manny's hand and slap him across the face.

"What is the matter with you?"

A splitting sound made everyone jump as the doors were kicked open. Klokov appeared, his face splotchy and swollen with red rage.

"Where's Resonance?" he thundered, calling Manny by his street-fighter name. His knuckles were turning purple.

Leg Up slipped in quietly behind him. Manny didn't look so cocky anymore. His face flushed, and Pasha could see his hands trembling. Klokov crooked his finger. Manny staggered towards him, nearly tripping over a chair in the process. The moment he was within arm's reach of his employer, Klokov struck him across the back of the head.

"What were you thinking?" He grabbed him by the collar and threw him towards the door. "Downstairs, now!"

Manny raced out the door. The room grew silent. Klokov took several steps forward, pushed a chair out of his way, and wrenched his head to the right. An audible popping noise resounded from his neck.

"What is my rule about harming women?"

All the street fighters in the room answered in unison. *"Any man caught raising his fist to a woman, child, or invalid will be killed."*

He raised his finger. "I don't ever wanna catch a single one of you doing something so stupid ever again!"

He exited, slamming the door behind him. The crowd dispersed, the noise gradually regaining volume. Faina stood there blankly for a moment, fingering her necklace with her chin tucked to her chest, looking very much like a lost child. The moment Pasha took a step towards her, she bolted for the door like a startled doe.

Pasha weaved through the crowd, shoving chairs out of his path. "Faina!"

"What'd I tell you?" chortled Joe. "One hundred percent certifiable! What a Dumb Dora!"

"Shut up, Joe!"

The bandleader's voice echoed over the speakers. "Ladies and gentlemen, we interrupt your tango to announce that the Finals for this month's dance competition will begin in fifteen minutes."

Pasha caught up with Faina halfway down the stairs outside. "Faina! Hey! Faina!" He grabbed her by the arm and towed her back. "Faina, this has to stop!"

Faina wrenched her arm away and leaned far over the railing. "What has to stop?"

"Your reckless behavior! Faina, don't pretend you don't know what I'm talking about! Ever since Leo and Jazmin died you've been darting out in front of cars, you've tried to start fights with grown men—"

"So?"

She reeled back up the staircase but tripped on her heels and caught herself on the bannister. Her shoulders shook as she sobbed.

"Why are you doing this?" Pasha loomed over her. "You're gonna get killed! You wanna get killed?"

"Sometimes!"

Pasha froze. The words he had stored on his tongue vanished, snuffed out by her unexpected declaration. Below them the traffic blared.

"I don't want you to feel that way." The words balled up in a cloud as they departed his mouth.

"Yeah, well, me either." She swallowed and exhaled out her mouth. The crying had made her sinuses swollen and she sounded stuffy. "But what can you do?" She rose from the stairs and crossed to the bannister.

"Why do you wanna die?"

"Because I'm cursed." She stared down at the Bowery, looking as though she might throw up. "Scratch that, I *am* the curse."

"You're not a curse."

"All my family's dead before their time. Leo and my parents were murdered under two completely unrelated circumstances. I'm a burden to my uncle …" Faina's brow crinkled as tears leaked down her face. "And I'm just so alone!"

"Faina, everyone adores you. Weren't you telling me the other day that Peggy always compliments you on your outfits?"

"Okay, so maybe everyone doesn't hate me … but I'm not close to anyone except you. You're the only friend I have, even though I've tried to make more. People are nice to me but that's it. No one wants to get close. I scare them away. People like me but nobody loves me. There's something wrong with me!" She sucked in a breath full of air. "It's just like Joe said! There's something off and everyone can smell it!"

Pasha was slow to react this time. He let her stand there and cry for a moment before pulling her into his arms once more.

"You think nobody loves you?"

Faina swallowed and nodded. Pasha wasn't sure how she would interpret his next words, whether she would see the deeper truth behind them that he had tried to fight, or not. He wasn't even sure what he wanted to come from it, but he had to say it.

"But I love you."

A long silence followed.

"Why?" came the muffled reply.

"Why?" He swallowed, and swayed her back and forth. "Because you're exciting." His eyes wound towards the hidden stars on the horizon. "And funny. You do things like … You just do things differently." He sighed. "You make sure everyone gets loved, even the people nobody pays attention to. People like me. Even if you don't get loved back. I don't think there's anything wrong with you. I think you're wonderful."

Faina was trembling with tears once more. She looked up at him. Everything came into sharper focus when she leaned towards him. Faina's freckles were brighter. All movement seemed to slow. A burning excitement flooded Pasha's chest. She was rising up on her tiptoes now, her lips puckered.

Faina was going to kiss him, and yet he couldn't be happy about it. There was a strange sort of dread building up inside him. He had exactly what he wanted in his arms. But the timing was incorrect. And it would be wrong to give in.

Before she could go any further, he cupped her cheeks and turned her face down, kissing the crown of her head. "You're my best friend."

Faina fell back on her heels with a thud. The wrought iron shivered beneath their feet. She stepped back from Pasha, her eyes cold and hurt.

Regretting what had passed, Pasha reached for her face but she moved away.

"Faina, you're not in your right frame of—"

"You're my best friend too, Pasha." She wrenched her head up and forced a grin to her lips. Then she turned and ran down the steps, leaving Pasha by himself.

Chapter 10:

Lydia's Wisdom

"You're home awfully early," remarked Lydia when Pasha came through the door. "I thought you had the dance finals with Faina tonight."

She and Katya were sitting in the parlor engrossed in piecework. He could tell from the way Katya slumped in her chair she'd been at it too long and was getting antsy.

"Change of plans." He grabbed a sleeve of Saltines from the tin and headed towards his room. He could feel his mother's skeptical gaze trailing him towards the hall.

"Why? What happened?"

"Ma," whined Katya, "I can't get this thread to knot!"

Pasha turned and watched her slide childishly onto the floor with a groan. Lydia held out her hand.

"Give it here."

Katya laid the garment in her mother's hand and stretched out on her stomach where she began fidgeting with a stray button made of pearl. Lydia did not take her eyes off her son.

"What happened?"

Pasha arched his neck and collapsed against the wall. "Nothing!"

She waved her hand at Katya. "Stop fidgeting with that button." She reached into her pocket and handed her a cheap brown one. "Use this one instead." She scanned him over briefly, then sat up. "If it were nothing then you would tell me."

The button rolled under her chair. Without thinking twice, Katya crawled after it, squeezing between her mother's legs with the carelessness of a dog.

"Katya! Please! Your brother is depressed!"

Having retrieved the button, Katya flopped back on her belly and tried to get it to stand on one end. "He's always depressed!"

Lydia's features were rapidly taking on the expression of a mother who'd reached her limit for the day. Pasha, on the other hand, could not help but snicker.

"Kid gets me."

The button rolled between them to the corner and slipped into the vent where it clanged noisily.

Katya's lips formed a little "O". "Oops."

Lydia shut her eyes in a slow, exasperated manner, signaling that she was at the end of her rope. She inhaled through her nose.

Pasha glanced at his sister. "How long has she been at it?"

"An hour and a half."

"You know she's completely useless when she gets to this point."

Lydia gestured to the extensive pile of clothes on the floor. "What choice did I have?" She snapped her fingers at Katya and gestured for her to stand. "Alright. You're done for the night." She kissed her head. "Thank you, my little helper. Go wash up and then you can do whatever you want until bedtime."

Alive with liberation, Katya flew up from the floor and dashed jubilantly down the hall with a cheer. Thinking that he, too had been delivered from his mother's authority for the evening, Pasha drifted towards his room.

"Faina have another of her breakdowns?"

Pasha turned to look at her. Lydia's gaze softened. She looked down at her lap.

"You don't have to tell me if you don't want."

Pasha hovered at the mouth of the passage with his hands in his pockets, struggling to decide what he wanted.

"No." He took a careless step towards her, crossing one ankle over the other as he did. "I don't mind that much I guess …" He looked down at the floor and shrugged dramatically.

Her dimples appeared with a gentle smirk. "You sure?" She cleared the pile of clothing off the sofa as he sat down.

"No. But I don't know who else I'm gonna talk to about it." He bent forward with his hands clasped and brushed his hand through his bangs. "Yeah. Faina had another of her breakdowns."

"Did you have a talk with her about it?"

"Yeah. I did." His tone was flat.

"And how did that go?"

"She tried to kiss me."

He took a chance by glancing back at her. Her expression was somewhat muddled, but he was relieved to see that she was more excited for him than disapproving. That being said, a part of him wanted nothing more than to disappear between the slats in the vent like Katya's button.

"Tried?" she finally said. "What stopped her?"

"I did."

Lydia said nothing, waiting for him to go on. His words came out with an exhale.

"She wasn't in her right state of mind. Her emotions were all over the place." Pasha swallowed, fighting against the redness in his cheeks. "I wanted to kiss Faina. But I don't wanna just be something to fill up the emptiness with."

"Well, of course not."

He hesitated, struggling to get over the reality that he was confessing all this to his mother. A feeling of sadness twisted inside his heart. He longed for Papa.

"I'm sorry I'm the only one you've got to spill your secrets to. It can't be any fun having to open up to your mother." She managed a weak smile.

"Did I make a mistake?"

"No." Lydia placed her hand on his shoulder. "You did the right thing, and I am so proud of you, *moya Patulya*."

"You are?"

She rubbed her hand up and down his back. "It couldn't have been easy to let that opportunity go. You are right, Faina is not in a good place right now. She is vulnerable, and there are many boys out there who would've taken advantage of such a situation. But I think it shows great maturity on your part, and a great respect for Faina to have held back, even though it is what you wanted." She reached up and stroked the cowlick at the nape of his neck. "And no, you do not want to be a bandage for Faina's pain. That is not real love."

Pasha nodded, feeling justified but no less disappointed. "It hurt her feelings I think."

"It probably did. But there are some hurts that are good for us."

"Do you think I've lost her for good?"

Lydia waved her hand with a quiet scoff. "Not at all. Faina has a little growing to do is all. She'll come back around, but she needs to heal first."

Pasha leaned back against the sofa while his mother put her arm around him.

"What can I do to help her get better?"

"You just keep being her friend. Do what you are doing now. Encourage her, protect her. Hold her accountable like you did tonight."

"What made you feel better after your father died?"

Lydia leaned her head back with a self-deprecating sort of laugh. "Unfortunately, it was a long time before I can say I was truly healed. I made a lot of mistakes. Many of them very similar to Faina's. And there were a lot of consequences I had to face. But when you came along, I think it helped to have something to care for."

121

Pasha looked up at her with an exceptionally wry expression. "So you're saying what Faina needs is a baby?"

Lydia gave him a playful shove while he laughed.

"She certainly does not." She scuffled his hair. "Her birthday is coming up in a few weeks. Maybe you can get her something to lift her spirits a little, eh?"

"Well, I do have one idea. But I'm gonna have to ask Uncle Matvei."

Chapter 11:

Dreamcatchers

It was well past midnight. Staccato was on his fourth cup of coffee as he poured over a copy of *Tales and Omens: An Anthology of Voilerian Folklore* beneath the dim light of Aunt Poppy's sitting room. The book had been borrowed from one of his aunt's friends from the Home Sweet Home Society, a moira who, like so many others, had taken to prophesying about the Firebird lately. Aunt Poppy had long since gone to bed, but Staccato was too absorbed in his work to sleep.

His finger slid silently along the page. Behind him the clock ticked rhythmically on the wall. He squinted his eyes. He was finding it difficult to keep them focused. The lamp was really not sufficient for reading, and he had been forced to rely partially on the thin stream of streetlight coming in from the courtyard.

The Firebird is considered the rarest of the seven Argentum, and is only ...

The text vanished beneath a passing shadow. Staccato swiveled towards the window. The last vestiges of an unidentifiable silhouette eclipsed the glass. Swiftly, he yanked back the curtains. Nothing. The fire escape was empty. For a moment, Staccato sat there, listening. All was quiet. There was no real reason to investigate further, and yet … and yet he could not shake the feeling that something was wrong.

He leaned against the panes. The glass fogged beneath his breath. Nothing. Still not satisfied, he opened the window and looked out upon the courtyard. The streets were still. Every window in the tenement had darkened save his own. He stood clinging to the sill. He blinked at the shadows. When nothing happened, he moved to duck back inside.

And then he saw it.

Illuminated by his own dull lamp. A tuft of coarse, black fur on the fire escape. Staccato's eyes flew to Lydia's window.

"Aunt!" he hollered without removing his gaze. "Aunt!! Aunt Poppy!!"

There was a shuffling noise from the bedroom. "What is it?" Aunt Poppy poked her head out the door. "What's wrong?"

Staccato held out his hand, signaling for her to stay put. "We have a visitor." He held up the shed fur. Aunt Poppy gasped and summoned her staff, which was disguised as a broom, into her hand.

"You stay here." He opened the window wider.

"You're not going out there, are you?"

"I have to protect Lydie and the children!"

Aunt Poppy nodded and shuffled towards the window. "I'll stand watch."

Staccato clutched his staff tightly by the neck and crept onto the fire escape, taking care to create as little noise as possible. He looked to the seam of the roof. A long shaggy tail whipped the air and vanished once more. Staccato continued up the side of the building. At the top, he peered over the ledge. Nothing was there.

A wet snarl cut the silence. Staccato looked to his right, and found himself staring directly into the many-toothed mouth of the beast, perched on the ledge. He narrowed his eyes.

"Ah. There you are."

The haig took a flying leap towards Staccato's head. Staccato thrust out his staff. The haig soared away from him. A chorus of shrieks from within the tenement rose up all at once, chilling his spine and splitting his ears. Unable to resist the call of his family, Staccato turned back to look down into the courtyard.

"Lydia!"

A force knocked him backwards onto the landing. Staccato's head rattled against the cold, damp iron. The monster rested its full weight on Staccato's shoulders. Its claws tore into his skin. The haig lowered its open jaws towards Staccato's throat. Staccato struggled to turn his head, avoiding the beast's breath, but it was no use. There was a peculiar, fizzling sensation in his veins as his power began to ebb under the pain. Below him he could hear Aunt Poppy shouting.

"Get back!" A burst of light glared in his peripheral vision. "Away with you! Before I call the police!"

The haig drew back and sniffed the air before threatening Staccato with one final snarl. Then it leapt down into the courtyard and bolted. With great effort, Staccato peeled himself from the landing. He clutched the railing, his muscles feeling weed-like and spent. One by one the screams gave way to conscious sobs as Pasha, Lydia, and Katya were roused from their nightmares. As their shrieks died out, Staccato was able to discern another voice coming from the window directly across from Pasha's. Staccato watched curiously as a lamp flickered on in the rimy panes of Faina's window, and the voices of Matvei and Anya extinguished the final cry.

That can't be, he thought to himself as he mustered the strength to climb back down the fire escape.

"I'm calling the authorities," said Aunt Poppy as she helped him back through the window.

"Aunt, you can't call the police! This is a Voilerian matter!"

"Our authorities," she corrected him as she leaned out the window and pointed her staff at the sky. A jagged jet of white light rippled out into the night forming a symbol of two spears crossed over a heptagon. It was only visible to Voilerians, and the Underground were bound to see it in no time.

Staccato waited patiently for her to finish, still keeping an eye on the courtyard below. He could see Pasha's silhouette through the curtains of his window as he returned to bed after checking on his mother and sister. Across the alley, Matvei still had his arms around his niece who appeared to be crying.

"Does Matvei have any Fay blood?"

Aunt Poppy shrugged. "If he does then he must not be aware of it. He's not a part of the underground community. Why?"

"Lydia, Pasha, and Katya weren't the only two screaming. It seems Matvei's niece was disturbed as well." He indicated to the window where Matvei continued to comfort Faina. "I heard her when I was outside."

Aunt Poppy stared curiously at the pair. "Well, Faina is a highly empathetic girl. It wouldn't surprise me if she's sensitive to such things. It has been known to happen, you know."

It wasn't long before the Underground Police were investigating the scene of the crime, and a uniformed seraph was soaring through their window.

"Miss Potemkin," began the winged man, "when I said I hoped to meet you under different circumstances, this isn't what I had in mind." Sergeant Colombera began removing his nicotine-stained gloves one finger at a time. "But I'm glad to find you not breaking the law for once." He nodded to Staccato. "Mr. Nimbus. A pleasure as always."

Staccato had become acquainted with Sergeant Celio Colombera long before he had begun arresting his aunt for risking the underground Fay community's exposure, as he was the younger brother of Angelo Colombera, the Guardian of Grand Central. When it came to family resemblance, Cielo favored his brother in form and figure, which is to say he was well-built with ochre-hued skin and a pair of thick, black eyebrows that matched his coarse hair. But he had the foggy, caffeine-soaked eyes of a person accustomed to shift work: heavily pocketed with dark bags.

Aunt Poppy rolled her eyes and gestured to a seat. "Very well, you've made your joke, now what did you and your boys find?"

"Not much I'm afraid. All we could find was a bit of haig hair."

Staccato stood behind his aunt, stroking his beard. "So no leads? No idea as to where it's gone, or who could have sent it here?"

Aunt Poppy jabbed him irritably in the ribs. "We know who's sent it! The same criminals who have been harassing every other Fay in the neighborhood! And who will continue to harass us until someone decides to make an arrest!"

Officer Colombera held his hands up defensively. "I understand your frustration, Miss Potemkin, but who do you want me to arrest? There's no evidence to suggest that the haig was operating under someone else's command. For all we know it was a stray. I have to have some idea of whom we're looking for, and so far there're no leads."

"You know perfectly well it wasn't a stray! Haigs don't just wander into Manhattan! Whoever is behind kidnapping Fay is using these creatures to sniff them out! And who else would want to hunt Fay besides Primals?"

Officer Colombera dragged a tired breath through his nostrils and passed a hand over his face. "We don't know that these attacks are connected to Primal activity. There have been others who have targeted Fay in the past. Occultists, conspiracy theorists, charlatans and snake oil salesmen like P.T. Barnum: people in the Other who got wise to underground Fay communities and tried to exploit them."

Aunt Poppy's fists were shaking. "So that's it? You're going to do nothing?"

Staccato put a hand out to steady her, and stepped forward. "Can't you at least set up some sort of surveillance for the next couple of days? A police watch of some kind? This is the second time a haig has been spotted on the premises."

"Under normal circumstances I would, but with all the kidnappings happening lately, we're spread too thin." Colombera turned to Aunt Poppy. "I'm sorry, Miss Potemkin. I understand why you're upset, but you gotta believe me when I say we're taking these incidents very seriously." He removed his cap to smooth back his hair and replaced it on his head. "We'll be keeping an eye out. You see anything else suspicious, give us a call." And with that he flew out the window and into the night.

***

The next morning, Staccato awoke from the sofa to find sparkling, golden vapors streaming from the kitchen, and a complex latticework of yarn, ribbons, and butcher's twine tangled over the window. Staccato moved towards the kitchen, waving away the clouds with a handkerchief.

"Aunt?"

Aunt Poppy hovered before an enormous stockpot on the stove whence the fog poured. At her elbow was a stack of dreamcatchers, and in her hand a pair of silver tongs.

"What's all this?" said Staccato, throwing out his arms.

"What does it look like? I'm cleaning my nets." She hung a dreamcatcher from a hook directly above the pot, allowing the humidity to moisten the fibers. Gradually, translucent, gold syrup began to materialize in the empty spaces so that the dreamcatcher began to resemble a suncatcher. Aunt Poppy worked her tongs into the crevices.

"The steam helps me to unstick it. I plan to give one to Katya and Lydia. Perhaps Faina too."

With some effort she pried the substance from the web. Staccato could hear the sticky gunk straining the fibers, resistant to let go. Aunt Poppy held the dream to the light. There was a loud hiss, and all at once the specimen shriveled into a hard, black resin.

"This one is a nightmare."

She turned to the kitchen sink and deposited it into a bowl of water beneath the faucet. An image of a scaly beast stretching open its jaws rippled across the surface. Aunt Poppy shuddered and looked away.

"Here." Staccato took the tongs. "Let me do that. No sense in you reliving your nightmares."

She patted his elbow. "My thoughtful boy."

Staccato could not help but smirk. "I'm fifty-four years old, Aunt. I'm not sure I qualify for that title anymore."

"Nonsense! To me you'll always be 'my boy.'" Aunt Poppy removed the quilt he had slept with from the sofa, and replaced it with a fresh one from the laundry basket. "I am surprised you haven't chosen to stay at the embassy like you usually do."

Staccato pinched the corner of a dream with the tongs and pulled. "Well, circumstances being what they are, I thought it best to be where I can keep an eye on everyone. You shouldn't be alone." The sticky substance shivered and stretched but refused to let go of the net. "Hopefully, this matter will be resolved soon, and then I'll be out of your hair."

Aunt Poppy snorted. "Well, don't start packing your bags. The authorities certainly aren't going to do anything about it, as we saw last night. And if they won't, who will?"

"I'm surprised at you, Aunt. It's not like you to be so defeatist. You know, I half expected to find you painting picket signs when I woke up this morning."

"With you around I didn't think it prudent," she looked at him harder. "You sound as though you have something in mind."

"The police say they're spread too thin, very well. We'll just have to lend them a helping hand."

Aunt Poppy dropped her laundry, suddenly inspired. "I could organize a neighborhood watch with the Home Sweet Home Society!"

"An excellent idea! In the meantime, I think I ought to plan a stakeout. At the rate Fay are being kidnapped it shouldn't take long before we run into the culprit again, not if we're keeping an eye out."

"What should I bring?"

"Actually, I want you to stay here. Someone needs to keep an eye on Lydia and Katya."

Aunt Poppy stared at him openmouthed. "But you can't go alone!"

A furtive smile spread across his face. "Oh, I have someone in mind."

Chapter 12:

Off the Rails

It was a week before Faina finally came around and went out stealing with Pasha again, and he could sense that she was no better off than before. In fact, things might have been worse. He had little evidence to go on, just a feeling, as they snuck onto a freight car at St. John's and rode their way up to the Bronx.

She may not have been particularly cold to him, but she wasn't warm either; in fact, she seemed devoid of any feeling at all. He wondered if she felt led on after he'd let slip that he'd thought her snoring was cute. Then there was his confession during her meltdown, but what was he going to do? Say nothing? She needed those words.

The sky was as cloudy as pasta water. Even the faces of passersby seemed indistinct and tinged with a gray sense of dread. Pasha wanted nothing more than to go home and lie in bed until the sun decided to show its face again.

They'd made the trek to the Bronx for one thing and one thing only: a one-hundred-year-old bottle of single malt scotch rumored to have been gifted to Andrew Jackson during his infamous inauguration party. Needless to say it was priceless. This rare and legendary gift was to be bestowed upon a corrupt commissioner to celebrate the triumph of his election. Never mind that it was most certainly rigged. While few would have dared dream of pulling off such a heist, Pasha and Faina were old hats. All it took was breaking into the apartment of his girlfriend—a jazz club singer of some renown—while she was away at a gig in New Jersey. It turned out she had hidden the alcohol in an old popcorn tin. Now, it was stored in Pasha's boot, double wrapped in an old tea towel. The truth wasn't all that exciting; Faina hardly said a word to him during the entire stint, but the rumors of how the pair had pulled it off were bound to be sensational.

When they had what they'd come for, Pasha and Faina wandered along the tracks towards the station where they would jump their next train.

Pasha kicked at the gravel, his hands shoved deep into his pockets. "How have you been sleeping?"

"Not great." She looked off into the distance. "A few times I slept in the back in Uncle Matvei's room."

"That window really scares you, doesn't it?"

Faina nodded.

He tried offering her an encouraging smile. "You know, I'm right there across from you though. I'll keep you safe."

Faina said nothing, just kept on walking.

"What about Anya? Maybe you two could share a room for a while."

Faina started to answer, but her words faded with her gait as she came to a halt in the gravel.

"What?" Pasha couldn't make sense of her hesitation. "What is it?"

"I just … don't think that's a good idea right now."

Pasha waited for the siren of an ambulance to pass in the distance before he asked his next question. "Would this have anything to do with Anya's new rebellious streak?"

Faina dragged her feet through the pebbles. "No … well, kinda."

It was all Pasha could do to keep from breathing a sigh of relief. Finally! He had found something to make her open up!

"Well, what happened?"

Faina shoved her hands in her pockets. "I caught her doing something else."

"Something else?"

"Or someone."

"You caught her doing something with someone else?"

Faina arched her back in frustration and stomped through the dirt; it was the most animated he had seen her all day.

"Not doing something, doing—" She stopped and covered her face in embarrassment. "Doing the horizontal tango!"

"What?"

"The horizontal—Pasha! Seriously?" She whispered through gritted teeth. "I walked in on Anya and Leg Up testing the mattress! Getting to know each other in the Biblical sense! *Polovoy*!"

Pasha's eyes widened. "You caught Anya … doing *it*? With Leg Up?"

Faina pressed her lips in a thin line and jerked her head up and down. Pasha's conversation with Leg Up from Tango Night immediately flashed through his mind.

It's not against the rules to fool around. You just have to be willing to marry the girl if she gets pregnant.

Guilt leaked from his gut and bled into his expression. He couldn't help but feel partially responsible. But then Leg Up had looked so awkward and uncomfortable after. Surely, there had to be some explanation!

"Are you sure you—"

"Pasha, trust me." Faina shuddered. "There was no way of mistaking what I saw."

Pasha opened and shut his mouth several times before getting his words out. "Are you sure it was Anya and Leg?"

Faina's eyes glazed over with sarcasm. "Huh. I never thought about that. I suppose it's just as likely that two complete strangers could have broken into our apartment and decided to use Anya's bedroom for a quick one."

"Oh." Pasha rubbed the back of his head. It had to be true then. They walked on in silence for a step or two more.

"So what did you do?" asked Pasha.

"I shut the door and ran away."

"And then what happened?"

"Nothing. They never knew I was there."

Pasha stared at her. "You didn't tell?"

Faina shook her head. When she offered no further explanation, Pasha grew as curious as a raccoon.

"But—If it had been Leo you walked in on you would've run straight to your uncle and spilled the beans."

"Yeah, I know."

"So why haven't you told him?"

Faina made a noise like "I don't know" and shrugged.

"Oh, come on! Don't give me that! Why are you being so secretive?"

Faina groaned and passed a hand over her eyes. "For several reasons! First … it's different with girls."

"What do you mean?"

"I just … I don't know, I can't tell a father that his daughter is having … relations! Can you imagine how humiliating that would be for Anya? I mean, intimacy … that's—that's a very vulnerable thing for a woman!"

Pasha scoffed. "You don't think men feel vulnerable in those situations?"

Faina tossed her hair over her shoulder. "No, not really. For men it's all about conquest."

Pasha threw up his hands, looking very much like a spooked horse. "Woah, woah, woah! Where did you get that idea?"

"Uh, from other men! From hearing them talk about it, I mean."

"What men?"

"Fellas down at the Foxhole."

"Those aren't men!" Pasha snorted. "The guys down at the Foxhole are full of it! They only talk like that because they think it makes them look tough. And if they do mean it, like Joe, then they're bad news. Men are just as vulnerable as women when it comes to that stuff. I mean, to be … *holyy*—" he stopped, realizing he had used the Ukrainian word. "I mean *golyy*—"

"Naked," Faina translated without the slightest bit of hesitation.

"Uh, *da*," yes, "with another person … to let them see parts of you that no one else gets to see … of course we feel vulnerable! We feel extremely vulnerable!" His cheeks flooded with scarlet. "I mean, not that I've … I mean, well, you'd know if I had." Pasha froze. "That came out completely wrong."

Faina's eyebrows nearly touched her hairline. "I would? I would know?"

By now, Pasha's cheeks were burning so profusely they were beginning to hurt. "What I'm trying to say, what I mean is … I've never even dated anyone, okay! So, obviously I haven't … you know!"

"Okay, well, when you do, do me a favor. I don't want to know."

"You know what I meant."

"Still, it's important to me that you know that I don't wanna know."

"Relax." He lowered his voice, looking exceptionally sheepish. "I'm *traditsonny*. Old-fashioned."

"I think that term only applies when you're female. It's never been taboo for a man to get his kicks before he's shackled."

"Again, you know what I mean."

They were silent for a moment, and then Faina lowered her voice, avoiding eye contact. "Yeah, I know what you mean." She hesitated. "I'm old-fashioned too."

Pasha stopped and looked at her. They could not have been having a more inappropriate conversation and yet Pasha couldn't imagine having it with anyone else.

"You are the only person I could ever talk about this with."

Faina replied with a weak smile, but remained quiet. In the near distance, a train heralded its approach with a groaning blare.

"So, I guess you and Anya haven't talked about it then if she didn't know you were there."

"No." Her voice was clipped and short.

"Are you gonna talk about it?"

Faina ducked her head down into her collar. "I don't wanna embarrass her."

"But Faina, if this is a regular thing between them, Anya could get pregnant."

Faina stopped and gave a desperate shrug. "Oh no! You mean Little Miss Perfect might actually get in trouble for once, and not Faina the Whore of Orchard Street?"

Understanding settled on his shoulders, heavy and uncomfortable. Pasha saw through her like thin ice. "You're hoping she does get pregnant."

Faina said nothing, but Pasha continued to push.

"Aren't you? You're sick of being the one who always gets in trouble, and now you want Anya to get it."

Faina directed her scowl at the gravel. "You know, if she wasn't always so self-righteous all the time I wouldn't care!"

Pasha shook his head. "Faina, this is serious. Anya's entire future is at stake!"

Faina coolly examined her fingernails. "You'd think she'd make better choices then, instead of criticizing everyone else."

But Pasha was determined to hold her accountable. He would fight for her better nature, even if it angered her. "This isn't like you. You haven't been yourself lately."

Faina made no reaction but slipped back into her impassive state once more. She became without character, like a stone buffed smoothed by an abrasive gale. With no smile pinching her cheeks it seemed her freckles would slide off like sand on marble, unanchored, as insubstantial as dust.

They could hear the even rhythm of the locomotive now, persistent and steady. Pasha waited a moment or two, then tried again, his voice stained with the unmistakable tremor of nerves.

"Can we talk about the night of the finals?"

Faina picked up her pace, refusing to look at him. "What's there to say?"

"Some of the things you mentioned … saying sometimes you wish you would die. I'm worried about you."

Faina bunched her mouth up and looked off in the direction of the approaching train.

"I don't really wish I were dead. Not exactly."

"Then why do you flirt with danger all the time?"

Faina at last turned to look at him with a smile that made his stomach turn. He knew that smile, and it always preceded something bad.

"Oh, lighten up! Just because I like a little adventure from time to time doesn't mean I have a problem!"

"You're not being honest with yourself. Last week, you were embarrassed after the incident with the knives. That's why you ran out … You scared me."

Pasha saw her spine stiffen. For a brief moment, rage eclipsed her eyes like shooting stars, then flickered and vanished. In its place was something far worse.

"I scared you?" She scoffed and danced ahead of him, skipping onto the tracks with a teasing smile. "Does this scare you?"

The train was in sight now. Pasha swallowed.

"Yes! Get down now, please."

Faina spun a lock of hair around her finger and waltzed backwards. "I don't think so!" She smiled coquettishly, her teeth sparkling like cursed treasure.

The volume of the horn blanketed his ears as Faina moved ever closer to the enormous moving wall of iron threatening to knock her flat.

"Faina!" Pasha's knees sprang into action. "Faina! Get off the tracks!"

But Faina remained where she stood, an insignificant shadow dancing before the yawning red jaws of a dragon.

"Faina!" Rocks flung from beneath Pasha's tread as his feet dug into the ground one after the other. "Faina, get outta the way!"

Pasha threw himself at Faina, their shadows swimming through the singular yellow headlight. They hit the pebbled ground and rolled through the gravel. The wind of the locomotive shaved against their flesh. Pasha bent over her like a gravestone angel, pinning her to the dirt. He opened his mouth to scold but a sob took its place, pulling tears from his eyes like ribbons from a spool. He rolled to his feet and grabbed the chain-link fence, turning his back on her.

Faina sat up, all at once sensitized to the risk she had just taken. "Pasha?"

Pasha ripped around to face her. "What the hell, Faina?!" Pasha never used strong language, but in this instance it just flew out.

Faina lowered her head in shame. "I was just—"

"*Yak ty mih tse zrobyty zi mnoyu?*" He stopped, realizing he was speaking Ukrainian. "You're not the only person who's lost someone! I watched my father get murdered when I was nine! Not a day goes by when

I don't remember it! Did you *want* me to see you get hit by a train? Is that something you wanted for me? To see your body being torn apart across the tracks? Did you wanna burn that image in my head too?"

Faina's mouth sank open with a sob as she realized what her behavior had cost him.

"You're right, I'm sorry! I don't know why I did it, it was stupid! I didn't mean to hurt you!"

"Well, what were you trying to do then? It's not funny! It's not cute! It's scary!" He pushed his hands through his hair and circled back to the fence. "It hurts to be close to you when you're like this! And I want to be close!"

Faina searched him with cloudy eyes, desperately trying to untangle the meaning behind his words. She staggered to her feet, gravel falling from her coat.

"Pasha—" Her lips wrinkled at the sides, and she gave another little whimper. "I'm so, so sorry!"

Pasha continued clutching the chain-link, watching his tears fall onto the rusted metal. Faina hugged her arms to her chest and bawled.

"Please, please don't stay mad at me! Please forgive me! I've never been sorrier for anything in my life! I should have thought about how it would make you feel!"

Her cries prompted another tear-filled moan from his chest. He ran to her and hugged her tight, pressing her wet cheek to his chest. They stood there, clinging to one another like two vines, soaking each other with tears.

"I know you feel alone because Leo and your parents died," Pasha whispered, "but there are people who love you and care about you!" He shook his head. "This has got to stop! You can't come on heists with me anymore if you're gonna do this."

Faina turned her head up to look at him. "But you need my help."

"I'm not gonna make it easier for you to hurt yourself. I'll get by. Come on. We're going home. We'll take the subway. The police are bound to come looking for us after that."

Chapter 13:
Oil

Matvei sat at the front counter of the shop, huddled over an open binder. He had a pen tucked behind his ear, and a dab of ketchup on his elbow. Lunch had been rather hurried. Though it had been a slow day for business, Matvei hadn't let it stop him from catching up on some much overdo work. He was just about to turn the page when a pair of legs crossed into his field of vision. Startled, Matvei sat up. It was Pasha.

"Pasha! I didn't hear the bell." He paused and glanced about the empty shop. "Where is Faina?"

"Faina is upstairs in bed with some tea."

"Why? Is she not feeling well?"

Pasha opened his mouth to say something only to sigh, his shoulders sagging. Matvei hastened to pull out the other stool and gestured for Pasha to sit.

"What happened? Is she hurt?"

"No. But she could have been." He wrung his cap in his hands. "Faina's just been really depressed lately. She's not acting like herself. She says she feels really lonely, and like she's a burden to everyone. And I think all these feelings she's having are causing her to act out. Today she …" he paused and looked down at his feet. "Well, she did something that could've caused her to get hurt really bad."

Matvei stared back at Pasha with wide eyes. "What did she do?"

Pasha's head drooped further between his shoulders. He chewed on his lip as though determined not to say. Matvei leaned forward.

"Pasha, what did Faina do that was so dangerous?"

It took him a moment, but Pasha finally brought himself to look Matvei in the eye. "Can you just trust me that it was bad? I don't want to get her in worse trouble. I told her if she's going to pull stuff like that she can't come help me. Not until she works through whatever this is."

Matvei sighed and looked away for a moment. Pasha didn't have to elaborate further. An image of his twin, Faina's mother, danced through his mind. Ariadne had always been the daring one, the adventurous one … the reckless one. She suffered from what their mother described as "an overabundance of feelings," and sometimes those feelings spilled over—not like water, but oil. Petroleum oil. It was the kind of sorrow that smothered and doused you until you grew so slick everything just slipped between your fingers. You couldn't hold onto anything. It just blanketed you, never integrating with the person beneath but sitting atop the surface, coating you in darkness. During those periods, his sister had seemed unreachable. You could try to claw her out of the muck. You could dig and dig with your fingers. Only they would slip beneath you.

It did not surprise Matvei that Faina should suffer the same affliction. The same spirit that had made Ariadne such a force of nature lived on inside her daughter. And Faina had much sorrow to bear.

"Alright." He passed a hand over his face. "I won't force you to tell me. I want you to know, you haven't gotten Faina into trouble by telling me this." He closed the binder. Perhaps he had not been prioritizing his niece like he should have lately. "She is lucky to have you, Pasha. Rest assured, I am taking this very seriously. I'll see what I can do."

Pasha stood and placed his cap back on his head. "Thank you for listening, Uncle Matvei. Let me know if there's any way I can help."

Matvei smiled and nodded, but the moment the door shut his expression sank. How could he not have noticed Faina was so bad off? How could he have been so blind? It was hardly past noon, but Matvei put up the closed sign and ventured upstairs to check on Faina.

The apartment was quiet save for the creaking of the floorboards as he turned down the short passage to Faina's bedroom. Not wishing to disturb her, he opened the door just a crack and peered inside. Faina was curled into a ball on the mattress, her arms positioned in such a way that she appeared to be hugging herself. She looked small. For someone whose presence could fill an entire room there was something noticeably diminished about her.

Uncle Matvei turned and shut the door. Something had to change.

Chapter 14:
The Haig Takes the Subway

"I sure could use a cigarette about now," whined Pyro as he and Staccato sat perched atop the roof of the tenement across from the Frasier.

"For the last time, this is a stakeout," snapped Staccato, shivering in the harsh breeze. "We don't want to give away our position with tobacco odors."

"The entire neighborhood smells like tobacco! If anything I'd be blending in!"

Staccato ducked his head inside his upturned collar as they were assaulted with yet another unbearable gale. Without looking at him, Pyro thrust out his hand.

"Give it here."

For the third time that evening, Staccato allowed Pyro to grab his wrist. Pyro gave a tight squeeze.

"Ow!" Staccato drew back and sprang to his feet. "Must you be so rough?"

"Do you want me to raise your temperature or not?"

Staccato relented with an irritable sigh, and allowed Pyro to use his powers. His shoulders dropped a measure or two as a current of warmth flooded back into his skin.

"You and Sonata," nagged Pyro, "can't tolerate a little chill for nothing!" The moment he said it he froze, his eyes dropping regretfully to the ground.

It was the first time he had made mention of Sonata that evening. Busy with the V.I.P.A., Staccato had had little opportunity to dig further into Pyro and Sonata's feud, and now jumped at the chance to discuss things further.

"Have either of you talked while I've been away?"

Pyro hunched down into his collar, his eyes narrowing. "What's to talk about?"

"You haven't returned the ring, have you?'

"What ring? I never bought one."

Staccato's eyes bulged. "You proposed three times without a ring?"

Pyro shrugged as though it weren't important. "Yeah, so?"

"Well, no wonder she turned you down! I'd turn you down too!"

But Pyro waved the idea away. "Nah. If it were because of the ring she would have said. Actually, she told me the reason why."

Staccato pressed his lips tightly together, striving not to look too eager. So Sonata had given Pyro a reason? This was news neither of them had thought to share … or more likely, preferred not to. Staccato gave a slow blink.

"Did she now?"

But Pyro was no fool. Never one to let his guard down, he clenched his fists with a surly glower. "I know what you're after, but I'm not going to tell you what she said."

"I understand. But do keep in mind that Sonata and I are very close. If you tell me her reasons for turning you down, I may be able to persuade her otherwise."

The tension in Pyro's mouth appeared to slacken. He uncrossed his arms. For a split second, it looked as though he would open up to Staccato. And then he sighed.

"I can't. She wouldn't like it." He coiled back into his original bunched up posture and looked away.

Staccato raised his eyebrows. Pyro could stamp and huff as much as he liked; it was obvious he still cared about Sonata, and her rejection had left a raw and tender wound in his heart.

"It's just as well," Pyro muttered under his breath. "She don't want me, then I don't want her."

Staccato's tone was dull. "I have a very hard time believing she doesn't want you."

"Why else would she turn me down?"

"It isn't because she doesn't love you. Whatever she said, she loves you, Pyro."

Pyro glanced up at him from the corner of his eye, and for a moment, Staccato thought he saw a glimmer of hope there. But Pyro quickly pulled down the brim of his fedora, making it difficult to see his face.

"It wouldn't have anything to do with you demanding she keep your relationship secret, would it?"

Pyro threw back his head and groaned. "Not this again."

"Because you know you can't possibly endanger Sonata by association. I've seen the bounties. You may be high on the C.O.N.'s list, but thanks to the incident with Sea-Splitter, Sonata has been declared Prime Adversary. If anything, she's endangering you."

"It's not that, okay? Just trust me."

Weary of the wind beating about his ears, Staccato lowered himself once more to a seat, the ledge shielding them from the worst of it. He was just thinking they ought to move to a new location, when Pyro snapped his fingers repeatedly in Staccato's face.

"What? What?!" Staccato shoved his fingers away. "What is it?"

Pyro pointed to the neighboring building across the street. "There's our beastie."

A figure emerged from the shadows of the airshaft, its shaggy tail dragging on the pavement behind it.

Staccato grabbed his staff and got to his feet, but Pyro steadied him with his hand.

"Wait. Let's see what it does first."

The haig slunk along the sidewalk, keeping close to the wall, and turned into the courtyard of the Frasier. It paused momentarily beneath the moonlight, offering them a full view of its breadth and size.

"Tongs and torches," breathed Pyro, "I reckon it's at least six feet long!"

"How long do they usually get?"

"I'd say no more than four and a half, maybe five feet." He shook his head. "Makes me wonder if this is a hybrid."

The haig crouched low to the ground before springing up on its powerful legs and jumping onto the fire escape outside Faina's window. It sniffed around the wall. Staccato stroked his beard, intrigued. This particular haig seemed fixated on Matvei's niece, a girl whom, by all accounts, was not a Fay at all. The beast lowered its head to the window, its boney snout almost touching the glass.

"Do it now," urged Pyro.

Staccato aimed his staff at the unsuspecting haig and gave a thrust. The haig shuddered and scrambled backwards as it was struck with the illusion that the fire escape was collapsing. It sprang from the landing and lighted down in the courtyard, its nails skittering across the pavement as it took off down the street.

Staccato dashed across the rooftop. "Quick! Before we lose it!"

They raced down to the corner and turned onto Delancey, the haig several leaps ahead of them.

"I think it's headed for the subway," managed Staccato between breaths.

Sure enough, at the end of the second block, the creature turned onto Essex and descended straight into the station.

At the top of the stairs, Staccato grabbed Pyro by the wrist and towed him back. "Not too loudly! We don't want it to hear us."

They made their way down the stairs as swiftly and as silently as possible, vaulting over the turnstile and tailing it down a second set of steps.

"How deep does this thing go?" hissed Pyro.

"There's a lower level for the Sixth Avenue Line."

A distant roar echoed beneath their feet, followed by the smooth, synchronized pumping of wheels rolling along a track. They made it downstairs just as the F train was sealing its doors.

"They run this late?" said Pyro in amazement.

"All night."

"Who in blazes is going to board a train at this hour?"

Staccato nodded towards the haig. "Apparently, our friend here."

The haig slid its lanky form onto the coupler between two cars, its attention drawn to the other side of the track. Staccato aimed his staff at a pair of doors, forcing them back open, and they fled inside. The car bolted forward, pitching an unsuspecting Pyro to the ground. Staccato, meanwhile, had the foresight to grab a pole.

"Where are we headed?" asked Pyro, his questions never ceasing.

"If I remember correctly, this line goes to Brooklyn."

Stop after stop, the haig remained on the coupler. When they were almost to Borough Hall, the connecting door of the car in front of them began to slide open. Staccato nudged Pyro.

"It's moving!"

Pyro and Staccato huddled together at the glass and watched as the haig entered the compartment, made its way to the other side of the car, and opened the next connecting door with its paw.

"It's moving up the train." Staccato pried open the exit. "Come on then."

Car after car, Staccato and Pyro tailed the haig, bouncing along on unsteady couplers until they had almost reached the front of the subway.

The car was just beginning to slow, but had yet to stop completely. Pyro jabbed his finger out the window.

"Look! It's getting off!"

As the platform came into view, the haig leapt off the coupler and made its way towards the exit. With the car still in motion, Staccato aimed his staff at the doors and summoned them open once again. Together, they bounded onto the empty platform. The mosaic tablet on the wall read Borough Hall.

Once they were out on the street, they pursued their quarry all the way to Atlantic Avenue, where a series of squat little apartment buildings crowded together in a neat row. From there, the haig made its way up the fire escape, and continued its route via the rooftops. Halfway down the block, the creature descended into the courtyard of a narrow brick tenement, traveled down into the walkout, and entered the building through the open door of the basement.

"We better be careful," warned Staccato, as they stood at the top of the walkout, wiping a bit of sweat from his brow. "I think it best if we have a little camouflage, don't you?" He waved his staff, but their bodies remained as opaque as ever.

Pyro looked down at his hands. "What happened?"

Staccato bent forward, huffing and puffing in an attempt to catch his breath. "Fatigue's setting in. It takes a lot of power to make one transparent."

"We'll just have to watch ourselves then."

Staccato led the way down the stairs, and peeked around the door. A dim light was flickering overhead, casting shadows on the dirty floor of a vast undercroft. The furnishings were sparse, but it wasn't completely empty. Several cases of illegal beer sat in the corner on the far side of the room, and there was an old wardrobe by the door. A stack of books propped up a three-legged sofa partially covered by a canvas tarp. Beneath the stairwell was a busted secretary and a leather armchair that had clearly seen better days. But the haig had already disappeared.

"Well," Pyro cracked his knuckles and made his way over to the secretary, "what do we have here?"

He began rummaging through the drawers, while Staccato opened the doors of the wardrobe. A leather leash dangled from a rusty wire hanger, but there was little else worth noting. His foot slid on a sheet of paper. Staccato looked down. A missing poster for Pearl Sulzbach stared up at him, freshly branded with his shoe print. The stairwell door creaked overhead. Pyro and Staccato locked eyes.

"Hide," they both mouthed at the same time.

Pyro dove onto the sofa and crawled up under the tarp just before the basement door opened. Staccato opted for the wardrobe, where he could just see through the cracked door.

"Escaped again, did you?" A man was making his way down the stairs with the haig. Staccato's eyes darted towards the sofa where Pyro hid. All was still. The man rounded the corner of the staircase and stood in the dim lamp light. When Staccato saw him there was no mistaking that he was an ophidian. He was a young, statuesque pillar of a man, elegant and symmetrical. His bone structure was like that of a Greek statue, and his canines were noticeably long. He crossed to the secretary and retrieved a large manila envelope from a drawer. The haig was staring at the wardrobe. Staccato's mouth went dry. He could try to strike it with an illusion, but it was so quiet he was afraid to move lest he make any noise.

Curiously, the haig crept towards the wardrobe. The man pulled out an address book from the secretary, and sat down in the armchair. After flipping through a couple of pages, he removed a pen from his pocket. The haig moved closer, its white soulless eyes like twin moons in a dark sky. Staccato could hear the pen scribbling rapidly across the paper envelope. How much longer would he be? The haig had its boney nose to the crack of the wardrobe. Staccato tightened his grip on his staff. He could feel the wet heat of its breath coming through the crack. All at once, the haig drew back. The man had grabbed it by the scruff of its neck, and was veering it back towards the stairs.

"You can hunt rats later!"

Staccato exhaled. The man turned around. Blood drained from Staccato's face. Somewhere outside, the engine of a motorcycle popped and chugged distantly. The man's eyes settled on the wardrobe. Uncertain if he was looking at him or something unseen, Staccato brought his staff closer to his body.

"I knew this would happen!" Sneering, the man flew towards Staccato.

Staccato extended his staff just as he was stretching out his arm. The man turned the lock on the wardrobe door.

"How many times have I said 'lock it back when you're done'?" He turned and marched towards the stairs, the haig following close behind. "Can't trust anyone."

Staccato waited until the door slammed and the footsteps died away before he breathed again. Why had the man cared so much about locking the wardrobe when all that was inside was an old leash? He could hear the tarp being peeled away and thrown to the floor, as Pyro emerged from his hiding place. The drawer of the desk slid open, and there was a sound like paper ripping.

"Hang on," whispered Pyro. The doors swung open as the wardrobe was unlocked. Pyro stood in the open space holding some sort of list that looked as though it had been torn from a notebook. "We have an address. We have a description. And now we have evidence." He stowed the paper in the inner folds of his jacket and jerked his head towards the door. "Let's blow this place!"

151

Staccato and Pyro hurried out of the basement, made their way back onto the roof, and bolted. It wasn't until they reached the subway station that they allowed themselves to stop.

"Alright," managed Staccato, doubling over to catch his breath. "What's this you've found?"

Pyro removed the paper and held it out so Staccato could see. It appeared to be a list of addresses.

"I reckon it's a catalogue of all the Fay in the Lower East Side. See? Here's the Frasier." He pointed to the address. "And that number at the end of it, that's how many Fay they think are living in the building: five. Your daughter, your granddaughter, your grandson, your aunt—" He paused. "Who's the fifth one?"

"I bet that's me. I have been there quite often as of late. Aunt would know if there was anyone else. I imagine she'll be able to confirm the rest of these numbers as well." A smug grin spread across his face. "This is it, Pyro! This is perfect! We'll take this to the Underground Police, and that's that!"

By now it was reaching the early hours of dawn. When Pyro and Staccato emerged from the subway in Manhattan the sky was beginning to lighten.

"You think I can have that cigarette now?" asked Pyro as they turned onto Orchard Street.

"You really should eat something first."

The door of *Opa!* swung open, and Matvei appeared, a broom in one hand, and a thermos of coffee in the other. The moment his bleary eyes registered Staccato, his face lit up with an enormous grin.

"Mr. K! What a pleasant surprise! I did not expect to see you out and about so early!"

Staccato resisted the urge to bite his lip, forcing a calm smile instead. "Doctor's orders, I'm afraid. A brisk early morning walk to keep the arthritis at bay." He beat his chest. "Wonderful for the respiratory system as well."

"Ah! I see! And who is this you have with you?"

Staccato took one glance at Pyro and pressed his lips together. "This … this is my …" A cool smile spread across his face suddenly. "This is my son-in-law!"

Pyro flashed him a look, but Staccato merely ignored him and placed his hand on Pyro's shoulder.

"Oh!" exclaimed Matvei. "Your son-in-law!"

"Yes, Py—Perry. Mr. Perry. Phillip Perry."

Uncle Matvei gave Pyro's hand an enthusiastic shake. "So good to meet you, Mr. Perry!" He could hardly contain his look of surprise as he returned his attention to Staccato. "I had no idea you had children!"

"Yes. Two girls. Phillip here is married to my youngest." He straightened his lapels. "Well, I'm afraid we must dash. Phillip's blood sugar is getting a bit low, and my aunt has a nice breakfast waiting for us. A pleasure talking with you as always, Mr. Dalka."

As soon as they were out of earshot, Pyro gave vent to his grumbles.

"I see what you did there."

"Just letting you know, that I'm not letting it go anytime soon."

"Does this mean I can start calling you Dad?"

Staccato scoffed. "Not if you value your neck!"

Chapter 15:
Sweet Sixteen

In the following weeks, Faina saw Pasha little. Not because they didn't want to see each other, but Pasha wanted her to take a break from thieving for a while, and Faina wanted to give him some space from her emotions. She owed him that, she figured, after the pain she had caused him from the incident with the train.

To the outside world she appeared numb: withdrawing into the tenement building, and withholding her thoughts from those around her. The reality was far different. To Faina, the thought of feeling nothing seemed a relief. It was the shame and humiliation that was suffocating. Suppose the train had hit her; not only would Pasha have lost her, he would have been scarred for life.

Uncle Matvei had taken to babying her lately. He knew some version of what had happened with the train, but he never really talked to her about it. She supposed he was frightened, afraid of handling her the wrong way lest she explode. Instead he treated her as delicately as piecrust.

"You've done enough work this afternoon," he announced one day, coming into the storeroom and clapping his hands. "Why don't you go next door and see if Pasha would like to join you for a float down at the drugstore? I hear he has the day off today." There was a metallic clang as he slapped a fistful of change down on the desk.

Faina looked up from her inventory sheet in surprise. It'd been some time since she'd seen this side of Uncle Matvei, and it warmed her heart to see him going out of his way to cheer her up. She slipped him a small but endearing smile.

"That's sweet of you, Uncle. But I don't really feel like going to the drugstore with Pasha today."

Uncle Matvei bent his bony frame over the desk and leaned his chin on his fist.

"What about with me? Would you go with me?"

Faina looked up at his goofy expression and spun round in her swivel chair, hiding her amusement.

"But you don't like floats."

Uncle Matvei reached over with his long arms and spun her chair back towards him.

"Perhaps not, but I do enjoy the occasional strawberry phosphate." His mustache stretched with his broad smile.

"Who's gonna watch the store?"

"It won't hurt to close up for an hour."

Faina glanced down at his watch. A float did sound tempting, and he was being awfully sweet to her. "What time is it?"

"Half past two."

Faina's face fell. She held the clipboard close to her chest and swayed in the chair. "School will be letting out."

"So?"

"The lunch counter will be busy."

Uncle Matvei seemed utterly lost. "Not if we leave now."

Faina turned the chair so that she was facing the wall again. "Maybe some other time, Uncle Matvei. I'm not sure I'm up for it."

The room was still. Uncle Matvei continued to lean on the desk, staring at her. Faina refused to let her eyes float up from the clipboard. Uncle Matvei exhaled. His knobby knees creaked as he stood. As he made for the door, Faina swiftly reached for his hand and gave it a squeeze. Uncle Matvei put his arm around her and hugged her to his side, then he kissed her head and departed.

***

The next morning was Faina's birthday. While most girls looked forward to turning sixteen, Faina had decided early on to lower her expectations, though it had done little to ease her disappointment on the eve of the dreaded anniversary.

So when Uncle Matvei burst through her bedroom door with a guitar shouting the words to *S Dnyom Rozhdeniya Tebya* at the top of his lungs, Faina was wholly unprepared for such revelry. She sat up so suddenly her hand got stuck in the lace curtain, and she nearly tore a hole in the material. It had been so long since she'd heard her uncle play guitar—not since Leo was alive.

Uncle Matvei gave one final flourish on the instrument, then plopped down at the foot of the bed.

"Happy birthday, *solnyshka*!" He grabbed the lump where her foot was and shook it affectionately. "When you're ready I want you to put on your nicest things because we are going to the pictures."

Faina couldn't have been more surprised if a traveling orchestra had come marching through her bedroom door—which it practically had.

"The pictures? But what about the shop?"

"*Opa!* is officially closed for the day!" He removed his guitar and leaned it against the bed.

"The whole day?" Uncle Matvei had never closed the shop for her birthday before, for any of their birthdays for that matter. They usually just ended up celebrating in the evening or on the following Sunday.

"That's right! The day is yours, *radost moya*!" My joy. "Just you, me, and the city!"

Her uncle smiled his kind, gentle, genuine smile, the same smile that greeted her at the kissing post, the one that had made her feel so known, and so loved in that brief first meeting. Faina felt her throat tighten. A tear trickled from her eye. She sat up and threw her arms around Uncle Matvei, burying her head in his chest.

156

Uncle Matvei understood entirely. He wrapped his arms around her and held her close.

"I'm sorry I haven't given you enough attention lately." He kissed her forehead. "I want you to know just how special you are to me, and how much I love you!"

Faina hugged him tighter. "I love you too, Uncle Matvei!"

It was the most eventful birthday Faina had ever had. They saw *Scaramouche* at the Capitol, ate lunch at a café in Midtown, and afterwards took a walk through Central Park and ate ice cream.

When they returned home, Anya and the Chevalskys were waiting to surprise Faina. Anya had saturated the entire tenement in streamers, and together she and Katya had made a pink strawberry cake. Mama Lydia had fashioned a crown of flowers for the birthday girl to wear, and arranged it on her head so that it did not interfere with her ribbon. When they had finished their cake, Pasha excused himself temporarily to fetch Faina's birthday present.

As they waited, Faina was instructed to sit in the armchair beside the victrola with her eyes closed and not to open them until Uncle Matvei said so. There was plenty of giggling amongst everyone as the door clicked open.

"I don't suppose you have any guesses as to what it is?" said Uncle Matvei with a chuckle.

Faina shrugged. "A hat?"

"Hold out your arms," instructed Pasha.

She could hear the smile in his voice. A warm, wooly bundle was placed in her arms. Something fuzzy wiggled back and forth. It was moving! Faina's eyes snapped open. There, curled in her arms was a mousy, grayish-brown puppy. He had a full, fluffy coat and a rounded, babyish face. The puppy whimpered excitedly and nuzzled his head against Faina's chest. Faina's mouth hinged open with a delighted squeal.

"Is it mine? Is it really mine?"

Uncle Matvei patted her on the shoulder and laughed. "He's all yours, *Faishka*!"

Faina hugged the puppy close, rocking him back and forth like a baby. "This is the most wonderful birthday gift anyone's ever given me! Thank you so much!"

Uncle Matvei nudged Pasha forward. "It was all Pasha. I merely gave the approval."

"Pasha," Faina leaned forward, "you did this for me?"

"Why do you look so surprised?" he teased. "You know I'd do anything to make you happy … and safe."

Chapter 16:

Proof of Intention

"I don't understand," said Staccato. "I've brought you the proof needed to confirm it was Primals who attempted to break into the tenement building that night, that they are in illegal possession of a haig, and that they used that animal to target the Fay in the vicinity. And you're telling me that no arrest can be made?"

Staccato and Pyro were sitting in Sergeant Colombera's office, the desk between them crowded with paperwork. With the address provided, the Sergeant was able to confirm that the man living in the apartment was in fact an ophidian and a known Primal, Salvatore Cantini. And though he'd never been charged with possession of a haig before, he had once been investigated in response to a disturbance call. But that was all.

Colombera handed them back the list of addresses, looking tired and regretful. "Look, Mr. Nimbus, I would love to help but it's complicated with Primals. The Other is considered outside the Ecliptic Council's jurisdiction. The Gateway Council is responsible for governing New York's underground Voilerian communities, but these days no one knows how to deal with the Primals. Everyone's got different ideas. In Capricorn, you can't hold a Primal criminally responsible for illegal actions due to discrimination. Meanwhile, in Sagittarius, the practice of Primal Instinct is banned outright."

Pyro jumped out of his seat. "That's shrapnel!"

But Staccato waved him back down. "Don't most gateway councils respond to Primal activity by holding their actions to the standard of the law in the country where the community resides?"

"To an extent yes, however laws can vary by state. Look, I understand your frustration but I can't arrest someone on suspicion alone. The haig was apprehended before any damage could be done. Therefore, you have no proof that the intention was a breaking and entering, or a kidnapping."

Again, Pyro began to shout. "What's the point of immigrating to the Other if you're just gonna let the thing they're running from terrorize them here?!"

"Pyro, calm down!" Staccato returned his attention to Colombera. "It is my understanding that breaking and entering is an illegal act in every state, like any civilized community!"

"And how, may I ask, did you obtain this evidence?" Colombera asked, gesturing to the papers strewn about on the table.

Staccato's eyes bulged. What had they done? How could he not have realized their actions were illegal? And here he was, the pot calling the kettle black. Did Sergeant Colombera know what had happened? Could they be arrested for this? Aunt would never let him hear the end of it.

When Pyro and Staccato did not answer, Sergeant Colombera pressed his lips together and sat back in his chair.

"Are we done here, gentlemen?"

Terrified to say anything more that might incriminate them, Staccato donned his hat and got to his feet.

"I believe so!" He gestured for Pyro to stand. "Come, Pyro. We don't want to waste any more of Sergeant Colombera's time."

He was just about to open the door, when Colombera stopped them.

"Mr. Nimbus!" He held up his hand as though to soften the blow. "You say you witnessed the beast entering the apartment. If it makes you feel any better, I can follow up on the illegal possession of a haig, but that's all." He shrugged. "Maybe it will lead to something more. You never know."

***

Staccato and Pyro sat at a table in the corner of a deli off Houston Street and nibbled dismally at their lunch.

"So according to Colombera," said Pyro between bites of his pastrami, "Angelo has decided to just let the Primals get away with everything?"

Staccato shook his head. "It's not Angelo. The Gateway Council is made up of several members. Even as Head Guardian of the Grand Central Gateway, Angelo can't control everything."

Pyro raised his eyebrows and scoffed. "Family dinners must be awkward."

"I know what it looks like, but believe it or not Colombera is on our side. It's just a matter of his hands being tied." He leaned back in his chair and stroked his beard. "I suppose the best thing any of us can do now is try and support the Home Sweet Home Society."

Ever since its inception, Aunt Poppy's neighborhood watch had taken off through the Home Sweet Home Society. A volunteer watchmen brigade had been formed, free self-defense courses were offered at the community center, and Poppy herself had headed off a miraculous donation drive for dreams, providing people with sweet reveries to protect them against haig-induced nightmares.

"That," he continued, "and push back the C.O.N."

"Speaking of pushing back the C.O.N.," Pyro set down his cup. "I don't know how much longer we can wait on Aries. Da's trying his hardest, but with all the territory the C.O.N. has accumulated their resources are overwhelming. Even when Aries hits him hard they're never down for long, and there have been reports of Primal activity not far from where we're staying now. They're onto us."

"What sort of Primal activity?"

Pyro sighed and shook his head. "Let's just say Manhattan's not the only place haigs are being sighted."

Staccato leaned forward and propped his chin in his hand, deep in thought. Pyro jiggled his foot impatiently.

"We have to move!"

At length, Staccato gave a slow blink and regarded him with heavy eyes. "Once you go, it will be difficult for me to reach you again. Most of the gateways near Aquarius have been shut down due to the Land Lock. Are you certain you'll be alright without me?"

"We will if we can get to the Floodgates."

Staccato sighed and let his hand drop. "If it must be done, then it must be done. We'll start making arrangements to move."

Chapter 17:
Class of 1925

The following weeks saw a change not only in Faina, but the entire Dalka household. Uncle Matvei made an effort to dote on his niece the way he had when she'd first arrived, taking every available opportunity to demonstrate to her how loved she was. Anya, too, lavished her cousin with attention, putting aside her homework to go to Vaudeville performances, or put on a jazz record and pour over magazines in one of their rooms.

Faina had named her dog Mammoth for his wooly coat, and tended to him with all the pride and love of a new mother with her baby. With her poorly mastered sewing skills she fashioned him outfits from hand-me-down clothes and took enough photographs with Leo's old Brownie to fill up an album. She walked him daily, and Pasha was sure that had she owned a baby carriage, Mammoth would have been paraded down Orchard Street in a bonnet.

He was an affectionate, cuddly creature who wheezed when he slept, which was often, and who could put away almost as much food as Pasha.

Though she couldn't stifle her impulsive nature completely, Faina grew more thoughtful, and Pasha noticed her taking extra care in his presence where danger was concerned. He often caught her looking at him as though to say "Are you okay? I haven't hurt you, have I?" She hadn't had a date since Steed, and didn't really seem interested in flirting with anyone, at least that's how it seemed to Pasha. By the middle of April, they were thieving again, and Pasha felt he had the old Faina back, safe and happy.

One day, after a long, wandering walk about the Battery, Pasha and Faina sat down upon a swing set, swaying absentmindedly, and splitting a bag of Circus Peanuts candy. Neither said anything. They didn't need to. But every now and then one would catch the other's eye and smile. When some time had passed, Pasha grew brave enough to ask Faina how she was feeling.

"You seem a lot better now."

Faina leaned her head against the chain and looked down at her feet. Pasha reached for her arm.

"Sorry. I didn't embarrass you, did I?"

Faina hesitated but soon smiled and shook her head. "No. You know me, I'm an open book." She hooked a hair behind her ear. "I am doing better, thanks to you."

"Thanks to me? I feel like I abandoned you. We didn't see each other much for a while."

She shrugged. "That's partly why. You cared enough to hold me accountable." She furrowed her eyebrows together, her expression growing pained. "I can't stop thinking about what you said after you pulled me off the tracks. About how if the train had hit me, you would've seen my body get torn to bits." She dragged the toe of her shoe through the sand. "I'm so ashamed that I hurt you like that. I don't ever want to do that to you again."

He squeezed her arm. "It's okay. I forgive you. I'm just sorry you felt so lonely before. I feel like I should've been a better friend."

"A better friend? How? Pasha, you're my *best* friend!"

"If that were true then you wouldn't have felt like that."

"You're wrong." She looked out at the Hudson. "You could never have prevented me from feeling the way I did. No amount of kindness can stop someone from grieving. It's not something you can fix. You just have to feel it. It's painful, yes, but it isn't evil. It's an act of love. It should tear us up and change us."

It seemed to Pasha she would have gone on tearing herself up until there was nothing left, unless someone had stopped her. She wouldn't have been the first person to be annihilated by grief, after all.

"Yeah, but you can't let someone grieve to the point of self-destruction."

"Well, you didn't. And thank goodness, because you can't afford to go on any more heists without me. Not now that you've landed yourself a warrant."

Pasha shrugged. It hadn't taken him long to slip up in front of the police after Faina had stopped tagging along. In fact, it had happened embarrassingly quickly. He hastened to change the subject.

"Did you ever tell your uncle about Anya and Leg Up?"

It had been some time since Faina had mentioned the two. Ever since Pasha found out Faina had caught them in the act, he'd had some difficulty facing Leg Up, though Leg didn't seem to notice. Over and over again, Pasha replayed their conversation in his head. At least Leg Up was aware of the rules, so he must have been prepared to marry Anya in case she got pregnant. Though, if anyone important ever found out he was a Buryat, or that Buryats were Mongolian, a marriage between them would be illegal.

Faina's chin dipped towards her chest as she looked away. "No. It's just … it was so long ago now. And I haven't noticed Anya sneaking out as much lately. So what if they stopped? What if it was just the one time? I don't want to make her go through all that if they've stopped."

Pasha nodded and twisted the swing around distractedly. She seemed sincere, and he supposed it would be rather hard on Anya to get her in trouble if she was no longer doing anything.

"But, let's not talk about that anymore," she insisted. "Sergei tells me you're close to making it into the top five bracket."

Pasha picked up his feet and let the swing unwind, grinning as he spun. If it hadn't been for Stayer Sochinsky's new baby, Pasha would never have gotten close. But with an infant keeping him up all night long,

Stayer, who had a ninety-five percent winning average, was too exhausted to maintain his stats.

"Yeah, just gotta beat Anastas before the quarter is up."

Faina leaned back in the seat, her hair nearly sweeping the ground. "Just think, you've been a Breadwinner for four years now! You're almost halfway through your sentence! What do you think you're gonna do when you graduate from street fighting?"

Pasha's smile faded at the edges. "What do you mean? I'll still be a Breadwinner."

"Yeah, but that doesn't mean you have to be a thug. Klokov said he's got all kinds of people working for the Breadwinners. I mean, Leo was just an associate, and Klokov was gonna set him up at the *New York Daily*!"

Pasha nodded and smiled politely, but was afraid to give it much thought.

"Come on," Faina urged him, giving him a playful nudge. "What happened to the dream of being a rich, self-made American philanthropist? What do you wanna be?"

Pasha brought his arms close and chewed his nail. "A police officer …" he mumbled.

"A what?"

Pasha shook his head. "Nothing, I didn't say anything."

"*Nyet*! Come on!" Faina pulled on his sleeve like a child begging their mother for one more bedtime story. "I just couldn't hear you! Tell me, please!"

Pasha lowered his head once more, his cheeks coloring. All traffic seemed to fall silent as he answered her. "A police officer."

Somewhere in the distance, a taxicab slammed on the brakes, its driver leaning out the window and shouting obscenities. There was no mistaking the look of absolute shock on Faina's face, despite her efforts to hide it.

"A police officer," she finally said. "What made you think of that?" Her smile was entirely too big.

"Don't tell anyone, okay?" He shifted and sat up straighter. "It's just … there are Breadwinners on the police force, right? So, it's not a totally crazy idea."

"No, I suppose not." She folded her lips over her teeth and made a popping noise with her mouth. "Why a police officer?"

"Because I want to help people. Remember that cop I was telling you about that first time I got arrested? Officer Liebowitz?"

Faina nodded, her smile finally becoming genuine. "Ah. Now I understand."

"It's just, he didn't treat me like I was a bad kid, or just some stupid hood. He saw right through everything. He knew I wasn't there by choice. And I just got to thinking … maybe if I were a police officer, I could help other kids like me. Maybe I could stop them before they ended up having to join the Breadwinners."

Faina said nothing, but beamed at him.

"I know it won't be easy," he continued. "I'd have to do a lot of physical training, but I'm used to that. Does that sound stupid?"

Faina shook her head. "*Nyet.* I don't think it sounds stupid at all. Just … a little contrary, is all, given that you work for a crime boss. But I guess it could work."

"Promise you won't tell anyone though, okay? I know the other fellas are gonna give me a hard time about it. They already make fun of me because I never smart off to the police."

Faina held up her right hand, her eyes still dreamy and kind. "Thieves' Honor."

A barge drifted across the water. The day was nothing short of vivid. The clouds hung low in the sky and had a painted quality about them so that they seemed more like set pieces than a genuine part of the landscape. It was almost as though they could've leaned a ladder against them, and climbed up into the heavens.

At last, Faina kicked off and pumped the swing back and forth. "Bet you I can jump off the swings further than you."

A rascally smile crept up the side of his face. "Oh, you do, do you?" Pasha pushed off from the ground and stretched his legs out. In no time he matched her rhythm. When they had reached as high as the swing set would allow, they counted together.

"*Raz … dva … tri!*"

The pair of them lighted into the breeze, their legs extended. Sunlight glared in Pasha's vision. Their shadows shrank. Without thinking, he grabbed Faina's hand. Soft ground slammed against their feet, knocking them both off balance. Sand sprayed in all directions as they tipped forward, their hands outstretched to catch themselves, wild laughter exploding from their lips. Pasha squeezed his eyes shut. He fell to his knees and rolled, colliding with Faina. When he opened his eyes, they were lying face to face on their sides. Only a few inches separated them. Dirt was smeared across Faina's cheek. The final drops of laughter evaporated from their lips, leaving behind a sweet taste in Pasha's mouth. Silence fell. Their eyes locked.

With a timid smile, Faina sat up and stared at the ground. Despite her bashfulness, Pasha was in no rush to move. Actually, he felt uncommonly relaxed. He couldn't say why. Neither of them said anything for some time. Pasha could think of no words to fill the silence. He feared that if he spoke the fragile perfection of that moment would shatter into a million irretrievable pieces. Instead, he was overcome with the urge to hold Faina's hand.

His arm felt heavy as he willed it to move towards her. His fingertips brushed the delicate bones of her hand and then pressed into something cold and metallic. Pasha drew back and lifted his head. A heavy gold ring stamped with the initials "SHS" was fitted to her finger. On the left side of the letters was the number two, and on the right was the number five.

Curious and amused, Pasha held her hand up to the light. "Where did you get that?" He fingered the fine texture of the embossed letters. "It looks like a class ring."

"It's Dmitry's."

"Why are you wearing—" The answer slapped him in the face before he could finish. He dropped her wrist.

"We're walking out together." Faina folded her hands tightly in her lap.

Pasha sat up. His mouth went so dry his lips nearly stuck together when he tried to speak. "Dmitry? As in Dmitry Vavilov? Whose family owns the drugstore?"

Though she clearly could not bring herself to look at him, her cheeks swelled with an all-too-genuine smile. "Mhm! That's the one."

"When—when did this happen?"

"A few days after my birthday. He took me to a Vaudeville show and then afterwards we went back to his place and ate ice cream, even though the drugstore was closed. We had the whole place to ourselves."

Pasha felt his head falling lower and lower between his shoulders. "Oh." He cleared his throat, forcing a lightheartedness into his voice. "That sounds nice."

Her smile faded for a moment, and she looked him intensely in the eye. "You don't have any sort of beef with Dmitry that I don't know about, do you?"

I might now, he thought to himself, but jammed a grin into his mouth instead. "No! Not at all. Dmitry is … a really nice guy."

And it was true. Dmitry Vavilov was one of the nicest kids on the block, and the least like anyone Faina had dated so far. He was kind, studious, an honor student, and best of all, he wasn't a Breadwinner.

Faina's intensity faded into relief. "Good! Because I don't want to find out later that he slugged you in the face or something."

"Of course not." He sank his teeth into his bottom lip. "Any guy would be lucky to have you, Faina. I'm glad you've found someone who is worthy of you." He rubbed the back of his neck and gestured down the street. "I, uh, better get back. I told Katya I would teach her how to play chess today." The moment he turned away and took his first step, Pasha felt so heavy he thought he might sink through the sand.

Faina's relationships never last very long, he reminded himself. *It won't last. You just have to wait it out. It will be over in a week.*

Chapter 18:
Pasha's Rival

"Why are we here?" Pasha sat at the lunch counter of Vavilov's drugstore with Sergei and Yuri, staring dismally at the opposite wall.

Yuri scraped his spoon against his glass and spoke between mouthfuls. "Because it's hot, and when it's hot you eat ice cream."

"Could we not have gone somewhere else?" Pasha twirled the bottle cap of his untouched Coke between his fingers. "Are you two trying to kill me?"

Yuri waved his hand as though Pasha were being dramatic, which, he was."Will you relax and drink your Coke?"

In the bright light of the drugstore's windows, Pasha noticed for the first time that there were dark circles under Yuri's eyes. "You look exhausted."

"Mila has colic."

"I thought you said she was a peaceful baby."

"She was. But she's three weeks now. That's when symptoms start showing." He pushed the cherry around with the end of his straw. "Should probably go stay with Olive."

"What about her parents?" asked Sergei. "I can't imagine you'd get much sleep avoiding getting caught."

"It'd still be more than I get at home."

"Well, you look awful." Sergei shook his head. "If you don't get some sleep soon you're gonna get licked your next fight."

"Trust me. I can handle it. I worry more about my sisters. Lana said the foreman almost caught Sonya falling asleep at the machine the other day."

Pasha put down his Coke mid-sip. "Sonya's working? How old is she?"

"Seven."

Pasha wasn't sure what to say, but Yuri seemed to already know what he was thinking.

"Be glad you only have one sibling."

Child labor may have been illegal but it was hardly enforced, at least in New York City. Pasha took an awkward swig of his Coke, and the conversation grew quiet. At length, he lowered his voice.

"So now that it's June I guess I can ask you guys … Did Klokov ask either of you to clear your evening for the twenty-sixth of June, possibly four months ago?"

Yuri abandoned his glass and leaned in further. "I thought I was the only one."

"He asked me too," added Sergei. "Any idea what it's about?"

Pasha shook his head. "Not a clue. But we're supposed to meet in his office at six apparently."

"All's I know is, I better be getting paid for it," declared Yuri.

Pasha sighed and hunkered down over his Coke, unable to resist casing the room one more time. The bell of the door jingled as it opened, and a dark-haired girl walked in holding hands with a boy. Pasha instinctively twitched.

"Will you cut it out?" Yuri practically shouted, finally losing his patience. "Faina and Dmitry ain't even—" Before Yuri could finish his sentence, they heard laughter on the stairwell leading to the flat overhead. Faina and Dmitry danced into the room, their fingers laced together and swinging between them.

"I hate you right now," muttered Pasha between clenched teeth.

Sergei gave him an apologetic pat on the back. "Sorry, Pasha. We should have listened to you."

Dmitry Vavilov was a handsome, pristine-looking young man with smooth, perfectly parted blonde hair, and eyes so blue and bright you forgot he was wearing glasses. His hands were always immaculately clean and his teeth were perfectly aligned. Without so much as a glance about the room, he leaned in and kissed Faina squarely on the lips.

"I really hate you right now," Pasha hissed again.

Yuri dropped his spoon down inside his empty cup and rolled his eyes. "Relax. Don't act like such a baby." He started to raise his hand. "Hey, Faina!"

Pasha grabbed his hand and slammed it down on the counter. "Shut up! Don't call them over!"

"This is your chance to show Faina what she's missing! Give her a little side-by-side comparison!"

"What's to compare? We're exactly alike only he's better! I can't compete with a better version of myself!"

Yuri shrugged. "At least she's dating someone halfway decent. And he ain't a Breadwinner."

Pasha sighed. "Another point against me."

"That's not what I meant."

"Pasha, calm down," said Sergei. "You said it yourself, Faina's relationships never last."

"It's been two months. Faina's never gone out with anyone this long."

"So find someone else." The three turned to see Roan sitting at the end of the counter. "Listen, Pasha, you're dodging a bullet. I've dated Faina, and she's a nice girl but she's completely starved for affection. No man wants a clingy broad."

Pasha drew back, trying not to look offended on Faina's behalf.

"Listen to the man," said Yuri, tossing his shoulders. "You're sixteen and you've been hung up on Faina for years. You've never even dated before! Have you even kissed a girl yet?"

Fortunately, Sergei stepped in before Pasha had to answer. "I think what Yuri is trying to say is maybe you should pursue someone else for a while."

Pasha propped his elbow on the counter and held his chin up with his fist. "Like who?"

By now Yuri was getting irritable with Pasha's pity party. "Oh, come on! I know Faina isn't the only girl you've ever been attracted to!"

"Nadia Berkowitz," answered Sergei, slyly indicating the girl sitting at a table near the window.

"Shut up!" Pasha practically pulled his cap down over his face. "Don't tell him that!"

Yuri narrowed his eyes at Pasha with an incredulous scowl. "Boy, you really have a type, don't you?"

"What are you talking about? They look totally different!"

"They look just alike!"

"Oh, what? Because they both have dark hair?"

"They're built similar!"

"I don't know, Nadia is kinda skinny," interjected Sergei.

Pasha enumerated their differences on his fingers. "Their noses are different, their eye color is different—"

"Alright, alright! Point is, if I saw them both from a distance I wouldn't be able to tell them apart."

"Hey, fellas!" Dmitry spotted them from across the room, and marched their way with an all-too-enthusiastic grin and a friendly wave. Faina hesitated at first before treading after him with an awkward simper.

Pasha tried to smile but it felt more like he was baring his teeth. "Hey!"

"We were just finishing up," Sergei hastily explained in an attempt to save Pasha the heartache.

"Already?" Dmitry noted Pasha's mostly full bottle of soda. "You've hardly touched your Coke. Does it taste alright?"

"Yeah, everything is fi—"

"I know what it needs," interrupted Faina. "It's missing a bag of peanuts."

Dmitry looked her askance, his arm fitted firmly around her waist. "Peanuts?"

"Mhm! Pasha and I like putting peanuts in our Coke. It's even better if you add it to a float with vanilla ice cream."

"Oh, yeah! I have noticed you two doing that before! That's right!" It didn't even seem to bother him that Pasha and Faina had a special dish they shared. The whole time the sunlight was dancing on Dmitry's class ring fitted to Faina's finger. Whenever he caught sight of that little glare, Pasha couldn't help but ache with jealousy, not just over Faina but the fact that Dmitry had a ring to give.

Dmitry was an excellent student, just as Pasha had been. But while Pasha was forced to drop out of school, Dmitry's academic achievements had earned him enrollment at the prestigious Stuyvesant. And it was well known that everyone who attended "Stuy," as it was so called, went on to attend college.

"It was my idea to try it." Faina made a display of placing her hands on her hips with a sassy expression. "Another of my genius ideas."

"Yeah, sure, Huncamunca." Pasha froze the moment the name left his mouth. He hadn't meant to call her that.

"Huncamunca?" echoed Dmitry with an amused and curious smile.

Pasha stared down at the counter and fiddled with the Coke bottle. There was no going back now.

"Yeah, that's uh, that's my nickname for Faina."

Again, Dmitry remained nonplussed, if not delighted. "Huncamunca! That's cute!" He squeezed Faina closer to his side. "Maybe I oughta start calling you that!"

Over my dead body, thought Pasha.

"Well, Faina and I better skedaddle. We've got tickets to a matinee." He pulled her away and waved goodbye. "You fellas enjoy! See you later!" The bell over the door rang as they departed.

Yuri stared at Pasha with his nose twisted up in disgust. "The hell's a Huncamunca?"

Chapter 19:
Pasha's *Ochi Chernye*

"*Ochi chernye, ochi zhguchie, ochi strastnye i prekrasnye* ..." Dark eyes, burning eyes, frightful and beautiful eyes … Faina sang before the mirror as she rubbed a towel through her hair and let the waves tumble down her back. "*Kak lyublyu ya vas, kak boyus' ya vas, znat' uvidel vas ya ne v dobryy chas* …" I love you so, I fear you so, for sure I've seen you at a sinister hour. She sang often these days, and those who heard her down in the grocery would remark to Uncle Matvei what an impressive gift she had.

It was sunset and Faina was especially glad to be clean after a full day of running around in the summer heat. The window breathed in a gust of air, causing the drapes to billow up like frilly ball gowns. Faina smoothed her clean, linen nightdress over her figure, which looked especially lovely against her tanned limbs. Feeling energized, she spun in place and danced over to the bookcase.

Anya wandered in through the open door just as she was plucking a title from the shelf.

"He keeps glancing over here, you know."

Faina froze on her toes, her eyes widening in utter innocence. "Who?"

Anya plopped down in the vanity chair and opened a Hershey bar. "Pasha."

"Oh." Faina let her heels drop. "Why?"

Anya covered her full mouth. "Maybe because someone is singing and dancing in front of the open window in her nightgown."

Faina dismissed her observation with a wave of her hand, and plodded over to the mattress. "Pasha doesn't see me like that."

Anya peeled back the wrapper of her candy bar further and stared at her incredulously. "Yes, he does."

"Shows what you know!" She waved her book at her in a playful gesture, then quickly sobered. "I tried to kiss him last February, remember? And he didn't want to."

Anya waved her hand and rolled her eyes. "Yes, you've told me the story." She rocked back in the chair, tilting it on its back two legs. "That doesn't mean anything."

"What do you mean it doesn't mean anything?" Faina lowered her voice, fearing that Pasha might hear her through the window. "If he liked me why wouldn't he let me kiss him?"

"You were hysterical! Can you blame him?"

Faina considered for a moment, staring down at her lap. The very idea sent a thrill down her spine, but she wasn't about to let herself get rejected again.

"Faina, he just didn't want to take advantage of you in such a vulnerable state. That's what good guys do!" She paused. "But I guess it doesn't matter now. You have Dmitry."

When Faina didn't answer, Anya grew suspicious. "What do you look so moody for?"

Faina hesitated, then glanced off at the wall. "Actually, I was thinking of dumping Dmitry."

Anya stared back at her in surprise. "I thought you were happy!"

Faina floundered for an explanation. "I mean, I *am* happy … kinda."

"You can't get over Pasha."

"Alright, fine!" Faina scooted over so that she was out of view of the window. "I'm in love with Pasha!" she mouthed, leaning against the wall in a dramatic display.

Anya raised her eyebrow and giggled. "You *love* him?"

"I do! I love him! I only started dating Dmitry because I thought I had scared Pasha off for good."

Anya snickered and shook her head.

"What?" Faina rose up on her knees, prepared to defend Pasha's honor. "Don't you like him?"

"Do I like him?" Her eyes slid towards the window. "I do. In fact, I've wanted you and Pasha to get together for a long time. He may not be the most romantic choice, but I think you would make each other happy."

Faina bounced to the center of the bed and scoffed. "Romantic? What do you mean?" She reclined back against her pillows.

"Well, Pasha may be alright for you but I'd rather have someone big and strong. Someone confident and charismatic, who tells me my hair is like silk, and my eyes are like stars, and all that." Anya propped her chin on her fist and gazed dreamily at the wall.

Faina eyed her as though she were half crazy. "Is that what Leg Up tells you?"

Anya's eyes glazed over. "Well, he checks off most everything else on the list anyway."

Faina scoffed. "So you want a hard-boiled poet. That's a tall order!" She turned over on her side. "And what do you mean, big and strong? Pasha's a street fighter, isn't he?"

"He doesn't have the build of one."

"Hmph!" Faina cracked open her book and rested it on her knee. "I like his build. And I don't want to be with anyone who I couldn't fight off myself if they got any ideas they shouldn't be having." Her expression softened. "Not that he would ever be that way." She looked up again. "As far as I'm concerned I don't trust a fella who acts like he's got it all figured out. Any man who walks up to a woman without blushing and tells her she's the most beautiful woman he's ever seen is lying. He's seen dozens of beautiful women. Flowers every day, jewelry, big romantic gestures," she shook her finger at Anya, "it's all symptomatic of a skirt chaser. And I should know. I've dated enough of them."

Anya scooted her chair closer and laughed. "I'm shocked at you, Faina! Since when are you such a cynic?"

"I'm not a cynic! I'm the opposite really! I just know what's important. Give me a man who stumbles over his words, who blushes when he speaks to me, who goes weak in the knees when I enter a room. That's a fella who's sincere." Her face grew serious for once. "All I want is someone kind, and patient. Someone I don't have to be afraid of, who never shouts, never strays, and never loses his temper. Someone who I can trust and depend upon. What can be more romantic than that?" She bit back a smile. "Besides, don't you think he's handsome?"

Anya stretched out her legs and crossed her arms. "Well, he's not bad looking."

Faina stretched her arms over her head and pointed her toes. "He has those big, brown eyes!"

"You mean his *ochi chernye*!" Dark eyes.

The two of them dissolved into giggles as Faina threw a pillow at her.

"And that thick, dark hair! And that adorable, doe-eyed smile!"

Anya took another bite of her chocolate bar. "His forehead's kinda big."

"Now who's the cynic!" She crawled to the edge of her bed and, grabbing Anya's wrist, guided it towards her mouth. "Give me a bite of that."

They lowered their heads and tittered. Faina fell back on the mattress with a snort. When she glanced over her shoulder she caught sight of Pasha sitting on his own bed with his own book, peering over the cover and staring at her. The moment he realized he'd been caught, he quickly ducked back behind his book with a rapid blush.

Chapter 20:

Shut Up and Kiss Me

Faina had it all planned out. She had already dumped Dmitry, and though he was certainly saddened by Faina's change of feelings, they were able to part amicably and remain friends. She knew it wasn't traditional for a girl to pursue a boy, but Faina was hardly traditional, and she was tired of waiting. Though her first instinct was to simply kiss Pasha, she didn't want a repeat of the events at the Foxhole. She would have to use her words this time, express to Pasha how she felt. Over and over again she had practiced what she would say until finally she came up with a plan. They'd go about their business like they did every day. When lunchtime came around, she'd let Pasha do most of the talking, and then she would interrupt him and say:

"I wish you'd just shut up and kiss me!"

When she'd told Anya her plan, her cousin was far from impressed.

"It's a little theatrical … but then again, so are you."

Faina decided to stick with it.

The day hadn't started out well. She awoke drenched in sweat and feeling as though someone had been putting out their cigarette on her throat. Had she not been suffering from such symptoms for the past several months, she would have been tempted to stay home. But Faina had waited long enough. With any luck, today would be the day she kissed Pasha Chevalsky.

They set out at their normal time, and together they pillaged their way through the Burroughs. Though she made no hint at what she was planning, Pasha was noticing her giddiness, and with good reason. She laughed a bit too freely at his jokes, and grinned when a simple smile would have sufficed. He said as much when they were taking the train back from Midtown.

"What are you so fidgety for?" he asked when he caught her jiggling her leg up and down in her seat.

He grabbed her leg to get her to stop, catching her so off guard she dissolved into a fit of giggles. The corner of his mouth curled up in amusement.

"Is there something you're not telling me?"

"Like what?"

"I don't know. You're just acting kinda funny. Like you're keeping a secret. Either that or you drank way too much coffee this morning."

Faina pushed her lower lip out and shook her head. "No secrets here."

Pasha leaned back in his seat and pulled his cap down over his eyes. "If you say so."

They got off at the Bowery Station and headed out into the sunshine in search of lunch. By then, the morning's exertions had finally started to wear on Faina, and she could feel sweat beginning to seep through her collar. The sun was bleeding through paper-thin clouds like a daub of yellow paint, boiling the moist air and sapping her energy. They stopped in front of the Pensky's café. Faina tried to swallow but ended up coughing instead. Pasha patted her back as she covered her mouth with her elbow.

"Are you feeling okay?"

She turned to answer him, but was still too choked to get her words out.

"You look a little pale." He put a hand to her forehead. "You're burning up!"

But Faina ignored him. She had to proceed with her plan. She took a deep breath and stood up straight, trying to look flirtatious, but she had a feeling she only looked delirious.

"Pasha … I wish …"

"*Pavlushka!*" a feminine voice sang out from the doorway. Nadia Berkowitz sashayed toward them, her pretty, lithe arms swinging merrily. "*Co ty tutaj robisz?*"

Pasha grinned and hurried toward her. "*Hej! Właśnie jedliśmy obiad.*"

Faina's eyes grew to the size of locusts as she gaped at the pair, panicked and helplessly unable to comprehend a single word of their conversation. She could only watch in horror as Nadia grabbed Pasha's hands and reeled him towards her with a coy snicker.

"*Chciałbym wiedzieć. Mogliśmy usiąść razem.*"

Faina cleared her throat, snatching away their attention and shattering their private moment with as much subtlety as a hammer on glass.

"Faina!" exclaimed Pasha, his face red. "*Znasz* Nadia."

Faina tucked her lips together in a sarcastic smile. "I don't speak Polish."

Pasha shook his head with a nervous laugh and corrected himself. "You know Nadia."

Nadia gave him a playful nudge. "Sorry. We speak Polish sometimes. In fact, Pasha asked me out in Polish. Isn't that sweet?"

The news hit Faina like a slab of concrete. "He what?"

"We have a date this Friday night," explained Pasha.

Faina stared wide-eyed at the two of them standing side by side, Nadia looking tall and statuesque with her long legs, and chewing on her bee-stung lips in a way that could've easily been an invitation for Pasha to kiss her, and Pasha with his hand resting casually on her waist as though they'd been dating for years. All at once Faina felt quite frumpy in her ill-fitting men's clothes, sweat collecting on the back of her neck and behind her knees, and her face growing pastier by the second.

"You have—I didn't know you were dating!"

"He just asked me out a couple days ago. We were thinking of going to the Moroccan. Have you ever been?"

Faina was polite but could not force herself to smile. "Nope. Can't say that I have."

"You would love it! Oh! Maybe you and Dmitry could come with us next time! We could make it a double date!"

Faina could feel her throat growing stiff. "Actually, Dmitry and I broke up."

Pasha's eyes stretched open. "What?"

Faina nodded hesitantly. "*Da* …" Yeah. She held up her hand, showcasing her ringless finger.

"*Kodga*?" When?

"*Neskol'ko dney naza*d." A few days ago.

"*Pochemu ty mne ne skazal*?" Why didn't you tell me? He drew back as soon as he said it, perhaps realizing just how loud he was being.

Nadia's eyes flickered awkwardly between them. Faina laced her features with another sarcastic simper.

"Sorry, we speak Russian sometimes. You know, because we're both Russian."

"Pasha is Crimean," Nadia corrected her.

Not used to having her wit challenged by other people, Nadia might as well have stabbed Faina with a fire poker.

"Which has been a part of Russia the majority of his life!"

"And then it became independent."

Pasha shrugged sheepishly between them. "Well, technically, both of you are right, in a way. My grandfather's side of the family is Polish but they lived on the estate in Crimea, my grandmother was Ukrainian, and my mother is Russian, so—"

Faina ignored him, continuing to address Nadia. "And now it's part of the Soviet Union! Should I start calling him 'Comrade?'" Without waiting for an answer, she returned her attention to Pasha. "*Ya kak raz sobiralsya tebe skazat'* ..." I was just about to tell you before ...

Faina took one last glance at Nadia. She was one of those girls who possessed that enviable ability to shine without any effort. She was taller, daintier, had a tinier waist, fuller lips, and bigger eyes. It was all Faina could do to keep her head up. She cleared her throat.

"Before I went home for the day."

Pasha squeezed his eyes shut and shook his head. "Wait, you're leaving?"

Faina began backing away. "Uh, yeah. I'm—I'm not feeling so good right now. I think I'm coming down with something." She sucked in an involuntary gasp as though about to cough, which seemed convincing, but in reality she was just trying not to cry. "You two have fun! I'll catch you later, Pasha!"

Faina sprinted home, packing down her sobs until the moment her bedroom door shut behind her.

Chapter 21:

The Worst Date Ever

Pasha hustled along the sidewalk beneath the tall evening shadows, his hands shoved into the pockets of his nicest dress pants, headed for Central Park to meet Nadia. To avoid running into Faina, Pasha had lied and told Nadia he would be visiting a friend just before their date and therefore could not pick her up at her tenement. It was a lousy thing to do, making her ride the train by herself, and Pasha was ashamed for having done so.

He spotted Nadia from a distance, standing in the Ladies' Pavilion with her pale, silvery hands folded in front of her. His feet seemed to resist as he pressed forward. There was no getting out of it now. It would have been rude to cancel, and even if it wasn't what Pasha wanted, he was determined to show Nadia a good time. At the very least, they would part as friends.

Pasha waved. "There you are!"

Nadia spun around on her heel and greeted him with an enthusiastic smile. Apparently, she had forgiven him for not escorting her to the park himself.

"*Pavlushka*! I was wondering when you'd get here."

Pasha shrugged his shoulders. "Sorry. Things ran a little late with my, uh, friend."

"It's fine. It's so beautiful here, I didn't really mind waiting." She studied the landscape with a romantic sigh. "So, what made you want to come here? I mean, it's not exactly close."

Pasha drew a blank. He supposed it would have been more convenient to meet in Columbus Park, or St. John's, or even Madison Park. But because of his heists with Faina, he was more familiar with Central Park than any of the others.

"I just like it here, I guess." He shrugged. "I take it you don't come here often?"

Nadia braced the railing. "Not really."

"Huh. Faina and I come here all the time." Pasha realized his blunder the minute it left his mouth. "That is, I mean, because of uh … work." He didn't exactly want to say "because there's a lot of rich people to steal alcohol from around here," not that Nadia didn't know the truth.

"Ah." She folded her hands in front of her. "That makes sense."

Pasha resisted the urge to check his watch. How could he pass the next two hours entertaining her without things growing too romantic? *It'll be fine*, he assured himself. *You asked her out, not the other way around. She's probably not all that interested in the first place.*

He offered his arm. "Wanna walk?"

Nadia grabbed it with both hands, and then, without prompting, kissed Pasha on the cheek. Pasha felt the lining of his gut turn cold. Evidently, she was more interested than he initially thought. Instinctively, he threaded his fingers through his bangs, horrified at the idea of having to disappoint her. And yet, he could not resist the very natural feeling of pride her admiration inspired, and soon fell prey to the temptation of showing off.

As they approached the bridge overlooking the lake, he picked up a flat stone from the pavement and pointed to a rock in the middle of the pond.

"Betcha I can skip this stone to that rock."

The moment he wrenched his arm back the stone flung backwards out of his grip and flew into the windshield of a police car parked by the curb. Pasha's jaw dropped. He hadn't even realized the vehicle was there. The officer and his partner got out of the car. Pasha recognized them at once. It was Officers Murray and Schneider. While some of the police went easy on kids caught up in the Breadwinners, Murray and Schneider wanted nothing more than to see them committed for life, and they especially hated Pasha.

As the cops made their way toward him, the reality of Pasha's situation dawned on him.

"Nadia, I'm really, really, really sorry for what I'm about to do." He took a deep breath and covered his eyes. "And someday I'd like to make it up to you."

Nadia stared back at him, utterly dumbfounded. "What are you talking about?"

"Hey! You!" shouted Murray. "I know you! Stop right there!"

Pasha turned to her with an apologetic shrug. "I have a warrant." And with that, he turned and hightailed it in the opposite direction.

"Pasha!" he could hear her hollering in the distance. "Don't just leave me here!"

Pasha cringed. He couldn't believe what he was doing. Heeled footsteps echoed close behind him. Pasha turned and looked over his shoulder. She was following him.

"What are you doing? Stay where you are!"

"Get the girl! Get Spichkin!" hollered Schneider. Pasha dug his heels into the ground and turned. They thought Nadia was Faina! Pasha grabbed her by the wrist and dragged her off the path.

"Pasha! What are you doing? Ow!" she squealed as the prickly brush scratched at her legs and face. She stumbled forward and slipped in the mud, grabbing onto Pasha's arm for support. "My shoes!"

"Shhh!" He yanked her back onto her feet and towed her down the slope towards a large stone. "They think you're Faina, just keep running!"

"They think what?"

Murray's voice cut through the bramble. "Come out with your hands up! We have a warrant for your arrest!"

188

Pasha pulled her down a set of stone steps leading into the rock. "Come on, we have to hide."

But Nadia just stood there staring at him as though he had just suggested they engage in an indecent act.

"Are you insane? That's Ramble Cave! Don't you read the papers? I'm not getting in there!"

Pasha didn't exactly blame her. Although Ramble Cave had started out as a fun, secret place for children to explore, it had earned a reputation for being associated with crime over the years, and had been the location of a robbery just two years prior.

Pasha grabbed her hand and tried again to tug her forward. "Nadia, please! I—"

Nadia wrenched her hand away with all the dignity she possessed and began marching back towards the road. "This is ridiculous!"

Pasha ground his teeth together and hissed. "Nadia! No!"

"There!" exclaimed Schneider, followed by a shriek from Nadia.

Pasha passed a hand over his face and groaned.

"You sure this is her?" said Murray, his voice uncertain.

"Oh, this is her, alright! Faina Spichkin. Tall, dark hair, always hanging around Chevalsky."

Pasha's eyes glazed over as he sighed. *Yuri is never gonna let me live this down.* He slipped quietly out of the cave and began climbing a nearby tree overlooking the bridge.

"I'm not Faina Spichkin," protested Nadia. "My name is Nadia Berkowitz! I live on Delancey!"

"Sure, whatever you say, Miss!" Pasha could see Murray forcing her other hand behind her back into the handcuffs. "You can explain everything down at the precinct."

Pasha hopped down from the tree and raced back to the police vehicle.

189

Well, if I wasn't in trouble before, I'm about to be, he thought to himself. He took out his pocketknife and eyed the tires. Pasha let out a small whimper. *I can't believe I'm about to do this.* Then he spied the keys in the ignition. Pasha's shoulders deflated with a sigh of relief. *Thank God.*

Pasha opened the door and plucked the keys from the slot. Then, he retreated back into the brush and waited for the officers and Nadia to reappear. Nadia continued to struggle as Murray opened up the back and helped her into the car.

"I'm telling you, I'm not Faina Spichkin!"

"Give us some credit, sweetheart. This isn't our first time running into you two."

He watched Schneider slide into the driver's seat. "What'd you do with the keys?"

"What do you mean, what I'd do?" said Murray. "They're right there in the ignition!"

"No, they ain't! Look for yourself!"

Murray fumbled around in his pockets.

"Well?" Schneider snapped impatiently.

Murray slammed the rear door and turned back towards the path. "Must've fallen out of my pocket. I'll be back."

Pasha waited for Murray to disappear. He picked up a heavy rock and threw it into the shrubs further down the road. Schneider flew out of the driver's seat and bolted in the direction of the motion.

"I got you now, Chevalsky!"

Pasha raced to the vehicle and flung open the rear door. "I am so sorry!"

Maybe it was just the dim light of the setting sun, but Nadia's teeth appeared sharp as she hissed, "Get me out of here now!"

Schneider's head popped out of the bushes. "Hey!" He bolted towards them.

In what was probably the stupidest move of Pasha's thieving career, he threw himself into the car with Nadia and locked the door. Schneider pasted his face against the window and tugged on the handle, shouting all the while. With impressive agility, Pasha tumbled into the driver's seat and locked the front doors.

Nadia couldn't believe his lack of thinking. "You locked us inside a police car!"

Pasha stared wide-eyed at the irate cop screaming and pointing his finger at the glass.

"Well, at least they can't get inside."

"What is wrong with you?!"

"Get out of that driver's seat!" thundered Schneider. "Get out of that driver's seat now!"

Pasha threw up his hands apologetically. "Okay, okay! I'm moving!" As he was climbing over the seat his foot collided with the gearshift.

For a moment Pasha thought he was imagining things as the car lurched backwards, or that perhaps he was just a little dizzy from all the running around. Slowly, the trees started moving past the window. He and Nadia locked eyes in horror. The car rolled backwards down the hill, quickly picking up speed.

"The brake! Pasha, the brake! Hit the brakes!"

The car slammed against a tree at the base of the hill, knocking Pasha and Nadia to the floor.

Chapter 22:

Hot and Sour Soup

Faina didn't have to ask Pasha how his date turned out; she learned everything from Anya. It was all over the neighborhood. The Breadwinners were able to get Pasha released from police custody within an hour, but Schneider was determined to hold onto Nadia. In the end, her mother had had to come down to the precinct to prove her daughter was who she said she was. And it didn't end there. Confined to her bed due to her summer cold, Faina got a front-row seat to Mrs. Berkowitz dragging Nadia to the front doorstep of the building and having it out with Pasha's mother. Faina was sorry to see Mama Lydia get maligned for her son's misfortunes, but she certainly enjoyed seeing the thick bandage covering Nadia's nose, which, due to her hands being cuffed behind her back, had come into pretty hard contact with the back seat when the car crashed. According to Anya, Nadia had sworn off Breadwinners for good.

By the sound of it, Mama Lydia was not happy with Pasha ditching a girl in the middle of Central Park to run from the police, and would rather he had turned himself in, considering the Breadwinners would have busted him out anyway. Now, because of the cop car, Pasha would have to go to Juvenile Court, forcing Lydia to take time off from work.

When Faina got up from her nap to take her medicine, Uncle Matvei was coming up the stairs with a little paper bag in his hand.

"Ah! You're awake!" He held out the bag to her. "Pasha wanted me to give this to you. He said to eat it immediately."

Faina took it and broke the seal. "It's a fortune cookie." She looked questioningly at her uncle.

"Don't look at me. He came into the shop, bought a box of pepper, and told me to give this to you after he left. I don't know anything about it."

Faina turned and headed back to her room. "Thanks, Uncle Matvei!" Once inside, she split the cookie open and removed the fortune. It was written in Pasha's hand.

A handsome thief will leave soup on the fire escape outside your window.

Faina rolled her eyes and smiled. She set the cookie on her nightstand and opened her window. An entire quart of hot and sour soup was sitting on the fire escape, along with the pepper he had bought from Uncle Matvei. Faina laughed aloud as she retrieved the gift and brought it inside. Pasha must have given the note to Mr. Fong and had him put it in a fortune cookie. On the top of the container was a folded paper fixed with tape. Faina opened it. There was no writing, no name. Just a heart.

Chapter 23:
Cold Medicine and Calderas

Staccato lay utterly spent on the floor of the loft, traces of magic staining his palms in smears of gold and silver. It seemed every spare moment these days was consumed with the crafting of dreams, protecting the company's minds against the nightmares of the haig beasts that hunted them.

Below him the others slept soundly swaddled in quilts and heavy blankets. Icicles dangled from the roof. The snow thickened. Twice now the wheels of the wagon had needed to be changed. Winter still breathed here. Winter was always breathing its rimy breath over Andromeda, even in the summer, albeit somewhat faintly. But the caravan was comfortably warm. Smooth, marbled, heat-producing boulders known as dragon stones toasted the interior, and blankets of scarlet wool shorn from Tupperkell sheep ensured that no one suffered a chill.

The company had made it as far as Mirach with their would-be assassins close on their heels. Food was often cold. Baths were limited to icy rub downs with a cold cloth. Dread crept behind them. Haigs wailed in the night. Whenever they neared a settlement the cries of the villagers stirring from their nightmares roused the company from their sleep. They had been traveling for a week and a half. It wouldn't be much longer before they reached Pegasus. Safety was near. Safety was coming.

Staccato's chest rose and fell at even intervals. His eyelids twitched. His hands relaxed. Rest had conquered his anxious soul. But then he had been particularly indulgent in his choice of dreams. To sweeten his sleep, Staccato had reached for a favored fantasy, one seldom employed outside of aggressive insomnia. In his mind, Staccato saw himself as a man in his early forties. His hair was still blonde. Or at least, it was mostly blonde. In place of his beard was a neatly styled mustache. And in his arms, clinging to his neck, was a long-legged child with coarse raven hair. A shelter of blue lilac surrounded them on all sides, tinting the shadows with shades of twilight and lavender. Beyond the hedge lay a meadow of poppies blooming in blush and scarlet.

The boy turned his head and addressed Staccato. "Is this where the unicorns are, Grandfather?"

"Just wait, Pasha my boy. Wait and keep still."

Pasha grew motionless. All was quiet save for the rhythm of his grandson's warm breath near his cheek. And then, it happened. The hedge on the far side of the meadow rustled and twitched.

"Ow! Tongs and torches! What in blue blazes was that for?"

Unwanted consciousness struck Staccato like a baseball between the eyes.

"Could you possibly make any more noise?" hissed Sonata in a voice that was probably meant to be quiet.

"What? What noise?" countered Pyro.

"Your snoring!"

"I can't help it! I've been sick!"

Staccato rolled over and buried his head in his pillow, hoping to drown them out.

"Please!" Sonata snorted. "I know for a fact you haven't been taking your medicine!"

But Pyro wasn't backing down. "For someone who's such a know-it-all, you seem to have a pretty poor understanding of what constitutes a fact versus an assumption."

"And you snore a lot for a person who has taken a decongestant."

"Considering you just assaulted me in my sleep, you're sorta asking a lot."

"I hit you with a pillow! Dramatic much?"

"You catch more flies with honey than with vinegar."

"I prefer a swatter."

"I'll bet you do!"

Staccato winced and sat up. Clearly, this would require his intervention. Before Staccato had returned to escort the company halfway to Aquarius, he'd had little interaction with Pyro and Sonata in the same room. Dominated by his quest to return Pasha to Voiler, he'd kept mostly to himself, or was away in New York. The pair had yet to mend things. This he knew. But when they'd all huddled into the caravan, Staccato was shocked to discover just how far things had escalated between them.

"You're keeping us all up!" snapped Sonata. "See? Skelter is awake too!"

"He's awake because of you!"

Cello, who had been asleep at the end of the mattress, raised his head up and stared at Staccato, as though inquiring whether or not he were going to do anything.

Staccato rolled over towards the open hatch. "What in Heaven's name do you two think you are doing?!"

Sonata was hovering near Pyro's bunk still clutching the pillow she had struck him with while Skelter sat up in the trundle covering his eyes.

"I can't sleep because Pyro refuses to quit snoring," answered Sonata, "and I have the next watch!"

Staccato stared back at her with exhausted impatience. "Now, Sonata, you know that isn't fair. Pyro is congested. He can't help it."

Pyro threw up his hands. "Thank you!"

But Sonata held up her finger. "He could take his decongestant like he's supposed to!"

Staccato put a weary finger to his temple. "Pyro, did you take your decongestant?"

Pyro tensed and glanced off to the side. "No …"

"What was that?"

"I didn't take it! Okay?"

"I knew it!" exclaimed Sonata, pumping her fist into the air.

"What's the point?" Pyro tangled his arms across his chest. "It doesn't do anything!"

"Oh, so instead you take nothing! It's a wonder you didn't go into the medical field! At the very least you should be taking it for the sake of everyone who's forced to share a room with you at night!"

Before they could bicker any more, Staccato threw out his hand. "Alright, that's enough! I'll take Sonata's watch."

Staccato sat up and tapped the ceiling with his staff. "I'm coming to relieve you, Melodious! You can come back inside!"

Staccato put his hand to his face and smeared his thumb across the inner corner of his lower eyelid. Gold, glittery light began to seep from his eye, until the entire dream spilled out and coiled into a little ball. The dream of Pasha rolled around in his palm, a soft glowing sphere. Staccato took his time getting it back into the vial, and locked it away into his cabinet of dreams. It was to be double-locked. No one must ever see it. Like his dreams of Evangeline, no one could ever know of the grandson he kept hidden away in his heart.

When Staccato had finished, he put on his winter gear and headed down the ladder with four fresh dreams he had saved for each of them. Melodious had just come through the door, and was sitting in his Murphy bed, peeling off his coat.

"Here you are, Reverend." Staccato handed him his dream. "Don't mind the rest of us, Sonata and Pyro thought we all needed a wake-up call." Melodious said nothing but yawned and settled back into his bed. He was still wearing his hat.

Skelter, who had already fallen back asleep, was curled in a ball with his blankets up to his chin. Staccato gave him a nudge.

"Wake up, Skelter." He placed a vial in Skelter's hand. "You still have to take your dream."

Without opening his eyes, Skelter uncorked the bottle and tossed the glittering substance onto his head.

"Really, I don't see why we have to take another dream just because we woke up," said Sonata, taking the vial. "Won't they just pick up where we left off?"

"Not with our sleep being so broken. We don't want to take any chances. And you—" he jerked the blanket off Pyro's head, "you take your medicine."

Pyro groaned and rolled up off the bed.

"Make sure you take the bottle with the unicorn on it," nagged Sonata. "the bottle with the toad will—"

"The bottle with the toad will make me drowsy!" finished Pyro, his eyes rolling skyward as he opened the cupboard. "I know, I know!"

Sonata slammed the doors to her little alcove.

Pyro narrowed his eyes. "If I take the bottle with the toad maybe I won't wake up next time you try to assault me."

The doors flew open with such force, they nearly hit Staccato in the face. "What was that?"

Skelter took one of his pillows and jammed it over his head where he couldn't hear them.

"Go back to bed, Sonata." Staccato shooed her back inside and shut the doors. Sighing, he reached into a cabinet and retrieved the thermos of coffee he had stored there. "Would you mind terribly?" he asked Pyro.

Pyro took the thermos between his hands and held it until steam began to rise from the vent. "Careful." He handed it back to Staccato. "The outside might be a little hot."

"I have gloves on." He reached into his pocket and held out the last dream to Pyro, who stared down at the vial with a dull expression.

"That better not be a dream of Sonata or else you might as well let the haigs get me."

"Just take it."

Staccato made his way back up the loft and, bracing himself, opened the hatch leading to the roof. The door tore backward with a loud bang. Icy wind scratched his cheeks. Wincing, he scrambled onto the top of the wagon. Drifts of snow strayed through the opening onto his mattress below. Staccato shuffled around the portal on all fours, fighting against the breeze until he at last managed to slam the hatch shut. By now he could not feel his face. He settled himself on top of the door, and sipped his coffee testily.

They had parked the caravan behind a thick copse at the edge of the wood. Beyond the barrier of fir trees, the landscape opened upon a vast frozen lake belted in stony ridges. Deer tracks punctuated the bank. According to Pyro, there was an extinct caldera somewhere along the border of the lake. They couldn't be far.

Traveling with Pyro and Sonata was beginning to wear on Staccato. Day and night they sniped at each other. In the history of the couple's romance, the pair had never stayed separated for more than a month and a half. Now they were going on three months. They showed no signs of getting back together, but neither did they show any signs of moving on. Over the years, Staccato had come to rely heavily upon Pyro and Sonata as a team. So in sync were they in battle, that the pair had taken to naming their maneuvers, such as the Boiling Spout where Sonata would manipulate water to fountain in the air, and Pyro would hit it with a stream of fire creating a sort of lethal geyser. Together they were unstoppable. Apart they were insufferable.

The wind howled in his ears, and Staccato felt that if he didn't brace himself he could easily be blown away. He looked down at the pegasi in their waterproof blankets. Their wings were fluffed up and folded close to their bodies for the extra warmth. There would be no flying in these conditions. Fifty miles by land.

Bit by bit, Staccato grew tolerant to the chill. The warmth of his thermos bled through his gloves, heating the tips of his fingers. The moon reflected off the lake. Despite his circumstances, Staccato soon began to feel sleepy. It was his own fault, really. He was known for going long stretches without sleeping only to collapse later when his body had hit its limit. He would think of something to keep him awake. Yes, that would do it. He would think of Pasha, and how best to get him to agree to come to Voiler.

The next thing he knew he was standing in the courtyard of the Frasier, looking up at Pasha's bedroom window. It was dark. Too dark, as a matter of fact. Almost as though it had been blacked out with paint. Curious, Staccato pulled down the ladder to the fire escape and began climbing. Rung after rusted rung, he scaled up the side of the building. After what felt like the sixth landing, he froze suddenly, a thought occurring to him. Wasn't the apartment on the second floor? He glanced over his shoulder. The ladder dangled down into the courtyard. He had only gone up one story. Staccato pinched the bridge of his nose as his head began to spin and sway.

He was standing outside the window now. Greasy black grime coated the glass in a thin film of darkness. He could just make out his grandson's lanky form lying on the rug before his bed. With some effort, Staccato pried open the window. Pasha's back was turned. He was exceptionally still. Slipping inside, Staccato rolled onto the bed and stood over the place where Pasha lay. Dread leaked into his chest. Something was wrong.

"Pasha," he called softly.

The boy did not stir. Sweating slightly, Staccato knelt down at his side and put a hand on his shoulder.

"Pasha?"

Gently, he rolled Pasha onto his back. The emaciated face of the weakened Pasha from the prophecy stared up at him with an almost lifeless gaze. His eyes were sunken and gray looking. Bruises burst in black and yellow blooms along his jaw and cheeks.

"Don't worry," Staccato exclaimed, his breathing growing shallow, "I'm going to get you out of here. I've come to take you home."

"It's in the closet …" he croaked in a wilting voice.

"What? What is it? What's in the closet?"

The closet door creaked open. Staccato looked up. A parched skull like that of a horse or a deer stared back at him with white pupil-less eyes. The haig beast.

Staccato didn't recall opening his mouth, but all at once a bloodcurdling scream was crawling up out of his throat, ringing into the vast night, echoing off the walls, and pinching his ears.

"Noooooo! Noooo!"

A massive hand closed over his mouth. A knee pinned him at the shoulder. Instead of the apartment, Staccato found himself staring up at an enormous expanse of evening sky flecked with silver stars.

"Hush!" Sonata's face floated in front of him, blocking out the moon. "Hush, now, it's alright!" Her hands climbed over his wrists and squeezed, subduing him with her tranquilizing power.

All at once, Staccato remembered where he was. He craned his head back and spied Melodious, who gently removed his hand from Staccato's mouth and unpinned his shoulder. Skelter was peeking his head over the edge of the roof, having climbed up the side of the caravan. Staccato's eyes widened in horror.

"What have I done?" he whispered.

Sonata put a finger to her lips. The four of them listened. All was still. And then it came. A howl cut through the air like the swift glide of a guillotine, echoed by another, and then another.

"Get inside!" Staccato scrambled to the edge of the roof and hopped down into the driver's seat. Melodious and Skelter did as told, but Sonata hesitated.

"Where will we go? We can't fly in these conditions!"

"I'll figure something out! Where is Pyro? I want him up front with me, ready to fire!"

"Still asleep in the caravan."

"Well, wake him up!"

"I'm trying," hollered Melodious from the interior, "he won't wake!"

"What do you mean he—Oh, for the love of stars!" Staccato hopped out of the driver's seat and ran into the caravan through the side door. "Skelter, take the reins, and head off along the bank!"

Sonata was just coming down through the loft. Pyro lay on his back, mouth open, arms thrown over his head, completely unconscious.

"Pyro!" shouted Staccato, bending over the bunk. He shook his shoulder. He tapped his cheek. For a moment Pyro's eyes fluttered open, completely bloodshot, before rolling back and shutting once more.

Furious, Sonata wrenched Staccato out of the way.

"I'll handle this." She grabbed Pyro's nose between her thumb and forefinger and twisted.

Pyro shot upwards, his hair wild, his eyes completely disoriented. "It was the chinchilla, I swear!"

Staccato stared back at him in abject confusion, but Sonata was seething like a tiger. "You idiot!"

But Pyro appeared not to have heard her—or remembered that they were separated for that matter. "Hello gorgeous! Looking for a pair of warm hands to toast your—"

Sonata struck him so hard with his pillow Staccato feared she may have disoriented him further. "You took the toad, didn't you?"

"What toad? What are you talking about?"

"The medicine, you brainless bottom-feeder! You took the bottle with the toad on it!"

"No, actually, it was the one with the baboon … The butterfly … What are we talking about again?"

By now Sonata's face was turning purple. "I'm going to kill—"

Staccato pulled her back. "Calm down and get your trident!"

Melodious stumbled forward with Staccato's thermos. "Here! Sober him up!"

"Good thinking!" He shoved the coffee in Pyro's face, practically forcing it down his throat. "Pyro, listen. We're under attack. I need you up front and ready to blast some haigs."

Pyro dug his fist into one of his eyes and nodded. "You got it, boss." He grabbed his empty chakram holster, hopped out of bed, and immediately swayed to the side.

Staccato pushed the hand with the thermos back towards Pyro's lips. "And for Heaven's sake, don't stop drinking that coffee!"

Moody meows sounded from under Sonata's arm as she carried Cello to her berth and placed him on the bed. "In you go, Cello." She shut the doors. "Stay where it's nice and safe."

A pounding noise on the other side of the wall shook the caravan.

"Curse Skelter's vow of silence!" snapped Staccato. "Sonata, go assist him!" He helped Pyro up the ladder after Sonata. "Melodious, get your knives ready!"

With a loud bang the caravan rocked severely to one side and then the other, knocking Staccato and Melodious to the ground. The ladder leading to the loft swung to and fro. Pyro sailed backwards into the trundle, Sonata tumbling after. Another chorus of howls rang through the trees, closer now. It was only a matter of time before they caught up. Drawers rattled with every bump. And suddenly they were sailing at an impossibly smooth speed.

Staccato was the first to make it to the ladder. He stuck his head out the hatch. The caravan was gliding along the ice.

"At this speed we could outrun a motorcar," observed Sonata, poking her head out.

"Yes, but we've no cover." Staccato climbed onto the roof and helped her up. "We're like a big, yellow chrysanthemum popping out of the snow."

"We'll be spotted in no time." Pyro squeezed his way through the hatch. "Why haven't we painted this bloody thing?"

"It's the original color," snapped Sonata. "This is an antique, Pyro, not a tank!"

"Then put it in a museum and get a real vehicle!"

"Enough bickering," ordered Melodious, pushing his way through. "Staccato, what's the plan?"

"I'll need to cast an illusion. There's no other way around it."

"What kind of illusion?"

"Something dangerous. Something intimidating. Something to send them running in the other direction." Staccato stared thoughtfully at the edge of the wood, struggling to ignore the raging howls which were growing louder and louder. "A dragon. I'll make it look as though the caravan is a big, yellow dragon."

"A big yellow dragon?" echoed Sonata. "Are you sure that's convincing?"

"We're going to make it convincing. Skelter, stop the caravan!" The pegasi slowed until they gradually came to a stop. "Don't go anywhere, Pyro. I'll need you."

Pyro raised an eyebrow. "You want me to use my powers on the ice?"

"Not just you. I want you and Sonata to perform the Blow Torch, and—this is important—when I say so, aim it directly at the spot where they appear. Do not, under any circumstances, aim near the ice!"

Pyro and Sonata took one look at each other and grimaced. Staccato knew he was asking a lot. An igneous's powers all came down to one thing: breath control. Born with larger than average lungs, mastery was achieved through breathing exercises and diaphragm work, as well as endurance and stamina exercises. Relaxation was key. The more at ease an igneous, the better they could control their breathing, and the more powerful they would become. A long time ago, Sonata got it into her head to use her tranquilizing abilities to create a surge in Pyro's power. The result was a fifty-foot stream of flame that could blacken a tree in under five seconds: the Blow Torch.

"Can't you just make that part of the illusion?" whined Pyro.

"Maintaining a spontaneous illusion of such size and magnitude will be difficult enough. You're going to have to carry some of the weight."

"But you did it that one time in the Other!"

"How many times must I remind you? Casting illusions in an environment with minimal exposure to magic is entirely different than one that thrives on it! Besides, they know I'll be using my miraculous powers for defense. But if we can strike them with real fire, not only will we have them convinced, but we can do them some real damage!"

Sonata crossed her arms. "Well, I daresay Pyro can do it on his own, now that he's plastered himself with cold medicine! He should be plenty relaxed!"

"Yeah," agreed Pyro. "If anything she'll only make me tense!"

"Both of you shut up, and do as I say! Go stand in front of the pegasi!" The thicket at the edge of the woods began to rustle. Staccato aimed his staff at the bank. "Now remember, it has to reach all the way to the other side. Pyro will need to be as relaxed as possible."

Staccato pictured the door of the hatch swinging open and evolving into a giant, curved spine. He imagined the shafts attached to the pegasi curling into a pair of long horns atop a triangular head. The spokes of the wheels rearranged themselves until they looked like deadly, curving claws.

A team of haigs lugging a black sleigh burst through the bushes at the crest of the bank. Four more were seated at the front with their masters: two ophidian men, while two women Staccato took to be liliths sat in the back with another pair.

"Get ready," hissed Staccato, but Pyro and Sonata weren't listening.

"Ow! Tongs and torches, Sonata! What was that for?"

"What was what for?"

"Look, just because you hate me doesn't mean you can dig your nails into my neck!"

"Don't be dramatic! I wasn't digging my nails into your neck!"

"I'm not being dramatic! You always do this! Whenever you're mad you always find sneaky little ways to get at me! Like that time you accidentally poured scalding coffee all over my lap!"

"You're an igneous, it couldn't have possibly scalded you!"

"Yeah, and a good thing too!"

Melodious signaled for them to stop. "Do you really think this is the best time to have this argument?"

"Alright," ordered Staccato, "now!"

There was a flash of light from the corner of his eye. But nothing more.

"What was that?!" sniped Sonata. "That was pathetic!"

Pyro's voice echoed with sarcasm. "Thank you, my pillar of support!"

"Again!" Staccato rolled his eyes. But nothing was happening.

The driver of the sleigh was standing in his seat now, looking as though he was trying to discern whether what he was seeing was real or illusion.

"Pyro! Now!"

"I'm trying!"

"Try harder!" barked Sonata.

It was all Staccato could do to keep from cursing. "Sonata, you're not helping!"

By now Pyro was furious. "Honestly, it would be more helpful if she just didn't touch me at all!"

"Excuse me?"

Staccato was beginning to sweat. He couldn't maintain the illusion much longer. In his mind, he could see the claws curling back into wheels, and the scales shrinking into the wood.

"Do it now!"

Finally, a limp stream, no longer than four feet, jetted out from Pyro's lips. The arm holding Staccato's staff began to tremble until at last the illusion broke apart, and the company was left completely exposed. The driver of the sleigh cracked his whip. Eyes glowing, the team of haigs sped down the bank and across the ice.

"Get inside!" ordered Staccato. "Go Skelter, go!"

But the assailants were too fast for them. The haigs cut them off, spooking the pegasi, and forcing the caravan to stop. Melodious hurled his knives. One embedded itself into the sleigh. Another grazed the arm of the driver. Skelter took up the whip, fending the beasts away from the pegasi. Not wanting to risk the ice, their pursuers attacked from the interior of the sleigh, with the liliths using their powers to fight. Sonata levitated into the air, but was quickly dropped when one of Melodious's knives came flying at her attacker's face. She ducked just in time to miss it. But Sonata easily regained her footing, as the prosthetics she was wearing were designed for snow and ice. Sonata ran at the sleigh, her trident held high.

"Frightened of a little hand-to-hand combat, are you?" She knocked the lilith upside the head and forced her out of the sleigh. "Or is it the ice you're afraid of?"

Meanwhile, Pyro was a different story. He had followed Sonata's example, running up to the sleigh but, barefooted and doped up on cold medicine, one kick from the driver sent him sailing across the lake on his back.

Out of knives, Melodious was now fighting off one of the haigs with his bare hands, and was poised to finish it off when another came barreling towards him. Bracing himself, Staccato leapt off the roof, his staff extended, intending to blast the haig in the opposite direction. But nothing happened. His powers had been completely drained. The haig snarled, and snapped at the end of Staccato's staff. But Staccato was too quick. He spun his staff in a perfect arc, bringing the crown down on the haig beast's head.

"Is that all you got?" growled Pyro.

Staccato turned. The driver had pursued Pyro out of the sleigh, apparently able to navigate the ice with perfect grace, and was now beating Pyro bloody. Pyro gave several pathetic swings, but missed every time. Staccato glanced down at the empty holsters at Pyro's hips and gasped. He didn't have his chakrams! He had grabbed the sheaths, but forgot the weapons! Staccato dashed towards the caravan, struggling to stay upright. Unaware of Staccato's proximity, Sonata swung her trident preparing to strike her enemy and accidentally knocked Staccato's feet out from under him. Staccato skidded across the ice on his front, directly into the path of another haig beast. The haig lunged for his throat. Grabbing it by the antlers, Staccato wrenched it onto its back. The beast gnashed its teeth, snipping at Staccato's sleeve, but a strike from his staff was enough to slow its movements.

Floundering to his feet, Staccato ambled to the back of the caravan. He wrenched open the bottom half of the Dutch door and slipped inside. Just as he was shutting the door, a pair of antlers plunged through the opening. Staccato was thrown back into the wall as the haig forced its way in. Trembling, he tried to back away but tripped over the trundle, landing on his back. Enormous paws sank into the mattress, its claws tearing at the sheets. Staccato scrambled backwards into Pyro's bunk as the haig charged forward. With a terrible splitting noise, one of its antlers gouged a hole in the upper bunk, the space too narrow to fit its head. Splinters of wood rained down upon him. Staccato's hands were shaking. If he wasn't careful he could easily be gored. He pressed himself against the wall, but the haig continued to try and squeeze its way through.

Staccato was cornered. His only hope was to drive the haig away. Mustering all his strength, he jabbed his staff at the monster, but the haig grabbed it with its teeth, tossing it far out of Staccato's reach.

Staccato swallowed. He was utterly defenseless. With no powers, and no staff, how could he possibly hope to protect himself? Instinctively, he reached for his pocket. His fingers enclosed around a wooden handle. His pocket knife! Staccato moved fast. He flicked open the blade and plunged it into the side of the haig's neck. The haig coiled back with a screeching cry. With a kick to the face, Staccato propelled the beast backwards.

"Now get out!"

The haig scrambled out the door, its tail between its legs. Staccato dove across the caravan, threw open the weapons cabinet, grabbed the chakrams, and dashed up to the roof. One of the haigs lay dead on the ice, Melodious was fighting off the other ophidian, Skelter had cornered a haig with his whip, and Sonata had just managed to defeat her opponent. Across the lake, Pyro continued to struggle. By the looks of it, he had managed to get in a few hits, but overall he was just too slow.

"Sonata," called Staccato, leaning over the roof and holding out the chakrams. "Get these to Pyro."

"Why don't you just use your powers?"

"The illusion drained me. I'm spent. You can run on the ice better than I can."

Sonata took the chakrams and sped off in Pyro's direction. "Pyro! Your chakrams!"

Winding her arm back, she chucked one of the discs in Pyro's direction. The blade spun past Pyro's head, narrowly grazing his skin. Catching it with his left hand, Pyro whipped round to face her.

"Woman, are you trying to kill me?" He chucked the blade upwards, slicing his attacker's arm.

"If I wanted to kill you I wouldn't have thrown them, you ignorant hothead!"

"Oh, sure! First you try to cut my neck with your talons—"

"Talons?!"

"And when that doesn't do the trick, you nearly do me in with my own weapon!" He bounced the blade off his attacker's shin, cutting open the skin and leaving him helpless.

"Well done! You've figured out my whole scheme! I'm secretly trying to murder you!"

Teeth bared, a haig ran at Pyro from behind. In one fluid movement, Sonata tossed the second disc at its head. With a metallic clash, the blade ricocheted off its antler.

"Oh, for the love of shrapnel!" Pyro reached out and caught the second chakram. "You take this one, and I'll take the other!" Raising his chakram over his head, Pyro ran off at an invisible enemy.

Sonata stabbed the haig with her trident and stared after Pyro, dumbfounded. Completely sloshed, Pyro swung his foot at his imaginary rival and slipped head-first onto the ice. Staccato was still cornered on the roof, fending off a haig using his powerless staff. With Pyro sedated and unable to use fire, and Staccato's powers sapped, it was unlikely they could hold off their attackers much longer. Suddenly, Skelter jammed his fingers into his mouth and whistled from the driver's seat. With the haigs away from the pegasi, they could drive the wagon again.

"Back to the caravan!" shouted Staccato.

Melodious tossed his opponent across the ice like a frisbee and hurried into the wagon. With a crack of the reins, Skelter took off, pointing a finger at Pyro and Sonata.

"Pyro! Sonata! We're headed your way!" translated Staccato, but the two were too busy arguing to have heard him.

"You're just jealous because Cello likes me more," screamed Pyro.

"Really? Well, as soon as this is over I'm never letting you see him again!"

For a moment, Pyro seemed too angry to speak. His fists shook. His freckles started glowing, and before anyone knew what was happening, steam was pouring out his mouth.

"THAT'S ILLEGAL!"

"Illegal?! What are you talking about?!

"You can't take the cat away from me! That is parental alienation!"

"Parental—? He's my cat!"

"He's *our* cat!"

"You weren't there when he was a kitten!"

"I WOULD HAVE BEEN IF I COULD!"

The caravan was coming up on their right.

"Pay attention!" exclaimed Staccato, leaning over the roof and hooking the back of Sonata's collar with his staff. Sonata glided alongside the caravan. From inside the wagon, Melodious threw open the side door, grabbed her hand, and towed her inside. Stranded, Pyro stood there staring after them in a drowsy haze. Meanwhile, their remaining opponents had piled back into the sleigh, and were quickly gaining on them.

"Skelter, get Pyro! Get Pyro!" Staccato dove down into the loft. The caravan swerved to the left. In seconds, Staccato slid down the ladder and shoved the end of a rope into Melodious's hands.

"Hold this."

Kicking aside the Dutch door, Staccato stood at the opening and waited for Pyro to come back into view. Silver shavings of ice sprayed from beneath the wheels. In a desperate attempt to catch up with the wagon, Pyro ran clumsily across the lake, slipping and sliding and never getting very far.

Staccato hurled the rope over his head. "Grab hold!"

Pyro caught the rope with both hands. For a moment, he was left to stand awkwardly as the moving caravan picked up the slack. Then, all at once, Pyro was jerked forward, and dragged on his belly with nothing between him and the ice but a thin undershirt and a pair of flannel pajama pants.

"Should I start pulling?" asked Melodious.

Staccato eyed Pyro uncertainly and bit his lip. "Let's see if he can get to his feet first."

Pyro wriggled around to his side. Gradually, he made it into a squatting position, pulling back on the rope. No sooner had he made it to his feet, than two of the haigs jumped out of the sleigh, running after him as if he were a drumstick on a string. Staccato narrowed his eyes.

"Sonata, bring me my rifle."

The haigs were on Pyro like dogs on a bone. With one hand he swung his chakram, but he was no match for the two of them.

"Your rifle?" echoed Melodious. "What for?"

"Two haigs are after him," explained Staccato to the blind man. "If he uses his powers he'll risk melting the ice. And I doubt he can hang on and fight them off in the condition he's in."

"Are you sure this is a good idea? You could hit Pyro."

"Trust me, I hunted reindeer for fifteen years."

Melodious raised an eyebrow. "You hunted reindeer?"

Sonata plowed forward with the firearm. "I'll do it!"

Staccato snatched it from her grip. "You *will* hit Pyro! Here, help hold the rope." Staccato looked through the crosshairs. "Start pulling him in."

The haigs snarled and snapped at Pyro's heels as he advanced forward. Staccato waited until he was safely out of range, then pulled the trigger. Shards of ice fountained into the air, but the haigs continued to run. He fired again. Halfway across the ice the bullet froze. Staccato squinted into the night. The lilith was standing up in the sleigh, her hand outstretched. Staccato's eyes bulged as the bullet turned and raced back in their direction.

"Get down!" Staccato slammed the upper half of the Dutch door shut. *Crack!* The bullet struck the exterior of the door. Pyro was sliding on his back now. Abandoning the rifle, Staccato fell to his knees and started pulling on the rope. At last, Pyro was able to clamber back into the wagon, coated with flecks of ice. Staccato watched in horror as the upper half of the door wrenched back open telekinetically. Legs still moving, the haigs levitated in the air and sped towards the caravan. Staccato yanked the doors shut again, holding fast to the handles.

"Melodious, head up to the roof and tell Skelter to fly us back to land."

"In these conditions?"

"We won't be going far. We just need to get off the lake. I'm going to have Pyro blast a hole through the ice."

Melodious dashed up to the roof, while Staccato bolted the door.

"Alright, Pyro, what I need you to do is—Pyro!" Pyro was lying in the trundle, completely passed out. Staccato turned to Sonata, gaping in astonishment.

"By thunder! What's in that medicine?"

Sonata shrugged. "Sedatives. Honey. Your typical cold medicine ingredients."

"That can't be right. Under no circumstances should he be *that* sedated!"

Sonata opened her mouth, then stopped. Her eyes glazed over with annoyance. "I think I know what happened." Grabbing the pillow from Pyro's bunk, she socked him in the face. Pyro's eyes snapped open.

"The moon has my cigar! Quick! Get the pitchfork!" Pyro froze. His eyes glanced from one side of the caravan to the other, remembering where he was.

"How much cold medicine did you take?" asked Sonata through gritted teeth.

"Two and a half tablespoons."

"That's the amount for the unicorn bottle! The toad bottle is half a tablespoon!"

"I thought they were the same!"

"So not only did you take the wrong medication, you took too much of it!" Sonata threw up her hands and growled. "Do you ever pay attention?"

"It was dark, okay? I thought it was the unicorn bottle!"

"Since when do toads bear a passing resemblance to unicorns?!"

Scraping noises like razor-sharp claws shivered across the roof. Sonata gasped.

"They're on the roof!"

An angry cry from Melodious echoed outside, followed by a yelp. Staccato turned to the window in time to see the haigs passing outside the glass.

"Not anymore." He grabbed his rifle and headed for the door again. "Pyro, when I open this door, I want you to blast the ice. Understand?"

Pyro jumped to his feet. "Got it!"

On the count of three Staccato hurled open the door. Pyro wasted no time. With a tremendous inhale, he leaned over the edge of the threshold and blew. Orange flames lit up the night, casting long, lean shadows across the ice. Cursing, the driver drew back on the reins, desperate to slow down. Cracking sounds split the air. Below them the ice was starting to fissure and break apart.

Staccato beat on the wall with the butt of his rifle. "Now, Skelter, now!"

Dark water began to gush through the gash. The caravan bounced once or twice. A hearty wind whisked across the lake. All at once the wagon wound into the air in an indistinct spiral.

Staccato drew Pyro back and slammed the doors shut. "Hang on!"

The wagon pitched sideways as the pegasi struggled against the harsh winds. Outside the window, the lake was shrinking beneath them.

215

Just when they thought they were safe, a formidable gale struck from the west with a shrill wail. The wagon was thrown ninety degrees, spun horizontally, and sent careening down from the sky. For a moment, the caravan was dragged along on its side through the snow before dipping down again and turning right-side up down a steep incline. At last, they slowed to a halt.

Staccato was lying in a heap on the Murphy bed, his fingers wrapped around the handle of a cabinet.

"Is everyone alright?" Staccato looked over his shoulder and froze. Pyro and Sonata had disappeared.

The door of Sonata's berth swung open, and Cello emerged with a yawn as though nothing had happened. But no Pyro or Sonata. Loud thumps resounded from under Pyro's bunk. Realizing that the trundle had slid shut, and that Pyro and Sonata were trapped inside, Staccato scrambled over to the drawer.

"Get your hands off me!" growled Sonata.

"Then get off my hands! And quit breathing on my neck!"

"Where else am I supposed to breathe?"

Staccato grabbed the handle of the trundle and wrenched it open so that their heads were visible. Pyro and Sonata had been thrown together face to face, tangled in a sheet, their arms wrapped about each other.

Smirking, Staccato couldn't help but tease. "Normally, I'd scold you, but what with all your bickering lately, I'm tempted to leave you like this."

"That's not funny," they snapped in unison.

The back door of the caravan swung open. Melodious and Skelter dashed inside.

"Is anyone hurt?" asked Melodious. Skelter took one look at Pyro's and Sonata's heads peeking out of the trundle and raised an eyebrow.

"We're fine," said Staccato airily. "Pyro and Sonata are a little stuck, but otherwise unharmed."

Sonata's teeth were bared. "Get me out of here now!"

"Ugh!" Pyro made a face. "You spat on me!"

"Keep it up and I'll bite you!"

Staccato raised his voice. "Both of you be quiet or so help me I will close this drawer!" He turned to Skelter. "Where are we?"

Skelter made a cone shape with his hands, then thrust his right arm upwards with his fingers splayed.

"We're in the caldera?"

"It is not a bad place to hide actually," assured Melodious. "We've shelter from the wind here. And I would be surprised if anyone came looking for us inside an old volcano."

"Did you hear that Pyro?" Staccato waited but Pyro didn't answer.

"Pyro, wake up!" ordered Sonata.

"Saddle up the potatoes!" There was a pause, then Pyro murmured in a confused tone, "Did we make up?"

"Quit falling asleep!"

"I'm trying!"

Rolling his eyes, Staccato grabbed hold of the handle again and pulled.

A piercing shriek split the air.

"Blue blazes, Sonata!" Pyro tried to wrench away from her but there wasn't enough room. "My ear is right here!"

"Stop! Stop! My hair is caught! You're pulling my hair!"

Sliding his hand under the bed, Staccato felt around for Sonata's curls.

"We can always cut it," quipped Pyro.

"You cut my hair, and I will rip your beard out!"

"How? With your teeth?"

Melodious leaned over the bunk. "Perhaps if we lift the mattress?"

Springs creaked as Skelter slipped around Staccato and raised the bedding, exposing the slats in the frame. A section of hair was stuck in the track. Gently, Staccato eased the strands out of the hardware.

"Alright, I'm going to pull again."

Sonata gave another shriek. "It's still stuck!"

"Hold on." Staccato tried pushing the drawer back in a measure, hoping it would slide the hair out.

"No, no, no!"

Staccato peered through the slats. Sonata's hair had been stuck in such a way that moving the drawer had pulled her head forward until her face was smooshed up against Pyro's.

"Don't you dare kiss me!"

Unable to contain his laughter, Skelter snorted and let the mattress drop.

"Ah, yes, because you are so kissable right now!" spat Pyro. "Could you be any more full of yourself?"

"Oh, you are such a hypocrite!"

"That's it!" A smell like burnt hair leaked out from under the bed. "Pull!"

Staccato tugged the trundle open. In a flurry of indignation, Sonata sprang up from the drawer like Dracula rising from his coffin. Black smoke billowed from her hair in a thin stream where Pyro had severed the lock.

"YOU BASS!"

"What are you upset for?" Pyro retorted. "It's not even noticeable!"

"Enough!" exclaimed Staccato, throwing his hand up. "I want both of you outside the caravan now! We need to have a little talk."

Pyro and Sonata begrudgingly did as told. When the door had been shut, Staccato turned to them, his expression as dark and ominous as a skull and crossbones.

"As you are aware, I am about to be gone for several months. Once we reach Alpheratz I must leave you to depart for New York, while you carry on to the Floodgates. It will be difficult for me to return after I am gone. I need to know that I can depend on the two of you to run things in my absence." His gaze intensified, and his tone rang with the threat of retribution and consequences. "This cannot happen again. Do you understand? Regardless of your feelings for each other, you still have to conduct yourselves like adults. You may hate each other for all eternity, but it is vital that you respect one another as teammates and keep your personal drama to yourselves! Is that understood?"

Pyro and Sonata fidgeted, and glanced down at the ground. "Yes, sir."

"Good." He adjusted his sleeves. "Now, I'm going to survey our surroundings. If all is well, we'll stay here for the night. In the meantime, Sonata, I want you tending to everyone's injuries. Pyro included!"

Pyro sneered and tangled his arms across his chest. "No thank you! I'll take my chances!"

"What did I just get finished saying?" thundered Staccato.

With a discomfited look, Pyro slipped his hands into his pockets. "Sorry."

"If we're attacked again, I need you in top fighting condition. And as far as I'm concerned you can dump that toad bottle out!" His lecture at an end, Staccato shooed them back inside, and set off to explore.

Minutes passed as he took his time investigating their new hideout. Melodious had been right. The conditions inside the caldera were far more tolerable, and the surrounding walls shielded them from prying eyes. It would do for the present. And hopefully, by the next morning the winds would have died down enough to fly.

When he at last returned to the caravan, Melodious, Pyro, and Skelter had all fallen back asleep. Staccato shook his head. Not wishing to disturb them, he would have to administer their dreams himself while they slept.

Sonata was poised on the edge of the bunk, having just absorbed the last of Pyro's wounds. By the looks of it, he had passed out a long time ago. Unaware of her godfather standing in the doorway, Sonata stared down at Pyro without a trace of hostility. Her hand inched near Pyro's forehead. Pyro lay utterly still, his chest rising and falling gently, completely unaware that Sonata was reaching out to touch him. In a soft, smooth gesture, she brushed her fingers through his hair. Pyro did not wake, but turned his head her direction, a subconscious longing. Something inside Staccato loosened and relaxed. There was hope. Forgetting himself, he shifted his weight. The floorboards squeaked. Sonata drew back at once, her cheeks red.

"A bit of dried blood in his hair," she hastily explained.

Staccato's eyes drifted coolly from Pyro to Sonata. "Ah."

Scowling, Sonata hunched forward. "You needn't look so pleased."

"I gave no such look."

"I know you talked to Pyro about the two of us splitting up."

"You knew that was bound to happen."

Her expression remained defensive. "Then you must know why I turned him down."

"On the contrary, I do not."

Sonata looked up in surprise. "You don't?"

Reaching out to her, he smoothed her singed lock of hair against her head. "My dear, he told me nothing."

220

"Nothing?"

Staccato shook his head. "He seemed to think it would be a violation of your trust." Taking off his hat, he turned towards the ladder. "I'll fetch the dreams, and then we can turn in for the night."

The mattress creaked as Pyro turned over with a jolt. "Hush, I'm hunting tax collectors!"

Staccato exchanged looks with Sonata before shaking his head and ascending the ladder to the loft.

Chapter 24:
Mammoth is Mammoth

Faina's cold ended up earning her a trip to the doctor where it was decided she would need her tonsils removed. An entire week passed before Pasha was able to see her again, and even then she was still recovering. On the twenty-sixth, in between stealing, he ended up joining her for lunch at *Opa!* with Uncle Matvei and Anya.

"So," began Faina as she picked at the crust of her baloney sandwich. "How much trouble did you get in?"

"Well, Ma was pretty upset when the judge assigned me a probation officer—"

Faina's eyes looked as though they would jump out of their sockets. "A probation officer?"

"Yeah, but he works for Klokov. He's got tons of them working for the Breadwinners, social workers too, for whenever any of us get caught. Anyway, she confiscated my record player for a week."

"So, does that mean you can never go to jail?"

Pasha swallowed a bite of his sandwich. "I wouldn't put it like that exactly. It's just harder. Take Anastas for example. Trifecta says he's been arrested so many times this year, there's no way he's staying out of jail."

Uncle Matvei emerged from between two shelves and plucked a celery stick from his plate by the register. "Anastas finally in jail, wouldn't that be nice?" He tossed the remaining scraps of his baloney sandwich to Mammoth, who happily accepted the treat.

With everything going on it had been some time since Pasha had seen Mammoth up close, and he was shocked to discover not only how much he had grown but how large he was overall. Indeed, Mammoth seemed full-sized for a four-month-old Chow Chow.

"Is my math wrong or is Mammoth supposed to be only four months old?"

Faina snickered. "I know what you mean." She reached under the counter and produced a book about dog breeds. "I got this at the library to help solve the mystery of his growth. According to the vet, Chows usually only weigh eighteen pounds at this age."

"How much does Mammoth weigh?"

"Sixty."

"Sixty?!" Pasha felt his baloney get sucked down his lungs. "That's three times the average!"

"Yeah, but the doctor says relative to his size he's healthy." She paused and glanced down at him. "Only, he's not supposed to be that big yet."

Uncle Matvei, who had been standing in the corner, narrowed his eyes thoughtfully on the dog and waved his celery stick.

"How old did you say Mammoth was when you got him, Pasha?"

The stairs creaked overhead and Anya appeared with a tray of glasses and freshly prepared lemonade.

"About nine weeks."

"Are you sure?"

"I mean, I don't know much about Chows but I didn't see anything to make me think otherwise."

"How big are Chows supposed to get, Faina?" asked Anya, who had already discerned that they were discussing Mammoth.

Faina opened the book and began flipping through the pages. "About …" She ran her finger down the text. "Fifty to sixty pounds."

Uncle Matvei rubbed at his chin and tucked his tongue in his cheek. "I don't think that dog is a Chow."

"You don't?"

Uncle Matvei took a swig of his soda and shook his head. "Who was this friend of yours who sold you the dog?"

"Yuri Mishkin," answered Pasha.

Anya threw back her head and scoffed. "That explains it."

Faina was already thumbing through the pages of her book again. "Wait a minute." She held up a finger. "It says here that all Chows have a bluish-black tongue." She tore off a piece of her baloney and leaned down towards Mammoth. "Here, *Mamoshka*."

Mammoth wrenched open his chops and happily chomped down on the deli meat.

"Well?" Anya peered over the counter. "What color is it?"

Pasha scratched his head. "Looks like just regular pink."

Faina reached for one of the glasses of lemonade. "Well, if he isn't a Chow, what is he?"

"He kinda looks like a Newfoundland," suggested Anya, turning the pages of the book until she came to a drawing of a massive, fluffy dog with hair the color of Mammoth's.

"Or maybe a Bernese Mountain dog," said Pasha.

"You're not likely to find it in any breeder's book, at least not in this country," said Uncle Matvei. "That is an *ovcharka*, a Caucasian Shepherd dog."

"A what?" repeated Anya.

"One of the oldest dog breeds in the world. People used to breed them to hunt bears."

"Bears?" Faina gaped at him. "You're saying Mammoth could take down an actual bear?"

Uncle Matvei gave a chuckle. "Maybe not now. But you give it a couple of months. He'll live up to his name."

Pasha finished off the last of his lemonade and checked his watch. "I better be on my way. I wouldn't want to show up to Klokov's empty-handed, not when I'm supposed to meet him in his office afterwards."

Faina reached down and patted Mammoth's head. "Ah! So today's the day we finally discover the mystery of June twenty-sixth!"

Pasha got up and reached for his satchel. "Looks that way. Whatever it is, he's asked Yuri and Sergei too."

"We've been scanning the papers for any upcoming events that might coincide with the date. But so far the only thing happening on the twenty-sixth is some doctor from Louisville attending a medical conference uptown."

"Doesn't exactly sound newsworthy."

Anya was quick to interrupt. "That's because Faina's leaving out the good part. My Junior Red Cross leader told me all about it. This doctor wants to open the first blood bank in the U.S. They've been a huge success in Great Britain."

Pasha chuckled. "Well, we know that can't be related. Not unless he's got some sort of blood-banking racket going on." He slung his bag over his shoulder and thanked Uncle Matvei for lunch.

Faina clung to his arm. "You have to tell me all the details tomorrow! Thieves' Honor?"

Pasha threw her a wink, prompting a bashful smile to find its way to her lips. "Thieves' Honor."

Chapter 25:

Boys with Guns

Pasha sat atop a crate in Klokov's office with several of the other street fighters, letting his legs dangle over the side. The box was so tall his feet didn't even touch the ground. He rubbed his nose and gazed discreetly down the row of boys, hoping to find some reason as to why they had all been summoned here. Both Yuri and Sergei were present, just as they had said, as well as Trifecta, Moneyrider, and the Savage.

Heads turned as the door opened, revealing not Klokov, much to Pasha's chagrin, but Anastas. Pasha forced his head away, trying not to sigh. So whatever they were doing, he was in on it too.

Pasha repeated the names over in his head, searching for the common link between all of them. They weren't in trouble, for they would've known it if they were. Nearly all of them had been Breadwinners for at least three years now. As far as physiques went there was quite a bit of diversity amongst them, Yuri being the smallest overall, and the title of biggest being a tough call between Sergei and Anastas. Finally, Yuri said what everyone else was thinking.

"Does anyone know why we're here?"

Before anyone could pose their theories, Klokov entered through the door. "Gentlemen." He turned the lock behind him.

Not a one of them responded but waited patiently as he took his place behind his large, oak desk and removed his cigar holder from his pocket.

"Got a job for you fellas tonight."

"A job?" echoed Sergei. "What do you mean, a job?"

"Yeah," said Yuri in his sneering, whining voice. "You ain't ever given us a job before."

Klokov held the cigar between his lips and raised a match to the end. "Trifecta knows what I'm talking about."

The boys looked questioningly towards Trifecta, who remained his usual quiet self.

"Though most of you younger fellas may not realize it, especially those of you who are still fresh off the boat, we've enjoyed an unprecedented season of peace and quiet the past four years here in the Lower East Side."

Pasha's eyes glazed over cynically. Sure, there hadn't been much activity from the Butchers as of late other than the string of disappearances, but it was hard to consider things peaceful when you were running from the cops every day and couldn't remember what it was like not to have a bruise. Klokov tapped the ashes from the end of his cigar.

"But this is the underworld, and peace is often short-lived. It was only a matter of time before the Butchers would rise up again and attempt to reclaim sections of their old territory." He held up one of the missing posters for Pearl Sulzbach. "Earlier this year, a few of you brought me an incriminating photograph of this girl discovered in a Butcher raid. We now know that it is the Bowery Butchers who are behind all these disappearances."

The Savage raised his hand. "So, what'd they do to the people who were kidnapped?"

"The details are sketchy, but we're pretty sure they've been trafficked."

Many of the boys stared back at Klokov with blank faces. Only Sergei had the bravery to ask, "What's 'trafficked' mean?"

"Sold, either into forced labor or prostitution. In the case of Miss Sulzbach I think it's safe to say she's been put up in a cat house."

"What about all them marks on her arm?" asked Moneyrider.

Klokov shook his head. "We don't know for sure what that's about yet, whether it's drugs or some form of abuse. But one thing I do know is that war is on the horizon." He paused to blow a smoke ring. "And it's time I begin preparing you boys for a bigger challenge."

Pasha clutched the box he was sitting on tighter. Before he could stop himself the words were flying out of his mouth.

"Wait, I thought not all of us had to be foot soldiers. Are you saying you're sending us out to fight the Butchers?"

Klokov showed no sign of reproach towards Pasha. His features remained arranged in the same stern pattern.

"Maybe not all of you are cut out to be foot soldiers, but in times such as these we need every man we can get. Tonight I'm sending you all on a mission. It may very well be the only mission you'll ever have to carry out. I have chosen each and every one of you for a specific purpose." He turned to Yuri. "Rail Runner. You got street smarts, kid. We're gonna need a slick like you to pull one over on these rats." Next was Sergei. "Broadshanks, you're the strongest."

Pasha chanced a glimpse at Anastas. The moment Sergei had been declared the strongest, his eyebrows had lowered another measure or two. Klokov went on to award Trifecta the title of leader. It was said the Savage had been included for his ferocity, and Moneyrider for his speed. Finally, he came to Pasha.

"And Stallion here …" He smiled. "Leo taught you well. Ain't nobody able to slip in and out of the city like you."

"Except Leo's sister," grumbled Anastas, who received no attention for his comment.

"As for you, Rogue." Klokov took another drag from his cigar. "You've got something special. Something none of the rest of us have."

Anastas cracked his neck as he sat up straighter, looking as though every exultation of praise was well deserved.

"You got connections."

Anastas froze. "I got what?"

"Your parents had Butcher affiliations. You know the ins and outs of the Butchers better than any of the rest of us."

Anastas fumbled for a response, then at last fell to scowling. "Yeah, whatever."

"Tonight, the Butchers will be passing off their victims to a client from down south. It'll be your job to stop that from happening."

Pasha felt as though the air in his lungs was only reaching a depth of three inches.

"But, I still don't understand. Why are you sending *us*? You expect us to stop a traffic? We don't have any experience."

Klokov was showing the first signs of irritation. He narrowed his eye and jammed his finger on the desk. "This is your experience. You gotta start somewhere."

Sergei flashed him a warning look, but Pasha refused to be put into a gang war if he didn't have to be. There had to be something he had missed. Something he wasn't understanding.

"Start? When I first joined you told me we didn't have to grow up to be foot soldiers. You said we could be anything."

Klokov aimed his finger at Pasha, his voice beginning to rise. "You'll be whatever I tell you to be, understand?"

Pasha fell silent. It was as though Klokov had reached down his throat and snatched the very soul from his heart. The reality of his boss's words began to sink in. He was trapped.

Klokov got up from his chair and retrieved a small crate from underneath his desk. He motioned for them to stand. "Get up. Hold out your hands."

Pasha's mouth had gone dry. Klokov taught all the boys how to shoot when they first joined, but Pasha had never thought he would actually need to know. What's more, shooting hardly seemed liked the minimum requirement to pull off such a mission. Most of the boys had never even heard of trafficking before tonight, and now they were expected to stop one from happening? Why hadn't Klokov trained them? Or was this his way of ensuring that none of them would try to back out and run away?

The sweat on Pasha's palm was clearly visible beneath the garish shine of the pendant lamp. Klokov placed a pistol in his open hand. Whether from the weight of the weapon or from sheer nausea, Pasha's wrist went weak. He was forced to grab the gun with both hands to keep from dropping it.

Anastas held his pistol admiringly towards the light, his teeth peeking through his lips as he smiled. Sergei exchanged fearful glances with Pasha from across the room. Yuri's eyebrows twinged slightly. He was rather good at masking his emotions, but Pasha could recognize the traces of fear in his posture.

Trifecta was the last to receive his gun. Pasha had always liked Trifecta, and understood why Klokov had made him the leader. There was a quiet authority about him, but Pasha sensed something more. A sadness. When his fingers enclosed around the handle, Pasha saw the imperceptible brokenness in Trifecta's eyes that Klokov did not, and likely never would.

***

The docks reeked of brine, fish, and whatever else had been thrown into the Hudson Bay to rot. It didn't matter how warm of a day it had been, it was always at least ten degrees colder down by the harbor, and several shades darker all around. The Savage turned over his wrist and checked his watch.

"Seven minutes past."

"The Butchers will be departing right about now." Trifecta lit a cigarette and shook out the match.

"How long you think it takes them to show up?" asked Yuri.

Trifecta shrugged. "I give 'em half an hour."

The wet, moldering wood groaned beneath his footsteps as he walked out to the edge of the dock. Pasha looked back at the delivery van parked in front of the warehouse. It was Anastas's expertise which had led them to the discovery of where the Butchers would be docking. Not long after arriving, a contact would show up to transport the victims to their next location. Klokov had arranged for more experienced Breadwinners to detain the contact, allowing the boys time to stop the Butchers in the act.

As they waited huddled together, Pasha felt as though he had been picked up and placed somewhere else, like a seed or a burr. Until now, the Breadwinners had been somewhat survivable. The bruises were nasty and the work was hard, but an hour ago there had been an end in sight. Now Pasha realized he had been cruelly misled. Bribed into servitude. When first he had voiced his concerns about his future all those years ago, Klokov had made it sound like an advertisement for joining the army.

You fight for us four years and we'll send you to college! We'll send you to business school! We'll get you a contract with MGM! Or how about a seat in the Senate? As though it were some Ivy League club! And sure, as an associate, Leo may have been lucky enough to be rewarded with such dreams, but such was typical for the ever-popular high-school heartthrob. Leo possessed the charm, the charisma, and the likability to get people on his side. Pasha on the other hand? What chance did he have?

"We're cattle," he finally burst, shivering in the harsh breeze. "We're all just cattle."

"Pasha …" Sergei breathed.

"No, we're worse than cattle! We're …" he stumbled for the perfect word. "We're game! Lured in to be stuffed in a cage! Like rabbits, like foxes, like—"

"Like horses," Trifecta finished, biting down on a cigarette and turning to look at him. "Like thoroughbred racehorses. Why do you think we're all named after things you only hear at the Kentucky Derby?"

231

The Savage pulled his cap down over his curly blonde hair and shoved his hands in his pockets.

"They takes us out of the wild, they breaks us, they rides us into the grave."

"He can't do this to us!"

The other boys stared at Pasha as though he'd lost his mind.

"What? This ain't what you signed up for?" scoffed Moneyrider.

Pasha dragged his breath through the back of his throat, lowering his eyebrows.

"Why would I sign up for something like this?"

"Gee, I don't know, to feed your family?"

"Typical Chevalsky," grumbled Anastas with a nasty smirk. "Bit of an idealist. Always used to getting his own way."

Pasha did not possess the tolerance for Anastas's remarks just now. He dared towards him with a threatening gesture.

"Shut your mouth, Anastas!"

"Hey, hey!" Trifecta stepped between them. "Break it up you two! Anastas, go walk it off! You're supposed to be on lookout anyway."

The Savage elbowed him in the side. "Hey, you gonna be okay, kid?"

Pasha shrugged him off and stormed over to the railing. "No! I just found out my whole future has been taken away!"

"Well, what kinda future were you expecting when you joined the Breadwinners?"

Pasha lowered his head, propping his foot up on the lower rung. "When you joined, did Klokov tell you that you didn't have to be a thug when you were finished street fighting?"

"Yeah, but I didn't actually believe him."

When no one else joined in to dispute the Savage, Pasha looked up at them in disbelief.

"Didn't any of you have dreams? Wasn't there something you wanted to be before you became a Breadwinner?"

Unable to take it anymore, Yuri took his cap and threw it down on the ground.

"Will you just let it go already?!"

Pasha edged back in surprise. Sergei reached for Yuri's shoulder.

"Come on, Yuri, leave him alone!"

Yuri shoved him away. "No!" He leveled his finger at Pasha's face, looking more rodent-like than ever. "As much as I hate Anastas, he has a point! You don't live in the real world, Pasha! You were born rich! You know what I was born with? Nothing! And my parents were born with nothing! And whatever their parents had—which was probably also nothing—was taken away from them during the Pogroms!"

Pasha turned his back on Yuri, hurt.

"We're not like you!" he went on. "We can't afford to dream! My gosh, you're so naive! You really thought you could join a group of thugs and grow up to be a firefighter, or a police officer, or an aviator, or some other stupid kid dream? I may be a thug, but at least I know what I am! At least I can accept that!"

"You're a real pal, Yuri," snapped Pasha, walking away from him.

Trifecta put his hands out. "You two done? Good! Yuri, get back to your station."

Pasha parked himself atop an old crate, cradling his head in his hands. He could hear Trifecta following him and wished he would just leave him alone.

"Hey." He nudged Pasha's foot with his shoe.

Pasha looked dismally up at him, leaning against the railing.

"Don't listen to him, kid." He rolled down his shirtsleeves and exhaled a puff of his cigarette. "You aren't the only one who Klokov's tricked into this operation, kay? It's just nobody wants to admit it." He lowered his head. "Moneyrider, you know what he wanted to be? A pitcher for the New York Yankees. And the Savage? He's lying. He wanted to go to Harvard and be a lawyer."

"What did you wanna be, Trifecta?"

Trifecta paused for a moment, as though deciding whether or not he wanted to share.

"A writer."

Pasha blinked at him in confusion. "A writer? That's not something the Breadwinners could stop you from doing, is it?"

"You'd be surprised." Having smoked his cigarette down, he threw the butt over his shoulder into the bay. "I won't say it's impossible to get promoted like Klokov was saying. But there's a type they generally prefer to boost up the ladder."

"You mean like Leo?"

"Yeah. Exactly like Leo. They want someone charming, a smooth talker, you know. Those are the guys they give the real jobs to."

A cold sinking feeling mounted in Pasha's chest. "Why would Klokov want Leo at the *New York Daily*?"

"You kidding? To keep his dirty business out of the media! Not that Leo would've agreed to any of it. But …" He looked up at the sky.

"But he wouldn't have had a choice."

Trifecta sighed and scratched the side of his head. "It's possible Leo could've found a way out of it, being an associate as opposed to an actual member. But make no mistake, he would've had to pay dearly for it."

The wind tore at Pasha's skin, and yet he felt utterly numb. The memory of Leo's face as he turned and waved before running off up the street passed before his eyes. Leo thought he had been handed the opportunity of a lifetime. Never mind that he was seventeen, never mind that he'd gotten his girlfriend pregnant, that he'd spent the last three years stealing to provide for his family; he had still managed to come within reach of his dream. He never knew the truth. Maybe it was better that way.

Pasha had never felt more stupid. He recalled his confession to Faina about wanting to be a police officer and cringed. Even if Klokov had allowed him to be on the force, the only person Pasha would have been helping was Klokov, covering up his crimes, destroying evidence. Yuri was right, Pasha was naive.

"Heads up, fellas!" Anastas was jogging back from his post. "Boat's headed this way."

Trifecta removed his gun from his waistband and snapped his fingers. "Alright, boys! You know what to do! Get in your places!"

With trembling hands, Pasha made his way up the steps of the warehouse. Trifecta had been merciful and placed him in charge of signaling to backup when the job was done. This meant he had to stand in front of the window on the second floor with a mirror and wave it back and forth in front of the light when the time came.

Pasha crouched below the glass and peeked over the sill. The waves came in choppier and quicker as the boat approached. He could see Trifecta and Moneyrider hiding behind their stations, guns at the ready. Pasha placed his hand over his forehead in an attempt to get a hold of himself.

It took a while for the boat to dock. A man in a gray Mackintosh emerged, shouting orders to a bunch of boys in bomber jackets and caps. They could've been Breadwinners. They were boys no older than themselves, who had more than likely found themselves pledging their allegiance to the Bowery Butchers under similar circumstances. Pasha trained his eyes on the cabin with frightened curiosity. If Klokov was correct, six people were imprisoned inside. Six of his neighbors. People he had passed on the street. People with whom he had stood in line at the butcher's. People like Faina or Mrs. Novak. Would he recognize them? Was Pearl Sulzbach among them?

As the first boy made his way off the boat, Trifecta and Moneyrider leapt from their hiding places, guns raised.

Headlights panned across the scene as a van sped into the parking lot. Doors flung open in perfect rhythm, and three men shot out of the back seat. They had massive black rifles raised to eye level, aiming at Trifecta and Moneyrider. The attempt to detain the contact had evidently failed. Pasha swallowed. He couldn't watch another death. Not sure what else to do, he shot at the upper right-hand corner of the window to get their attention. The glass shattered. Pasha saw the men swivel around before ducking back under the sill.

Bullets fired one after the other, spraying through the window and knocking out whatever glass remained. Pasha fell flat on his face. The shouting trailed off into the distance. Pasha lifted his head. Movement drew his eye towards the ground where the floorboards were wide enough to peer through. Yuri sprinted down the aisle, two other boys chasing him.

Pasha scrambled to his feet. His eyes scanned the shadows for some sort of solution. A thin metal sheet covered a hole in the floor a yard or two in front of him. Beside it was a stack of old, rotting crates. Pasha bolted across the room and kicked the metal sheet aside. He waited until Yuri had passed, then pushed the crates through the hole. The boxes landed with a deafening crash, slowing Yuri's pursuers.

Another round of gunfire ripped through the air, followed by angry cries. They couldn't wait. They needed the backup now. Pasha still had the mirror in his pocket. He ran back to the window and thrust the glass over his head, directing it towards the streetlight. Puddles of seawater mingled with blood were soaking into the dock. Someone pointed their finger at him.

"Hey!"

Pasha jumped back just as the shot was being fired. Showers of splintered wood sprayed past his cheek, cutting his face. He raced towards the other side of the room. His foot plunged through the rotting floor. Pasha fell through the ceiling, landing on the tarp of a boat and sliding onto the asphalt.

Pasha was lying in the narrow space between the vessel and the wall. Voices echoed off the ceiling. From beneath the trailer he could see the shadows of figures running past.

"Come on! Let's move, move, move!"

A van was parked at the other end of the dead space. Pasha lifted his head. People were being rushed into the vehicle at gunpoint. The hostages. Little stood between them save for a couple of barrels, and the boat that kept Pasha from view. They were in such a hurry to be gone that no one was there to cover the gunman's back.

Pasha's breathing stalled. He was aware of the noise around him and yet it all seemed distant and muffled. His vision sharpened. All he could see was the gunman. Pasha's chest felt hot and prickly. The task had fallen to him. Klokov had dispatched seven Breadwinners to thwart the Butchers, and somehow this opportunity had fallen to Pasha. The least capable. The least willing.

He stood. He reached into his waistband for the gun. The metal was still warm. His tongue felt dry and leaden, as though carved out of wood. He aimed the barrel. His finger settled on the trigger. Was he really about to do this? Was he about to shoot someone?

The final captive, a petite girl of Pasha's age, dug her heels into the pavement when her turn came. The Butcher with the gun cocked his pistol and aimed it directly at her chest.

"I said move!"

Pasha could just make out her features in the spare streetlight. It was Pearl Sulzbach. He remembered how his mother had shot the Red

Army soldier holding them captive. She had saved their lives. Who else was there to save Pearl? It had to be Pasha.

Pasha swallowed once. He began to sweat. He steeled his arm and pulled the trigger. The bullet exploded out of the chamber, seemingly louder than before, and with it the noise of his surroundings blared back into existence. The gunman jumped as the bullet skipped across the pavement past his shoes, yellow sparks spitting in its wake. Pasha couldn't believe it. He had missed.

Startled, Pearl whipped her head around in the direction of the bullet and saw Pasha hiding in the shadows. Pasha let out a soft gasp. Their eyes locked on one another, and for a moment Pearl appeared relieved, as though she knew Pasha had come to rescue them.

Their gaze was unceremoniously broken as the gunman shoved Pearl into the van, hurled himself in behind her, and slammed the door. Pavement crackled beneath the wheels. Desperate, Pasha shot again, this time aiming for the tires. But he was met with nothing more than an empty bang and shrinking taillights.

The gun felt heavy in his hand. He dropped his arm to his side, his ears still ringing. He had failed.

Someone whimpered beside him. Pasha jerked his head around. Yuri was huddled down between the boat and the wall, his gun held close to his chest.

"Yuri?"

How long had he been there? Pasha must have missed him in the excitement of the moment. There were visible tears streaming down his face. Pasha lowered himself to the ground and squeezed through the narrow space toward his friend. Something warm and wet soaked the knees of his trousers and dampened his hands. He looked down at his fingers. Red fluid stained the tips. His eyes followed the trail to a hole in Yuri's trousers near the back of his calf. Pasha couldn't tell if he'd been shot or just badly cut. When he turned his head, there was a trickle of blood running down from his temple as though a bullet had grazed him.

Pasha felt his eyes widening but Yuri put a finger to his lips and shook his head. The sound of approaching footsteps echoed down the passage. Pasha scurried further behind the boat, closer to Yuri.

"Look!" he heard one of the Butcher boys holler.

A flashlight shined on the hole where Pasha had fallen. Their voices lowered.

"You check behind the boat. We'll look further down."

Yuri's chest began to heave. The hand holding the gun trembled. They could hear the others walking away. Pasha felt sick as the figure of a young man about seventeen appeared around the corner aiming a firearm at the two.

Neither of them had a chance to react. Tires squealed outside the building. A large, black Ford tore under the warehouse, crashing through the stack of barrels. One of the containers hit the boy, knocking him to the ground. The gun flew out of his hand, landing far out of reach.

Yuri saw his opportunity and dragged himself to his feet, leaning against the wall for support. The boy was unarmed, but Yuri raised his gun all the same. Nearby, Breadwinners were scattering out of the car, ready to take control of the situation. Words could not have described the look of helplessness possessing the Butcher boy's eyes. Pasha covered his face and tried to focus on taking even breaths. Yuri's lip curled over his teeth. He let out another whimper, this time louder.

"Don't do it," Pasha mumbled. "Just don't do it, Yuri."

Yuri wrenched forward with a strange wheezing noise. His eyes pinched closed as he let out a sob.

"Get out," he growled at the boy.

There was something bestial and inhuman about the noise which came from Yuri's throat.

"Get out!" Yuri screamed, sounding almost feminine in his desperate shriek.

The boy scuttled to his feet like a newborn deer, and was gone. Boots slammed against the pavement. An older Breadwinner appeared around the corner followed by Trifecta and Moneyrider. As if on instinct, Yuri raised the gun on them, a wild look in his eyes.

"He's been shot!" Pasha quickly explained, fearing what might happen to Yuri if they thought his tears and defensive demeanor were born out of fear. But his words were unnecessary. Unable to stand any longer, Yuri's leg gave out beneath him, and he fell to the ground, blood pooling on the asphalt.

Chapter 26:

The Kodak Mermaid

An hour later they were standing in the garage, helping unload the last of the boxes pulled off the Butchers' abandoned speedboat. Yuri had been taken downstairs to the basement to get his bullet removed, along with the Savage, who had suffered a minor gunshot wound.

Sergei dropped the crate he was carrying on the floor in front of the last stack and dusted off his hands.

"Just one more left."

Pasha was sitting on a stack of boxes near the table, still trying to recover his nerves.

"What all's in these boxes, anyhow?" continued Sergei.

"You mean besides alcohol?" Trifecta pried another lid off one of the crates. "Whatever other contraband they've been transporting. Found a box of Cubans just a second ago in that one over there." He tossed the crowbar on the ground and made his way towards the door. "Come on, I'll help you out."

Moneyrider turned towards Pasha. "You coming, Stallion?"

Trifecta shook his head. "Let Chevalsky sit this one out. He needs a break."

Their footsteps died away. Pasha sighed and wandered aimlessly towards the table where an assortment of contraband was laid out. In addition to the Cubans and alcohol, there was a considerable assortment of weapons, some Pasha had never seen before. After examining a semi-automatic Colt, he picked up what looked like a club studded with shark teeth. Pasha knew better than to go nosing through illicit materials gleaned from a raid, but curiosity got the better of him. He picked up the club and held it to the light. He ran his finger along the surface of a parchment-hued spike, noting the dry, hard texture. Pasha raised his eyebrows. They truly were shark teeth.

Well, that's one I've never seen before.

As his eyes wandered the table, he became aware of several more peculiar items distributed amongst the loot. There was a hand mirror of no discernible worth, various unlabeled jars with substances Pasha assumed to be beauty products, and a crate of unidentified fruit that smelled like vanilla wafers and looked like honey-colored butterfly wings. At one point, Pasha found himself studying a particularly large conch shell. As he neared the place where it was sitting, he could have sworn he heard a soft melody drift past his ears.

He came across a large manila envelope, and carefully opened the contents. Pasha drew back at once. The envelope fell to the ground, scattering photographs like Pearl Sulzbach's all over the floor. Pasha's face grew florid. He peeked back at the open garage door. The last thing he needed was the other boys teasing him about scandalous pictures. He dropped to his knees, trying to avoid looking as he swept them back inside, but when he caught sight of a girl dressed like a mermaid, he simply could not tame his inquisitiveness—not because he was enticed by her, but because she looked like a real mermaid.

It wasn't just the seashell top, or the wavy hair cascading over her shoulders; from the waist down the girl was outfitted with an incredibly lifelike mermaid tail. She was lying on her back with it raised and curving over her head. Due to the severe arc at which the tail swooped over her, it seemed impossible for her to angle her legs in such a pose. Her knees would have had to have been bending in the opposite direction! Indeed, there was no sharp corner to indicate her knees at all like in a regular costume; instead, the silhouette was soft and floppy like a fish. Nor was there any clean line where the waist of a fabric tail would've ended; rather, it appeared to fade into her skin with scales that sparkled even in sepia.

From behind the photograph of the mermaid girl, the face of another with wings growing from her back peeked out at him. Before

Pasha could see any more, he pushed the photograph back down into the stack, accidentally forcing another picture to free itself and flutter to the floor. The image landed face-up before he had a chance to look away. At first, Pasha instinctively shielded his eyes, but as his brain registered the photograph, he dropped his hand.

The image was not of a scantily clad girl, but a boy, fully dressed with daisies growing from the tips of his fingers. Pasha raised an eyebrow. It was obvious the photo was not intended to seduce. He glanced back at the envelope. What if he had misunderstood the nature of the photographs? He pulled the angel-girl from the stack. She wasn't naked. In fact, she was wearing a dress similar to one Faina often wore. Relieved, Pasha began leafing through the prints. There were many like the boy with the daisies, and a considerable amount of mermaids. Only a few of the pictures were of a suggestive nature.

As he flipped another angel to the back of the stack, Pasha's fingers stiffened at the image that had replaced her. In the photograph was a man standing inside a tank of water, his hands bound. A muzzle was fitted over his mouth. Pasha felt his tongue go dry. Regret germinated throughout his body like overturned ink. He should not have been looking at the photographs.

He shivered and put the pictures away. There was no telling what other violent images were hidden in the stack. He would let Trifecta know in private. Perhaps it would shed more light on the disappearances.

Pasha set the envelope aside, his attention now drawn to an ornate gold snuff box. Curious, he turned it around, admiring the cameo, and flipped open the lid. Inside was a thin bit of paper holding a measure of white dust. Pasha stepped back immediately, his hands retreating to his sides.

"You know what that is, don't you?" Anastas crept out from behind a stack of boxes. Pasha took one look at him and continued to wander down the length of the table without an answer.

"You know what that is?" Anastas repeated.

Pasha gave an irritated sigh. "It's dope." He only answered in hopes that Anastas would leave him alone.

"They sell it in the brothels."

Pasha grunted, not sure what else to do. He watched Anastas pick it up and hold it to the light, admiring the sheen of the box.

"Mellows you out. Just a pinch is enough to take out a thug twice your size." He turned and smiled in a way that made the hair stand up on Pasha's neck. "Ever tried it?"

Pasha eyed him as though he were crazy. "No." He stepped back. "Don't let Klokov catch you talking like that. There's no telling what he'd do."

Anastas maintained his foul grin. "Prude."

Pasha didn't say anything.

"You know …" Anastas dumped the contents of the box on the table and moved towards Pasha. "You look like you could use a little winding down."

Before Pasha could try and get away, Anastas grabbed him by the back of the neck, dragged him over to the box, and slammed his head down on the table. Pasha's nose was inches from the pile. He refused to breathe.

"Get off!"

He tried to wriggle away, but Anastas pinned his arms behind him and rested his full weight on Pasha's back.

"Not until you take a whiff."

Pasha could feel his lungs constricting. The more he struggled the faster they seemed to shrink. He tried to move his head back. The friction from the tabletop burned his skin.

"Hey!" thundered Trifecta from behind them.

Pasha slipped onto his knees as Anastas was ripped off of him. Pasha fell onto his haunches, gasping for air and coughing.

"What's your problem?" Trifecta slammed Anastas against the wall, pressing his face into the brick.

"I ain't got a problem!" Anastas twisted around and shoved Trifecta back.

"Go downstairs and see how the others are doing."

Anastas begrudgingly did as told, muttering all the while.

Sergei helped Pasha up by the elbow. "You alright, Pasha?"

Pasha nodded breathlessly and covered his eyes, pressing his cool fingers into his eyelids. He slid his hand under his cap, feeling lightheaded.

"I just wanna go home."

"Go home." Trifecta nodded understandingly. "You're dismissed."

Pasha walked, then ran to the door. The lights in the alleyway seemed dimmer. Pasha doubled over his knees and cursed. It was happening again. He could feel it coming on. How much time did he have to make it back to Orchard Street before he passed out?

He charged down the sidewalk, ignoring the sweat gathered on his neck. His only instinct was to get away from the Bowery as quickly as possible.

There was no leaving the day behind. No forgetting what had passed. For he now knew the reality, and the truth had not set him free. No, the truth had only enlightened him to his enslavement.

Chapter 27:
Blind and Bloodstained

Faina hugged her pillow to her chest and continued to stare at the clock on her bedside table. The second hand was dragging its way around the face with agonizing slowness. Rubbing her eyes, she rolled towards the window and looked out across the courtyard. Had Pasha arrived home, the ladder of the fire escape would have been pulled down. There was no telling what Klokov wanted with him. Anything could have happened. Her mind grasped helplessly at dates and events, hoping to extract some reason for why Klokov would need Pasha on the night of June twenty-sixth. But all that stood out to her was the doctor advocating a blood bank Anya had mentioned.

A flurry of movement drew her attention back to the window. Pasha sprinted into the courtyard, his long legs struggling to brake at the base of the fire escape. He grabbed the bottom of the ladder and doubled over, his chest heaving. Fearing the worst, Faina threw open the window.

"Pasha!" she called in her loudest whisper.

Pasha raised his head to look at her. Faina's eyes doubled in size. His face was boiling red, like a stoplight in the dark. His lips parted to speak but he couldn't seem to get enough breath in. With one disoriented sway, his knees weakened, his fingers slipped from the ladder, and he fell back on the pavement, unconscious.

"Pasha!" She grabbed her wrapper and beat on the wall. "Anya! Wake up! Pasha's fainted in the courtyard!" She thrust her leg through the window and sailed down the fire escape, not even stopping to put on her slippers. With anxious breaths, she threw herself down by his side. Up close she could see that his face was cut up and caked with blood. Gravel had been ground into his clothes, and there was a tear in his shirt. But most alarming was the dried blood staining the knees of his trousers. She cupped his face with her hand.

"Pasha? Wake up! It's alright now, I'm here."

His eyelids twitched but he did not respond. She tried lightly slapping his cheek.

"Come on!"

Pasha gave a soft groan. His head rolled to the side. "*Faya …*" His eyes fluttered open. Faina raked her fingers through his bangs in a soothing gesture.

"What happened?"

Pasha blinked several times. His breathing grew shallow, and he grabbed her hand and squeezed it as though it were some kind of anchor.

"Can you see?" said Faina.

"Not much. Everything is blurry." He tried to sit up but immediately began to swoon.

"Woah!" Faina pulled him back down. "Take it easy. It's alright. I'm here now."

He squeezed his eyes tighter and covered them completely with his hand. His chest pumped up and down as he struggled to take even breaths. Faina placed her free hand on his cheek.

"I don't know what's happened, but you're home now. You're home, and I'm right here. You're safe."

Pasha shook his head. "I'm never gonna be safe again."

Faina felt her pulse quicken. What could he mean by that? The bell over the door rang as Anya and Uncle Matvei emerged in their robes.

"Good heavens, Pasha," exclaimed Uncle Matvei at the sight of him. "What happened?"

Pasha tried to sit up again, wincing and holding his head. "I don't want my mother to see me like this. I just need help getting into the apartment."

"He can hardly see," explained Faina. "He fainted."

"Get him inside." Anya gestured for Uncle Matvei to take one of his arms. "I'll have a look at him."

Faina and Uncle Matvei each took an arm, hoisted Pasha to his feet, and helped him upstairs into the apartment. Anya immediately began fishing through her first-aid kit in the bathroom.

"There, there, my boy," Uncle Matvei helped him onto the sofa. "What you need is a drop of wine. Something to relax your nerves. I believe we still have a bit of cabernet left over from the good old days."

As her uncle disappeared behind the kitchen wall, Faina sat down beside Pasha and placed a hand on his knee.

"What happened?"

Pasha swallowed, his head stooping beneath her chin. "We were shot at."

Faina's breath caught in her throat. "Shot at?"

Pasha nodded. "The Butchers are the ones responsible for the disappearances. Klokov says they're kidnapping people and … and selling them. He sent us to rescue some hostages before they were sold." His voice shrank. "We failed."

"Are you okay?" She began searching him for more injuries. "Did they hurt you?"

Pasha shook his head. "No, I'm fine." He drew a ragged breath. "But Yuri got shot in the leg, and the Savage got hit in the arm."

"I don't understand. I thought you didn't have to become a foot soldier."

Pasha's movements grew idle and gravid, as though his soul had grown too heavy for his body. "I thought so too." There was something more troubling him, but before Faina could inquire, Uncle Matvei reappeared with a full wineglass.

"It might help if we turn the lights on."

He pulled the cord on the lamp and placed Pasha's hand on the glass.

"Here you go, my boy."

"Thank you, Uncle Matvei." His voice was hoarse.

"Should we give him laudanum?" asked Faina.

Anya rounded the corner with a flashlight, shaking her head. "No, wine will do just fine."

When Pasha had taken his first drink, Anya had him open his eyes so she could shine a light on his pupils. Pasha tensed the minute they opened.

Faina placed a hand on his shoulder. "It scares you to open them, doesn't it?"

Pasha dropped his head slightly. "Mhm."

"Don't get worked up," Anya reminded him in a singsong voice. "They're responding just fine. Can you see anything?"

"Not really."

Anya turned off the flashlight and stuck it in the pocket of her robe.

"Well, you should be able to sleep it off."

"I can help him back to his apartment," volunteered Faina.

Uncle Matvei nodded. "That's fine. Go on and finish that glass, Pasha. You take all the time you need."

When Pasha had finished the wine, Faina escorted him back to the apartment. Together, they crept quietly to his room. Pasha grabbed hold of the bedpost and lowered himself onto the mattress.

"Thanks, *Faya—*"

Before he could finish, Faina knelt down on the floor and began untying his shoes. When Pasha realized what she was doing, he reached down to do it himself, but Faina swatted him away.

"Relax." She removed his shoes, and helped him into a reclined position. "Let someone take care of you for a change, even if it's only for five minutes." She leaned over him. "Can I get you anything?"

Pasha shook his head. "I think I've got everything I need."

"You wanna try opening your eyes one more time?"

Pasha gave a tentative blink, then opened them wider. Faina couldn't tell if he was seeing or not. His eyes fixed on her. One by one the muscles in his face began to relax.

"Can you see anything?" she asked.

Faina felt a rush of butterflies as he reached up and placed his hand on her cheek. She could see his pupils focusing.

"I see you."

Chapter 28:

Sliding Into Home

When Pasha opened his eyes the next morning he had forgotten he lost his vision the night before. He rolled over and arched his back until he heard a satisfying crack. Something was digging into his waist. Pasha reached down and felt the loose strap of his suspender bunched up beneath him. It was then that he realized he was still in his clothes from yesterday. The memory of the previous night resurrected itself beside the hellish nightmares that plagued his sleep. The gunshots. The blood. The weight of the gun in his hand as he took aim. The van pulling away. Yuri's screaming voice. The revelation that Klokov had tricked him, and that his future was doomed.

He recalled dreams of mermaids trapped inside glass bottles. Some cloudy and narrow, others clear and round. Each a prison. Like model ships, they were being auctioned off as priceless works of art to a crowd of bidders. Visions of Pasha holding the Red Army soldier his mother had shot at gunpoint had haunted him throughout the night. Again and again he would fire. Bullets burnt through his uniform. But the soldier continued towards him, bloody but unaffected, until he at last slipped a noose around Pasha's neck.

Pasha covered his eyes, wishing the dreams had stay buried in his pillow. And then Faina rose from his thoughts like a beautiful phoenix. Pasha squeezed his blanket. It had taken every ounce of remaining nerve just to reach up and touch her face. So what if they had touched a thousand times before? It mattered little. His fingers were copper wire and Faina's skin was a bolt of vibrant electricity. Every freckle had been a spark of light, igniting his skin and awakening his nerves.

Pasha flew out of bed. He grabbed a set of clean clothes from the closet and raced to the shower. How long would his life measure? In the services of Klokov it was unlikely to be very long. He knew that now. And

Pasha did not wish to waste another second without Faina knowing his true feelings. He wanted more. He wanted to drag his fingers through her hair, to kiss her again and again until they both grew dizzy.

When he had finished grooming himself, he tiptoed into the bedroom shared by his mother and Katya, and bent over his sleeping little sister.

"Hey," he whispered. "I'll be right back, okay?" He bent down and kissed her head.

Katya stirred and rubbed her eyes. "Where are you going?"

"I'm just gonna pop by Faina's for a minute." He smoothed her hair. "Go back to sleep, Little One."

Pasha sped out of the tenement and down the hall to Faina's apartment. He was raising his fist to knock when the door swung open. Faina stumbled back in surprise.

"Pasha!" She placed her free hand over her heart and laughed aloud. An apron was tied around her neck, and in one hand she carried a covered plate. "You scared me!"

Pasha smoothed his hair and laughed. "Well, aren't you a sight for sore eyes!"

"Very funny. I take it your eyes are all better then?"

"Perfect, twenty-twenty." He stepped aside, indicating to the covered plate. "I didn't know you were going someplace. I'll get out of your hair."

"Actually, I was going to check on you."

"Oh. Then who's the plate for?"

Faina peeled back the cloth. "You. I made you breakfast. I thought you might not be feeling well after last night."

Pasha's eyes swelled like sponges as he soaked up her sweetness. "You made me breakfast?"

"Mhm!"

Pasha ran a hand through his hair. "Gosh. You didn't have to do that."

He hadn't realized it but he was staring at her rather tenderly, causing Faina to blush and pin a stray hair behind her ear.

"You wanna come in and eat?"

They sat down at the table and Faina poured them each a cup of coffee.

"So, it was the shootout that caused you to faint last night?"

Pasha shook his head. "Not exactly. Everything had been building up I guess. What really set it off was when Anastas tried to shove my face into a pile of dope."

Faina set her mug down harder than intended. "He what?"

"I'm fine. Don't worry. I didn't get any on me, or breathe any of it in."

Faina propped her chin on her fist with a desperate look. "*Pavlushka*," she practically whispered. He watched her fingers extend and retract, as though she wanted to reach out and touch him but stopped herself.

"I'm just glad it was you who found me," he added. "You're sorta my home base."

"Home base?"

"You know, like in baseball when you slide into home and the ref yells 'Safe!' Whenever I look at you, or feel you near me, it's like someone's there yelling 'Safe!' And I can stop running."

Faina leaned in closer and was about to respond when the door to the stairwell opened and Uncle Matvei appeared.

"I smell bacon!" he declared cheerfully as he crossed the threshold. "Ah! Good morning, Pasha! Feeling any better today?"

Pasha smiled and nodded. "Much better, Uncle Matvei, thank you."

Uncle Matvei leaned over the serving plate. "Is that *blini*?" He reached eagerly for a pancake but Faina smacked his hand away.

"You already had breakfast."

"You don't mean to tell me the two of you are going to eat all that by yourselves!"

"Oh, I'm full. I'm not gonna eat any more," Pasha insisted, but Faina ignored him.

"Uncle Matvei!" She flashed him a pleading look.

Uncle Matvei lowered his voice, grumbling, and poured himself another cup of coffee. Out of habit, he switched to Russian, forgetting that Pasha too spoke the language. "You are taking this whole 'the way to a man's heart is through his stomach' thing entirely too seriously." The moment he said it, Uncle Matvei's face fell, realizing what he had done.

"Uncle Matvei!" Faina's face was as red as the bacon.

Not sure what else to do, Uncle Matvei kissed her on the head and stole a sausage link from her plate before escaping out the door.

Faina sat stiffly in her chair, looking mortified. Pasha had cleaned his plate now. Inside, his heart was singing nervously. He wasn't sure how seriously he should take Uncle Matvei's words. After all, he could have just been teasing her. It was no secret their families had been championing their union for some time. But judging by the rosiness of Faina's cheeks, the way she had avoided him after he asked out Nadia Berkowitz, and Anya's own assurance, Pasha thought he had a pretty good shot. He rose with the intention of helping put away the dishes.

"You done?" he asked Faina, reaching for her plate.

Faina forced a smile, still flushed with embarrassment. "Oh, yeah, I'm done, but don't trouble yourself with all that. Uncle Matvei will want my leftovers."

"You sure?"

"I'm sure!" She hurriedly got up and dumped the other dishes in the sink. Pasha followed her. She struggled to untie the knot of her apron at the back of her neck. Pasha reached for the tie.

"Here, let me help."

Faina held up her hair, revealing a patch of freckles Pasha had never noticed. As he tried to untie the knot with shaking hands, he could smell the scent of soap on her skin.

"I didn't know you had freckles here."

He traced his finger over the nape of her neck. Faina flinched.

"Oh." She laughed awkwardly. "I've got 'em everywhere. There are a lot you haven't seen." She froze. They both turned as red as strawberry phosphates. At last the knot came free. Pasha pulled the cord loose at her waist. The white apron slipped off her shoulders and fell to the floor between their feet. Neither bothered to pick it up.

"Thanks for breakfast." Pasha rubbed the back of his neck. "And for last night."

Faina stared down at his shoes. "Guess you better get back to Katya."

He shuffled and shoved his hands into his pockets. "Guess so." He turned towards the door. "I'll catch up with you later."

"See ya."

Pasha paused. He bit his lip. He had to do something.

With shaking hands, Pasha pivoted back around and pressed his lips against her warm cheek. Her eyelashes brushed the tip of his nose. He stepped back, his knees feeling weak and wobbly.

"I—I'm sorry!" he sputtered. "I shouldn't have done that!" He was ready to turn and run out the door, but Faina took a step closer, wearing the expression of a child who'd just had her teddy bear snatched away.

"Wait—what do you mean? Why?"

255

Pasha raked his fingers through his hair and struggled to get his words out. "I—I just thought I might have been being too forward." He tried to take a deep breath but was too nervous. "Look, Faina, I … remember how I said any guy would be lucky to have you? Well, I want to be that guy. I've wanted to be that guy since the day we moved in. I want to be yours." He swallowed, unsure of what to say next. "How do I be that guy?"

Faina stared at him, her eyes the widest he'd ever seen. "You already are."

An uncontrollable smile was taking over Pasha's mouth. "I am?"

Faina giggled as her skin grew more and more cherry-like. "You've always been!"

They stared at each other, grinning giddily with flushed cheeks and trembling knees. Faina threw her arms around Pasha's neck, drawing him closer until he could taste her sweet breath, still tinged with hints of maple syrup. The moment their lips made contact, Pasha could feel his eyes rolling back. It was as though his skin were knit with supernovas and stardust.

Wow … he kept thinking. *Wow* …

She kissed with such surprising force, Pasha had to grab the back of the chair to keep from falling over. Her breath was warm on his lips, and he could feel the full weight of her body leaning against him. Pasha couldn't remember how many times he had imagined this moment, only that he had been dreaming of it for six years. After several seconds, she drew back, throwing Pasha so off balance he dropped backwards into the chair.

He'd never expected his first kiss to be so passionate, not that he was complaining. Though as long as it was with Faina, it was bound to be dramatic in some fashion. He felt as though he had electricity running beneath the surface of his lips, sizzling and reacting to the slightest caress.

They gaped at each other for a moment with flushed faces before flinging themselves at each other again.

Chapter 29:
Starry Cheeks

Pasha's steps were smaller and softer than usual as he emerged from the washroom. Hair still damp from the shower, a bead of water dripped down his forehead. It had taken a few strokes with the comb, but he'd finally gotten it to stay put in a neat side-part without sacrificing the slight bit of wave he had.

"Do I look okay?"

Lydia looked up. She was perched on the sofa in the sitting room, mending one of his shirts. Beaming with an over-abundance of pride, Lydia's voice went squeaky with emotion. "Okay?" She jumped to her feet and flowed towards Pasha in a way that made him want to retreat back to the bathroom. "You look like a prince!" She grabbed him and crushed him to her heart in an embrace that was sure to wrinkle his freshly ironed shirt.

"Ma! Ma! Take it easy, I just combed my hair!"

"Oh! Right, right! I am sorry!" She edged back. Her hands zipped to her chest, where she fiddled with the ribbon on her collar.

Pasha smoothed his lapels and looked down at his clothes. Light bounced off his freshly shined shoes. The knickerbockers he was wearing had just been purchased earlier that day. He was clean. He was fresh. He was a boy about to embark on a date with a pretty girl. Holding out his arms, he turned in a slow circle.

"You're sure I look okay? No stray threads? No holes? No buttons coming loose?"

Lydia stepped back and examined him up and down. "Perfectly manicured. A true gentleman."

Pasha smiled, the air cold against his mouth. He had just brushed his teeth. "Thanks, Ma."

With soppy eyes, Lydia cocked her head to the side and simpered sappily. "My baby's very first outing with a girl!"

"Does this mean we're not counting my date with Nadia? Because I'm all for pretending it never happened."

"This is different. This is your first date with someone you love." She sighed dreamily as she surveyed him. "It seems like just yesterday the two of you were playing pretend out on the fire escape! And now look at the two of you!"

Pasha shoved his head down and brushed past her to the sitting room. "Ma! You said you wouldn't make such a big deal out of it!"

"I know, I know! Not another word!" She followed after him and gestured to the sofa. "Come sit down for a minute."

Pasha grabbed his cap from the hook on the wall. He knew what was coming. He had to get to the door quick. Maybe if he acted like he was in a hurry she would let it go.

"I can't. Faina is waiting for me."

He reached for the handle. His fingers brushed the metal. But his mother latched onto his braces with a gentle tug.

"It's ten minutes till. I want to have a quick word with you before you go. It will only take a minute."

Pasha's eyes darted around for his little sister. "Where's Katya? Didn't she want to see me off?"

She towed him to the couch and nudged him to a seat. "I sent her to retrieve something from Aunt Poppy. She'll be back in a few minutes."

Blin! The woman had thought of everything. Pasha could already feel his cheeks reddening as she sat up straight and cleared her throat.

"I do not wish to make you uncomfortable, but you are sixteen years old—"

Pasha gripped the arm of the sofa and squirmed. "Ma, I already know how babies are made. We talked about this when I was twelve—"

"You didn't have a girlfriend then."

Pasha folded his lips over his teeth and glanced off to the side. "Well, unless biology has changed I'm pretty sure things still work the same way." He rose from the sofa. "So I guess I'll just be—"

"Pavlo!" She grabbed hold of his suspenders once more and yanked him to a seat. "I was only a year older than you are now when I became pregnant with you following an impulsive decision to elope in a ceremony I knew had no legal standing. Now, I know you know the rules in this household. You know what I expect from you." Her expression softened. "But I know too that sometimes things just happen, even when we don't intend for them to." She placed a hand on his shoulder. "Sweetie, I just want to know that you're being careful."

Pasha took a slow inhale through his nose, shutting his eyes. "I understand what you're trying to say. But you have nothing to worry about." He got up from the couch.

"Pasha—"

"Trust me, Ma."

"Can you hang on just a second please?"

"Faina and I are not—we're just not, okay?"

"I know you're in a hurry but—"

"You know me! Nothing is going to happen!"

To his abject horror, she reached into her pocket. "Here, I want you to take—"

Pasha wrenched himself in the opposite direction, throwing his hands over both eyes. "MA! I'M A VIRGIN!"

At that exact moment, a floorboard squeaked in the entry. Slowly, Pasha twisted around. Katya stood in the doorway. He hadn't even heard the door open. Relieved by her sudden appearance, and hoping she hadn't heard him, Pasha returned his attention to his mother. A couple of dollars sat in her outstretched hand. Pasha cocked an eyebrow.

"What's this for?" He couldn't have been more confused if she had handed him a chicken foot.

"In case you need it." His relief must have been obvious for his mother squinted at him in confusion. "What did you think it was? Did you—Oh, sweetie, did you think I was about to give you—"

"What's a virgin?" Katya's voice sang out from the kitchen.

Pasha's eyes bulged. Boiling water could not have turned his skin redder. Lydia pinched the space between her eyebrows.

"It means … someone who's never been kissed."

Katya popped her head around the corner and stared up at her brother incredulously. "You've never been kissed?"

Jaw clenched, Pasha turned and marched through the entry. "Goodbye!"

Lydia hastened after him. "You forgot the—"

"I've got my own money, Ma." He wrenched open the door. "It's alright," he quickly added. He didn't want to make her feel bad. Knowing his mother, she hadn't offered it to him because he needed it, she had offered it to him as a gesture of love. It was Pasha's paycheck that kept them afloat, after all. And while Pasha was happy to provide for his family, he knew she often felt as though she had failed him.

Pasha waited for Faina downstairs with Uncle Matvei, nervously rocking on his heels as he stood before the counter. Uncle Matvei kept up a casual conversation with him but he could hardly pay attention. His nerves would not allow it.

The top of the staircase creaked and Faina emerged in a simple white cotton dress, looking breezy and lovely. It was casual enough for a romantic outing at Coney Island, but still feminine. She had styled her hair into perfect ringlets like the Miss America winner of the previous year. She was a summer night: full of fireflies and cricket songs, clean and crisp like a fresh sheet laid out on the grass for stargazing.

"Don't you look swell!" She could hardly keep from smiling as she neared him.

Pasha removed his hat. "You look beautiful."

Uncle Matvei teased them by pretending to clear his throat. "My, my! I feel like I'm intruding!"

"Uncle Matvei!" Faina covered her face and giggled.

He patted her back. "Alright, alright. I'll let you two be on your way." He smoothed a stray hair over her forehead and kissed her cheek. "Be careful. And I'd like you back no later than ten, okay?"

"Yes, Uncle."

Pasha stuck out his chest. "I'll take good care of her, Uncle Matvei."

"Good man! That's what I want to hear!"

The moment they stepped outside they were struck with a case of foolish grinning as they took each other's hand. It seemed odd that a little thing like holding Faina's hand could have Pasha feeling so giddy when just yesterday they had been kissing in the kitchen. At first all he could focus on was the warmth of her palm, and whether or not he was holding on too tightly or too loosely, but he soon grew accustomed to the feeling.

"I, uh, have something to show you before we hit the subway." He pulled her down the next block and stopped before an apartment building air shaft. "Look up there!" He pointed to a space above a second-floor window. "You see that?"

Scrawled onto the brick in white was the inscription "P+F" encircled by a heart. Faina stood back with her hands on her hips.

"Aw! Would you look at that! Peggy and Franklin must've finally got together."

Pasha's mouth went slack. "Peggy and …? Uh, no, it's supposed to be—"

Faina bent forward with a laugh. "I'm teasing, *Patulya*!" She drew him towards her with both hands. "You really did that for me?"

"Yeah, of course I did!"

"Pasha Chevalsky, I can't believe you went out of your way to paint our initials on the side of a building."

Pasha held his breath. "Yeah … paint."

"What? What is it?" Faina looked back at the initials again. "You didn't use paint?"

"I used chalk. I didn't even think about using paint! No wonder nobody's made a big fuss about it … What's so funny?"

Faina rested her head against his chest and let out a long laugh. "Just when I think you couldn't be any more adorable!"

"But it's not permanent. Doesn't that sorta spoil the romance?"

"You think you have to commit a crime just to impress me?"

"Well, I just thought the risk would have made it … I don't know, a little more exciting."

Faina wrapped her arms around his neck and giggled. "In that case every day spent bootlegging with you is a romantic getaway!" She kissed his cheek. "As if you need anything else on your rap sheet. I love it more knowing you didn't break the law!" She tugged him towards the subway station. "Come on, we better get moving, Tiger."

The air grew cool and moist as they descended down into the tunnel. As they waited for the train to pull in, Pasha's eyes snagged on another missing poster for Pearl Sulzbach pasted to a column. The image of Pearl locking eyes with him just before being tossed into the van flashed through his mind.

"Pasha?" Faina squeezed his arm. "You alright?"

Pasha swallowed and deliberately turned his back on the poster. "Yeah." The sound of gunshots was still echoing inside his head. "Yeah, everything's jake."

It was clear from Faina's expression she remained unconvinced, but thankfully the subway pulled in before she could ask any more questions.

They reached the Reigelmann Boardwalk at the first signs of sunset. The seam of ocean and sky became gilded with light, and the shadows grew rosy. The clouds were red and feathered like the outstretched wings of a phoenix. Beneath the brash timbre of the waves a calliope could be heard in the distance, pumping out twinkling notes to "On the Sidewalks of New York".

Boys and girls together
Me and Maimie O'Rourke
Tripped the light fantastic
On the sidewalks of New York ...

The salty breeze and burnt sugar clouded together in a sweet incense as young lovers promenaded down the boardwalk, their blossoming romance like the first fruits in a tribute to the solstice. Before they could get very far, Faina dragged Pasha under the pier and pinned him against a pillar, flinging her arms around his neck and kissing him. Kissing Faina was like plunging into a pool at the advent of summer. All at once you were immersed in something new and rare, something you had waited all year for. And the coming up for air was no different. Faina stumbled back with a giggle as Pasha braced the pillar, feeling breathless and invigorated.

"Race you to the carousel!"

She bounced on her toes with an anxious energy that might have intimidated other boys. But Pasha wasn't a fool. He knew what he was getting into. He didn't have to date Faina to be at the receiving end of her intensity, but it didn't bother him the way it did others. Where Roan might have seen Faina's feelings as a threat to his freedom, Pasha saw conviction and devotion, things he cherished and desired. At the same time, he couldn't help but wonder if Faina had been this attached to all the boys she'd dated.

Faina took off in a dash, playfully glancing over her shoulder to see if he was following. They scampered beneath the boardwalk, weaving in and out of the columns, tripping over seashells, and laughing. When Pasha finally caught up with her, he grabbed her from behind, lifting her off the ground and swinging her in a circle.

Faina laughed and squealed as he tried to kiss her cheek but missed and instead kissed her neck. They laced their hands together and made their way to the carousel, which they rode twice. When they were hungry they bought hotdogs from Nathan's and ate them while sitting on the railing looking out at the ocean. When Faina nearly got ketchup on her white dress, Pasha swooped in with his handkerchief like a true gentleman and saved her attire. Afterwards, they ate kettle corn and played games.

A surge of confidence inspired Pasha to try his hand at the High Striker, an ill-advised endeavor, but thankfully Faina wasn't disappointed when he lost, and she certainly didn't make fun of him for it. Instead she won him a little chalkware horse by knocking over a pyramid of bottles with a baseball. In turn, he got her a Kewpie doll in a game of Skee Ball.

"We'll take the one with the black hair," he told the vendor after achieving his victory.

Faina leaned against the counter. "Why the one with the black hair?"

"I wanted to get you one that looked like you." The vendor handed Pasha the doll, and he thanked him. "See? A miniature Faina."

Faina laughed and admired the doll beneath the lamplight. "Now I just gotta get my hair bobbed."

"Knowing you, I'm surprised you haven't already. Not that I'm complaining, that is! I mean, I think you look gorgeous either way, but—"

he reached out and smoothed a curl over her shoulder—"you've got hair Mary Pickford would be jealous of."

Faina blushed with a self-deprecating scoff. "Mary Pickford? The most iconic curls of the twentieth century so far? That's sweet but I don't think so."

"It's true!"

"Well," she bit her lip and adjusted the doll's skirt, "it's not going anywhere anytime soon. It's my favorite thing I inherited from my mother." She ran her finger along the s-shaped wave in the doll's hair. "It sounds silly, but I always thought it was such a shame that she had to put her hair up. I didn't see why she couldn't just wear it down all the time. It's funny, isn't it? Now the only way a grown woman can wear her hair down without being inappropriate is if she cuts it all off! And that's considered daring!" She stretched her arms over her head and hung from the lamppost. "If I could have my way, I'd keep my hair long and loose forever!"

As Pasha stood there watching Faina swing from the post like a Maypole, he understood at once what she meant about her mother. Faina's hair roiled and squalled from her head like the inky swells of a rough sea. The idea of tying up and pinning down those dense, unruly waves seemed stifling, especially when Pasha wanted nothing more than to wade through the wrought-iron surf.

When the last of the sunlight had disappeared from the horizon, Pasha and Faina boarded the Wonder Wheel. Pasha was a bit nervous about riding the Wonder Wheel, as it wasn't designed like your typical Ferris wheel. The carts were built on a track so that when the wheel moved they would slide back and forth down a little slope and swing the passengers. There were stationary carts for those too afraid of the swinging variety, but when Faina confessed that she, too was a little nervous, they made the decision to brave it together.

Pasha and Faina stood behind the salt-scoured gate and watched the kaleidoscopic cars make their unhurried revolution. At length, the motley whirlpool eased to a stop, and Pasha and Faina were ushered forward. The cart was candy-apple red, and seesawed beneath them when they stepped inside.

They shared the bench facing the outside, their hands wound together. Faina huddled close to him, and he couldn't help but notice her leg pressing into his. The door creaked shut, and the car floated above the boardwalk like a radiant red balloon. About a quarter of the way up the gears clanked and the ride slowed to a stop. The car gave a little sway, then careened over the track, sending Pasha and Faina flying backwards. They grabbed onto each other, shouting and laughing, enthralled with a strange, euphoric terror that left them giddy.

When they reached the top, the Ferris wheel halted to board more passengers. Together, Pasha and Faina grew still and relaxed, taking in the view.

"I don't know why I thought we'd see stars," Faina confessed with a sigh.

"It's still New York City."

"Yeah."

"Well, you know what that means."

Faina's eyes were wide and blooming like the Kewpie doll's as she looked up at him. "What?"

"Don't you remember? When we were little you said you gotta look other places to find the stars."

Faina snickered and looked out at the ocean. "Oh, you mean Grand Central."

"Yeah, like the skyscrapers knocked the stars out of the sky, or something like that." He looked down at the boardwalk and smirked. "I always thought that was neat the way you described it. I used to think to myself, 'maybe that's how she got her freckles.'"

Faina swerved her head around to look at him. "What?"

"You know, like maybe some of those stars that fell out of the sky landed on you." He traced a patch of freckles on her cheek with his finger. "You got starry cheeks. Star catchers."

Faina stared at him with mounting intensity. Pasha swallowed and withdrew his hand. Had he offended her?

"I mean, of course I didn't ever think that that's really how they got there, I mean, I know you were born with them. I just like to pretend that that's what happened. Not that that's better or anything, I was just—"

Faina clasped his face and flung herself at him with such force the cart rolled backwards over the track. Pasha had to grab hold of the latticework to keep from sliding to the floor.

It was a kiss like the ones he'd seen in the pictures, the kind where the maiden ends up fainting afterwards, and all the girls in the theater sigh dreamily.

When they'd finished, Pasha was slumped down in the corner of the seat with his head smooshed against the cage.

"I love you!" she blurted, her hands still cupping his cheeks. Pasha's astonishment must have been evident, for she quickly plastered a hand over her mouth and blushed. "I mean—I know that makes me look fast but—"

Pasha pulled himself to an upright position. "Fast? We've known each other for six years."

"I know, I know." She lowered her head slightly. "It's just, I know that's what everyone thinks about me. I know they say it all the time. I don't want you to think that too."

A breeze swept up the boardwalk carrying the scent of buttered popcorn to the top of the Ferris wheel.

"Faina, you dumped Steed because he was moving too fast on you. And you wouldn't go out with Joe because you knew he would try to get physical."

Faina shrugged. "But people still say it anyways."

Pasha didn't know what to say. It was true. The Kissing Cat Burglar, as well as the incident with Lena Kuznestov, stuck with Faina for better or for worse.

Faina shifted uncomfortably in her seat, and pinned a hair behind her ear. "Um … I think … I think boys might get that impression from me because I can be a little intense. Like the things I say, maybe I come on too strong? I think they get afraid I'm trying to pin them down, or stifle them, and they—they don't want that." She stared down at her lap, looking as though she wanted nothing more than to crawl under the bench and hide. "But that's not my intention." She was talking very fast now. "It's just—ugh! It just sort of explodes out of me! It's just how I am, I don't know how to stop! I'm just … a lot, I guess."

Pasha shook his head. "I don't see you that way at all."

"You don't?"

Pasha took her hands in his and leaned in closer. "You're not fast. You're passionate! And I love that about you!" He squeezed her hands as though to emphasize the point. "I love hearing all your thoughts and feelings! I love your intensity! You don't have to tone down anything with me, because I love you! I've always been in love with you! Don't you know that?"

Faina made a noise somewhere between a laugh and a sigh of relief. "I thought you might have stopped."

"Never."

"Thieves' Honor?"

A smirk bled into the corner of his mouth. "Thieves' Honor." He leaned down and kissed her. His neck grew warm, and her hands slid into his hair. They pulled away, their eyes still shut, foreheads touching, breathing from their mouths.

"I told you you'd fall in love with me someday, didn't I?" he at last whispered in a hoarse voice.

Faina kissed the end of his nose. "Except I was already in love with you then."

Pasha's chest swelled with a sigh of contentment, and suddenly he found himself wondering why he had been so afraid. How much time had he wasted? He leaned forward and pressed his lips against her forehead, feeling ashamed that he had ever doubted her. Just then a strong breeze tore through the air, snatching the white ribbon from Faina's curls. Before it could blow away, Pasha caught it in his right hand, the tail tangled between his fingers. He handed back the ribbon with a playful squeeze.

"Now, uh, you gonna kiss me again?"

Just as they were closing their eyes the Ferris wheel began to move again and the cart slid violently in the other direction. Pasha and Faina let out an involuntary yell and fell against each other, laughing.

Chapter 30:

The V.I.P.A.

Staccato moved swiftly through the throng gathered on the concourse. His hand was clenched tightly around the token in his pocket, and his hat was pulled down low. The collective moisture gathered on the raincoats of crowded bodies overwhelmed the already musty subway tunnel, competing with the ever-present electrical odor. Boots squeaked on the cement. Clicks echoed from the turnstile. Across the tracks a rat was running along the seam of the wall with a crust of moldy bread wedged between its yellow teeth.

Beside him a weathered flier for the missing Pearl Sulzbach was peeling away from a column. After the police had searched Cantini's apartment, the haig sightings had come to a complete stop, and no one had been reported missing for quite some time. No evidence of a haig possession had been discovered. Staccato wasn't sure what to think. Had Cantini caught wise to the police before the investigation and gotten rid of the beast? Or had something happened to it? Assuming there was only one. It was possible there could have been more hidden away in some secret place. Despite all this, no one had found the girl, or any of the others who had disappeared for that matter.

A blast of air barreled down the tunnel as the train finally pulled in. Staccato removed the token from his pocket as he shuffled with the crowd towards the open doors. If he wanted to get to the V.I.P.A. it was imperative that he not lose it.

As he stepped across the threshold, the man to his right melted into thin air, and Staccato found himself inside a completely separate train altogether. A gang of igneous youth sat huddled on the far side of the train sharing a bag of stolen tobacco and making eyes at two young mermaids. A wheeled water tank sat between them, in which a bioluminescent sea serpent was struggling to remove a pet cone from around its neck.

He was about to take a seat in the front corner when a spastic snorting sound came bubbling from below the bench.

"I wouldn't sit there if I were you, sir," warned one of the igneous. "That's Train Track Jack's bench."

Staccato raised an eyebrow. "Train Track Jack?"

"Or Benny the Bench Troll if you're from Brooklyn," said the igneous with the cap. "In Queens they call him Bug-Eyed Larry."

A rattling sound of claws scraping the ground echoed in Staccato's ears as a bug-eyed monster with an enormous head, underbite, and patchy fur stuck its head out from the shadows. It was a feral goyle, a creature that could've easily passed for a bobblehead of a Chinese Crested Bulldog that had been pulled from the remains of a burning car wreck. It narrowed its eyes at Staccato.

"Yeah, he sorta lives there," explained the youth. "The Magical Wildlife Department has tried to remove him several times with no luck. Now he's sort of a beloved mascot."

Staccato took one look at the scowling creature whose breath reeked of garbage, and gaped at the boy. "A beloved mascot?"

"Yes, sir." He reached into his lunch bag and pinched a bit of pastrami off his sandwich. "But if you feed him he'll let you sit anywhere you want. He'll even let you pet—"

Staccato raised his hand in disgust. "Say no more!" He took the seat on the opposite side. "I'll just sit here."

"Suit yourself." The boy tossed his scrap into the creature's mouth where it hung from its crooked teeth. It spent the remainder of the transit staring at Staccato with narrowed eyes.

The train stopped at Rocklobster Station, a depot for immigrant Fay located beneath Wall Street and owned by one of Voiler's wealthiest mermaid families. In an outstanding display of despicable government bureaucracy, the V.I.P.A. office was located not within the convenience of

Grand Central Terminal where the New York Gateway Council and the majority of its municipal facilities were located, but rather, it was all the way downtown in the Financial District, in a completely separate building adjoining the train station.

Half the concourse was closed off where several esperites and sylphs were attempting to tile over the previous architecture, in which the entire ceiling was a one-sided worm's-eye view of Wall Street. The whole affair had proven to be a huge scandal at its grand unveiling, when the shocked public observed that the view offered not only a sweeping view of Wall Street, but a clear view up several women's skirts as well. It did not help, of course, that the whole project had been encouraged by Adagio Rocklobster, the eldest son, who was a notorious scoundrel and philanderer.

Staccato shook his head in annoyance as he made his way through the concourse towards the municipal offices. With such a high number of Fay immigrants these days, the government was overrun, and the people who relied upon it were suffering as a consequence.

Once inside the V.I.P.A. building, Staccato was directed to a waiting room on the second floor overlooking the street. It was a large chamber with many seats, and yet only one other person was present: a woman with a black shawl embroidered with a Mexican floral motif. *Maybe this will go by quicker than I expected*, he thought to himself.

An elderly seraph woman at the window presented him with a sign-in sheet. When he was finished filling out his information, she handed him a numbered ticket. Staccato stared back at her in confusion.

"What's this for?"

"That's your number."

Staccato narrowed his eyes. "I can see that it's a number."

"When your number is up you can come on back."

"But I have an appointment."

"You're number fifteen. You got two numbers ahead of you."

Staccato's eyes darted about the empty room. "But there's only one other person here!"

"Wait until your number is called." And with that she slammed the window shut.

Staccato exhaled slowly through his nostrils before shoving the number in his pocket and taking the seat opposite the woman.

"I hope you brought a book with you," she muttered without looking up from her own volume.

"I'm afraid not." He checked his watch. "How long have you been waiting?"

The woman looked up. She was somewhere around his age, with a few blades of iron running through her black hair. She had a curved nose, a full, smirking mouth, and a beauty mark above the left corner of her lip.

"Forty-five minutes." She held up her number. "I'm number seventeen."

"And no doubt you've been the only one here the entire time."

She closed her book. "Precisely." The moment she sat up straight they both stared at each other with unmistakable familiarity in their eyes.

"So," began Staccato when the silence grew awkward, "what brings you here, if you don't mind my asking?"

"You know the Puck on West Fifty-third?"

"Ah, yes! The theater for the Voilerian underground. They do Variete performances, don't they?" Variete being a sort of Voilerian type of Vaudeville. "I've never been but I've heard great things."

She smiled. "I own it."

"That's a lot to be proud of. From what I understand the Puck has been quite successful."

"Thank you, I am proud of it. It's all I have, really, and so I'm very protective of it." She pinned a stray hair behind her ear and leaned forward. "We've had some trouble with gang activity lately."

Staccato's face grew serious. "You don't say?"

"Primals. I'm certain of it. There have been rumors you know."

"Oh, yes, I know all about that. But what do they want with your theater?"

She cast her eyes downward and tucked her shawl more tightly about her. "I don't know exactly. Money, maybe? All I know is they stand outside my establishment night after night intimidating customers, and just last week they vandalized my entrance and broke a window."

"That's terrible!"

She threw a reproachful glare at the desk window. "This is the second time I've been here, and the V.I.P.A. still hasn't done anything about it."

"You've tried the Underground Police, I'm sure."

The secretary at the desk called out the number thirteen. When no one answered, the woman rolled her eyes and sighed.

"I did. All they would say is it's—"

"Complicated with Primals?" Staccato finished for her.

The woman gave a grim smile and nodded.

"They told me the same thing. And that was in response to a haig attack."

"And I can't just have them arrested for standing outside my entrance. As far as the vandalism goes I'll have to prove they did it."

"Can't you get them for loitering?"

The woman scoffed. "I doubt a fine for loitering would do much to discourage them."

"True." Staccato shook his head. "The system is clearly broken, that's for certain."

275

"If anything it's overwhelmed. So many are immigrating to the Other to escape the violence carried out by the C.O.N. You'd think the Gateway Council would be more willing to protect its citizens from potential threats."

"Number fourteen," called the secretary. Staccato and the woman exchanged dull looks.

"Forgive me," said Staccato after a beat, "but you seem awfully familiar."

"Funny, I've been thinking the same of you this whole time." She offered him her hand.

The window slid open again. "Number fifteen!"

Staccato gestured to the door. "You were here first."

The woman waved her hand. "Don't worry about it. They won't allow it anyways." She held up her reading material. "Besides, I've got a book, whereas you, my friend, do not."

Staccato chuckled and tipped his hat. "It was nice talking with you." He rose and handed his ticket to the secretary.

"First door on the right."

Staccato followed her instructions and knocked on the door. The nameplate read *Pradeep Mitra, Voilerian Immigration Attorney.*

"You may enter, Mr. Nimbus."

Staccato turned the knob. Mr. Mitra was a surprisingly cordial man who wore a pair of coke-bottle glasses, a red tie, and a pristinely pressed suit. He invited Staccato to sit and removed a file from the drawer.

"Good news! The paperwork has been approved!" He handed Staccato the folder. "The V.I.P.A. now legally recognizes the Chevalskys as having legitimate Voilerian heritage."

Staccato took the file with mounting excitement. "Excellent! I couldn't be more pleased!"

"Now, to apply for their Visas, I'll need a member of the Soter family who knew Lydia to sign some paperwork."

"Of course! If you'll just give it to me, I'll mail it at once."

Mr. Mitra reached under his desk and retrieved, with some effort, a stack of papers as thick as a seven-layer cake. It hit the desk like a block of cement, rattling a jar of pens. Staccato resisted the urge to sigh as his chest deflated.

"And after I get these signed? How long will it be then?"

"The approval process is very thorough. It could be anywhere from six months to two years."

"Two years?!" Staccato snapped, his eyes bulging.

***

Staccato plodded his way down Orchard Street, the stack of papers threatening to burst his valise. Two years. Two years! Anything could happen in two years! In two years, Pasha would be eighteen, old enough to vote, and more importantly old enough to legally marry. Aunt Poppy was right, it was all a bunch of bureaucratic nonsense. Lydia was a natural-born citizen of Voiler, therefore she should not have needed a Visa to reenter in the first place. But seeing as Lydia had been a baby at the time of her immigration, the V.I.P.A. wanted signed witness statements that Lydia was born in Voiler, ideally from her parents. Which, unless Staccato wanted to admit they had lied on her birth certificate, would be impossible. Instead, they would have to rely on Theo, Javaid, and Estella.

Normally, the V.I.P.A. required an in-person interview, but because of the Land Lock, everything had to be done by mail. *Mermaid* mail. As in good-old-fashioned message-in-a-bottle mail. Staccato would need more than a glass jar to forward these documents. It would take a whiskey barrel! And what with the weight, he couldn't just toss it in the ocean, no! He'd likely concuss a porpoise! No, he'd have to use special services to deliver the paperwork. Staccato cringed at the thought. The shipping was bound to be astronomical!

There had to be a way around this. As Aunt Poppy had pointed out, Staccato had friends in high places. There were exceptions for those seeking asylum under dangerous circumstances, people like refugees. Certainly, Pasha would qualify. His life was in danger, after all. But then, how would the V.I.P.A. feel about Pasha's criminal record? As far as they would be concerned, Pasha had brought it on his own head. Ultimately, he was the one who had volunteered to join a gang of thugs. No, he couldn't let the V.I.P.A. find out about the Breadwinners. It was too risky. Otherwise, Pasha might never get in.

A pair of adolescents shot across the sidewalk in front of him, hand in hand. Staccato tensed like marble. It was Pasha and Faina. He glanced back at the building. So distracted was he, he hadn't even realized he had been standing in front of the Frasier. Laughing, the pair dashed into the courtyard, completely unaware of his presence. With a wave of his hand, Staccato made himself transparent and watched from around the corner of the wall. He didn't dare enter until they had passed. As they turned to face each other, Staccato could not help but notice how closely the two were standing.

Are they ...?

"I'll, uh, see you tomorrow," said Pasha, reluctantly letting go of her hand.

Faina was twisting one foot into the ground as she looked up at him sheepishly. "See you tomorrow."

They leaned in somewhat uncertainly, with that sort of hesitation characteristic of new couples, that early stage before a goodbye kiss has yet to become commonplace and automatic, when there is no such thing as a casual peck, and even something as simple as brushing hands feels explosive. Their lips touched for a brief moment, turning both their faces red.

A delighted smirk tugged at the corner of Staccato's mouth. His grandson had gotten himself a girlfriend. Did Aunt know? Why hadn't she said anything? And then as quickly as his heart had soared, it soured. Pasha had a girlfriend. Potentially bringing them one step closer to the prophecy.

Chapter 31:

A Nice Set of Pipes

Monday morning, Uncle Matvei found himself sweeping up the glass of a broken window yet again, only this time with his head held high. Mammoth was laying in his bed behind the dog gate separating the back room. When he saw Uncle Matvei smiling at him, he wagged his tail.

"That's a good boy, Mammoth!" Uncle Matvei's chest swelled with pride.

While his back was turned, the bell over the door rang. Matvei turned and found himself almost chest to chest with an immaculately dressed little bald man.

"Mr. Klokov!"

Klokov removed his hat, and bowed his head respectfully. "Mr. Dalka, a pleasure to see you as always." He held out his squat, muscled hand.

Uncle Matvei shook it, hoping the mobster did not notice the trembling in his fingers.

"The same to you, sir, uh, may I ask to what I owe this visit? Is there anything I can help you find?"

"I hear you had another break-in last night."

"Well, I—" Uncle Matvei was cut short by a low growl. Mammoth was rising up from his bed, his head lowered, his lips peeled back in warning as he stared Klokov down. Matvei's heart jumped into his throat, terrified of how Klokov might react.

The mobster gave an amused chuckle. "This must be the hairy hero I've heard so much about, the one who chased off your burglars."

Matvei started to cross his arms over his chest, but scratched his head instead, not sure what to do with himself. "Uh, you'll have to excuse him, he's still a bit shaken up." He cupped his large hand over his mouth. "Anya!"

Thankfully, Anya was already in the process of turning the corner before he finished calling her name.

"Can you take Mammoth upstairs please, darling?"

At the sight of Klokov, Anya's eyes grew wide. Her gaze shifted unblinkingly between her father and the thug, as though trying to soak in every detail.

"Yes, Papa."

She clipped Mammoth's leash to his harness as he continued to hold his aggressive stance. Matvei coughed into the back of his hand and waved towards the hall.

"Take him out the back way, if you please, *Annushka*."

Anya nodded, gently coaxing Mammoth away, a treat in her hand. Uncle Matvei slicked his hair and looked down at the floor.

"I apologize, Mr. Klokov."

"Oh, no. No apology necessary. He's doing what he's bred to do. I may be a proud man, Mr. Dalka, but I will not deceive myself into believing that I project a savory nature. I have chosen the path of a lawbreaker, and that is my cross to bear."

Matvei gestured to the stools behind the counter. "Would you care to sit down?"

Klokov nodded, and Matvei ushered them to a seat. Klokov cleared his throat.

"I understand you were able to catch a glimpse of your attackers last night?"

"*Da*." Matvei's voice was raspy. "I mean, yes. They were two men, both tall in stature, one thin and one large."

"How old were they?"

"I'd wager somewhere between thirty-five and forty. The larger one was heavily bearded, and missing his eyeteeth."

Klokov leaned back with the satisfied expression of one who'd just solved a particularly difficult riddle. "Ah. And did this man have a large birthmark on the right side of his forehead?"

"As a matter of fact he did."

"Just as I suspected. Mr. Dalka, it appears you have been a victim of the Bowery Butchers yet again."

"I have?" Uncle Matvei adjusted his tie, feeling rather claustrophobic. "Wait, you're not saying this has something to do with the kidnappings that have taken place, are you?"

Klokov nodded his head. "I'm afraid so, Mr. Dalka."

Matvei's lungs constricted as he recalled Faina's terror after the first break-in, how she had insisted that there had been a man in a mask at her window, and that he was trying to take her away. Then there was everything Pasha had shared about the trafficking incident.

"But why? Why my family?"

"That is what I intend to find out." Klokov rose. "Our neighborhood is being targeted, Mr. Dalka, and I won't stand for it any longer." He donned his hat once more. "You see anything else, give me a call." He slipped Matvei his business card. "You know where to—"

He paused and looked up. Outside, the street was as silent as Manhattan could make it. Somewhere upstairs Faina was singing. When Klokov did not finish, Uncle Matvei nodded.

"Yes, Mr. Klokov, I know where to—"

"Shhh!" Klokov held up his hand. "That ain't a record, is it? Is that singing?"

"Oh! Um, that would be my niece, Faina."

An easy smile spread across Klokov's face as he stared up at the ceiling, listening.

"She's got a nice set of pipes on her." He sniffed and removed his hat once again. "Bring her down here."

Matvei stood gaping at him as though he hadn't heard Klokov correctly.

"You—you want me to have her come down here?"

"Yeah." Klokov stroked his chin. "Yeah, bring her down."

Uncle Matvei tucked his lips over his teeth and turned awkwardly towards the stairwell.

"Okay." He shuffled hastily up the steps. "Faina!" His voice cracked calling her name.

"Yes, Uncle Matvei?"

"Could you come down here please, *Solnyshka*?" Sunshine.

"Yes, Uncle. I'll be right down."

Uncle Matvei stood for a moment on the stairwell, wringing his hands, wondering what on earth Klokov could want her for. Surely, it couldn't be to merely compliment her. After collecting his thoughts he made his way back down.

"She's on her way." Matvei assured him, taking his place behind the counter once more.

After a moment of waiting, the door creaked open at the top of the landing, and Faina's hurried footfall could be heard echoing down the passage. She rounded the corner and froze, making much the same expression Anya had when she first came in.

"You've met Mr. Klokov, Faina darling, haven't you?" Uncle Matvei paused, sliding his tongue across his upper teeth. It seemed such an odd thing to say.

"Yes." She inched forward, then appeared to have suddenly remembered to smile. "How do you do, sir?" She shook his hand.

Klokov nodded, still wearing his amicable simper. "Very well, young lady. Thank you. May I say that's quite a lovely voice you've got there."

Faina opened her mouth in surprise. "O—Oh!" She hooked a hair behind her ear. "Thank you."

"You enjoy singing?"

"I love it. I sing all the time."

"Have you ever thought about singing professionally?"

Uncle Matvei regarded the back of Klokov's head with a raised eyebrow. Where could he be going with this?

"I'd like to become an actress and sing for the theater."

"Ah! A fine ambition! I know many young women in the theater."

Uncle Matvei found his fingers creeping nervously towards his hairline. Was this where they were headed next? An audition procured by thugs for his sixteen-year-old niece? No good could come of it! No matter how chivalrous the Breadwinners claimed to be.

"I may have an opportunity for you actually."

Uncle Matvei covered his eyes and braced the counter with one hand, feeling absolutely helpless to stop what was happening. Faina gasped and rose up on her toes.

"Really?"

"Nothing serious, mind you, but it might get you a little experience."

Uncle Matvei peeked out from behind his fingers. Klokov continued.

"How'd you like to sing with the band on the top floor of the Foxhole sometime?"

"I'd love that!"

"It's a thing we're doing, letting some of the kids showcase their talents. I'll speak to the bandleader, and we'll see what we can come up with."

Uncle Matvei breathed a sigh of relief, wanting nothing more than to collapse back in his seat. So it was a talent show, a sort of Vaudeville for the other adolescents in the neighborhood. Perhaps this was a good idea after all!

"That would be wonderful, Mr. Klokov!" Faina clapped her hands together. "Thank you so much!"

"Don't mention it." He placed his hat atop his head once more and turned to Matvei. "Let me know if you spot anything else."

Uncle Matvei forced a weak smile to his lips and waved. "Will do, Mr. Klokov."

Chapter 32:

Stars and Stripes

There's something to be said for declaring one's love early on in a courtship; it tends to make one doubt the sincerity of the confession. Such was the case with Pasha and Faina. Even if they had known and pined after one another for years, they had yet to adjust to the nuances of a romantic relationship.

Pasha, who had never dated anyone before—except for his one abominable date with Nadia—found himself completely floundering within the first week of their relationship's onset. As her best friend, Pasha had been quite at ease with Faina, even if he had been swooning on the inside. Their interactions were organic and uncomplicated. Now, he found himself second-guessing his every word and gesture. The truth was, now that he had her, he was terrified of losing her. Faina may have claimed to love him, but what if he proved to be an unsatisfactory boyfriend? What if he bored her? What if after dating Dmitry she came to realize just how little Pasha had to offer her as someone doomed to a life of criminal activity? If he wanted to keep her, he himself had to be worth keeping.

As it happened, the Fourth of July landed on their one-week anniversary. For their second date, Pasha invited Faina to the annual party Klokov threw for the street fighters in Great Neck. No one was quite sure how he managed it, though there were plenty of rumors, but Klokov had some sort of "in" with a person who owned a waterfront mansion in Sands Point where the party was held, and where the Breadwinners would stay the entire weekend.

It was a grand soiree; there was live music, fireworks, and the entire celebration was always catered by an associate who had worked for the Ritz. Pasha had never attended, but it was common for the street fighters to bring their girlfriends, and even more common for them to stay the weekend … though Pasha and Faina had no such plans.

Thus far, Pasha had made no mention of his relationship with Faina to the other Breadwinners, though they had noticed a difference in his demeanor. After winning a particularly nasty fight with Moneyrider one day, Sergei couldn't help saying something as Pasha sat at the bar and waited for his pay.

"How hard did the Savage hit you?"

Without thinking, Pasha had grinned back at him as though he hadn't seen Sergei in months. "What? What are you talking about?"

"You're sitting there with that goofy smile while you got blood oozing down your front teeth!"

Pasha held his handkerchief to his mouth and dropped the simper. "Would you rather I scowl at you?"

Sergei merely shook his head and smirked. "You're hiding something."

"Whatever you say."

It would be a milestone, their first appearance as a couple amongst their friends. But a part of Pasha didn't want to share her yet. There was something rare and romantic about the privacy of a secret courtship, something safe even, and he wanted to protect it.

The train ride to the Bronx was long and quiet, so quiet that Pasha actually fell asleep at one point. With his defenses lowered, nightmares stormed into his subconscious, only this time instead of Pearl Sulzbach being shoved into the van, it was Faina. Again and again, Pasha fired the gun. But nothing happened. Not even a click. Just like the dream of the soldier.

Pasha awoke with a gasp, startling the passengers in front of them. Faina clutched at his elbow.

"Are you alright?"

He wrung the brim of his hat in his hands. "Bad dream."

The second break-in at *Opa!* had done little to ease his nerves. Now that he knew what the Butchers were after, it nauseated him to think that Faina could've been next. Was it possible someone was keeping tabs on her?

"You haven't slept well since the break-in," observed Faina.

Pasha shook his head, afraid to say more. The truth was he hadn't slept well since the shoot-out. But he didn't want to frighten her further. Overall, she had coped well with the second incident, something she attributed to Mammoth's presence. Pasha felt her fingers curling around his.

"I still have Leo's gun." She scooted closer. "Uncle Matvei has one too now."

Pasha now kept the pistol Klokov had given him under his mattress. After the failed mission at the pier, Klokov had suggested they carry at all times. This seemed especially stupid to Pasha, considering if any of them were to be arrested they would then be charged with possession of an illegal firearm in addition to stealing, which could easily land them in jail. Now a part of him craved the security.

There were whispers amongst some of the other street fighters that Klokov had been acting rather unhinged lately, though Pasha detected little deviation from his usual behavior. He had always been ruthless, never shying from extremes, and persisting in his black-and-white perception of the world. If that was the definition of unhinged, then by Pasha's reckoning, he had always been so. And yet, Klokov's suggestion that they carry their guns at all times seemed reckless advice for someone so calculated. Perhaps they were right.

He kept his arm around Faina's shoulder the rest of the ride, and she seemed comfortable. Anya, who would also be attending the party for the first time with Leg Up, would be arriving later when Leg had finished helping his mother with the lunch rush at the family restaurant.

When they arrived in the Bronx, a car was waiting to pick them up and chauffeur them to Sands Point at the behest of the Breadwinners.

"Have you ever been to Sands Point?" asked Faina, her hands pressed to the glass.

"No. This is my first time going to the party at all. Everyone says the mansion is huge. Franklin says there are fourteen bedrooms."

Faina pivoted around. "Fourteen? There's no way!"

"That's what he says!"

"What would you even do with fourteen bedrooms?"

"I don't know. House a bunch of adolescent street thugs from Manhattan every Fourth of July, apparently."

As they made their way further into the village, the houses swelled in size like giant balloons, until mansions became castles, and castles became palaces. They seemed less like houses and more like jeweled treasure chests, awash with finery. Faina couldn't point her finger fast enough.

"Look at that one … No, wait! Look at that one! … Did you see the one with the green shutters?"

At last, the car pulled into a driveway whose length seemed more suited to horse racing than parking cars. The massive lawn was as thick and green as the felt of a pool table, and a three-tiered fountain blossomed from a large hedge circle at the center of the drive. The pavement was hot and bright as they emerged from the back seat. Pasha and Faina grabbed their beach bags and stared up at the mansion in awe.

It was a Georgian manor of red brick, grand yet elegant, with stucco columns like bleached redwoods. A sleek pair of greyhound statues flanked the entrance, which was crowned with a fan-shaped window of stained glass.

"Still think it has fourteen bedrooms?" said Faina.

Pasha shrugged. "We'll just have to count them ourselves. If it doesn't then you owe me a milkshake. If it does, I owe you one."

"You're on."

"And a kiss," he quickly added.

Faina smiled. "And a kiss." She scrunched up her nose playfully. "And you better pay up in full, or I'll charge interest."

He nudged her towards the garden path that wound around the house. "Trifecta said not to bother with the front door until later. Everyone's gathering at the beach while they set up for the party."

Pasha reached over and grabbed Faina's hand. His grip felt tremulous and weak, as it had a week ago when they'd left *Opa!* for Coney Island. In just a few short steps, an entire crowd of people would be gawking at them.

The garden was fresh and lush with colossal hedge walls of fortress-level thickness. Blue and yellow butterflies idled amongst hydrangeas and baby's breath, turning the garden into a summer paradise. The brick path opened upon a vast expanse of pale shoreline edged by the Long Island Sound. The sky was painted in a thin blue wash, with clouds so fluffy and wooly that one could practically hear them brushing past one another.

Pasha was surprised by how many of the other boys had already arrived. Sergei and Ida Blonski were sharing a bottle of root beer beneath an umbrella—Maimie Kessler had been history for some time. Trifecta and the Savage were having a smoke in the surf. Moneyrider had parked his car directly on the beach and was sitting on the hood with Tillie Mazur in his lap, and the foals were scattered about.

"Hey, fellas!" Pasha greeted them with a bashful wave, his other hand still holding Faina's.

The chattering ceased as everyone turned and stared. Eyes darted from Pasha's face, to Faina's, to their twined fingers. Desperate for something to say, Pasha held up their clasped hands.

"I brought Faina."

All at once the entire gathering broke into a chorus of rapturous hoots and hollers.

"Finally!"

"It's about time!"

"Chevalsky's got himself a girl!"

Sergei was perhaps the most excited, jumping up and shouting, "I knew it!"

Moneyrider nudged Tillie off his lap and jumped off the hood. "You know what that means!"

Pasha grabbed Faina's hand tighter and immediately began backing up. "Oh, no! Guys, no, no, no! Not a Rodeo!!"

Moneyrider waved his cap over his head and hollered, "Rodeo! Yee-haw!" as everyone closed in around them. "Come on, Pasha, it's tradition!"

"Do it in the car!" shouted Jacob.

Manny and Elmer held the doors open. Faina, who thought it all in good fun, was easily coaxed into the passenger seat by the girls. But poor, introverted Pasha fought like a cornered raccoon. He dug his heels into the sand as his arms were pulled, causing his feet to slip out from underneath him. Before he could scramble away, Franklin and Jacob each grabbed a leg, while Sergei hoisted him underneath the arms.

Together they carried Pasha to the driver's side, singing:

"Oh, you beautiful doll, you great big beautiful doll, let me put my arms around you, I could never live without you!"

The Savage loomed over him and held his hands up like a conductor. "On the count of three, boys!"

291

Pasha continued to squirm. "Is this really necessary?"

The crowd chanted in unison as they swung Pasha back and forth. "One, two, three!"

Pasha sailed in through the door like a javelin, his head landing in Faina's lap. The sound of doors slamming echoed in his ears. Pasha scrambled upright and jiggled the handle but the other Breadwinners held the doors fast, refusing to let them escape. Pasha spat sand from his mouth and laid on the horn.

"Come on, you idiots! Let us out!"

"You know the rules," insisted Moneyrider. "Not until you lay one on her!"

The crowd chimed in. "Kiss! Kiss! Kiss! Kiss!"

Pasha turned and looked at Faina. The beating of his heart was reverberating into his throat. This was exactly what he had been dreading. Eager to get everyone's eyes off them, Pasha leaned in and pecked Faina on the lips. The others whined in disapproval.

"Boo!"

"That's not a kiss!"

"You can do better than that!"

Faina lowered her voice. "You know, they wouldn't tease you if they didn't think they could get a rise out of you."

Pasha hunched his shoulders. "I just don't like everyone staring."

"So? If it's a show they want, give them one to remember! Then they'll leave you alone."

Pasha grumbled and glared at the crowd. "I guess you have a point."

Faina playfully batted her eyes. "Don't you wanna kiss me?"

Pasha eyed her neck as she tilted her head to one side. He did want to kiss her.

He turned back to the window and playfully rolled his eyes. "Alright! Alright! You want me to kiss her?"

The crowd cheered and clapped their hands. With mounting jitters, Pasha scooped his arm around Faina's neck and dipped her backwards until her hair brushed the seat. Faina's fingers dug into his shoulder as she struggled to keep from falling over.

The cheers were so loud they drowned out the radio. When Pasha drew his lips away, Faina was staring at him breathless. A bashful thrill tunneled through Pasha's veins, causing him to snicker when he met her gaze.

"I don't think I've ever taken your breath away before."

"Trust me, you have."

Pasha turned and blared on the horn. "Alright! Now let us out before she dumps me out of sheer embarrassment!"

"She ain't dumping you after that kiss!" teased May.

Satisfied, the others backed away from the car. Pasha scrambled out of the seat as several of the street fighters clapped him on the back.

"Alright, alright, that's enough!" said Trifecta, breaking up the crowd. "Give the lovebirds some space!" He beckoned to Pasha and Faina. "Come on, and get yourselves something to drink."

He led them to a beach blanket under an umbrella, and removed two bottles of lemonade from an ice chest.

"So, you finally made it to one of the Breadwinners' famous Fourth of July parties!" He handed them each a bottle and plunked down on the blanket, inviting them both to sit.

"I'm starting to feel like I'm the only one who's never been," said Pasha. "Looks like everyone is here." He squinted his eyes. "Guess Yuri's still recovering from his injury?"

Moneyrider started to open his mouth, but Trifecta cut him off, speaking louder than usual.

"Actually, Yuri's visiting his family upstate for the summer."

"Oh." Pasha set down his drink. "I didn't know he had family outside the city. But now that I think about it, I do seem to remember him mentioning something about upstate when his uncle's dog had puppies." Was that what he'd said? He specifically remembered the words "upstate" and "uncle" being mentioned.

Moneyrider wiped a bit of sand out of his eye. "Anastas ain't here."

Pasha shrugged. "Can't say I'm surprised." Anastas may have been a Breadwinner, but he would've sooner paraded down the Bowery dressed as the Easter Bunny than take part in a holiday celebrating the United States.

"Yep." Trifecta leaned back on his elbows and squinted at the horizon. "Got sent to jail last Tuesday."

Faina couldn't swallow her lemonade fast enough. "Jail?"

"Jail."

Pasha felt a wave of relief trickling over him. "It's finally happened." His voice was tinged with such rapture it was almost comical. No matter how many times Anastas had been arrested that year, he had never allowed himself to think it was possible. But his tally of warrants had finally caught up with him!

"You mean jail like a holding cell, or jail as in an actual penitentiary?" pressed Faina.

Trifecta took a drag on his cigarette. "The big house. The Juvenile Penitentiary for Boys."

"But I thought it was next to impossible to get a street fighter in jail."

Moneyrider scoffed. "Not if you're stupid."

"You just have to try really hard," snickered Trifecta. "And boy, did Anastas try."

"How long is he in for?" The question flew from Pasha's mouth.

"Not sure."

"But if you had to guess."

Trifecta exchanged an amused glance with Moneyrider. "Glad to see the back of him, eh? Can't say I blame you. What do you think, Money?"

"Hard to say. Could be anywhere from a month to six months."

Pasha shut his eyes with a dreamy sigh as he imagined six whole months without Anastas. Six whole months without him barging into private conversations with hateful remarks. Six whole months without his relentless attempts to degrade and humiliate Pasha. Six whole months without him mocking every achievement.

"Is Klokov gonna try to get him out?" asked Faina.

"At this point, I'm not sure Klokov even wants to deal with him anymore." Trifecta sat up. "Anastas has always been more trouble than he's worth."

The sun was high in the sky now. Hot and lightly dusted with sand, Pasha was eager to get into his bathing suit if only to cool down. When they'd eaten the sandwiches they'd packed, the boys directed them to a pair of changing tents.

"Or you can always change up at the house if you want," suggested Trifecta. "The party ain't started yet but you're welcome to explore."

"Plenty of bedrooms if you're looking to, uh … rest from the road." Moneyrider indicated to Faina with his eyes and threw Pasha a wink. Faina didn't notice.

"Ah, go on back to your girlfriend, Petrov," said Trifecta, waving him away, "before she finds someone more interesting." He pulled Pasha aside. "In all seriousness, if you're looking for a little privacy … you know, if you wanna enjoy the beach without these bozos harassing you, go a little further down. There's a cove past the rocks. No one will know you're there."

Pasha thanked him. It was nice to have his desire for privacy acknowledged without someone making sexual innuendos for once.

The inside of the changing tent was musty and dank. Pasha removed his new ribbed wool bathing suit from his bag, which he'd bought especially for the occasion. Seeing as he had never learned to swim, he'd had no need for a bathing suit until now, and was rather nervous about wearing one. While many of the other boys had opted for flashier styles with daring patterns and bright colors, Pasha kept it simple. The top was white with dark blue trim at the neck and arm holes. The shorts, which were to be worn overtop the white one-piece, were navy-colored with a white belt.

One by one, Pasha removed his socks and shoes. He could feel motes of sand scattered about the warped, moldering wood floor. Something cold and metallic jabbed into his shoulder blade. A nail had been embedded in the wooden frame. Pasha hung his clothes on the hardware, and set about getting dressed.

The ensemble was surprisingly complicated to put on, at least in the dim light. When he finally managed to wrestle the thing on, he sighed and stared down at his bare legs. He tugged at the tight fabric and watched it spring back to his skin. He wished he had a mirror. Wind beat against the weathered canvas prompting the frame to creak and groan. Pasha stood frozen at the tent flap, too nervous to move. It was no different than walking out in his underwear, except his drawers were longer!

Why did I think this was a good idea? I can't even swim! A voice answered back. *But you get to see Faina in her bathing suit.* Admittedly, Pasha had spent the better half of the morning picturing just that. *What if she's embarrassed too?*

The idea struck him with a twinge of shame, though knowing Faina, it seemed unlikely she would be anything but eager to get his attention. But what did he know?

Pasha rocked back on his heels with a deep breath, and plunged into the sunlight. The tide gnawed at the shore. Gulls glided overhead. Not a soul looked up. No one stopped to laugh at him. No one pointed at or teased him. The world kept turning. He allowed himself to exhale.

Faina had yet to emerge from the opposite tent. Perhaps she truly was nervous. Or maybe her swimsuit was difficult to put on like his had been. Pasha plunked down on the outer deck and waited with his elbows on his knees.

He hadn't been sitting long when the candy stripes rippled on the flaps of the changing tent. Faina appeared in a plain red jersey bathing suit that just covered the tops of her thighs. Her shoulders were bare with the exception of two thin straps, and when Pasha's gaze inevitably dropped to her legs he noticed she had no stockings on. She wasn't the only one. Several of the other fillies had foregone their stockings as well. Had they been at a public beach, Faina would've been asked to leave if she were caught barelegged. It was a stupid rule. Most people thought so. Pasha would've died if Faina knew just how happy he was that she was breaking it, and tried his best not to stare. Prickly waves of adrenaline ebbed up and down his spine as she approached.

"How do I look?"

Pasha jumped to his feet. "Like I wanna kiss you!"

Faina fiddled with her fingers. "Cash or check?"

"Pasha! Faina!" Sergei jumped up and down in the surf. "Franklin just caught this huge horseshoe crab! You gotta come see it!"

Faina winked at Pasha. "Better be check then." She grabbed his hand and towed him towards the gathering.

The next couple of hours were a blur of sand, salt, and gingham. Croquet balls as red as valentines glided under canvas folding chairs and across picnic blankets. There were strawberries, and blackberries, and watermelon so fresh and chilled that it made one's teeth ache upon first bite. Once they had sufficiently mingled, Pasha felt it safe to wander away without anyone noticing.

"Where are we going?" asked Faina as they neared the rocks.

"I thought it might be nice to have a little privacy." Pasha climbed atop a large boulder and held out his hand. "You know, just the two of us."

"I see." She grabbed ahold and let him tow her up. "Looking to cash that check, are you?"

"Nothing gets past you, does it?"

The cove was tight but cozy. Fir trees fringed the boundary and scratched the pale blue sky. Buffed and polished by the tide, the wet sand appeared smooth enough to glide upon. Black stones ribboned with rusted brown were clustered around the edges, fencing them off from the outside world.

Faina clasped her hands behind her back and cased the perimeter with a mischievous smile.

"How intimate." She snapped her hands onto her hips. "Alright, Tom Thumb. What are we gonna do here?"

Pasha pushed his fingers through his hair and chuckled. "Uh … well, we could—"

"Why don't we get in the water?"

Pasha balked at her. "Weren't we just—"

"I mean, further. Up to our waist." She grabbed his hand. "Relax! I won't let you drown! If you start to get scared we can always turn back."

He allowed her to lead him across the mirrored glass surf, their cloudy reflection materializing at their feet. With every step, their toes ground deeper into the damp, velvety coastline. Before Pasha could brace himself, the icy water raced towards them, submerging their feet. Still, Faina continued to pull. The water traveled up to their thighs, dampening the fabric of their bathing suits, and pasting the material against their skin.

Faina smiled down at their feet, her forehead resting against his chin. "Can I tell you a secret?"

"What is it?"

"You look really handsome in your bathing suit." She sank her teeth into her lower lip and giggled, unable to look him in the eye.

Pasha raised his eyebrows, a dumbfounded smile unwinding across his face. "You think so?"

She nodded and hid her blushing grin in his chest before reaching up and stroking his bicep.

"I can see your muscles better." She ran her hands down his arms, bending them at the elbow, and examining his fingers as though they were a work of art. "I've always admired your hands."

"You have?" Pasha bit his tongue. He was beginning to sound like a parrot.

"Mhm." She splayed his fingers and stroked the center of his palm. He watched in fascination as she brought his hand to her lips and kissed the center. She turned her head, pressing it to her cheek.

"I love you."

He cupped his other hand to her face, turning it up to his. "Every time you say that I feel like it can't be real."

She smirked. "Then I'll just have to keep saying it, won't I?"

She sank back into the tide, allowing her hair to spread around her like raven-colored angel wings. Pasha watched her floating beside him with a persistent ache, his arms tightly folded around his chest. She peeked open an eye.

"Come on, I won't let you drown."

Her legs dropped back to the sand. She rose to her full height, water spiraling down her dampened waves and beading at the tips. Slowly, she unfolded his arms and placed them on her waist. Her fingers, chilled from the water, walked across his shoulders and met behind his neck. Pasha closed his eyes as their noses brushed, and he felt the gentle pressure of her lips inviting him to sink down into the water with her. The sea closed in around them as they kissed, carrying them into deeper water. Faina's body was weightless in his arms. He could feel her hair floating up and enveloping them, soft, and feathery. The tips of her toes swept his ankles.

Water thundered in their ears as a wave plowed into their side, temporarily lifting them up and setting them back down, but Pasha wasn't afraid. Faina drew away and rested her head on his shoulder.

"I love you," she said again. "Thieves' Honor." He could feel her fingers in his hair. "Believe me. This is real. I love you."

Pasha cradled her close, sinking his fingers into the soft skin of her back.

"I love you," he echoed.

They remained like that for some time, with the feel of her cheek warm and wet against his shoulder, her damp hair sticking to his arms in starling-hued coils and spirals. Salt kissed the corners of his eyes with a faint sting, and his sinuses tingled.

"You're so quiet," she finally murmured. "What are you thinking?"

Pasha shut his eyes, squeezing her tighter. "How badly I've wanted this."

"Why didn't you do something about it sooner?"

The question caught him off guard. He loosened his grip around her, letting her feet return to the sandy floor. Pasha ached with shame as he remembered Anya's words.

"I was afraid you didn't really like me."

"Didn't like you?" she scoffed. "Pasha, I couldn't have been more obvious."

"It's just …" He paused to scratch his forehead. "… You're sweet, okay? And you like to joke around. And you and I have always been very close. I didn't want to misinterpret things." He grabbed her hand. "I was afraid if we dated, you'd think I was too boring for you."

"But how could I think you're boring? I've known you for years! It's not like we just met."

"Look, don't read too much into it, okay? You know how I overthink things."

She stared at him with cloudy eyes. "But what about when I tried to kiss you the night of the dance finals?"

Pasha tensed. He didn't want to tell her the whole truth. Something told him Faina might not appreciate being told that he didn't want to be a bandage for her pain, so he decided to leave that part out.

"You were emotional. I didn't want you to do something impulsive that you might regret later, or feel like I had taken advantage of you when you calmed down."

Faina softened a bit. "That's what Anya said." She appeared to shrink slightly as she crossed her arms. "I'm sorry if I made you uncomfortable."

"Trust me, you didn't." He shook his head with an exaggerated sigh. "I gotta tell you, it was really hard to resist you though."

This made her smile. "You're cute." She brushed the wet strands of hair from his forehead. Her knuckles traced the height of his cheekbone. "Those eyes …" Her voice was a wistful sigh that seemed more suited to gazing into the eyes of a film star than those of Pasha. "Every time I look at them, I think of that quote from Romeo and Juliet." She continued smiling, but her eyes darted back and forth from his gaze to the waves below as she tried to remember the words. "That part where it says, 'Take him and cut him into little stars, and … he will make the face of heaven so fine, everyone will fall in love with night.'" She covered her face, an uneven titter blurring her words. "Sorry. A beautiful boy asks me to a Fourth of July party, and all I can do is moon over him."

Beautiful? The things she said, the words she used—quoting Shakespeare, for goodness' sake—how could she possibly be describing him? He knew Faina was passionate, but this was a depth he'd yet to explore. He was tempted to think she was joking. But her eyes! The way she looked at him! No girl had ever looked at Pasha like that. But Faina didn't just look at people; she saw them.

"Come here, princess!" Pasha bent down, locked his arms around her knees, and lifted her into the air. Faina scrambled forward, hugging his neck with one arm, while the other dangled down past his back.

"Pasha!" she squealed, trying not to fall.

Chapter 33:
Bombs, Brisket, and Barbecue

Faina strolled down the hall, dressed and dry, counting quietly to herself as she passed each bedroom. The interior of the house had certainly not disappointed. The upstairs alone had more crystal than a diamond mine, and two bathtubs that could've easily been mistaken for a small pool. The beds all had quilted headboards with gilded frames, the kind that had cherubs carved into the wood, and a vase of fresh roses was on every nightstand. So far she had counted eleven bedrooms. Just three more and she would owe Pasha a milkshake.

She came to a set of double doors at the end of the hall and paused. Was it a bedroom? She wasn't certain. All the other doors had been ajar, and she didn't want to interrupt anyone who may be using it by barging in. Faina looked over her shoulder to see if anyone was coming and put her ear to the wood. The door behind her sprung open suddenly, revealing a diminutive young lady in a sleeveless dress of blue cotton.

"Anya!"

The moment Faina said her name, Anya stumbled back as though Faina had been pointing a gun at her.

"Faina!" She wrenched the door shut behind her, her hand squeezing the knob until her knuckles turned white.

"I didn't mean to startle you!" Faina's eyes swept from the strap sliding off her shoulder to the ribbon coming loose from her hair. Faina backed into the wall, wanting nothing more than to melt through the molded wainscoting.

"I was just getting changed." Anya leaned against the door and pulled one of her shoes on.

"I don't remember seeing you down at the beach."

"We must have just missed each other." The door handle turned behind her, but Anya grabbed it and held it in place.

Faina pretended not to notice. "Guess so." She backed down the hallway, nearly turning over a priceless vase. "Well, I better go find Pasha. I'll catch up with you later!" She turned and sped across the gallery, her eyes crossing as she scanned the checkered floor for any signs of Pasha.

"Fourteen!" shouted Pasha.

Faina grabbed the bannister before she could trip down the spiral staircase. Behind her, Pasha was racing to catch up.

"There are fourteen bedrooms! Someone owes me a kiss!" He grabbed her by the wrist. "You'll never guess where the last one is! Come on, I'll show you!"

"*Nyet*!" Faina pulled back. "I mean—Not right now! Maybe later!"

Pasha stared at her with one of those doe-eyed, befuddled expressions that made her heart pound. "What's wrong? I thought you wanted to see—"

Faina seized him by the hand and dragged him down the stairs. "Later! We can see them later!"

Pasha hastened to her side. "Alright, alright!" He lowered his voice. "Did something happen?"

Faina passed a hand over her eyes and groaned, trying to rub the image of Anya and Leg Up from all those months ago out of her mind.

"Anya is here … with Leg."

"That's great—"

"No!" She ground her teeth together. "*With* Leg!"

Pasha bumped his eyebrows together. "What? Just now?"

"Mhm!"

"So … they are still doing it."

"Apparently! When she stopped sneaking out as much I thought she had stopped! I guess I was wrong." She wrung her hands. "I wasn't lying when I said I don't want to tell Uncle Matvei!"

Pasha took a thoughtful pause before reaching for her hand with a shrug. "Let's not think about it right now. You can worry about all that when you get home. For now let's try to enjoy ourselves." He ushered her towards the patio door.

"Easier said than done." She sighed and shook her head. "I don't understand. Klokov wants to teach all these boys to be outstanding members of the community and then he sets them all up in a house with fourteen bedrooms for the weekend and tells them to bring their girlfriends! It's like he's inviting them to … you know."

"Klokov thinks boys need to let off steam."

Faina lowered her voice. "Klokov is a walking contradiction. How can boys learn to respect women if they're told they're there to 'let off steam'?"

Pasha tensed and glanced about the room. "I understand what you're saying, but maybe let's not talk about it here." He pulled her behind a pillar. "I think I'll take that kiss now." Without waiting, he closed his eyes and leaned forward with his lips puckered, looking just as he had when he'd tried to kiss her on Fifth Avenue when they were ten. Feeling playful, Faina pulled his hat down over his forehead and giggled.

"Looks like you're gonna have to charge interest." She sashayed towards the door.

Pasha set his hat right and grinned. "Playing hard to get, are we?"

Faina beamed. "I can't make it too easy for you!"

Pasha caught up with her and took her arm. "In that case, you just wait. By the end of the night, you'll be begging to kiss me."

Faina tilted her head to one side, intrigued. "You're on."

Outside the band had already begun to play, luring them towards the back patio. The doors were held aloft as they crossed over into a glittering world of money and merrymaking.

A symphony of fragrances toasted the twilight with notes of maple, vinegar, and smoke.

Grand banquet tables lined the garden, flush with a bacchanalia of sizzling, luscious barbecue.

Mountains of sausages with taut, blackened skin overstuffed with a savory blend of spices crowded platters. Rosy hunks of fatty pork ribs with crisp, charred crusts were piled together in a tower of meat. There were drumsticks the size of clubs fried in fragrant garlic and pepper, with meat juicier than a navel orange, and skin so crispy one bite was loud enough to be heard two seats down. But the best by far were the red slabs of brisket, marbled with pink ribbons of fat, encrusted in a brown sugar glaze, and generously coated with an excess of mahogany-hued barbecue sauce.

Brash timbres of trumpets and bold percussion ensured that not a single foot stood still amongst the gathering. Faint odors of gunpowder mingled with the barbecue, promising a splendid show of fireworks the second the sun melted into the horizon.

Pasha and Faina sat at a table with Sergei, the Savage, Trifecta, Moneyrider, and their girls—Ida, Tillie, and Danica—though Trifecta was solo as usual. Their plates were sloppy with barbecue sauce. White tablecloths rippled against their calves as the bay breathed in and out. The food alone was enough to make Faina forget her troubles for the evening, and she soon found herself relaxing under the influence of the summer twilight.

Mouth still full, the Savage reached across the table for the potato salad. With a startled cry, Sergei and Moneyrider grabbed his arm and drew him back.

"No, no, no!"

"What? What?" The Savage wrenched his arm free. "Did you two idiots do something to the potato salad?"

Sergei shook his head. "Trust me, you'll regret it."

"You'll burn your taste buds off."

The Savage rolled his eyes. "I eat horse radish all the time."

"It ain't the horseradish," explained Trifecta. "It's got Serrano peppers in it. Cook's an Italian."

Faina stared back at them in surprise. "I didn't notice anything."

Sergei's mouth fell open. "You had some?"

"Yeah. Of course." She reached across the table and spooned some onto her plate. "It's good." The others watched in horror as she picked up her fork and took a bite. True, there was heat, but not enough to make her tear up or anything.

"Burn my taste buds off, eh?" The Savage glared at his companions and scooped a heaping spoonful onto his plate. "Nice try, fellas."

No one tried to stop him this time as he shoveled a forkful into his mouth. Scarlet splotches bloomed across his face. He doubled over, chunks of potatoes sputtering from his mouth as he coughed. The others could hardly keep themselves from laughing.

Trifecta pushed his chair back and handed him a napkin. "Geez! Get a hold of yourself, Sav!"

Moneyrider shoved a glass of water into his hand. Tears streaming down his face, the Savage tossed back his head, draining the glass, and slammed it down on the table.

"What? Is your mouth fireproof or something?"

Pasha wiped a laughter-induced tear from his eye. "Faina has a really high spice tolerance."

Faina laughed and took another bite of the potato salad. "Really, it doesn't seem all that spicy to me."

For a time, after her tonsils had been removed, Faina's cravings for spice had ebbed somewhat, though she continued to be able to tolerate intense levels of heat. But as she nibbled at the potato salad, she felt a sudden surge in her appetite for fiery flavors, and was secretly happy no one else wanted it.

"You good now?" asked Moneyrider, when the Savage finally managed to quit coughing.

The Savage shook his head and wiped his eyes. "I think so." He sniffed. "Sure clears up the sinuses."

Moneyrider stretched an arm around Tillie and raised his glass. "Tillie, darlin', tonight you are feasting with the best of the best." He gestured to the other fellas. "You ladies happen to be sitting in the presence of the top five ranking street fighters this quarter."

Trifecta tore a piece of meat off the drumstick he was eating. "Way to brag about yourself, Money, seeing as you currently rank as number one."

"You're just sore you came in second," he tipped his head towards the Savage, "followed by the Savage …"

The Savage looked up from his plate. "Hey, don't forget I beat you last quarter."

He pointed to Sergei. "Then there's old Broadshanks here. And last but not least we have the Stallion!"

Pasha wrinkled his nose. "Ugh. Don't call me that."

"Why not? You earned it!"

"Hey, I hear you, Pasha," Trifecta took a swig of his root beer and sighed. "Street fighter names are stupid."

The Savage rolled his eyes. "Oh, you want I should start calling you Ivan then? Eh? You've only been answering to 'Trifecta' for the last seven years!"

"Alright, alright! You wanna know why I go by 'Trifecta'? Because no one here can pronounce Ivan! It's all *I-vuhn, I-vuhn*! And then I introduce myself as *Ee-vahn* and people think it's a girl's name!"

The others couldn't help but laugh at his expression as he offered his explanation.

"Sometimes I wonder if Klokov was making fun of me when he gave me that name," said Pasha with a snort.

The other boys scoffed and waved their hands.

The Savage snapped his napkin. "Give it a rest. We all know you're Klokov's favorite!"

Faina turned to Pasha with a teasing smile. "Are you really?"

"Psh! No!"

Again the boys protested and made a fuss.

"How?" Pasha persisted. "How on earth could I be Klokov's favorite?"

Trifecta tilted his chair back on two legs. "You're the teacher's pet!"

"What do you mean?"

"You never do anything wrong. You don't drink, you don't smoke, you don't talk back—"

"So? Neither does Sergei!"

Sergei crossed his arms over his chest. "Yeah, but you bring in way more money than me."

"He brings in more dough than anybody," added Moneyrider.

Pasha remained unconvinced. "But I'm not tough!"

"What do you mean you're not tough? Ever since you took a shot at the Butcher down at the pier you're all anyone can talk about!"

Faina hastily wiped her mouth. "Since Pasha did what?"

"Since he tried to shoot the gunman holding the hostages at gunpoint."

Pasha put down his fork and stared irritably at his plate, but it was too late now. Faina could only gape uncomprehendingly.

"Wait, you haven't heard the story?" The Savage threw down the rib he had been gnawing on. "Pasha's a hero!"

Moneyrider and the Savage went on to describe in detail the events of the night of the twenty-sixth, or at least everything Pasha had left out: how he had bravely taken aim at the Butcher thug before he pushed Pearl Sulzbach into the van, how he tried to stop the vehicle by shooting at the wheels.

"You saw her then?" Faina could hardly contain herself. "You saw the girl from the missing posters?"

Pasha clenched his napkin in his fist and bit his lip. "Yeah. And now none of us will ever see her again."

Faina lowered her head, regretting that she had asked. Clearly, it was not something Pasha was comfortable discussing in front of other people. Still, it bothered her that he hadn't mentioned it before.

The Savage waved his hand. "Ah, don't be so hard on yourself, Chevalsky. You did more than any of us. You're a hero!"

"What are you talking about? I failed. There's no telling where any of those people are now, or if they're even alive!"

Everyone fell silent. Faina reached under the table and slid her hand across his knee in a comforting gesture. At length, Sergei eased the tension with an awkward smile. "How's about a toast for Sochinsky's little girl?" Sergei lifted his glass. "To baby Helen, for keeping her Pa outta the top five so we could have a shot!"

The others found this quite amusing, and soon they was talking and laughing again. The meal was polished off with copious amounts of pie and creamy scoops of vanilla ice cream. The pies were almost too beautiful to be eaten, and tasted even better. And yet Pasha remained withdrawn.

After a while, the gathering dispersed across the dance floor like scattered seeds. Pasha and Faina wandered away from their noisy peers and stood beneath a magnolia tree at the edge of the garden. Faina ran her fingers along the edge of a branch, admiring the enormous blossoms.

"I'm surprised more people aren't exploring the garden."

Pasha gave a distant shrug, his back turned. "I'm not. They all want to party. That's all they ever want to do. Dance, drink, beat the crap outta each other, and hit the sheets."

Faina paused, preparing herself before she asked her next question. "Why didn't you tell me about what happened with the van?"

She watched his shoulders tense. Hesitating, he plucked a fallen petal from the bird bath and stroked it between his fingers. "I didn't want to talk about it."

"Not even with me?"

Pasha crossed his arms and leaned against a tree. "Don't take it personally. I didn't want to talk about it with anyone."

"But I'm your girlfriend—"

A shadow crossed his features, and for a moment he didn't even look like Pasha. "We've only been dating a week!"

Faina drew back, as though his words had physically stung her. The hardness evaporated from Pasha's face so quickly it was as though it had never been there. Suddenly, his eyes grew wide and his mouth fell open.

"I'm so sorry, I don't know where that came—"

"Well, we've been in love a lot longer!"

He reached for her shoulder, burying his gaze at her feet. "I know, you're right—"

Faina wrenched away, refusing to let him touch her. "Or at least that's how I thought you felt!" She now felt embarrassed by everything she had said on the beach.

"I did feel that way! I mean, I do!"

"You used to tell me everything! Have the rules changed now that we're together?"

"Of course not!" He took another step towards her, but Faina edged away, turning her back on him. "Faina, I am so, so, sorry. I don't know what made me say that. All I want is to be close to you, and that means sharing my feelings with you. I—I failed you. I'm sorry."

Faina could feel him moving closer, feel his shadow on her shoulder. When he saw that she wasn't going to sidle away, his arms closed around her from behind.

"Please don't be mad at me, love."

Faina clenched her jaw. She didn't want to end the evening this way, but she didn't want to make it too easy for him either. She wished he had never said it. His words had shocked her; it wasn't like him to be so cold. At a loss for what to do, she pulled away and plopped down in the grass, her arms crossed over her chest. With a regretful sigh, Pasha sat down beside her. Faina flashed him a warning glance. He scooted over a foot and a half.

"Sorry," he wrung his hands. "I'll try to give you your space."

For a moment, they sat in silence. Faina could tell she was making Pasha uncomfortable, and the thought brought her sweet satisfaction. At length, he cleared his throat.

"I, uh, I guess I didn't do such a good job of making you desperate to kiss me by the end of the night."

"You think?"

Pasha chewed on his lip. "I didn't tell you about the van. What if I told you about some other stuff I've been feeling? Like, how happy I get when you laugh at my jokes."

Faina glanced at him curiously, still maintaining her prickly expression.

"It's kinda embarrassing actually," he continued. "I don't know if you've noticed but whenever I get you to laugh at my jokes … I guess I get so nervous and excited that it makes me laugh harder. And I always end up laughing waaay too hard. I look ridiculous every time."

Despite her determination to hang onto her anger, Faina felt her body relaxing. "I did notice." She allowed herself a little smile. "But you don't look ridiculous."

"I don't?"

Faina shook her head, still trying to resist but completely helpless to his charm. "You look cute."

With a humble smirk, Pasha scooted a little closer. "You promise?"

Faina leaned towards him. "Thieves' honor."

Their noses were inches away.

"I am so sorry," he said again, his eyelids half lowered. "I can pay for the milkshake."

A shrill rocket whistled and whined as it twisted up the stratosphere and burst into a scintillating fountain of rubies. Pasha and Faina wrenched their heads towards the horizon. Blush-colored smoke billowed up from the beach, flecked with sparkling red embers. People were beginning to gather towards the opposite edge of the patio.

"Looks like the fireworks are starting," said Faina.

Incandescent cords of light were tattooed across the firmament, searing their eyes with a blaze of splendor as they flowered into gold and scarlet asterisms, fresh and blooming. A kaleidoscopic umbrella of sound and shine dripped down through the heavens like liquid stars. Rockets glared in lambent surges around them, casting colored shadows on their cheeks and foreheads as though they were sitting beneath a ceiling of stained glass.

Faina glanced back at Pasha, and found he was still looking at her. Arcs of light were streaking across the sky and yet she had his full attention. His fingers raked from the part of her hair to the ends of her waves. She tilted her face to his, her eyelids lowering as he leaned down to kiss her. Their lips touched just as another firework thundered against the horizon.

"I love you," he murmured, his lips still touching hers.

Faina was just about to return the sentiment, when she was struck with the faint sensation of being watched. She peeked open an eye, the sky blurry with light, and saw half the gathering staring at them with oversized grins.

"Chevalsky's at it again!"

"Having ourselves a petting party, are we?"

Pasha pulled away and pointed in the opposite direction. "Show's that way, fellas."

While the others returned their attention to the fireworks, Faina noticed Anya focusing in on her with a disapproving glare. Faina gave her a confused shrug, but Anya just shook her head. Faina felt her gut turn to ice. Without thinking, she tightened her grip on Pasha's hand.

"What's the matter?"

Faina shook her head. "Nothing."

"Are you sure?"

Faina forced a smile. "Mhm."

Chapter 34:

The Shovel Insults the Poker

The fact that Anya never mentioned Faina's behavior at the Fourth of July party mattered little. Faina was livid. And as the summer played out, others could feel the tension like a cord pulled tight between them. Faina's smiles were too large to be genuine. She laid Anya's plate down with a little too much force when setting the table, and was hasty to remove it when she had finished. Whether Anya herself noticed these alterations in her behavior remained to be seen, for she gave no indication one way or the other. And as for telling her uncle about Anya's dalliance with Leg Up, Faina refused to consider it.

It was mid-August when things finally came to a head. It was Pasha's day off, and the two had just come from the drugstore where Faina had agreed, begrudgingly, to pick up a magazine for Anya.

With bottles of Coke in hand, Pasha and Faina raced upstairs to Faina's tenement.

"Anya, we're home!" Faina tossed her purse on the floor by the coatrack, completely forgetting about the magazine. The floor was cool against her feet as she slipped off her shoes and led Pasha to her room.

"We?" Anya called from across the hall.

"Pasha's with me!"

The door creaked as she cracked it behind them, and set her keys on the vanity. Before she could turn around, Pasha's arms were around her waist, and his lips against her cheek.

"I haven't kissed you enough today," he murmured.

Faina rolled her eyes and smiled. "What about all those kisses you gave me under the archway? Those don't count?"

"Of course not! Those were out-and-about kisses. Now I have you all to myself!" Without warning, he lifted her into his arms and dipped her backwards as he kissed her. Faina's legs flailed as she laughed and squealed.

"I'm gonna spill my Coke!"

The hardware of the door rattled as Anya swung it open, her hand clenching the knob.

"Faina, why is the door closed?" Anya demanded.

Faina scrambled out of Pasha's arms, pulling the skirt of her dress down.

"It wasn't closed, it was cracked."

Pasha cleared his throat and nudged her foot with his. When she turned to look at him he discreetly gestured to his thigh, his head turned in the opposite direction. Faina glanced down and, blushing, realized part of her skirt had bunched up around her garter.

Blin! She hastily smoothed it down.

"You shouldn't have Pasha in your bedroom," said Anya without a single trace of irony. Faina could feel her face reddening. The bottle grew heavy in her hands, and if she wasn't careful she could have easily slung it across the room at Anya's head.

"Pasha and I are in each other's bedrooms all the time. What's the difference?"

"You aren't children anymore! You know what the difference is!"

Faina exhaled slowly through her nose, and looked Anya directly in the eye.

"Pasha, take our Cokes over to your apartment. I need to speak to Anya alone. I'll be over in ten minutes."

Pasha did as Faina said, ducking awkwardly between them. Faina waited until she heard the front door close to address her cousin.

"First off, the thing with the garter was an accident—"

Anya squinted at her. "What thing with the garter? What on earth were you two doing in here?"

"We weren't doing anything! Why are you treating me this way?"

"Treating you what way?"

"Like a whore!"

Anya did not raise her voice but lifted her hands in surrender. "I don't mean to hurt your feelings. I'm only trying to protect you."

"From what?"

"From getting hurt."

"Pasha would never—"

"I don't mean Pasha." There was real concern in her voice as she continued. "Look, your reputation is hanging by a thread—"

"We're not doing anything wrong! Just kissing—"

"Didn't you get your fill of that at the Fourth of July party?"

Faina had had just about all she could take of Anya's hypocrisy. It was a wonder she hadn't said anything before now. She certainly had every right to.

"If you don't lighten up, I'm gonna tell Uncle Matvei about the new little habit you've picked up." She forked her fingers, holding an imaginary cigarette. "I'm sure he'd love that."

Anya pinched her lips together. "Fine. But it'll be nothing compared to the fuse he's gonna blow when you wind up pregnant!"

Faina plowed forward, towering over her petite cousin's slim frame with muscle, conviction, and a rage that could have rivaled the force of a thousand sticks of dynamite. "Excuse me?"

"I know how you are, Faina. I can't help but be concerned!"

Faina felt a fire uncurling inside her that she didn't even know she had. "No! You don't know me at all! I've never fooled around with anybody!"

Her words must've shocked Anya, for the edge in her voice began to wane. "I didn't mean that exactly." She held up her hands as though trying to calm an angry bull, but it was too late. "I just meant that sometimes you can be a little impulsive … take things too far."

Faina's instinct was to yell "The shovel insults the poker," but she didn't think her cousin would be familiar with the Russian idiom. Instead, she shouted, "I'm not gonna stand around here and take insults from a hypocrite!"

Despite everything, Anya remained impassive. "What are you talking about?"

"I know about your secret, Anya! I've caught you twice now! Your beau wasn't the only one with a 'leg up'! And who are you to accuse me of doing anything at the Fourth of July party when you and Leg were locked in a bedroom together! I'm not stupid!"

At last, Anya turned as white and as chalky as porcelain. One might have thought her fingers would chip away from the force as she hastily shut the door.

"Alright, fine," she hissed. "I'll admit it. I've been sleeping with Leg Up!"

Faina's temper peaked with an impassioned shriek. "And you have the nerve to accuse me—"

"Shhh!" Anya waved her arms about. "I'm not finished yet! Hear me out!"

Faina lost none of her volume as she shouted, "Why should I?"

"I know I seem hypocritical, but—"

"*Seem?*"

"—Believe it or not I am only looking out for you!"

"You sure have a funny way of—"

"I know how easy it is to give in!" she exclaimed, her voice finally overpowering Faina's. "And how difficult it is to stop once you've started!"

Faina wanted to shout back, but Anya had left her speechless.

"When you're in love, every little touch becomes irresistible," she continued. "It consumes you. It's all you think about, all you can dream about. You and Pasha may have decided to wait, but when you're in the moment …" She clenched her fingers and sighed. "Your reputation can't afford any more hits."

Faina looked away, pretending to stare out the window, wishing she would just leave.

"I see how much it hurts you to get judged by people you don't even know. I see how lonely you are. And if you stick with Pasha, there's no way you're ever getting out of New York. Not while he's a Breadwinner. Whatever happens you'll have to stand and face it."

When Anya finished, Faina finally allowed herself to look back at her cousin. There was nothing insincere or harsh in her countenance. But Faina couldn't soften completely. Her pride forbade it.

"Aren't you afraid you'll get pregnant?"

"Of course, I'm afraid!" She sighed. "I got one of those books though."

"What book?"

Anya held up a finger and disappeared into the hallway. Faina took a seat on the bed to wait. When Anya returned, she handed Faina a blue book with a simple cover.

Married Love
A New Contribution to the Solution of Sex Difficulties
By Marie C. Stopes

Faina's eyes grew large with a mixture of fear and curiosity.

"I thought this book was banned in the U.S!" She dropped it on the bed, afraid to be caught holding it. "How on earth did you get a copy?"

"We live in a city of immigrants." Anya sat down on the bed with her head in her hands. Faina reached for the copy, then drew back. What forbidden and scandalous information was packed between the covers? Would she be shocked?

Anya cleared her throat. "I want to lend it to you."

Faina jumped to her feet, preparing to leave. "Don't bother. I don't need it."

"Don't get mad. I'm only trying to protect your reputation."

"And what about yours?"

"Mine can afford it."

Faina stopped in the doorway and turned to face her. "Here's a life lesson for you, Babycakes: being on the honor roll isn't gonna stop people from pointing a finger at your back!"

And with that, she left to retrieve her purse and made her way to the Chevalsky's apartment.

Chapter 35:

Obsession

"Everything alright between you and Anya?"

Faina dragged her feet as she followed Pasha down the hall to his room. All she could manage in reply was a groan.

"That bad, huh?" He held open his door for her.

"Yeah …" She paused at the threshold. Pasha had his new phonograph perched on top of a chair and was playing a record. "Where's Katya?"

"Playing quietly in her room."

Faina slunk towards the dresser with a knowing smirk. "What'd you promise her this time?"

"That we could play dolls for an hour later." He shut the door behind them, and removed a bag of peanuts from his pocket. "I'd say it's worth it." He handed her the Coke off the windowsill with a kiss on the cheek. "Still cold."

"Thanks, Tiger."

They sat down on the floor in front of the bed. Pasha picked a peanut out of the bag and aimed it at her mouth. Faina tilted her head back and opened her mouth just in time to catch the peanut on her tongue.

"Perfect catch!"

Faina smiled, and threw her arms out dramatically. "Thank you! Thank you!"

Pasha leaned back against the bed and sipped his drink. "So, what exactly did Anya say to you?"

Faina's face burned with a facetious scowl. "She thinks you're gonna get me pregnant."

Pasha nearly dropped his Coke. "What?!" He passed a hand over his reddening face. "Because of the gar—because of your—it was an accident! I looked away! I promise!"

"Not because of the garter. There's more to it than that." Faina crossed her arms. "She's lucky *she* isn't pregnant, seeing as she's been sleeping with Leg Up for six months now."

Pasha stared thoughtfully at the wall and stroked his chin. "You know, I didn't think about it before, but maybe they're not doing that part."

"What are you saying?" The meaning dawned on her the moment her words left her mouth.

Pasha swallowed and looked away. "I just meant—there are other things you can do that aren't …" He raked his fingers through his hair. "Never mind."

A string of static ground beneath the needle of the record player, filling the awkward silence between them.

"Better start it over." Pasha scooted towards the player and removed the needle from the disc. Eager to busy her hands, Faina opened her purse for something to fidget with. A groan slipped from her throat.

"I didn't give Anya the magazine."

"You can always give it to her later … that is, if you two are still speaking."

"It's her fault anyway." She laid the edition in her lap and flipped through the pages.

"I don't have to start this one over if you want," said Pasha, sitting back on his haunches. "I can play something else."

"What else you got?"

"Uh … Fannie Brice, more Irving Berlin, Eddie Cantor—"

Faina looked up from the magazine. "Ooh! Is it *The Sheik of Araby*!? I love that one!"

Pasha made a face. "Um … how about another one? That song scares Katya."

"It scares her?"

"Yeah, she thinks a Sheik is some kinda monster. And then there's that part where it says, *At night when you're asleep into your tent I'll creep*."

Faina doubled over with laughter. "That is adorable!"

Pasha chuckled. "Yeah, Ma and I had a pretty good laugh at that."

"Put on some more Irving Berlin then. You can't go wrong with Izzy."

Faina watched him as he set the record beneath the needle, admiring the sweet, placid look in his eyes she was so attracted to. Her eyes wandered along the curve of his back, taking pleasure in the wide angle of his broad shoulders. Faina froze, her thoughts grinding to an abrupt halt as she remembered her exchange with Anya.

I know how easy it is to give in.

Pasha set the sleeve aside and crawled towards her on all fours. Faina was admiring a pair of shoes when she felt Pasha's lips against the corner of her jawline. The magazine flew across the room.

"Sorry!" Faina put a hand to her head. "I, uh, thought I saw a bug." She forced a smile. "False alarm."

Pasha chuckled and brushed the hair from her shoulder. "You scared me for a minute."

She felt his breath near her ear. His lips brushed her cheek.

I know how easy it is to give in, Anya's voice repeated.

Faina snorted like a pig and doubled over into her knees. The heat from Pasha's proximity faded as he drew away. She was too embarrassed to look him in the eye.

"Is everything alright?" His hand traced the space between her shoulder blades, awakening the nerves in her spine one by one, as though he were lighting a row of candles. Faina pressed her lips together, suppressing a squeal as a shiver danced across her shoulders.

"Everything's jake!" She smoothed her hair. "Why do you ask?"

323

"You're a little jumpy, is all."

She covered her eyes. "I know."

"It's kinda cute."

She splayed her fingers, at last daring to meet his gaze. "It is?"

Pasha giggled. "Come here!" He grabbed her and drew her forward, cupping his lips against hers with a satisfied hum. His mouth was sweet and cold from the Coke, and she could feel his bangs tickling her forehead. Faina had scarcely pulled away for a breath before he laid another on her lips, and then another. He circled his arms around her waist. "I wanna hear you laugh again …"

Faina squealed as he pulled her down to the floor and started tickling her.

The doorknob turned, and the door flew open. Pasha and Faina sat bolt upright, their faces scarlet.

"Katya!" Pasha scolded. "Why didn't you knock?"

Katya ignored him with a smug little smile and rocked back on her heels.

"Why are you on the floor?"

Pasha's face was growing redder. "We were playing a game."

"What were you playing? Vampires?"

Faina's hand flew over her face in embarrassment. Pasha swallowed, struggling to keep his features even.

"Katya—"

"Does this mean you're not a virgin anymore?"

"WHAT?!" Faina practically shrieked.

"KATYA!" Pasha thundered. Faina had never seen anyone turn red so fast. Not even a traffic light. "It's not what you think," he pleaded, turning to Faina with desperate eyes. "Ma told her that a virgin means someone who's never been kissed."

Faina lowered her chin, her mouth falling open. "Ah." Part of her wanted to laugh, while the other half wanted to hide under the bed.

Annoyed that she had been duped, Katya stomped her foot. "Well, what does it mean then? Tell me!"

"You're too little!" insisted Pasha, his face still the shade of spaghetti sauce.

"If you don't tell me I'll tell Mama you and Faina were smooching on the floor!"

It was Faina's turn to go red now. She couldn't bear the thought of Mama Lydia thinking badly of her. Pasha's complexion had gone from florid to positively snowy. Faina couldn't be sure, but it looked as though he had forgotten how to breathe.

"That is not what we were doing! We weren't even kissing! We were just playing!"

"Well, it sure looked like that's what you were about to do!"

"Katerina Ruslanovitch Chevalsky, if you dare say anything to Mama—"

But Katya merely threw her arms around herself and started making kissing noises.

"Katya!"

Suddenly, an idea struck Faina. "Alright, alright! We'll tell you!"

Dropping her arms down by her side, Katya stared at Faina in disbelief. "You will?"

"We will?" Pasha flashed her a questioning look.

"Mhm!" Faina sat up straight, and looked Katya very seriously in the eye. "A virgin is someone who isn't a mama or a papa yet … well, usually."

All at once the muscles in Pasha's face relaxed. "Yes! That's exactly what it means."

Understanding dawned in Katya's enormous eyes. "Oh! And you're not a papa yet."

Pasha gave her an emphatic nod. "Exactly. But you can't go around talking about it, alright? I don't want to find out you're going up to people with children and telling them they're not virgins!"

Folding her hands behind her back, Katya flashed them a cool smile. "Fine. I won't."

"Now can you please leave?"

Katya said not a word but took her time shuffling out into the hall.

"Shut the door, please!"

A pair of suspicious eyes stared at them as she cracked the door.

"All the way!" Pasha called out. It clicked shut. "Now move away from the door!"

When her feet had pattered into the distance, Pasha sighed and rolled his eyes, plopping his head in Faina's lap.

"Sorry about that."

Faina gazed off into the distance, twisting her hair around her fingers. "It's alright." She swallowed, desperate to shake off Anya's shadow, and bent down to kiss his nose.

Pasha's mouth stretched into an exaggerated grin as she pulled away.

"I know we better be heading out soon, but you're making it really hard for me to get motivated."

Faina slumped forward as the feelings came flooding back like a tidal wave.

"Hey," Pasha rolled over on his stomach, "you alright?"

Faina shrugged. "I'm trying to be."

"Anya got in your head, didn't she?" He sat up and placed a hand on her knee. "Faina, I have no intention of doing anything like what Anya suggested. And I'm kinda disappointed she has so little faith in me."

"I don't think it's you she's worried about. She says when you're in love it can be hard to resist, and once you start it's hard to stop. She said she was just looking out for me."

Pasha stared thoughtfully for a moment. "Maybe she is." His fingers cupped her hand. "If I do anything that makes you uncomfortable, please tell me."

His palm was cool from holding the bottle of Coke. Faina laced their fingers together and smirked. "I'm not sure uncomfortable is the word …"

He combed his fingers through her hair and snickered, looking especially pleased with himself. "I never thought I could make Faina Spichkin weak in the knees."

"Please. Don't pretend like you're not an absolute sheik." She wrapped her arms around his neck. "Every time you kiss me, I feel like I'm gonna melt through the floorboards."

He pinned his forehead against hers with a quick kiss. "Well, as much as I'd like to turn you into a puddle, we better start heading towards the Foxhole. You don't want to be late for rehearsal."

Faina closed her eyes and drew a deep breath, her excitement threatening to spill over. "I can't believe I'm finally gonna get to sing in front of an audience."

"I can." Pasha kissed her nose. "Now we better get going."

Outside, the ground was hot but the sky had turned cool, with heavy clouds looking like wet, gray rags that needed wringing out. Children were splashing beneath a busted fire hydrant, and as they passed, Faina could smell the heat in the puddles, warmed by the sun-baked asphalt.

They arrived at the Foxhole earlier than they anticipated. As the bandleader began to set up, they waited from the loading bay outside the garage where no one would disturb them. Faina thought they were alone when Pasha bracketed her against the wall.

"Feel like melting?"

Faina eagerly touched her lips to his, her excitement building as he pressed back. She slid her arms around his neck, prompting him to scoop her up and seat her on a stack of crates where he could reach her better.

"You know I once saw him eat a sandwich with just mayonnaise and bread." teased Sergei, passing in front of the door carrying a large box. Faina immediately blushed and hid her face.

"Oh, uh, hey, Sergei," greeted Pasha, looking just as bashful. He hopped atop the crate next to Faina. "What are you up to?"

"Just helping carry some band equipment up to the restaurant." He turned his attention to Faina. "Speaking of which, I heard you got a gig coming up here in a couple of weeks. Congratulations!"

"Thanks! That's why I'm here as a matter of fact, I've got rehearsal today."

"It was only a matter of time before she got discovered," said Pasha, putting his arm around her and kissing her cheek.

The moment Sergei was distracted again, Pasha put a finger to his lips before leaning in for another.

Footsteps rattled on the landing. "Hey, what's the holdup?"

Anastas leaned over the railing with a snare drum under his arm. At the sight of Pasha with his hands all over Faina, the drum fell from Anastas's grip and rolled down the stairs. Sergei gasped and ran to stop it, catching it as it bounced into the air.

"What's the matter with you? That's a thirty-dollar drum!"

"Seriously!" hissed Pasha, his smile shattering. "He's already out of jail?"

In the past three years, Faina had given Anastas as little attention as possible, but for some reason, when she saw him staring at them with such shock and intensity, a little lump of fear rose up in her throat. The door behind Anastas clicked open again and Blinkers stuck his head out.

"Faina, the band's ready."

Faina smiled and nodded. "Okay, I'm on my way." Her eyes slid back to Anastas on the landing. She swallowed and slid off the crate. Pasha grabbed hold of her hand and tugged her gently back.

"You'll do great." He roped her in by the waist and kissed her full on the lips one last time, Anastas still watching.

Faina's smile was nervous, but not because of the band. "Thanks."

She made her way up the stairs, keeping her eyes pinned to the ground as she passed Anastas. A wave of relief flowed over her as she closed the door. She walked down the hall toward the staircase leading to the restaurant. The door opened, and footsteps flooded in behind her.

"Since when are you and Chevalsky swapping spit?"

Faina sneered at the expression and hurried down the corridor.

"Hey! I'm talking to you!" Anastas's footsteps grew closer. "How long has he been grinding your coffee?"

Faina reached the bottom step and turned towards him with a glower. "That's none of your business!"

"Oh-ho! So you are giving him the goods!"

Faina hurried up the stairs. "I'm not giving anyone anything!"

"Then why'd Chevalsky have his hands all over you, huh?" He climbed up after her.

She stopped and faced him from the landing. "Because he's my boyfriend, and we're in love! And just so you know, he's a perfect gentleman!"

"I don't believe that for a second! Not after the way he was kissing you just now!"

"What do you care? We haven't been friends for years!"

Anastas's temper abated slightly. "That doesn't mean I don't think about you sometimes."

Faina couldn't believe what she was hearing, and her face showed it. "Think what? All you do is harass me!"

"Look, I know we've had our differences the last few years, but maybe I care too much about you to stand by while you waste your time on Chevalsky."

"As opposed to someone like your old buddy, Steed? I don't seem to remember you putting up a fight then."

Anastas scoffed as though it were no big deal. "I knew Steed wasn't gonna get anywhere!"

"You are completely sick! You know that? You've bullied me, harassed me, called me names for three years, and now that I'm dating Pasha you try to convince me you're this caring person concerned for my well-being!"

Anastas's scowl returned with renewed ugliness. "What are you trying to say? That I'm obsessed with you or something?"

Faina threw back her head and laughed. "Not me! Pasha! You've always been!"

This was apparently the wrong thing to say. He stomped onto the landing, towering over her and almost stepping on her feet. "I always knew you were a little whore."

"You're playing a dangerous game here, don't you think? Coming after me like this in the Foxhole!"

He put on a fake smile. "Wait. I ain't being aggressive or nothing." He reached towards her, his fingers caressing the ribbon in her hair. Faina's stomach did a queasy flip. Without thinking, she rammed her knee into his groin. Anastas sank to his knees with a grunt, tearing the ribbon out as he went. Faina grabbed it from his hand and, turning, ran up the stairs.

"I ain't finished with you yet, Spichkin!" The railing rattled as he grabbed hold of it. "You hear me?"

Faina wrenched open the door to the restaurant and slammed it behind her.

Chapter 36:

The Snapshot

Faina's debut performance was scheduled for a Friday night at the end of August. She saved her bootlegging money and bought the most stunning white evening gown she could find. When she modeled it for Pasha in the sitting room of the Dalka's apartment, Pasha could hardly believe the dress was real.

It had that satiny, pearl-like sheen that begged to be touched. The kind that tortured young, curious fingers to reach for and feel. The barest traces of blush and lavender rippled across the fabric at the slightest gesture. It reminded Pasha of the glossy opaline glaze left in the wake of a receding tide. If that pearly sheen, with its lustrous bubbles of sea foam, could have been peeled off the sand and knit into a gauze, it would have looked exactly like Faina's gown.

"You look gorgeous! Where on earth did you find it?"

"A place Aunt Poppy recommended. Madame Barnacle's, on Mott Street."

Pasha raised an eyebrow. "Madame Barnacle's? Is that really her name?"

"As far as I know. But promise me you'll never go over there, her daughters are too beautiful! They all look like they walked straight out of a fairytale, like mermaid princesses or something!"

Pasha's eyes glazed over with a skeptical smile. "You have nothing to worry about. Turn around, let's see the whole getup."

The moment Faina turned her back, Pasha's brain had to sift through three languages before he could form a verbal response. The back of the dress was cut down so low, the material grazed just beneath her shoulder blades. His reaction did not escape her notice.

"Well, what do you think?" She stepped towards him with a teasing grin.

The door to the stairwell opened and Uncle Matvei appeared, smiling and relaxed. "Alright, *Faishka*, let's see this dazzling new dress you've been talking about!"

Turning to face him, Faina glided her hands over the smooth material and struck a pose. Even Uncle Matvei seemed genuinely impressed.

"Stunning! Absolutely stunning! Give us a twirl!"

Pasha tensed his jaw, preparing himself for the inevitable. Faina spun round, as innocent as a five-year-old with a new party dress. At the sight of his niece's exposed back, Uncle Matvei let out a cry so comical Pasha was torn between laughing and ducking for cover.

"Faina Adrianovna Spichkin!" He snatched a coat from the rack and threw it over her shoulders as though smothering out a fire.

"What? What?"

"You can't—" Uncle Matvei hesitated, his eyes darting from Pasha to the dress. "Where on earth did you get this dress?"

Pasha was just about to excuse himself when Faina cut him off. "From Madame Barnacle's, on Mott Street."

"Well, Madame Barnacle forgot to put in the back!"

Just then Anya emerged from her room, drawn in by all the ruckus. She took one look at the coat draped over her cousin and placed a hand on her hip.

"I told you he'd have a cow."

Faina whirled round to face her uncle with the most pathetic look she could muster. "You're not gonna make me return it, are you? It was made custom for me!"

Again, Pasha tried clearing his throat so he could sneak away to the bathroom, but nobody heard him. Uncle Matvei hesitated, his eyes drawn toward the sheen of the breathtaking fabric.

"Why can't she just wear a shawl?" suggested Anya. "Or a kimono? I'm sure we have something that will cover it up."

Uncle Matvei rubbed a hand over his forehead and sighed. "Alright, fine. But I have to approve it first! Deal?"

Faina eagerly jerked her head up and down. "Deal!"

All at once Uncle Matvei seemed to have remembered Pasha was in the room, for he did a double-take when he caught his eye, raising his eyebrows. Pasha quickly looked away, pretending to be occupied with a stain on the ceiling.

As Faina turned her back once more, Uncle Matvei shook his head and muttered something Pasha could not quite make out.

"Well, they make backless corsets, you know!" Faina burst out in response.

"Faina!" Anya and Uncle Matvei both shouted in unison.

"I better go!" Pasha quickly got to his feet and headed for the door before Faina got them both in trouble.

***

When the time came, all of Pasha and Faina's friends showed up at the Foxhole to see her shine. Everyone had heard about Faina's fancy dress, and was eager to see it in person. In order to surprise everyone, Faina had arranged to arrive at the Foxhole in her street clothes, and change backstage before the curtain went up.

When the trio first stepped through the doors of the restaurant, they found themselves shoulder to shoulder with a crowd of people.

"Jiminy!" exclaimed Anya. "When's the last time you've seen this place so crowded?"

"It's a good thing we asked Sergei and Leg Up to save us a seat!" Pasha waved to Sergei and Leg Up who had secured a table right in front of the stage.

Anya roped her arm around Faina. "You're gonna do great! Just look how many people showed up to see you!"

Faina had said little of Anya since their argument, but based on their interactions things seemed to have improved.

"You aren't nervous, are you?" asked Pasha.

Faina squeezed his hand. "Not when you're around."

"You better get back there and change." Pasha brushed her hair behind her ear. "You don't wanna keep your adoring public waiting."

Faina snickered and gave him a kiss, then made her way over to the bandleader at the front of the stage. It was a small, cabaret-style stage that was really just a platform enclosed with a velvet curtain, and the band had to clear out in order for Faina to dress.

Pasha and Anya took their seat at the table.

"There's my *Annushka*!" Leg Up leaned over and greeted her with a kiss.

"So, Pasha," Sergei took a swig of his drink. "What's it like to be shackled to a big star?"

"Pasha's gonna be her manager now," teased Anya.

Pasha folded his hands and put on a mock snooty expression. "That's right, from now on all inquiries about Miss Spichkin's performance must go through me first."

Everyone snickered except Leg Up, who appeared to be distracted by the table behind Pasha.

"What on earth is that joker doing?"

Sergei looked over his shoulder. "Who?"

"Anastas. Do you see that? He brought a camera."

Pasha took one look and rolled his eyes. "I'm starting to think he's a little obsessed with Faina."

Anya narrowed her eyes. "Maybe we oughta keep an eye on him."

335

"Hey, Pasha!" Someone tapped him on the shoulder. It was Joe Cherney's little brother, Eugene, who often helped with the sound equipment. "Faina's asking for you backstage. Said she needed something from you."

Pasha got up from his chair and started towards the stage. Eugene stopped him.

"But, uh, use the back entrance instead of the side." He pointed towards a door. "Just go out into the hallway and the door is immediately to your left."

"Oh, okay. Thanks, Eugene." Pasha pushed through the crowd and made his way into the hall. Maybe Faina had stage fright, and she needed him to calm her down. He entered through the stage door.

"Faina?"

He took a step forward into the dimly lit space and ran smack into a figure. Faina shrieked.

"Pasha!"

Pasha looked down and immediately shut his eyes. Faina was completely naked from the waist up. Her dress was down around her ankles and she had only her bloomers and stockings on. Pasha reached for the door handle but it was locked! Just as Faina turned her back on him, the curtains opened, showcasing Faina's naked chest to the entire restaurant. A camera flash exploded with light at the front of the stage, causing a multitude of spots to cloud Pasha's vision. A series of gasps, squeals, and wolf whistles echoed throughout the crowd. Faina screamed and shielded herself with her hands.

"Look, they can hardly keep their hands off each other for five minutes!" someone shouted.

"Way to go, Pasha!"

"I always knew he had it in him!"

"I always said she was a hussy!"

336

Not knowing what else to do, Pasha grabbed one of the curtains and pulled it closed while Anya leapt onto the stage with her coat and covered her cousin, allowing her to yank the dress up. Leg Up pulled the other side of the curtain closed, and Sergei jerked Pasha off the stage. The crowd was absolutely raucous with shouts, and soon there was a chorus of male voices shouting:

"Encore! Encore!"

As Anya and Faina hurried off the stage, they collided with a waiter carrying a tray full of wine, saturating both Pasha and Faina. The liquid spilled down the front of the sparkling gown.

Pasha slid his hand over his face. "I am such an idiot!"

Chapter 37:
The Book

"After everything we went through with your brother! How could you let this happen?" Uncle Matvei stormed down the hallway towards Faina's room. It was the morning after the incident. Anya and Faina had not explained what had taken place at the Foxhole, and refused to answer Uncle Matvei's questions as to why Faina had returned home in tears. But things soon came to a head when the next day Uncle Matvei found an eight-by-ten photograph of Faina taped to the front door of *Opa!*

"But Uncle Matvei, it's not what it looks like!" Faina pleaded, chasing after him. Anya followed behind her.

Uncle Matvei stopped and turned in front of her door. "Not what it looks like? How gullible do you think I am?" With flared nostrils, he shook his head back and forth. "This is my own fault!" He ripped open her door, flinging it so hard it crashed against the wall. "I've been too soft with you!"

Anya stepped forward. "Papa, she's telling the truth! I saw the whole thing!"

"You stay out of this, young lady! I found your cigarettes in your sweater pocket in the laundry this morning!"

He threw open the window, grabbed the tin-can phone running across the alley to Pasha's window and ripped it from the wall. He raised his finger in the air.

"You are never to see that boy again!" His voice shook with rage. "Do you hear me? From now on your window stays locked! You don't leave this building without a chaperone, is that understood?"

Faina stared up at him helplessly. "Uncle Matvei, you're not listening! I never did anything like that with Pasha, or any boy for that matter, I swear!"

"*Vran'ye!*" Lies! "Do you know what I found in the bathroom this morning?"

Faina stared up at him in utter confusion. Uncle Matvei momentarily disappeared into the hallway. When he reappeared he was holding the Marie Stopes book. Faina's face turned red.

"It's not mine!"

"Then whose is it?"

Faina started to say something but stopped herself. Her eyes flashed desperately towards Anya. Anya leaned against the wall, wringing her sleeve. When no one said anything, Uncle Matvei's nostrils flared.

"How could you disrespect me by lying like this?"

Anya staggered forward and swallowed. "Papa, it's not Faina's, it's mine!"

The knot between Uncle Matvei's wooly eyebrows unwound and rose. "What?"

"There's a perfectly sound explanation, although, you're not going to like it. I got the book from a friend at school." She put out her hands to steady him. They were shaking. "It was morbid curiosity. I know I shouldn't have been reading it, but the book is banned in the United States, and I just wanted to see what all the fuss was about."

It was a clever lie, and certainly plausible for an adolescent girl. But unfortunately, Anya was a bad liar, and it was obvious to anyone who knew her that she was not telling the truth.

"Annabelle Dalka, you look me in the eye and tell me that's the truth."

Anya twisted her sleeve until her hand had all but disappeared. Reluctantly, she met her father's eyes. "It's the truth." Her voice broke.

"Neither of you have any respect for me, do you?" He returned his attention to Faina. "Faina, do you realize what you have done to yourself? To your future? This mistake will follow you the rest of your life!"

Faina dropped to the ground, hid her face in the side of the mattress and wailed. "But it's not my mistake! I'm telling you!"

Anya broke between them, her face defiant. "Papa, listen! Last night, Anastas and a few other boys tricked Pasha into walking in on Faina while she was changing, then he snapped the photograph! He set the whole thing up!"

"That sounds awfully elaborate for Anastas!"

Anya's mouth hinged open. "You don't believe me?"

"I don't know what to believe anymore! In the past six years I've had my apartment searched by the police, a thirteen-year-old driving without a license so she could steal from an Ivy League Club, a pregnancy out of wedlock, and two underage smokers! The lies never stop in this house! So, you tell me, my girl, who am I supposed to trust? Hmm? Who am I supposed to believe?" He jabbed a finger at Pasha's window. "You are never to speak to him ever again! Either of you!" And with that he slammed the door and left.

Faina gaped at Anya, her eyes wet and burning with betrayal. "How could you?"

"Faina, I tried—"

"You threw me under the bus!"

Anya's countenance evolved from apologetic to outraged. "I did no such thing! I told Papa the book was mine. I can't help it if he didn't believe me!"

"You could've told him the whole truth!"

Anya balked at her. "You expect me to tell Papa I lost my virginity to a street fighter?"

"So you're gonna let him think I lost my virginity?"

"I'm sorry that Papa thinks it was you! But you can't expect me to tell him the real reason why I had the book! You would do the same thing if you were in my position!"

"Not if it meant someone else was taking the blame!"

"It's not my fault Papa finds it easier to believe you were the one sleeping around than me! You're the one who chose to go breaking the law with Pasha!"

"And you're the one who chose to sleep around! The only reason Uncle Matvei doesn't believe my story is because of that stupid book that *you* brought into the house! And the only reason he thinks the book is mine is because he knows you're lying!"

"I can't help it! I'm a bad liar!"

"Then you shouldn't have done something you were gonna have to lie about! Now get out!"

Chapter 38:
Solutions

Lydia stared down at the photograph and sighed. Pasha was sitting across the table from her, wringing his cap and swaying slightly. She had known something was wrong when he'd come home early the night before and locked himself in his room.

"What are you doing back so early?" she had asked him from the sofa.

"Something bad happened," he'd mumbled, hardly slowing down to look at her.

"What? Is everything alright? Is Faina okay?"

"I don't want to talk about it." And with that, he had slammed the door.

Lydia knew it was best not to pressure him. If left to himself, Pasha was more likely to open up to her once he had time to process. That's just how he was. So she said no more. She went to bed. The next morning, she went to work. The day passed as usual. Evening fell, and when she emerged the lamp posts had all been plastered with incriminating photographs of Pasha and Faina.

Now the apartment was deadly quiet. Katya was in the tub, but she didn't seem to be making much noise.

At length, Lydia turned the picture over and laid it face down on the table.

"I'll be honest," she pinched the space between her eyebrows, "this does not seem like you."

"I didn't do it, Ma," Pasha insisted. "I know what it looks like, but I promise we didn't do anything."

"Sweetheart, you told me you were not sexually active but—"

"I'm not! I haven't been!"

Lydia held up her hand. "Listen to me for just one second. I want you to know that if you *have* been, you can be honest with me. Okay?" She sat up straight, trying to make her face appear as calm as possible. "Things happen. I'd rather they not happen again. But if they *did* happen—"

"They didn't! Ma, if my word isn't enough, consider this: if I were going to fool around with Faina, why on earth would I do it five minutes before her performance, behind the curtain on a stage in a room full of people? That doesn't even make any sense! I know hormones can make people act stupid, but they can't make you act that stupid."

Lydia nodded. She knew he was telling the truth, but she was going to need a good explanation.

"Alright then. Why don't you tell me what did happen?"

Pasha went on to explain the whole ordeal. How Anastas and the other boys had tricked Pasha into walking in on Faina while she was changing, pulled the curtain, and then snapped the photograph. Lydia shut her eyes with a long exhale.

"Anastas did this?"

"Anastas, Joe, and Steed. Anastas was the one with the camera. I didn't see them do it, but Sergei and Leg Up said it was Joe and Steed who pulled the curtains."

Lydia could feel her blood boiling. She wanted to stand up. She wanted to grab the pots and pans hanging over the stove and throw them at the wall.

"And what did Klokov do?"

"He congratulated me."

Affronted, Lydia's mouth sank open. "He congratulated you?"

"Told me he didn't think I had it in me."

Lydia's nostrils flared. "What did he do to Anastas and the others?"

"Nothing."

"Nothing?" She jammed her finger at the back of the photograph. "This is sexual harassment."

Pasha shrugged. "I don't know what he thinks about the photograph. That was last night that he congratulated me on my way out. I haven't spoken to him since then."

Desperate to calm herself, Lydia took a deep breath. "Oh, *Patulya*." She rubbed her temples. "Have you talked to Faina?"

Pasha opened his mouth to speak but winced. Lydia reached for his hand just as his eyes were reddening.

"Baby, it's alright!"

Pasha swallowed, refusing to let himself cry in front of her. "I'm fine." He withdrew his hand, and cleared his throat. "Um. Matvei doesn't want me anywhere near the apartment … or his side of the building for that matter."

"So he hasn't heard your side of the story?"

Pasha threw up his shoulders and stared down at the table. "Well, he's bound to have heard it from Faina. And if he didn't listen to her, why would he listen to me?"

"I will talk to Matvei, alright? We can fix this."

"Fix it?" Pasha stared back at her, open-mouthed. "Faina's picture is all over the city! What are we gonna do? Get on the radio and make a public announcement to please disregard the naked photographs of my girlfriend because it was all staged?" He hunched over the table, covering his face. "Her reputation is ruined, and it's all my fault! I mean, *blin*, I don't even know that she wants to see me anymore! She probably hates me!"

Lydia put her hand on his arm. "Don't say that word."

"It's not the real word."

"I know, but it sounds like the real word."

"Only if you speak Russian—" he paused and exhaled. "Sorry. I don't mean to argue with you."

"You're just upset." She scooted her chair around the edge of the table, trying to get closer to him. "We could go to the police and see if they'll help take the photos down."

Pasha threw his head back with a mirthless laugh. "Are you kidding? If anything Lynch will use it as an excuse to arrest the both of us! He's tried to charge Faina four times now with public indecency—for wearing pants. What do you think he's gonna do when he sees the photos?"

"Alright, calm down." She paused to chew on her lip. "Here's what we're going to do. I'm going to talk to Matvei. Why don't you write Faina a letter, and try to think of a way you can pass it along? Perhaps you can have Aunt Poppy give it to her?"

Pasha's shoulders rose and fell as he heaved a grievous sigh. "Yeah … Yeah, okay."

She traced her nails over his back. "There, now. Everything is going to be just fine. I'll make you some tea."

Chapter 39:

The Negative

Faina pinned the dustpan to the floor with the ball of her foot as she scraped the broom against the dirt. She sniffed and wiped a stray tear from her eye. That morning someone had painted the word "slut" on the storefront window. A week had passed since the incident, but her picture was popping up all over the neighborhood, pasted to telephone poles, nailed to doors, and scattered along the sidewalk like fliers. Uncle Matvei had tried to get the police involved but they blamed Faina and refused to help find the person responsible.

After his initial outburst, Uncle Matvei's sympathy had overpowered his temper, and he was often soft with Faina. However, Faina had not forgiven him for his mistrust. But then why should he believe her? Anya was right. She'd broken the rules too many times. She wouldn't deny the truth. That's how Anastas had ended up the way he was, refusing to ever believe his actions were wrong, or that he had caused any of his own misfortunes.

The front door of *Opa!* opened, and Uncle Matvei appeared in the hallway with Mammoth on a leash, having just returned from a walk. Faina glared at him.

"I can't even walk my own dog?"

Uncle Matvei drew a deep and tired inhale. "*Faishka*, things are going to have to die down considerably before you can go out again. I don't want you getting hurt."

She knew he was right but didn't want to give him the satisfaction of thinking she was over it, so she didn't answer.

"That's enough sweeping. You can go upstairs if you'd like."

Faina set the broom against the door and pushed past him toward the stairs. When she got to her room she noticed an empty bottle had been placed on the fire escape outside. Faina narrowed her eyes. Inside was a coiled up piece of paper. She crawled over to the sill and tried to throw open the window. It wouldn't budge. An irritated growl escaped her throat as she fell back on her haunches. Of course it wouldn't budge; Uncle Matvei had glued it shut.

She hopped off the bed and wandered over to Anya's room. The door was open and the room was empty. She crawled out the window and climbed the short distance to her own fire escape. Carefully, she plucked the note from the bottle and sat against the wall. It was in Pasha's handwriting.

Faina, I'm so sorry about what happened. I know you're not allowed to talk to me or see me, but I don't care. I'm not giving up. We shouldn't have to suffer when we didn't do anything wrong. Your uncle may not believe us but that doesn't mean we have to accept his punishment. I love and respect your uncle, and I'm angry that Anastas has hurt our families. But I'm not going to accept a punishment for something I didn't do. I love you, and I want to be with you. I can't stand not being able to see you! Do you still love me?

Love, Pasha

P.S. Just so you know, my mother believes us, and knows we didn't do anything. She tried to talk with your uncle but he wouldn't listen. Mama says she loves you and misses you. Katya does too. They send you hugs and kisses.

Faina squeezed the note to her chest. She knew all about the skirmish between Uncle Matvei and Mama Lydia, because she had been eavesdropping from the stairwell the whole time. Their words were still fresh in her mind.

"Matvei," Mama Lydia had pleaded, "this boy Anastas is responsible for putting a permanent scar on my son's back. His idea of a prank is slamming my boy's head into a pile of heroin. He had no qualms whatsoever about trying to get Pasha blacklisted by challenging him during his first fight. And he tried to take advantage of your niece. Faina even says that Anastas knew about the incident on Wall Street before it happened and didn't warn Leo! Anastas has it out for your family and mine. His behavior towards Faina is obsessive, like that of a stalker, and his vendetta against Pasha frightens me. There isn't much I would put past him."

"Look, Lydia, what would you have me do?" Her uncle had replied in a wearied tone. "Give her the benefit of the doubt again? Do you think I don't know what everyone says about me? 'Oh, Matvei, he lets his children walk all over him!' Well, it's true! And look where it's gotten me! I have no control over my own family! These kids … Well, they're destroying themselves! You can afford to be dismissive of your son's behavior because he's a boy. I don't have that luxury! My poor Faina will be labeled the rest of her life!"

It had been Mama Lydia's turn to raise her voice then. "Dismissive? If I thought for one second Pasha had behaved towards Faina in a sexual manner, believe me, he would be hanging from the laundry line by his ears! And how can you accuse me of ignorance? I'm a woman, aren't I?" The sound of her chair scraping out from under her had seemed like a roar. "And it may not be my place to tell you how to raise your niece, but the last thing she needs from her uncle right now is to be called a liar! She is the victim in this situation!"

"I'll say! She's a victim of your son!"

The edges of Faina's mouth wrinkled. When she thought of what Anastas had stolen from her, tears burned her skin. Not only had he taken away her innocence, but she felt as though he'd robbed the innocence from her relationship with Pasha. They were each other's first loves. There was a thrill in discovering things for the first time together, at their own pace, by their own decisions, testing the water to feel when the temperature was right. But then Anastas had come along, spurred by his own jealousy, and pushed them into a dark territory Faina had not yet wanted to explore.

She wondered how much Pasha had seen but was too embarrassed to ask, and at the rate her photograph was being circulated around the neighborhood he was bound to catch up on anything he'd missed the first time. When she thought of all the people who had seen her naked, a sob forced its way through her throat. And how had Anastas and the others known when to pull the curtain? One of the boys had to have secretly been watching her undress! She now saw the full scope of Anastas's plan. He hadn't set out to spoil her just for Pasha. He wanted to see to it that Faina was spoiled for anyone, anyone who wasn't himself. And now he had a piece of her. A piece he could look at any time he wanted, to lock inside a drawer, or show off to his friends, and Faina had no say in any of it!

She slunk back to the fire escape outside Anya's room and crawled back through the window, sobbing. As she trudged back to her bedroom the floor rattled beneath her feet. There was a sound like the bell popping off *Opa!'s* door and clattering to the ground.

"Go on, you!"

It sounded like Anya. Faina raced down the stairs to the shop. Anya was dragging Anastas's little brother Alexei by his collar towards the counter. She pointed out Mammoth behind his gate.

"In case you get any ideas about changing your mind! This is our family pet!"

Mammoth barked, though more out of confusion than aggression. Uncle Matvei stood behind the register gaping at his daughter in astonishment.

"Anya, who is this?"

"This is Anastas's little brother." She gave Alexei another shove. "Tell him what happened."

Alexei sighed and ducked his head down. "My brother Anastas tricked Pasha into walking in on Faina. He set the whole thing up. Him, my brother Vadim, Joe Cherney, and Steed."

"Steed?"

"Vlad Gershkovich. Anastas was angry because Faina was walking out with Pasha. Joe wanted revenge after Faina made him look bad in front of everyone. And Steed was mad because Faina had dumped a milkshake on him when he'd tried to get fresh with her. Vadim didn't really care but he goes along with everything Anastas says." He swallowed. "Faina is always nice to me. My brothers are bad people. I don't like what they do, but I gotta do what they say." He reached into his pocket and produced an envelope. "This is the negative of the picture. And just so you know, I destroy any copies I find when they aren't looking. Without the negative they can't make anymore."

Uncle Matvei took the envelope and slipped it into his apron pocket.

"Thank you, Alexei. You've done a good thing by coming here and confessing all this to me. I appreciate that."

"Can I go now?"

"Yes, you may go."

"Alexei!" Faina whispered as he passed.

Alexei stopped and looked over his shoulder. Faina blew him a kiss, mouthing the words "thank you." Alexei smiled and nodded, then hurried out the door. Uncle Matvei sighed and collapsed back into his seat. He had his hand covering his eyes.

"What have I done? After everything she's been through, she'll never forgive me."

The floorboards creaked under Faina's footsteps. Uncle Matvei looked up. A pained expression broke across his eyes.

"*Faishka!*" He reached out to her. Faina approached him. He grabbed hold of her hands and drew her close, his head bowed below her chin. "Can you ever forgive me, my darling?"

"Of course, Uncle." She swallowed. "I'm sorry I gave you reason to doubt me. I understand why you found it difficult. I haven't exactly made it easy for you."

Uncle Matvei threw his arms around her and hugged her close.

"Never you mind, my girl! Never you mind!"

***

Later that evening, Anya appeared in Faina's doorway. "May I come in?"

Faina set her book aside and sat up in the bed. "You may."

Anya pulled up the chair from the vanity and sat by the bedside, her head bowed. "I'm sorry for what I said earlier … and that my book got you in trouble … and well, for a dozen other things."

Faina sighed. "You got me out of trouble though."

Anya wrinkled her mouth as though it still weren't enough. "Eventually." She glanced back at the door, then lowered her voice. "I want you to know I really was trying to look out for you all those times I was patronizing and critical … guess I could've handled it a little better. The truth is I was a jealous."

Faina stared at her incredulously. "Jealous?"

Anya hesitated for a moment then winced. "I wish I hadn't folded so quickly with Leg Up. When we started fooling around … well, I hardly knew him. I was caught up in the moment, in the feelings. It was so hard for me to resist, and yet for you it's easy. And that frustrated me. I'm supposed to be the level-headed one, after all."

"I wouldn't say it's easy for me exactly …"

Anya shrugged. "If I could go back and do things differently I would've slowed down a lot more. And I wouldn't have been so condescending towards you."

Faina picked at a loose thread in the afghan at the end of the bed. "You didn't want to tell me about you and Leg Up."

Anya shook her head. "No. But maybe I should have."

"That would've been a big risk."

"But one I could have trusted you with. You knew for months, and you never told anyone."

Faina crossed her arms in front of her chest and looked away. She wouldn't accept praise for it; she *should* have told. She had looked the other way while Anya and Leg Up did it for six months! After such a time without conceiving most women would have been inclined to think themselves infertile … of course, Anya had that book. And then there was the darker truth that lay at the heart of the issue, one Faina hardly wanted to acknowledge herself.

You wanted Anya to get pregnant …

If Faina could have physically shoved the thought away she would have. Instead, she clenched her fists.

"I didn't mean to imply that Pasha was irresponsible, or that you were loose," continued Anya. "Only that it's harder to resist than you think." She sighed. "You know, I used to turn my nose up at girls like Kitty Perkins, and Reyna Herzl … even Jazmin."

Faina's eyebrows lowered in defense at the mention of her late sister-in-law. When Jazmin had become pregnant at the age of seventeen, it was Leo who Faina had directed her wrath towards, not his girlfriend. But perhaps that hadn't been fair either. After all, Leo had done a great job of beating himself up, and was already reaping the consequences.

"Then I met Leg Up."

"I understand now," said Faina, eager for the conversation to be over. "I mean, if someone as perfect as you can give in to a guy … well, love is a pretty powerful thing I guess." She could hardly keep herself from rolling her eyes as she uttered the word 'perfect.'

"I'm not perfect, Faina." She smoothed her dress over her knees. "I'd think you would know that by now."

Faina shrugged, still not making eye contact. "Close enough, anyway."

Anya offered a weak smile and got up to leave. Faina was just about to let out a sigh of relief, when Anya paused at the door.

"I'm breaking up with Leg Up, by the way."

"What?" Faina pivoted around. "After all that? I thought you loved Leg!"

Anya shrugged. "Leg is special. But I don't know that I ever really loved him. Just the idea of him, I think. Anyway, there's no future in it. It's not worth the risks anymore. I want something different for my life."

When Faina continued to stare at her in disbelief, Anya shook her head and snickered.

"What?" Faina was beyond confused. "What are you laughing at?"

"You know something? You really are a romantic." And with that, she shut the door.

Faina threw herself back on the bed with an enormous sigh.

"Thank you, God!" Faina dug her fists into her eyes and slid onto the floor. "Thank you, thank you, thank you!"

She wouldn't have to tell! Who would have thought after all that, Anya and Leg Up would call it quits? The thought was revitalizing … and then it wasn't. After six months of dating, of risking everything—her future, her reputation—Anya was sending Leg Up on his way.

Faina didn't know what frightened her more: that she could lose control so easily in her passions, potentially forfeiting her reputation, or that the same passion that drove her to risk it all in the first place could just vanish.

Chapter 40:

No One Likes a Canary

Pasha slid his winning loaf of bread into his satchel and hooked it over his shoulder, eager to get home. It had been especially hot that day, and the Foxhole smelled worse than usual.

"Hold your horses there, champ." Klokov stopped him as he was sliding off the barstool. "I was wondering if you could deliver a message for me."

"A message?"

Klokov leaned forward with his elbows on the counter and beckoned him.

"The boys responsible for Miss Spichkin's, uh … the incident with the photograph, have been held accountable for their conduct."

Pasha stared at him for a moment. "What did you do to them?"

"They were flogged."

"Oh." Pasha tried not to swallow. Last he heard, Klokov hadn't planned to do anything, and was nothing short of proud where Pasha was concerned. He wondered what had changed his mind. "And you wanted me to tell Faina?"

"There's more. I'd like to give Miss Spichkin another opportunity to sing upstairs." He bit his lip in what seemed to be a regretful expression. "It's not much, but it's the least I can do seeing as her big moment was ruined."

Pasha was stunned. It appeared Klokov had truly had a change of heart.

"I'll tell her … but I can't guarantee she'll do it. Faina likes the spotlight but it was pretty traumatic for her."

"That's understandable. But let her know anyway. And tell me what she decides."

Outside, the temperature was just beginning to settle to a comfortable degree. The sun had set almost completely, and a third of the sky had turned pale violet. Pasha hoped Faina would take Klokov up on his offer. She enjoyed singing, and he didn't want to see her give up her dreams on account of a couple of hoods.

Pasha turned on to Delancey and froze. There, stapled to a telephone pole, was another missing poster for Pearl Sulzbach. Unlike the other posters which had grown crinkled and bleached by the sun and the rain, this one was pristine and new. The bottom of the page now read:

Reward: $600

Pasha ran a hand through his hair and turned away, wincing. Pearl's family had yet to give up, even nine months later. What had Pasha done wrong that night? How could he have missed at such close range? Were it not for him, Pearl might be safe at home with her family now. He leaned against a brick wall, his hands buried in his pockets.

Why had it fallen to Pasha to shoot the gunman? Why had it fallen to any of them? Shouldn't the police have been there? Surely, Klokov didn't believe in taking everything into his own hands! After all, according to him there were Breadwinners on the police force! Why trust a bunch of adolescents who had never even had the need to fire a gun before, to rescue a group of hostages? The mission had been doomed from the start!

Pasha narrowed his gaze on the sidewalk and hurried past the telephone pole, refusing to look up again for the rest of the journey home. He found most people ignored him when he kept his eyes down, so he was rather surprised when a pair of footsteps quickened close behind him.

"Well, look who it is!" Joe Cherny sidled up beside him and threw his arm around his shoulder. Pasha drew back in alarm only to bump into another equally close figure. Steed was grinning at him with a wicked smile and a massive lash mark across the side of his face.

"Where you going, pal?" He grabbed Pasha by the elbow.

"Off to see his little girlfriend, no doubt." Joe took his other arm. Pasha tried to struggle away.

"What do you want? Get off!"

But the boys merely tightened their grip. Had Pasha not just won a fight against Sergei, he might have had the strength to fight them off. But it had taken all his might and energy to get Sergei to the ground, and his arms felt like noodles.

They dragged him down a flight of stairs into the basement of a boarded-up shop. It was a cramped little room, with the only light coming from the street lamp through the shallow window.

"Bring him on down, boys!" Anastas was waiting at the far side of the room with Vadim, and two others whom Pasha did not recognize. Through the dim film of light he could see that Anastas's posture was different. He held his back a little stiffer. Pasha wondered how badly they had been flogged, whether they were given twenty lashes, or less. They threw him down on the floor and closed in around him.

"What do you want with me?" He tried to stand up but Joe shoved him back down.

"What do you think?" Anastas snorted.

"You got what you deserved! And you have nobody to blame but yourself! So, clear out and let me go!"

"Or what?" Steed smacked the back of his head. "You gonna tell your mommy?"

Anastas threw back his head and laughed. "Yeah, Chevalsky! You let your ma fight all your battles for you?"

Pasha stared back at them, completely lost. "What are you talking about?"

"Your ma convinced Klokov to teach us a lesson. She came down to the Foxhole and said we oughta be put in our place!"

Pasha's face burned. "She did?"

"Stan heard the whole thing through a vent in the next room, said your ma accused us of harassment. Klokov wasn't buying it until she pointed out that one of us had to have been watching her undress behind the curtain, and that if Faina's brother had been alive he would've wanted justice."

Pasha squeezed his eyes shut, visibly cringing. For all his mother's wisdom, she could be downright impulsive if her emotions ran too high. And though her intentions were obviously good, Pasha would now pay the price for her thoughtlessness.

"I didn't know." His eyes snapped open. "Not that I'm sorry you got what was coming to you! Had I thought of it I would have done it myself!"

"Oh, yeah?" Anastas grabbed him by the collar. "Well, now you're gonna get what's coming to you!"

Anastas drew back and clocked Pasha in the side of the head. Pasha reeled back, only for Joe to kick him forward onto his face. Pasha staggered to his knees, but a number of hands were grabbing him at once. He was kicked in the stomach, thrown up against the wall, and beaten repeatedly.

They tore the sleeve from his shirt, whipped him across the cheek with his own belt, and stomped on his arm. When they grew tired of tossing him around, they pinned him to the ground. Anastas bent over him with a knife. Pasha tried to wrench away, but Steed reached over and grabbed him by the chin to keep from turning his head.

A cloud of dust showered from the ceiling as footsteps stampeded above them.

"Hey! What's going on down there?"

Lights flickered through the slats in the floor above them.

"It's the cops," hissed Vadim.

"Let's go!"

They released Pasha, tripping over him to get to the door. A whistle pierced through the night. Pasha had no strength to get up; he could only lie there letting the blood trickle from his wounds. The door was kicked aside. A flashlight seared in Pasha's eyes.

"Jiminy!" The officer raced down the stairs. "You alright, kid?"

Pasha could not answer. His breath grew asthmatic. The cop knelt down at his side.

"Say, I know you!"

Pasha squinted up at him through the shadows. He couldn't believe it.

"Officer Leibowitz."

Pasha had met Liebowitz at the age of thirteen, the first time he was arrested. Rather than sending him to the precinct, the cop who had arrested him had taken him to the Tombs, the Manhattan detention complex famous for housing murderers and serious criminals. Liebowitz, the officer assigned to take Pasha's particulars after arriving, had been nothing but kind to Pasha, even going so far as to encourage him that he might not always be a Breadwinner. But here Pasha was, three years later. Where had Liebowitz been? Bloodied and weak, Pasha was suddenly overcome with sickening bitterness.

The muscles in his stomach contracted. Pasha scrambled onto his side, gagging. Officer Leibowitz grabbed a nearby bucket and helped him to his knees.

"There we go, kid." He patted the space between his shoulders. "Get it all out."

Pasha's mouth instinctively forced open as he bent over the bucket and vomited. The cold, acidic feeling in his stomach immediately subsided.

"You good?"

He spat a bit of blood into the container and sat back on his knees. "I think so."

"Who did this to you?"

Pasha glanced up at him with a contemptuous expression. "Jack the Ripper." He'd never been so bold with a cop before.

"Alright, enough with the wisecracks. I'm just trying to help you."

He wiped his mouth on his torn sleeve. "How long you been on the force?"

"Fifteen years."

"Then you know you can't help me." He tried to stand but staggered.

Officer Liebowitz caught him before he hit the ground. "You know I had hoped to see you better off next time I ran into you."

"You know what they say, the key to happiness is to lower your expectations."

Liebowitz slung his arm over his shoulder. "Boy, you have gotten worse. You didn't use to have such a mouth."

Pasha closed his eyes and drew in a deep breath. There was still a part of him that wanted the officer's approval, to hold his head high, to stand out.

"Sorry, I guess I'm a little sore on account of I'm about to get arrested."

"What are you talking about?"

"You aren't gonna arrest me?"

"What am I gonna arrest you for? Bleeding all over the place?" He steered him towards the exit. "C'mon, let's get you outta here."

"But I have warrants!"

"I don't check for warrants unless I suspect someone's committing a crime." He helped him up the first stair.

"Like when my girlfriend's wearing pants in public?"

"You must be thinking of Officer Schneider. I'd like to think I'm a little more progressive than that. You don't look very suspicious this evening."

"It doesn't look suspicious that I was bleeding my guts out in a basement?"

Liebowitz threw up his free hand. "Kid, do you *want* me to arrest you?"

"No."

"Then keep your mouth shut. I ain't about to put another kid in jail. That's the last thing you need."

Pasha pointed him in the direction of his tenement and they began their trek. He was grateful for the twilight. There was no telling what would happen if another Breadwinner saw him being helped down the street by a cop.

"You gonna tell me who did this to you?"

Pasha didn't answer, but continued to limp towards Orchard Street. Liebowitz snorted.

"So, it was your own kind then."

Pasha did a double take. Liebowitz gave a grim smile.

"Fifteen years."

Pasha scowled and wiped another trickle of blood from his nose. "You won't be doing me any favors by trying to bring me justice, so you might as well stop asking questions."

"'Nobody likes a canary.' See? I know the rules."

Pasha took one look at him and couldn't help but laugh. "Yeah, you're on your way to becoming Arnold Rothstein."

Liebowitz snickered. "You think they'd let me do undercover work?"

"You're a Slav, aren't you?"

"I'd fit right in!"

Traffic breezed past on the road beside them. Once or twice, Pasha thought he saw another street fighter, but each time it turned out to be someone else.

"I thought you worked in a different precinct."

"I got transferred."

"When?"

"Two months ago."

Pasha lowered his eyebrows once again. "So you were here when my girlfriend's uncle asked you to help him get rid of all those photographs of her that were being put up all over the city."

Liebowitz remained nonplussed. "Who'd he talk to?"

Pasha softened, realizing where he was getting at. "Lynch."

"There's your problem. By the time I found out your girlfriend's uncle had been asking for help, all the photos were gone. Schneider wanted to charge you both with public indecency but I wouldn't allow it."

"Oh." Pasha looked down at the ground and blushed. He wanted to explain to Liebowitz that it had all been set up, that he and Faina hadn't done anything, but decided it was best to get off the subject altogether. "I appreciate that."

They stopped in front of the tenement. Pasha lowered his head slightly. He was grateful for Liebowitz's help, even if he didn't want to show it. It was hard enough for Pasha to get taken seriously even without sucking up to a cop.

"This is me."

"You gonna be okay, kid?"

Pasha slid on his cap and sighed. "I'm never gonna be okay." He looked Liebowitz in the eye. "But I appreciate you asking anyway."

Liebowitz held his gaze. "You're a good kid, Pasha."

Pasha snorted and turned towards the door.

"You can laugh, but I know the difference!"

Pasha stared at him a moment or two longer, then tipped his cap and went inside.

When Pasha burst through the apartment door, his mother gasped as though she had been under water for too long.

"Pavlo! What happened?" She flew towards him, forcing his face to the light, but Pasha wriggled away from her.

"Where's Katya?"

"In the bath."

"Good!" He tore the rest of his sleeve off and threw it in the wastebasket. "Did you go to Klokov and demand that Anastas and the others be punished?"

She stared back at him with uncomprehending eyes. "Yes."

Pasha threw out his arms, showcasing the extent of his damage. "That's what happened!"

"Klokov had you beaten?" She flew towards him again but Pasha held up his hands, refusing to let her touch him.

"No! He had Anastas, Joe, and Steed beaten, and then *they* beat *me*! With the help of three other fellas!"

Lydia's hand flew over her mouth. At last she was beginning to understand. "Oh, *Patulya*!"

"What did you think was gonna happen?"

"Well, I just thought—"

"This is a street gang we're talking about, Ma! You can't fight my battles for me! This isn't the PTA! Klokov's not my teacher, he's my boss, and if he wants to he can kill me! Why didn't you just tell me to talk to Klokov instead of doing it for me?"

She held her head in her hands. "You're right, I wasn't thinking."

"No, you weren't! I'm in a street gang that beats kids for not being manly enough, and now they all think I'm a Mama's Boy!" He stormed off to his room and slammed the door.

***

An hour later, Pasha lay on his bed with the door cracked. He had an icepack plastered to his abdomen, and a tissue stuffed up his bleeding nostril. Every time he thought he heard his mother's footsteps nearing the door, he tensed. He couldn't bear the idea of speaking with her just yet. She may have meant well but the consequences of her actions frightened him. He was lucky he didn't have to go to the hospital!

The memory of Anastas flicking open his pocketknife flashed through Pasha's mind. What had he been planning to do with it? Pasha's stomach turned. Who knows what would have happened if Liebowitz hadn't shown up!

Pasha winced. He could feel the skin around his bruises growing stiffer. But he could hardly feel sorry for himself, because whatever he was going through, it was nothing compared to what Faina was having to put up with. He sighed and looked out at her window. The bottle he had left on the fire escape was now empty. How much time had passed since she'd received his message? Enough time to write a response? Was it possible she was ignoring him?

There was a knock at the front door. Pasha listened as his mother crossed the kitchen and removed the latch.

"Yes?"

"Lydia, I know you're upset with me. I've come to apologize."

Pasha sat up, the icepack sliding to the floor. It was Matvei!

"Please, come in and sit down. You don't have to stand there."

Pasha yanked the tissue out of his nose—it had stopped bleeding anyway—and tiptoed to the doorway, straining his ear.

"One of Anastas's brothers came and told me everything," he heard Uncle Matvei say. "He even gave me the negative of the photograph so the boys can't make any more copies. You were right. Pasha and Faina are innocent. They didn't do anything. I said so many awful things to you, and so many awful things about your boy. Can you ever forgive me?"

Pasha raised his eyebrows. So she had gone to bat for him. She had said she was going to talk to Matvei, but Pasha had never really thought about what she would say. He shoved his hands in his pockets, regretting that he had yelled at her.

There was a pause in which Pasha could imagine his mother reaching out and placing her hand on Matvei's.

"Of course!"

Cautiously, Pasha stepped out into the passage. At the sound of his footsteps, Matvei turned around in his seat.

"Pasha!" Matvei's eyes darted from injury to injury. "My word! What happened?!"

Pasha bowed his head. He was still finding it difficult to look Matvei in the eye. "I got jumped. It's a long story." He fidgeted with his sleeve. "Alexei told you everything?" He was sure it wasn't Vadim.

Matvei nodded. "I've done you a great disservice. After all you've done for my family. Splitting your earnings with Faina—"

"Faina earns that money—"

"That is neither here nor there. I am so sorry. I should have trusted you. I know you, after all. I know you to be responsible, respectful, kind, and mature. I should have known better than to accuse you. Can you ever forgive me?"

At last, Pasha was able to look him in the eye. "Of course I forgive you, Uncle Matvei. I'm just sorry that I was gullible enough to fall for Anastas's trap."

Uncle Matvei waved his hand. "I don't know that anyone could have foreseen what would happen. Anastas is quite a troubled soul. Don't beat yourself up about it."

Pasha took another tentative step forward. "Um, so does that mean I can still see Faina?"

Uncle Matvei chuckled and nodded his head towards the door. "You can see her now, if you like. Goodness knows she's dying to see you."

Without meaning to, Pasha grinned. "Right now?"

"Go right ahead."

Pasha moved towards the door, then, remembering his mother, turned back to kiss her cheek. He bolted out of the apartment to the Dalkas' residence. So eager was he that he banged more than knocked on the door. It took a minute, but soon Faina was peering timidly through the gap.

"Pasha!"

Her fingers flew to unlatch the lock. The door swung wide. Pasha threw his arms around her, pressing her into his chest, and covering the crown of her head in kisses.

"*Moya Faya!*" My *Faya*, he crooned gently. "Baby, I'm so, so sorry! This is all my fault! Are you okay? Are you doing alright? I can't imagine what all you must be going through."

"Me?" Faina wriggled free, taking in his battered appearance. "Sweetheart, what happened?" She cupped his cheek, fingering the tender bruises along his skin. "You look like you just narrowly escaped being murdered!"

Pasha had been so excited to see her, he'd completely forgotten about his appearance. Surely, he must have looked a fright.

"Yeah. I, uh … I was jumped coming home."

"Jumped? By who?"

Pasha gave a brief summary of what had happened with his mother, how his attackers had surprised him as he was making his way back from the Foxhole.

"*Patulya!*" Moved by pity, Faina circled her arms around his waist, grabbing him in a tight embrace, pressing into the place where he had been kicked. Pasha flinched and gave an anguished groan.

"Sorry!" She edged back. "I didn't mean to hurt you." She placed a hand over his side where his shirt was sticking out, gently lifting the material so she could examine the injury. Surprised, Pasha stiffened, unsure of how to react. At the sight of the puffy, yellowing bruise along his abdomen, Faina gave a cry.

"*Blin!* They could have ruptured your organs!" She ran her finger along the tender skin, prompting goosebumps to rise along his flesh.

Pasha stepped back. Faina dropped her hand, blushing in embarrassment.

"Sorry. Ticklish," he lied. Eager to move on, he cleared his throat. "I'm fine. Really." He reached out to her, running his fingers along a wavy lock of hair and smoothing it over her shoulder. "It's you I'm worried about."

Faina cast her eyes down and turned away. "It's too bad I stopped my education. Boarding school sounds like a paradise right about now."

"But then we'd be apart." He slipped his arms around her waist, hugging her from behind and burying his face in her neck. "I don't want you to go away."

"I wasn't serious. Besides, we could never afford it."

He pressed his lips along her shoulder. "Well, we're together now. I'm not going anywhere. Whatever else happens I'll be right here beside you to support you."

Faina turned just as he was moving to kiss her cheek. "Thieves' honor?"

He kissed the tip of her nose. "Thieves' honor."

Chapter 41:

Discipline

By the time Staccato reached the Floodgates, he had never been more travel-weary. It had taken him four gateways, all a considerable distance apart from each other, just to reach Aries. And did it end there? No. From Aries, he had boarded a boat to Pisces and, after consuming copious amounts of mermaid's breath, he had leapt from the bow straight into the ocean. Needless to say, it was a good thing his luggage was waterproof. His clothes, however, were not, but he made plans to change once he reached land. Beneath the surface, he met Calliope, who escorted him to a secret gateway twenty miles outside of his destination where his pegasus Lancelot awaited him. It was all Staccato could do to keep his head up during the ride. Never had he been more relieved to see the caravan in all its gaudy, oversized glory … that is, until he saw the smoke.

Black clouds billowed from the side of the barn where a fire had recently burned. Acrid odors of burnt wood and singed hay stained the air. The moment Lancelot's hooves touched the ground, Staccato dismounted and stared in horror across the field.

"Staccato! Staccato!"

Melodious ran towards him. As he neared, Staccato was shocked to find tears running down his face. His stomach lurched.

"What is it? Is anyone hurt?"

Melodious ground to a halt and dabbed at his eyes with a handkerchief. "You have got to make them stop! I cannot take it one more day! It is too awful!"

"Make who stop?"

"Pyro and Sonata! All day, all night they say the most horrible things to one another! My heart cannot endure any more!"

Staccato's eyes glazed over with one long, seething exhale. "Are they responsible for that?" He jabbed his finger at the smoldering barn.

"It was an accident. Pyro went to get a bucket from the barn, and Sonata was there tending to Scheherazade. They started bickering, and Pyro was standing next to the propane for the tractor and—"

Staccato held up his hand. "Where are they?"

Melodious said no more but pointed towards the caravan. It was parked beneath a tree. The side door had been left open, and now swayed lazily in the breeze. A path of singed grass wound about to the other side. Staccato plowed forward, his head bent like a hawk diving for prey, and his eyes burning. Drawing closer, he could hear Pyro and Sonata's impassioned arguing growing louder. He rounded the corner of the caravan.

Sonata and Pyro were standing so close to each other that under normal circumstances they would've looked as though they were about to kiss. Pyro was completely drenched. Wet clothes were plastered to his skin, and white steam was rising off his shoulders. A discarded bucket rolled at Sonata's heels. A pair of chairs lay discarded in the grass alongside a folding table which had been overturned. So engrossed were they in their argument, they didn't even notice Staccato standing there.

"You selfish, insolent—" Sonata was practically screaming.

"I'm selfish?! I'm selfish?!" Pyro speared his finger at her nose. "Do you realize how entitled—"

"ENOUGH!!!" Birds flew from their trees as Staccato's voice boomed across the valley with a level of rage any of them had yet to witness. Light flickered from the head of his staff. A great surge of energy poured from his body, bending the grass at his feet, and blowing Pyro's and Sonata's hair back.

In an uncharacteristic moment of foolishness, Sonata hissed to Pyro, "Now you're in trouble!"

The whites of Staccato's eyes flashed like gleaming swords as he turned on his goddaughter. "I SAID ENOUGH!"

369

With the barest gesture of his staff, the chairs flew towards Pyro and Sonata, and they were forced to sit like two naughty children beneath Staccato's volcanic glower.

"I could not have made myself clearer when I told you what I expected of you. It was your responsibility to lead in my absence. I depended on you! Both of you! Never have I been more disappointed! I've half a mind to send you both packing!"

Pyro raised a timid finger. "I know what it looks like, but you weren't here the whole—"

"The barn is on fire!"

"Actually, we put out the fire, it's just smo—"

"THE BARN IS ON FIRE!"

Pyro jumped and clutched at his seat.

Staccato's nostrils flared. "And you made the Reverend cry!"

"We made Melodious cry?" Sonata was too afraid to look him in the eye.

"Yes! You did!"

For a brief moment, Pyro and Sonata glanced at each other, their eyes filled with regret. It took some time, but Sonata finally managed to speak up.

"You're right to be disappointed in us. And I'm so sorry we let you down."

"Yeah …" agreed Pyro, his head bowed. "I'm sorry too. You were counting on us, and we got carried away."

Too angry to relent yet, Staccato could only stare at them. At last, he managed to reply, "Good. I'm glad you're sorry. You should be!"

"If you aren't going to fire us, may I ask …" Sonata stopped and winced, "… what our punishment will be?"

Staccato's furious countenance cooled into something sinister and much more unnerving. He turned away from them and examined the head of his staff, enjoying the effect he was having on them. He was rather good at doling out punishments. Too good. And they all knew it.

"I shall have to give it some thought. It may take a while."

Pyro couldn't help himself. "How long?"

"Oh, never you mind, Pyro. You'll know it when it happens."

Chapter 42:

The Star Catcher

"He still wants me to sing?" Faina gaped incredulously at Pasha from across the register. Uncle Matvei was leaning against the wall biting his finger.

"Only if you want to." Pasha twisted the loose end of the bandage on his arm. He would be in pretty bad shape for a while. Faina looked questioningly at Uncle Matvei but he said nothing.

"Well …" She shook her head and went back to wiping down the counter. "I can't."

Pasha raised his eyebrows. "Can't or won't?"

"If I get up there and sing, it's only gonna make things worse." Faina sprayed the counter with a bottle of solution. "It's best I stay out of the spotlight. Not just for me but for my family."

Uncle Matvei opened his mouth to say something but Pasha cut him off.

"Faina, are you sure you don't want to think about this for a while?"

Faina paused. She set aside the solution and stared down at her shoes. "I gotta change, Pasha. I mean, look where I've gotten myself." She hooked a hair behind her ear. "None of this would have happened in the first place if I hadn't been so wild."

She could see by the way he was staring at her that she wasn't getting through.

"What I mean to say is … I think maybe I need to rein myself in a little."

Pasha, always intuitive where his loved ones were concerned, was quick to point out the deeper issue behind her words.

"Sounds to me like you want to be something you're not."

Faina threw down the rag, frustrated. "No, not at all! I just want to be content with less … I want to be content with being quiet."

Pasha did not say he would tell Klokov her answer, but he kissed her goodbye and left. Faina hung the rag back on the hook and seated herself on the stool again, burying her nose in a book. When she realized Uncle Matvei was staring at her, she looked up and forced a smile.

"Was there anything else you needed me to do?"

Uncle Matvei scratched his chin. His brow was somewhat furrowed.

"*Nyet*. Er—" He waved his hand. "You can take this grocery order up to Aunt Poppy if you like, but only if you want to. Otherwise I can do it myself."

Faina hopped off the stool and scooped the bag up in her arms. "I'd be happy to pay Aunt Poppy a visit."

Faina made her way upstairs through the cramped hallway. At the top of the landing she stopped and covered her eyes, trying to catch her breath. The stress of everything that had taken place was beginning to manifest in her body. She hadn't felt truly ill since her tonsils had been removed, but she was often plagued with anxiety, and suffered from headaches on occasion. What's more, she had skipped her period, though she pretended to be on it anyway lest Anya suspect she was pregnant, which of course was impossible considering she was a virgin. She looked up again and sighed. She had forgiven Anya for her behavior but she wasn't sure she would ever really trust her again. Striving to maintain an even breath, Faina hoisted the bag higher and made her way down the passage to Aunt Poppy's door.

Faina gave a knock. "Aunt Poppy? It's me, Faina! I have your groceries!"

"Come in, darling!"

Faina turned the knob and pushed open the door. Aunt Poppy was seated in an armchair before the window, a heavy, midnight-colored blanket draped in her lap. A red pincushion sat on the arm with several needles sticking out in different directions.

"What are you up to today?"

Aunt Poppy dipped her aged fingers into a tall jar of tiny, silver beads.

"Oh, just sewing dreams into this blanket for a friend of mine. She has been suffering from nightmares."

Faina's eyebrows stretched. "Oh." She set the groceries down on the table and looked over her shoulder. "How creative!"

Aunt Poppy shook her head and beckoned for her to come sit. "I would say it is more tedious than fun. But some company will help to pass the time! I would so enjoy it if you would sing for me."

Faina hesitated and lowered herself into the chair. "Oh, Aunt Poppy, I don't know if I feel like singing just now."

"Not now? Then when? It has been some time since I have heard you sing."

Faina's eyes darted about the room, eager to change the subject. "I don't know. Maybe later."

"And by later you mean never!" She tucked the needle into the blanket and set it aside. "You needn't be so coy with me, my dear. I know all about what happened."

The sting of shame twisted like a knife in Faina's chest until her knees felt weak.

"Of course you do! The whole of New York knows!" Remembering that Pasha had also been caught in the picture, Faina covered her face and turned away.

Aunt Poppy reached out and rested her hand on Faina's shoulder. "Don't you be embarrassed in front of me, darling. You dare think I would judge you?"

Faina dug her fingers into her skin as she felt the tears flooding her eyes. "Well, it looks pretty bad, doesn't it?"

Aunt Poppy chuckled. "Do I look like the sort of woman who believes everything she sees? I know you, and I know Pasha, and I know that boy! That Nasty-as, or Ana-nasty, whatever his name is! Something Nasty!"

Faina peeked out from behind her hands and giggled, unable to help herself. Aunt Poppy took her hand and squeezed it.

"You can't let him take away your happiness like that!"

Faina sighed and wiped away her tears with the back of her hand. "I don't know, Aunt Poppy. Do you ever … do you ever feel like sometimes you'll never be happy again?"

Aunt Poppy looked as though she had suggested something truly astonishing. "Never be happy again?" She leaned back and shuffled, as though the very thought made her uncomfortable. "No! I could never accept that! And neither should you!" She leaned forward and cupped Faina's cheek with her hand, wiping away a tear. "You are too smart, and too talented a girl to think like that! You have big things in your future, my darling. You were meant to do something truly great!" She stomped her foot. "Don't you let that Nasty boy win!"

Faina laughed again. "Thank you, Aunt Poppy."

"Let me tell you a story." She smoothed her hand across the blanket, her wizened fingers filing through the silver beads that looked like stars. "Long ago, in a time few can remember, there were no stars in the night sky. The sun would set, and the world would grow dark and cold.

"The night sky—a beautiful, angelic woman—saw the creatures suffering down below. She watched them hiding away in the shadows, sad, frightened, unable to see the beauty that only blossomed after sunset. They knew nothing of the owls in the trees, or the moths floating on the breeze. It pained her that they could not see what she could. It pained her to watch their suffering. And with this pain came silver tears … the first stars!

"'Perhaps I can use this to bring light to the people down below,' thought the night sky. And so she continued to cry, catching the tears and braiding them into her dense, black hair. Soon the night sky began to shine, and the creatures below were no longer in darkness. Whenever people cried, the night sky would collect their tears, and as they slept she would braid them into her hair, determined that every tear should be used for a purpose. Not a single sorrow would be wasted, and would, in fact, be used for good.'"

Her voice was full of wonder as she leaned in and smoothed a lock of Faina's raven hair over her shoulder.

"My dear, when I see you, I am reminded of the night sky in the story. So young, and yet you have lived a life few could imagine. There is much pain in your past, it is true. And yet you have not wasted any of it."

"I haven't?"

"Do you think there are many people who would bother showing kindness to an old woman like me?" She waved her hand. "It is your pain that allowed you to show kindness to the Nasty boy, to befriend him when no else would, to give him grace when he deserved none. It was your pain that helped you make Pasha feel at home in New York City. It is what has brought the two of you together in love: the ability to share your sorrows and empathize. It has made you bold, compassionate, and rare, and you are better for it. Darling, you bring light to everyone you touch. Do not let these boys dim your light. People need to hear your song!"

Faina sniffed and choked on a sob, but these were no longer tears of hurt; they were tears of gratitude and strength. She threw her arms around Aunt Poppy and hugged her close.

Chapter 43:

The Last of the Red Hot Mamas

That evening, when Faina had finished making supper, she went downstairs to fetch Uncle Matvei. *Opa!* had just closed, and as usual the storefront was empty. She expected to find him standing at the register counting out change, but no one was there.

"Uncle Matvei?" As she poked her head around the aisles, her ear picked up the strains of a female voice leaking from the back room.

"*I'll never forget it, you know ...*"

She tiptoed down the hall towards Uncle Matvei's room.

"*I says one night to my boyfriend, Ernie, I says Ern ...*"

She peered around the door. Uncle Matvei was on his knees in front of his bed, pouring through an old magazine on the floor.

"Uncle Matvei? Is that Leo's old Sophie Tucker album you confiscated when he was sixteen?"

Uncle Matvei jumped, flinging the magazine in the air. "Faina!"

He scrambled towards the record player just as Sophie was telling the punchline of her shockingly dirty joke. Faina gasped and threw a hand over her mouth.

"That was a really bad one!"

Uncle Matvei removed the needle and shoved the record back into its sleeve.

"Faina, darling, we need to talk. There's a reason I'm listening to Leo's old record." He got up and motioned for her to sit down on the bed.

"Faina, I want you take Klokov up on his offer and sing at the restaurant."

Faina looked askance. "But Uncle Matvei, I can't sing in front of all those people! Not after what happened! What will people say?"

"Never mind what they say!" He rubbed his large, knobby hands over his eyes and sighed. "My sweet one, I am worried I may have given you the wrong impression of what I expect from you in this family. What you said to Pasha concerns me. Sweetie, I don't want you to change." He threw up his hands. "And change into what? What did you mean when you told Pasha you needed to change?"

Faina rolled her head forward and massaged her fingers. "Well, I'm wild, and loud, and intense. I come on too strong and scare people off with my emotions. I should be thoughtful and reserved. Stop drawing so much attention to myself. Like Anya!"

"Honey, I don't want you to be like Anya. I want you to be like you."

"But look where that's gotten me! Look at what that's done to our family! Don't you want me to change?"

Uncle Matvei sat down beside her on the mattress and took her face in his hands.

"Darling, I wouldn't change a hair on your head! Never in a million years! I love you just the way you are! And the best thing you can do for this family is be yourself. Be kind, be funny, be loud and wild! Be you! There is nothing wrong with the way you are. As for what happened at the restaurant …" He shrugged. "You didn't do anything wrong. People may think you did, but that doesn't mean you have to go around pretending like what they believe is true."

Faina got up, her face contorted in an uncomprehending expression. She crossed her arms over her chest and stared at the wall.

"But I still don't understand. I'm supposed to just go up there and pretend like nothing happened?"

"Not exactly. That's not how you are. The Faina I know is honest about everything, even when it makes other people uncomfortable. It's a strength that I believe we should take advantage of."

"What do you mean?"

"When Mama Lydia was in the store the other day and made a comment on that deformed looking carrot. What did you say?"

"I told her it looked pornographic."

"Precisely! You made a joke about it!"

"I wasn't joking! I was just saying what you two were thinking! Anyway, you told me not to say stuff like that!"

"Even though I did laugh."

A glimmer of pride came into her features. "You did laugh."

"My point is, Faina, you have a way of dealing with controversial topics that makes them more approachable. You use your sense of humor to diffuse tension. That's what comedians do!" He flipped open the magazine he had been looking at to an article about Sophie Tucker. "Did you know when Sophie Tucker first started her comedy routines in Vaudeville the producers didn't want her because they thought she was too overweight? So Sophie Tucker incorporated her weight into her routine. Not only that, but she turned it into a positive!"

"You mean like when she performed the song 'Nobody Loves a Fat Girl, But Oh How a Fat Girl Can Love'?"

"Exactly! She rose above her critics! She took the cruel things people were saying about her, and she used it to create something good! It's true that if you go up there you are bound to raise a few eyebrows, so rather than pretend like it didn't happen, what if you acknowledged it? Made a few jokes about it like you do at home? Do a comedy routine between songs! Not everyone is gonna appreciate it, of course, but I think there are many who would enjoy something like that." He stood and faced her, placing his arms on her shoulders. "The important thing is, my darling, that you get back up and fight. Don't let them think they've won. Don't give them the satisfaction."

Faina tried to imagine what Uncle Matvei was describing. She saw herself going up on stage, introducing herself, and cracking a few jokes before her opening number. She thought of Sophie Tucker, and wondered what "the Last of the Red Hot Mamas" would think about Faina's predicament. An amused sort of smile formed in the corner of her mouth.

"You know something, Uncle Matvei? I think I like that idea!"

Chapter 44:

The American Gulag

When Pasha limped into the Foxhole Monday evening and laid his goods on the trading table, Klokov took one look at him and dropped his pen.

"What happened to you?"

Pasha scratched at the tightening skin around his eye. "I don't wanna talk about it."

Klokov stared at him for a moment, then nodded. He seemed to understand perfectly. It'd been a miserable day for Pasha. Faina had tried to help him thieve, but things went south when a lady on Grand Street recognized her from her picture and started pointing and whispering. Then when he'd taken her home, he'd tried to kiss her in the privacy of her room but Faina drew away and started sobbing. It was as though he were tainted. He was afraid to breathe on her the wrong way.

Klokov counted out Pasha's pay and dismissed him for the evening. Before he left, Pasha stopped to check the roster. Underneath the day's heading was the name "Rail Runner." For a moment, Pasha brightened a little. So Yuri had returned and would be fighting that evening. Perhaps he should stick around and catch up with his old friend. As he passed the bar, Anastas propped his leg up on the opposite chair, blocking Pasha's path.

"How's that black eye healing up, Chevalsky? Your mommy put some ice on it?"

Pasha's chest pounded with hatred. It was becoming more and more difficult to ignore Anastas these days.

"Move."

"Ah-ah. What's the magic word?"

Pasha narrowed his eyes. A flare ignited somewhere deep within him. "The magic word?" Pasha kicked Anastas's chair out from under him with a declaration so foul his mother would've cut his tongue out had she heard him. "Is that the magic word?"

The entire Foxhole went quiet, but Pasha didn't balk beneath their stares. Anastas stayed down on the floor, too stunned to react. Trifecta quickly stepped in and put his arm around Pasha.

"Alright! Hey! Nothing to see here!" He ushered Pasha to a table in the corner where Sergei, Moneyrider, and the Savage were sitting. "What's gotten into you, huh?"

Pasha rolled his eyes. "What? Aren't I acting normal for a Breadwinner?"

Trifecta pulled out a chair and made him sit.

"Hey, Pasha," started Sergei. "What happened to your face?"

"What do you think happened to my face?!"

"Alright, alright!" Trifecta held up his hand. "Ditch the attitude. You ain't got nothing to prove to us."

Pasha cradled his head in his hand and stared down at the table. "I was jumped, alright? That's all I wanna say about it."

They all exchanged knowing looks.

"So it was Joe, Anastas, and Steed then," said Moneyrider.

Pasha flashed him a look.

"Don't worry!" He held up his hands in defense. "We ain't gonna say nothing."

The Savage took a swig from his beer. "We knew that was gonna happen after your ma came in."

"They have a nickname for her now, you know. They call her the Alpha-Mare."

"I don't wanna talk about my ma," hissed Pasha through gritted teeth. Overhead, the bell rang and Klokov ascended the podium.

"Uh-oh." Moneyrider lit a cigarette. "Looks like Mishkin's up against Stan."

"When did he get back?" asked Pasha.

Trifecta held out his cigarette for Moneyrider to light. "Uh, two days ago I think." He was oddly stiff when he said it, and Pasha couldn't help but feel he was holding something back.

An unfamiliar figure stepped into the ring. He was a slight, emaciated-looking boy with his head shaved down, and a grayish tone to his skin.

Pasha turned in his chair. "Who is that?"

On the other side of the platform, Stan made his way up the steps. Pasha looked back at the roster, confused. "Where's Yuri?"

Klokov gestured to the unfamiliar boy as he roared over the crowd. "… As we welcome back an old favorite, Rail Runner!"

Pasha's mouth dropped open. Yuri was completely unrecognizable. He looked as though he'd spent the summer in a labor camp. The boys around the table fell silent, their lips pressed tightly together. Pasha lowered his eyebrows.

"You all told me he was upstate visiting relatives."

No one said a thing but stared awkwardly down at their feet. Angered, Pasha pounded his fist on the table, causing their beer bottles to shake.

"What happened?! Why aren't you telling me the truth?"

Trifecta took a drag on his cigarette, still not making eye contact with Pasha. "We were afraid it would upset you too much."

"Yeah," agreed the Savage. "We didn't want a repeat of the shootout."

Sergei looked up at him apologetically. "We were just looking out for you. We know how emotional you can get, and we didn't want Klokov to think you were weak."

Pasha's nostrils flared. "For the last time, what happened to Yuri?"

Trifecta sighed. "Yuri was sent upstate for what Klokov likes to call 'rehabilitation.'"

Pasha knit his eyebrows. "Rehabilitation?"

"It's when they take kids who ain't meeting expectations and try to retrain them into tougher soldiers."

Pasha gaped at them uncomprehendingly. Sergei cleared his throat and looked down at his hands.

"It's a gulag, Pasha."

"Or at least, it's meant to mimic one." Trifecta dabbed the end of his cigarette into the ashtray. "Got his own little arrangement up north."

"What do they do to them?" Pasha's voice was almost a whisper.

"Hard labor mostly. You see his new 'do there? They shave your head so they can strip you of your identity. Take away your feelings, your emotions. Make you into a killing machine. And you don't exactly get three square meals a day either."

Pasha turned and looked at Yuri again. Yuri had been scrawny to begin with. Now he looked sick.

"But I don't understand. What did Yuri do to get sent there in the first place?"

"Klokov wasn't too happy with Yuri's little breakdown after the incident down by the docks. And he was angry that he let the Butcher kid go."

"The Butcher kid? What did Klokov want with him?"

"He wanted information. All the others had gotten away by then."

Gunshots echoed through Pasha's mind as the night of June twenty-sixth flooded back to his memory.

Don't do it ... Just don't do it, Yuri, Pasha had implored him as Yuri pointed the barrel at the Butcher. A chill ran down his spine as he recalled Yuri's bestial voice ordering the kid to get out.

"But—that kid was hardly sixteen! No different than any of us! He was just following orders, same as us."

"Careful, kid." The Savage leaned back in his chair. "It's that kinda thinking that gets you sent upstate."

Pasha put a hand to his forehead. His fingers were shaking. Sergei leaned forward.

"Pasha? You gonna be alright?"

Pasha swallowed and tried to smooth his hair back, but the twitching in his fingers was getting worse. Trifecta moved forward with a sense of urgency.

"Woah, woah." He shoved his flask into Pasha's hand. "Here, take a swig of this before you keel over."

Pasha tried unscrewing the cap but his hands were trembling to such a degree, Trifecta had to do it for him. Pasha winced and downed the bitter-tasting liquid, shuddering in the process.

"You really need to start drinking whiskey more often."

Pasha handed him back the flask and rose. "I gotta go."

Pasha barreled out the door and sprinted down the Bowery. When he reached the halfway point, his head began to spin. Pasha stopped and dug his heels into the ground. He turned into an alley and leaned up against a wall. He wasn't about to let himself faint again. He braced his head and felt his temples throbbing. He was beginning to wish he'd had more whiskey. It was always the first thing anyone shoved in his face when he was having a panic attack. Maybe there was something to it.

As he stood there waiting for the dizziness to subside, he felt the tears coming on. Pasha ground his teeth together and clenched his fist. He'd heard what happened to Yuri. Did he want the same fate? If someone as tough and as aggressive as Yuri could wind up in a gulag for not being manly enough, then what chance did Pasha stand? Never mind sending

Pasha away, they'd kill him! He had to be merciless, unfeeling, tough enough to do what others could not. His hands began to shake again.

But how? I can't just stop feeling! He thought to himself. *What's wrong with me? Other men aren't like this!* He squeezed his eyes shut. *You're just gonna have to suck it up and be a man!*

Pasha felt a whimper in his throat. In a desperate attempt to distract himself from the turmoil raging inside him, he pinched his bruised hand until he cried out. Pasha stared at the mottled, purple flesh and sighed with relief. As he stood there allowing the tight skin to throb beneath his touch, an unwanted thought rose to his consciousness.

Faina shouldn't be involved in all this.

His stomach dropped. There wasn't enough strength in him to consider such a thing. Not now. Hadn't he been through enough? He diverted his attention to a couple walking their dog down the street.

Faina shouldn't be involved in all this, repeated the voice.

Pasha ground his teeth together as he argued with the voice inside his head. *Faina's not the one working for the Breadwinners, I am! She'll be fine!*

And before his conscience could get the final word in, he turned and ran the rest of the way home.

Chapter 45:

Chevalsky Snaps

September drew away like a breath, leaving behind a world of orange and black in its wake. For several weeks Pasha had remained withdrawn and quiet. He slept often, and yet he never felt truly rested. His mind was starved for a reverie. In his misery his dreams had become thin, parched things, offering no more satisfaction than a dried-up soup bone.

He clung to Faina like a spider stranded on a buoy, never saying much but hungering after her affection. Presently, she sat cross-legged on her bed behind him, a pin sticking from the corner of her mouth as she sewed beads onto a pair of butterfly wings for Trifecta's birthday party Halloween night.

"Just two more stitches here … there!" She plucked the pin from her mouth and swept the wings around her shoulders. "What do you think?" She got up from the bed and posed coquettishly before the looking glass.

Pasha looked up at her, squinting through his swollen eye. Weeks had passed since his run-in with Anastas and the others, and the injuries they had inflicted had more or less healed. But he'd lost several street fights as of late, resulting in a black eye, a three-inch gash mottled with black and yellow above his right eyebrow, broken blood vessels in his forehead, and a bad limp. Given his misfortunes as of late, he had not been able to maintain his top-five ranking this quarter, and had dropped down to twelfth place. Pasha offered her a reserved smile.

"Cute."

It was an understated compliment that would never satisfy Faina, and he knew it. Predictably, she dropped her hands down by her hips in disappointment.

"Cute?" She sank to her knees beside him. "Just cute?" She crawled into his lap, wrapping her arms around his neck. "Not devastatingly gorgeous?"

Pasha couldn't help but chuckle. "Alright—"

"Not breathtaking?" She dragged her fingers down his sides, tickling him until he was forced to laugh.

"Hey! Cut it—ow! Sweetie? Sweetie! You're digging into my bruise!"

Faina hastily rolled off his lap as Pasha dropped his head back against the side of the mattress with a pained sigh.

"I'm sorry." Her voice was timid and small. Pasha felt her fingers tracing the height of his cheekbone. He opened his good eye and softened.

"You look like a fairytale princess," he at last conceded.

Faina laid her head on his shoulder. "Have you decided what you're going as yet?"

Pasha sighed and stared at the opposite wall. He didn't want to go at all, and was half entertaining the idea of feigning illness the night of the party to avoid disappointing Faina.

"Don't you wanna wait for things to die down a little more?"

Faina shrugged. "It's been at least a month since the incident. I can't hide forever."

"When are you supposed to sing at the Foxhole again?"

"Not until the week before Thanksgiving."

"Why don't you wait until then?"

Faina made a face. "And not go out for two whole months? Besides, you know me, I never miss a costume party."

Pasha dropped his hands by his side. "I can't imagine Dmitry will be happy to see us."

Trifecta's party was to be held at the Vavilov's drugstore. Though Dmitry did not know Trifecta particularly well, he was good friends with several of the younger street fighters who were throwing the party, and had graciously agreed to host.

"Oh, now don't be like that. Dmitry and I parted amicably. And he has nothing against you. As far as the business with the photograph, he knows how Anastas is, and he knows how I am. He knows we were set up."

They sat in silence for some time, Pasha continuing to stare at the wall, while Faina ran her fingers through his hair.

"I wish you'd tell me what's wrong."

Pasha's voice and expression went completely monotone. "Nothing is wrong."

"That's not true." She caressed a bruise. "Klokov shouldn't make you fight today in the state you're in."

"I said I'm fine!"

Faina drew back in surprise. Inwardly, Pasha cringed. He hadn't meant to sound cross with her, it just flew out. A patch of inflamed skin drew Faina's attention to his arm. Before he could stop her she was pushing back his sleeve. It looked as though he'd laid his arm in a nest of hornets.

"Pasha, what on earth?"

Pasha hastily drew back and pulled his sleeve down. "*Nichego.*" It's nothing. "I'm fine."

"Did you get stung by bees?"

Pasha stammered and shook his head, searching for an explanation.

"Have you been picking your skin?" she persisted.

"I don't mean to do it." He stared down at the floor and turned away. "I don't wanna talk about it."

Faina reached out to put her arms around him. "Baby, I can't just ignore it!"

390

But Pasha drew away from her, bringing his injured arm close to his chest. "It was an accident, alright? It's not like I'm doing it on purpose! It just happens! You know, like biting your nails."

There was a long silence in which Pasha sat cradling his head. Faina rubbed her hands over his shoulders.

"You're stressed. You need a rest. *The Thief of Bagdad* is playing this week. Maybe we could go Friday night."

"I'm not sure I feel like it."

"Okay then. How about we go out to eat?"

"No."

"Walk on the Pier?"

"No."

Faina paused. Pasha could sense a fight coming on; it was his own fault. Faina wasn't about to back down just because he had given her a bunch of petulant one-word answers without explanation, no matter how badly he wanted her to.

"Well, how about we order Chinese takeout and stay home? We can do my place."

Pasha raised his eyebrows. That was exactly what he wanted. He pictured the two of them half-asleep and snuggled beneath a quilt, Chinese takeout boxes scattered across the floor. Rain sluiced down his bedroom window, lulling them to sleep, while the taste of sweet-and-sour sauce stained their tongues. And there would be no Klokov, no cops, no missing posters of Pearl Sulzbach, no reminders of his bleak future as a two-bit hood with a gun shoved in his waistband.

"That would be perfect."

To his surprise, Faina didn't mutter or sulk but hugged him from behind, laying her cheek between his shoulder blades.

"That sounds more restful, doesn't it? You need to let that leg heal anyway." She released him and, climbing back on the bed, returned to her sewing. "And then we can plan what you're gonna wear to the party!"

A kaleidoscope of garish colors and loud, brash music paraded through Pasha's mind like an invasion of clowns. He saw the other Breadwinners snickering, pointing, and teasing, pouring beer on each other, and spitting tobacco on the floor.

"Enough about the party, Faina! I'm not going!" Pasha's voice bounced off the walls and echoed back at him, shocking him out of his impassioned state. Mammoth, who had been sleeping in the corner, lifted his head to stare at him. Pasha turned and looked at Faina. She dropped her sewing needle on the mattress. Pasha passed a hand over his face.

"Faina—"

"Did you hear yourself just now?"

Pasha slowly rose to his feet. "I know, I'm—"

"Because I'm pretty sure everyone else in the building just did!" She jumped off the bed, standing on her toes in an attempt to meet his gaze. She probably didn't even realize she was doing it.

"Faina, I'm sorry, I don't know where that—"

But Pasha knew Faina wasn't stopping. He'd lit the candle and there was nothing to do but let her burn.

"What is wrong with you? You act like a totally different person! You're completely deadpan all the time! You're cold, you're sulky, and you won't tell me anything anymore! You act angry whenever I ask about the Breadwinners, or your injuries—"

"Because I don't wanna talk about it! And I tell you I don't wanna talk about it but you keep pushing!"

"You can't expect me not to care when you're hurt!"

"I keep telling you I'm fine! If I tell you I'm fine then you don't need to be concerned! Besides, I'm not gonna sit here and whine and cry about it!"

"Because you're too tough for that now. Is that it?"

Pasha froze with a silence that rang like a million decibels. "I'm a Breadwinner, Faina," he finally managed to get out. "This is how I am. I'm a thug."

Faina stared at him unimpressed for a moment or two before answering quietly. "No, you're not."

Pasha didn't know what else to say. He sat down on the bed, leaning over his knees. Faina looked hard at him, as though forcing herself to say something she was afraid of.

"Do you even want me anymore?"

"Of course I want you! I love you!"

"You never wanna do anything with me!"

"Well, why we always gotta do stuff? Don't you get sick of being around people all the time?"

"Are you ashamed of me?" Tears spilled from her eyes. "Is that it? You're too embarrassed to be seen with the neighborhood slut?" She wrenched away from him.

Pasha seized her by the hand. "*Nyet, Radnaya!*"

Faina whipped her head around. It was a word for which there was no English translation. My blood, or perhaps, my soul were the only definitions which came close. Though it described a family bond, it was not a phrase one used to address family members. Rather, it was an expression which meant "you are the one I am closest to, closer than my own blood." It was by no means a casual declaration, and Pasha hadn't meant for it to be.

393

"*Radnaya*," he repeated, pulling her in until he had his arms about her waist, and his cheek resting against her stomach. "I love you, *Faya*." He nuzzled his nose against the fabric of her dress.

Faina raked her fingers through his hair, pinning him closer. "Thieves' Honor?"

He kissed her abdomen and towed her into his lap. "Thieves' Honor."

She placed her hands on both of his cheeks, her gaze falling to his mouth. "*Radnoy*," she whispered the words between his lips. They remained tangled for some time, kissing and listening to each other breathe, and would've stayed like that for the rest of the evening had Pasha not been scheduled to fight.

"I'll come with you," she insisted when Pasha got up to leave. She grabbed her purse just as he was headed out her bedroom door.

Pasha paused at the threshold and shut his eyes with a barely perceptible exhale. The last thing he desired was another fight. Faina had not been inside the Foxhole since the incident. She may have been scheduled to sing at the restaurant, but Pasha no longer wanted her downstairs watching his fights where the crowds were rough, and the majority of the room was inebriated. Someone was bound to shoot their mouth off and hurt her feelings.

"Faina, I'd really rather you not come watch me fight this evening."

Faina tensed but refrained from any outbursts. "Why not?"

Pasha opened his mouth to answer but paused and scratched his neck instead. "I just—I'd rather not linger, okay?"

Apparently, this was the wrong way to go about it, for any symptoms of defense vanished on the spot, and she picked up her purse again. "Okay. So we'll leave as soon as you're done."

Pasha took a deep breath, his shoulders heaving. He was too tired to argue and couldn't stomach another fight. "Alright."

They made their way to the Bowery with Pasha keeping her close at all times. He thought about the Butcher kid Yuri had let get away, how Klokov had wanted to interrogate him. Did the Butchers feel the same way about Pasha, the kid who had taken aim at one of their own? His thoughts drifted to Faina. Who was watching them as they walked down the street together? Thugs thronged to the Bowery. What if one day someone from a rival gang tried to hurt Faina to get to him? Pasha now understood why Yuri had kept his girlfriend away from the Foxhole. It was to protect her from his job. And if Pasha wanted to make things work with Faina, he would have to start doing the same.

Pasha and Faina entered just as someone near the door was exhaling a cloud of smoke. Inside, the Savage was finishing up a fight with Moneyrider, accounting for the larger crowd. The Savage was entertaining enough on his own with his blinding speed and brutal tactics, and Moneyrider hardly ever lost. Punches echoed over the sea of men as the Savage delivered strike after strike to Moneyrider's face. Finally, Moneyrider charged at the Savage, driving his head into his abdomen and flipping him upside down over his back. The Savage hit the floor, spent and disoriented. The bell clanged overhead as Klokov scurried down his podium with a loaf of bread for Moneyrider.

Pasha looked up at the roster, scanning the chalk letters for his name.

The Stallion vs. Rail Runner

Pasha's hands shrugged at his sides as though to say "Why me?" *I can't fight Yuri!*

"Pasha?" Faina laid a hand on his shoulder. "What's wrong?"

Pasha shrugged her off. "Nothing."

She glanced up at the roster, a smile crowning her lips. "You didn't tell me Yuri was back!"

"Hey, Pasha!" Leg Up clapped him on the back as he passed by. "You better get ready. You're after Franklin and Trifecta." At the sight of Faina, Leg Up gave a start. "Faina! Haven't seen you since … it's been awhile!"

Pasha narrowed his eyes as Leg Up smiled awkwardly, but Faina was happy to ignore his flub.

"Hey, Leg. Sorry about you and Anya."

Leg Up responded with a somewhat downhearted smirk. "It's alright. Never expected a classy broad like Anya to stick around forever, but we're still friends."

"I'm glad."

The bell clanged once more as another fight began. "Better get a move on." Leg Up tipped his cap and disappeared amongst the crowd.

Pasha's lips pressed together in a thin line as he quickly shed his coat and hat. "Hang onto these for me, will you?"

Faina took his outer layers, a crease forming between her eyebrows. It would be foolish to think she hadn't noticed Pasha's reservations after reading the roster. Sensing another question, he swiftly pecked her gaping mouth.

"Thanks, darlin'. I'll try to be quick."

He made his way to the bench where the street fighters often congregated awaiting their turn. Pasha was grateful to see Trifecta parked at the end, leaning forward with a cigarette hanging from his mouth. He took his place beside him, relieved to be sitting by someone who wouldn't pester him with overzealous cheering.

"Guess you saw the roster, huh?"

Pasha lowered his head. "Mhm."

"Do me a favor. Don't go easy on him, okay? Everyone's gonna notice, and Klokov's gonna know why."

Pasha rubbed his hands over his face with a loud exhale, as though he could drown out Trifecta's advice with his breath.

Irons and Joe made their way to the opposite ends of the stage as Klokov sprinkled salt onto the ground.

"What's up with you and Spichkin lately?" Trifecta pressed. "I noticed you acting a little distant."

Pasha's nostrils flared. "You know, if I'd known you were gonna ask so many questions I wouldn't have sat next to you."

Trifecta held up his hands in defense. "No need to get touchy. I'm only looking out for you."

"I don't need looking out for."

Trifecta looked him over. "Boy, that business with Yuri really got to you, huh?"

Pasha crossed his arms over his chest, refusing to answer. Trifecta pushed his cap back and took a long drag from his cigarette.

"Not everyone's suited for this kinda life, you know—"

"But we're stuck with it anyway."

"… And for that reason, you can't do it alone."

Trifecta's words draped around him like a warm quilt. His eyes drifted involuntarily towards Faina sitting at the bar across the room, his coat laid safely across her lap. People were staring, whispering, and he could see from the way Faina held her shoulders their glances hadn't gone unnoticed. It was bound to happen, but she had come anyway. And why? All to support Pasha. Pasha swallowed and scratched the bridge of his nose, fighting the urge to give in to Trifecta's questioning.

"It feels a little selfish."

Trifecta popped his eyebrows. "What's that?"

Pasha ground his teeth together, angry that he had folded so easily. "It feels selfish to drag her down with me."

Trifecta tossed his shoulders and sniffed. "I don't think you have to worry about that with Faina. Some girls ain't cut out to be a filly. And were it any other fella but you, she might not hack it. But Spichkin's tough, and she's obviously crazy about you."

"Won't she be in danger?"

Trifecta plucked the cigarette from his mouth and put it out on the bench. "Not willing to risk it, eh? I get that."

"So, you agree? It's a risk to date one of us." He struggled to mask the fear in his voice.

"We're thugs. No matter how Klokov tries to spin it. At the end of the day, we break the law, and we fight other gangs. We cross people we shouldn't cross. Even if we are 'thugs with principles' as Klokov puts it, that don't apply to all the other hoods out there."

"Have any Breadwinners ever had their sweetheart targeted before?"

Trifecta hesitated, reluctant to share the truth with him. "You know Backstretch? Former street fighter. A couple years older than me."

"Yeah, I know who that is."

"A few months back the Blind Bulls took a shot at his wife. Clipped her arm but she wasn't seriously injured. Then there was Tony Moscowitz. A couple of hoods from the Shark Teeth were harassing her at work for a while, but the Breadwinners took care of it before anything serious happened."

"Has anything serious ever happened?"

Trifecta scratched his head beneath his cap and looked away, pretending he hadn't heard him.

"Trifecta?"

Trifecta cupped a hand over his mouth, cheering on Irons. "Go for the knees!"

"Trifecta!" Pasha pressed.

Trifecta sighed and rubbed his nose. "Not for a while. Not since 1919. A girl was shot by the Bowery Butchers."

Pasha's stomach turned. Trifecta steadied him with a hand on his shoulder.

"Look, I know that's … scary. But don't let it stop you. Be smart about it. Like I said, this ain't the kinda life you wanna do alone."

Pasha threw off his hand, angered by, what seemed to him, reckless advice. "Then where's your girlfriend? If it's no big deal, how come I never see you with anybody?"

Trifecta's laidback expression shattered. For a split second, secrets rippled beneath his eyes like fish swimming too close to the surface. The bell clashed noisily overhead. Joe had Irons pinned by the neck. Trifecta stood and, composing himself, straightened his braces.

"I'm up." He turned and hollered to Franklin who was sitting on the other end of the bench. "You ready for this, Frankie boy?" He removed his cap and nodded at Pasha. "Remember what I said about Yuri." He turned and made his way up the stairs as Joe departed the ring with his loaf of bread.

Before the two could take their stance, Klokov met Trifecta at the center of the ring and placed his arm around his shoulder.

"Before we let these two go at it, I'd like to say a few words." The roar of the crowd dulled somewhat, but never went completely silent. "This here is Trifecta's last month as a street fighter, seeing as he turns twenty-one on the twenty-fourth." He put a hand up as several in the crowd began to whine in protest. "I know, I know. This young man has been with us a long time, seven years now. Trifecta came to us when he was just fourteen. His father had died serving in the Great War, killed early on in the Battle of Cambrai, and with four mouths to feed, his mother was struggling to pay the bills. Over the years, Trifecta has shown courage, discipline, and leadership. Just recently he led five other street fighters on a mission to rescue hostages from the Bowery Butchers, risking his life in the process." The Kopeck occupying his eye gleamed as his cheeks ballooned with a proud grin. "But best of all, Trifecta has exemplified obedience."

From his vantage point just below the stage, Pasha could see Trifecta swallow. His knuckles turned white as he clenched his hands behind his back.

"I've never known greater loyalty," Klokov continued. "Trifecta has always done what was asked of him, never once hesitating to fulfill his obligations to this brotherhood. And though his time as a street fighter is now ending, I am happy to see him graduating to bigger and better responsibilities. No doubt, he will carry them out with honor." As the crowd roared with applause, Klokov held out his hand for Trifecta to shake.

If Klokov saw the moisture gathering at the rim of Trifecta's eyes, he must have attributed it to pride, for he gave no indication that anything was amiss. As Pasha watched his fellow street fighter grab hold of their employer's hand, he had never felt sorrier for anyone in his life, not even Yuri. Trifecta may have been looking Klokov's direction, but his eyes were as empty as a dead man's.

Pasha had seen men come face to face with the reaper before: his own father, and later Leo. He'd witnessed that moment of bitter resignation. The point where the truth sinks down and settles like a rock at the bottom of a pond. The point when one realizes they are going to die. But Pasha hadn't expected to see it on the face of Trifecta, not now, not at this moment. There was more than loss in his expression, there was doom.

Klokov ascended the podium and the crowd blared back into existence as the bell rang. Sweat beaded down Pasha's forehead as the room grew unbearably hot. He undid the buttons of his shirt, preparing himself for his turn. A glass clanged noisily against the table behind him, causing Pasha to flinch. He glanced over his shoulder. Anastas was just sitting down at a table with Steed and Clyde.

"So how did you land yourself in the cooler?" asked Steed, lighting a cigarette. "You never mentioned."

"It's really not worth mentioning." Anastas's chair scraped the floor as he scooted closer.

"I hear you got caught stealing from a councilman."

"I didn't get caught. The elbow who arrested me couldn't prove I was the one who did it. He was gonna let me go when his buddy decided to check me for warrants."

"Was it Schneider?"

"Nah, some Pole. A real prig. In the end, one of Klokov's probation officers was able to get me out early." He snickered, and Pasha could hear his chair creaking as he tilted it back on two legs.

The roar of the crowd crescendoed as Trifecta pushed Franklin against the ropes. Pasha leaned forward on his elbows, raking his hand through his hair.

"You must be thinking of Liebowitz," said Clyde.

Anastas snorted. "Yeah, that's the one!"

"He's a real schmuck, locking up his own kind."

There was an audible *thwack* as Trifecta's body slapped against the mat, slippery blood oozing from his lip. Franklin was on him in no time, raining down hit after hit until Klokov finally rang the bell.

Pasha rubbed the space between his eyebrows and sighed, summoning the energy to stand. He dragged his feet up the steps. From where he stood, he could see Yuri making his way from a shadowy corner of the bar where he had been sitting all alone. Pasha forced a deep breath into his lungs, focusing his energy on keeping the look of pity off his face. Klokov's voice was an unintelligible growl thundering down from the podium. Yuri appeared over the top stair. His undershirt looked baggy.

Yuri bobbed his head in Pasha's direction, the gesture much slower than usual. "Long time no see, *Pavlushka*." His voice was weakened and hoarse. All trace of his usual sardonic smirk was lost.

Pasha managed a feeble simper. "Hey, Yuri. Glad to have you back."

The bell rang. Pasha raised his fists but found himself unable to move. Yuri, however, struck like a cobra, his lithe arm jabbing at Pasha's abdomen with surprising intensity. Pasha managed to block another blow, but one look at Yuri's wiry ribcage staid his hand. A jolt of electricity shot through his sinuses as Yuri's fist slammed into his nose. The crowd gasped as though able to feel Pasha's pain. Pasha wrinkled his nose as his eyes watered, blurring his vision. In that moment, he could see Yuri's stance. His knees were tight. It was a clear shot; all Pasha had to do was knock him in the shins and Yuri would be on the ground. Instead, he just stood there with his fists up.

"What are you standing there for?" someone in the crowd exclaimed.

Pasha whipped his head from side to side, trying to bring his focus back to the fight, but Yuri boxed him in the side of the head, further disorienting him. They went on like this for some time, Yuri getting in hit after hit while Pasha struggled to lay a hand on his friend. At last, Yuri was able to knock Pasha onto the ground with a kick so hard to the abdomen there was no way he could get up before the time ran out. There was an unmistakable grate to Klokov's voice as he declared Yuri the winner. When Pasha turned to look up at the podium, his eye was clearly fixed on Pasha, narrowed with seething disappointment.

Pasha hurried to vacate the ring and retrieve his shirt, making his way down the stairs as quickly as he could. He grabbed Faina by the elbow and yanked her off the barstool.

"What happened to Yuri?"

"Never mind that. Let's get outta here before Klokov decides to add another scar to my back."

They turned and headed for the door when Anastas stepped between them, walling off their path to the exit. He slowly plucked his cigarette from his mouth, his eyes dropping to Faina's chest.

"What's shaking, Spichkin?"

Faina stepped back, pulling her coat tighter about her. All around them the crowd seemed to be growing louder and louder. If Anastas hadn't been standing so close, they might've had to resort to lip reading. Heat bloomed against Pasha's neck as the man behind them lit a cigarette, poisoning the air with the stench of cheap nicotine, not caring that Pasha was less than a foot away. More than likely he was too drunk to notice.

Anxious to leave, Pasha didn't bother with trivial remarks but got straight to the point.

"Move."

Pasha flinched as another man forced his way past, stepping on Pasha's foot. Anastas ignored Pasha and continued to address Faina.

"I hear you got a performance in November. Gonna do another strip tease?"

Perhaps it was the crowd, or the stream of smoke clouding Pasha's vision, or the sore spot in his abdomen where Yuri had kicked him, but at that moment, something inside of Pasha snapped.

Everything was a blur. Pasha snatched Anastas by the collar and slammed him into the bar. Glass exploded around them but Pasha couldn't hear it. A bottle may have hit him in the side of the head. He wasn't quite sure. He was faintly aware of Faina grabbing his shoulders, shouting something to the effect of, *"Pavlushka,* stop!"

The room had gone completely silent. Pasha didn't notice. Next thing he knew, Anastas was on the floor. Somewhere in the chaos, Pasha grabbed a barstool. He lifted it high over his head, prepared to smash Anastas like a bug. Someone wrenched the chair out of his grasp, but Pasha could not be stopped. He threw himself on top of Anastas. Blood wet his knuckles as he pummeled his adversary's face. Finally, someone snatched him by the ankles and dragged him across the dirty bar room floor, away from his victim.

Pasha writhed onto his back, and was shocked to see Klokov holding his legs. Klokov dropped his ankles to the floor and doubled over, trying to catch his breath. Normally, his boss didn't care if boys came to blows. In fact, he encouraged it. Boys needed to vent once in a while. He only intervened if someone was in danger, and that almost never happened.

All at once the world slid back into his awareness. A multitude of eyes bore into his skin like fish hooks. Glass crunched beneath him as he sat up. Shards of broken beer mugs were scattered across the floor like shed scales. Off to the side, Trifecta and the Savage were holding the barstool. Joe and Steed helped Anastas to his feet. Red smears stained his teeth and dripped form the corner of his mouth.

"So much for not fighting outside the ring," quipped Steed.

Most disturbing of all was the way Faina stared at him, open-mouthed and pale, as though he were a complete stranger to her. He staggered to his feet, uncertain of what to do.

"Go home," ordered Klokov with quiet authority. "Cool down."

Pasha nodded and swallowed. He took one timid step backwards. A hand clutched his arm. It was Faina. The crowd parted, allowing her to guide him swiftly towards the exit.

Outside, the autumn air was crisp and forgiving. Faina said nothing but handed him her handkerchief. Pasha took it with a stupid expression.

"Your nose is bleeding."

Pasha touched his fingers to his nose and felt the warm gush of fluid running down his skin.

"Thanks." He held the handkerchief to his injury and stared down at the ground, too embarrassed to look at her.

"I don't think you have to worry about Klokov punishing you anymore." Her tongue seemed to struggle against her words. "I won't come to watch you fight anymore if it makes you feel better." She furrowed her brow and looked away. "I didn't mean to cause trouble."

Pasha shook his head. "It wasn't your fault." He took her hand and they made their way back home.

Chapter 46:

The Moth and the Butterfly

If Pasha had seemed withdrawn before, it was nothing compared to now. In the weeks following the incident, he had grown as reclusive and detached as a spider, retreating to the dark solitude of his room as often as was possible.

He hid from his mother, evading her questions with swift, one-word answers, and disguising his bruises beneath layers of clothing. Invitations from his sister to play were repeatedly ignored and dismissed. Even Faina was avoided to some extent, though she could not be brushed off entirely, not when there were heists to be planned. And Pasha still craved her company. It was the only thing that comforted him.

Pasha had become little more than a shadow on the wall. Insubstantial. Bodiless. Flat darkness in the shape of a sixteen-year-old boy. He felt odd, weightless, as though he might dissolve into ash at the slightest breath and scatter across the earth. And in a way, he wished he could.

Despite everything, he agreed to attend Trifecta's birthday party with Faina. When he couldn't come up with a costume, he tasked Faina with creating one for him—a bold move for someone who didn't want to attend the party in the first place. What's more, she had kept the details a secret. The only instruction she had provided was that he had to wear his favorite gray-and-brown-striped sweater. The dingy thing rarely saw the light of day, for it was too tattered to wear outside the house, with stray threads sticking out in odd places, and, truthfully, it was far too big for Pasha's lanky frame. But it was softer than a baby blanket, and by far the most comfortable thing he owned. Over the years he'd grown accustomed to wearing it over his pajamas on rainy days when he could curl up beneath his quilt with a good book.

Just before the party, Pasha ventured over to Faina's side of the building to try on his costume for the first time. Faina had him stand before the cheval looking glass in his mottled, oversized sweater and close his eyes while she swept about in her lovely butterfly attire. Mammoth sat beside him, his head leaning against Pasha's hip.

"Are you ready?" Joy and excitement glittered in her voice like a host of twinkling fairies, before she doubled over in another coughing fit.

Pasha furrowed his eyebrows. He had begun to notice her coughing again lately, and it seemed to be getting worse.

"You alright? You sure have been coughing an awful lot lately."

Faina waved her hand. "I'm fine. It's mostly happening at night, especially when I lay down for bed, so I'm pretty sure it's just allergies." She clapped her hands together excitedly. "Now, close your eyes!"

Pasha kept his eyes closed and tried not to look worried. "Work your magic."

There was a rustling noise as she pulled something from a box. "*Nyet*, Mammoth, this is not your blanket." Mammoth gave a disappointed whine.

She draped something heavy and warm over his shoulders and tied it at the neck. An elastic string snapped the back of his head as she fitted what was most likely a mask over his face.

"Ta-da!"

Pasha opened his eyes, and immediately recognized the likeness. Faina had transformed him into a moth, and quite successfully. The first thing his eyes were drawn to was the pair of wings stretching across his eyes. It was more than a mask … it was a work of art. Molded from papier-mâché, the mask had been hand-painted in soothing shades of ash and almond. A pair of fuzzy feelers branched out from the brow, creating an elegant frame about his head. He turned so that he could better see the cape. His jaw dropped. Strips of old furs in various weights and textures had been stitched together to form a shaggy pair of wings.

"Faina, how did you make this?"

Faina beamed with pride. "I cut up bits of old furs I bought from a pawn shop. They were practically falling apart so they were pretty cheap. I spent maybe a dollar fifty."

Pasha turned in the mirror again. He could simply not get over the sheer artistry and attention to detail. She was rather genius when it came to costumes, for although she was a poor seamstress, she was artistically inclined.

"And for the finishing touch …" She unfolded the collar about his neck and pulled it up over his head. It was a hood!

"Anya had to help me with that part." She twisted the ball of her foot into the floor and bit her lip. "Do you like it? The idea was to make something comfy that you could sort of hide in … seeing as you didn't really wanna go in the first place. And this way we can match! It isn't too feminine, is it? I don't want you to be embarrassed in front of the other Breadwinners."

Pasha fingered the base of his fur hood. Not only had she labored and planned to craft him this beautiful costume, and paid for the materials herself, but she had tailored it to suit Pasha's preferences so he would be comfortable in an uncomfortable setting. The entire costume had been fashioned for his well-being, accounting for his introversion, his love of privacy, and his delight! She had even managed to incorporate his favorite sweater!

Pasha turned and, placing his hands on her shoulders, kissed her. "I love it!"

Faina was all glitter and grins. "You do?"

"It's perfect!" Pasha hugged the fur collar closer about his neck. "I wanna hang this up in my room where I can see it every day! Heck, I wanna wear this every day!"

As the two made their way to the party, Pasha had never felt more at ease in a public place, with his hood covering his peripheral vision, his mask concealing his face, and his fuzzy cape cocooned around his shoulders keeping him warm and secure.

When they arrived at the Vavilov's drugstore, Dmitry, who was dressed like a cowboy, took one look at Pasha and drew a blank. Noting his confusion, Pasha quickly pushed back the mask and hood.

"It's me."

Much to his surprise, Dmitry behaved exactly as Faina had expected. He gave no signs of jealousy or animosity towards Pasha but maintained his usual sunny and welcoming attitude.

"Ah, Pasha!" He clapped him on the shoulder. "Clearly, it's been too long!"

Within ten minutes of being at the party, Pasha quickly learned that, had he not been accompanying Faina, the others would not have been able to place him from a distance. This made Pasha smile. Though he still would have rather spent the night in with Faina playing cards and drinking cider while they handed out candy, once he saw Trifecta he was glad he had come. It might not have been clear to everyone else, but Pasha was painfully aware of the anxiety tightening Trifecta's friendly smiles. He clenched his cup a little too tightly, and wasted no time flitting from conversation to conversation when he was ordinarily quite happy to sit in contented silence. As soon as there was an opportunity, Pasha raced to greet his friend.

"Happy birthday, Trifecta." He removed his mask. "I sure am going to miss you."

In true Trifecta fashion, he had opted for a simple pair of cat ears as opposed to a flashy costume. He gave an easy smile, though there was a caged look in his eyes. "Don't sweat it, Stallion. I ain't going anywhere. We'll still see each other around. Just not in the ring."

"That's true, I suppose. It's not like you're dying."

Trifecta's smile shrank, and he hastily whipped a cigarette out of his pocket. Pasha's eyes darted about, making sure no one was close enough to hear their conversation before asking quietly, "Are you gonna be okay?"

Trifecta lit the end of his cigarette and took a drag, his movements too quick. "Hm?"

Pasha leaned in towards his ear. "I said, are you gonna be okay?"

Trifecta paused, his face finally relaxing into his natural feelings. "I've been preparing for this for a while, kid. I'll be okay. But thanks for asking."

It was not an overly unpleasant way to spend the evening. There was plenty of good food and music. Faina seemed to understand intuitively that Pasha would rather not dance and was happy to let him sit contentedly off to the side looking like an old pile of furs. While Faina was chatting happily with Peggy and Franklin, Sergei sat down with Pasha, took out his fake fangs, and started up a conversation.

"She seems to be doing pretty well since the incident." He nodded in Faina's direction. "With the photograph, I mean."

It was true. Faina's reception at the party had gone better than Pasha anticipated. There were still one or two people who snubbed her, but most of the guests were the sort who knew Anastas was no good, and understood they had been set up.

"She's pretty resilient. Nothing keeps her down for long."

Faina appeared to have transfixed her audience with a lively story. Her hands flew about while her face remained vivacious and animated.

Nobody else seemed to have noticed that she had drowned her deviled eggs in pepper until the yolks were more black than yellow. But Pasha had observed her loading up on spicy foods all evening.

"You really love her, don't you?"

Pasha struggled against a shy grin. "I do."

"I'm happy for you, *Pavlushka*."

Dmitry joined in the gathering that had formed around Faina. Pasha couldn't hear what they were saying, but evidently Dmitry made a remark that struck Faina as particularly funny, for suddenly she couldn't stop laughing. They looked so sharp together, Dmitry with his shining confidence, and Faina with her creativity and wit. It was obvious there was a shared history between them. He wondered what inside jokes they had shared, what ridiculous nicknames they had given each other, if Dmitry ever thought about Faina.

"You doing alright?"

Pasha gave a start as he was sucked out of his ruminations. He nodded, causing the feelers on his mask to bounce around. "I'm just fine."

"I only ask because you've been a little … well, off lately."

Pasha resisted the urge to exhale irritably through his nose. His voice turned deadpan. "Yeah?"

Sergei fiddled with his cup and looked down at his feet. "I didn't think you would show tonight. Me and the other fellas … well, we've been sorta worried about you. You act different."

"I assume you're referring to the fight with Anastas."

Sergei paused. "You scared us, Pasha."

Pasha peeled his mask off and pinched the space between his eyebrows. "Alright, so I snapped one time."

"It's not just that. You don't come around much anymore unless you have to. You're sarcastic, angry; you bite off everyone's head all the time."

411

"Look, I can't just be the innocent, naive Pasha forever. Not as long as I'm a Breadwinner."

"So you're gonna be mean, scary Pasha instead?"

Pasha set aside his drink and rolled his eyes. "You wouldn't understand."

"Why wouldn't I understand? I'm a Breadwinner too!"

"Everyone thinks you're tough!"

"And you're not?"

"Well—Look at you!" Pasha gestured to Sergei's physique. "You're huge! You're seventeen and can grow a beard!"

"Pasha, we *both* ranked in the top five street fighters out of twenty-five last quarter! What are you trying to prove?"

Pasha exhaled and lowered his voice. "It's not about proving myself, *Seryozha*, it's about surviving. If Yuri can get sent upstate for letting that Butcher kid get away, then what's Klokov gonna do to me next time I mess up?" He was whispering now, but his voice lost none of its emphasis. "I'm the one who told him not to shoot!"

The gentle concern in Sergei's countenance multiplied and seemed to weigh heavily in his eyes.

"Pasha, it's not your fault Yuri got sent upstate. He was never gonna shoot that kid. He was scared out of his mind. He was hysterical. Yuri may put on a tough face but underneath all that bravado, he's just as scared as we are, maybe more. Yuri cracked under the pressure. But not you. You nearly took out the gunman and saved all the hostages."

Pasha's jaw tensed. "Stop saying it like I'm some big hero! I *nearly* took out the gunman. I failed."

"But you tried, and that's worth something."

Pasha worked up the courage to meet his friend's gaze. There was genuine worry tucked into the creases of Sergei's brow.

"I don't wanna lose another friend, Pasha."

"What do you mean?"

"Yuri's never gonna be the same again. It's always been the three of us together. Now you're all that's left. I don't want what happened to Yuri to happen to you."

"Well, I don't either. And that's why I gotta change."

"And what does Faina think about that?"

Pasha blinked. Maybe he should talk about Faina with Sergei. Surely, he wasn't the only Breadwinner concerned about their sweetheart's safety.

"You know, I didn't realize until recently how dangerous my life is, and what that means for Faina."

Sergei guessed what he was getting at and frowned. "Don't tell me you're thinking about breaking up with her?"

"I—"

"You love Faina! I didn't put up with all your sighing and belly-aching for six years just so you could dump her over some crap about doing the noble thing!"

"Hold on, I don't *want* to break up—"

"But you're thinking about it because you wanna do what's right."

"*Nyet*! I just wanna know what the risks are, and if I can do anything to prevent them from happening."

Sergei shrugged. "Well, you can always do like Yuri and keep your love life as private as possible."

"I would like that."

Sergei put on a knowing smirk. "But you're dating Faina."

Even under the circumstances, Pasha couldn't help but smile a little. "She's not exactly the type to sit at home."

"No, she's not." He rubbed his chin. "Have you talked to any of the other fellas about it?"

Pasha sighed and eased back into his chair. "I asked Trifecta if anything had ever happened to a Breadwinner's sweetheart. He said not since 1919. Then he told me to be smart about it … that being a Breadwinner isn't something you handle on your own."

"Trifecta told you that?"

Pasha sipped his drink and nodded. "Mhm."

"Trifecta's a romantic."

"A romantic?" Pasha scoffed. "I would've pegged him as a loner more than a romantic. I've never seen him with anybody!"

Sergei's amused simper dried up and vanished. "You don't know?"

"Don't know what?"

Sergei turned to make sure Trifecta was on the opposite side of the room, then turned his chair so that the back was facing Pasha, and straddled the headrest. "What all did Trifecta tell you?"

Surprised by Sergei's reaction, Pasha could only shrug. "All he said was a girl got shot by the Bowery Butchers."

Sergei nodded. "Trifecta's girl."

Pasha's mouth fell open. "What?" He leaned in so he could hear better, and shifted so that he was facing Sergei completely. "What happened?"

"You ever heard of Eagle-Eye Gallagher?"

"Yeah. He works for the Butchers."

"Well, Annie was his daughter. And Trifecta fell head over heels with her."

"How'd they meet?"

"At Coney Island. Annie had lost a bet to her friends and had to ride the Giant Racer. She was terrified of rollercoasters, you see, and none of her friends would go. Trifecta overheard the whole thing and offered to ride with her. They hit it off right away. Trifecta didn't tell Annie about the Breadwinners at first but when he found out who her dad was, he knew

414

they had to break it off. But by that point they were already in love. They tried to stay away from each other but they just couldn't help themselves. They started sneaking around, but after a while they got sloppy. Annie's brother caught Trifecta sneaking out of his sister's room one night. He barely avoided being killed. When Gallagher found out his daughter had been fooling around with a Breadwinner, he sent out his men to abduct Trifecta."

"But they never caught him."

"No, they did! Snatched him right outta his apartment! Held his ma at gunpoint and everything. He beat Trifecta within an inch of his life and then chained him to a dock just before high tide. Annie managed to free him right as the Breadwinners were arriving to take him home. And then Annie distracted her father while Trifecta and the Breadwinners escaped."

"Well, what happened to her?"

Sergei held up his hand. "I'm getting to that part. Trifecta wanted to go back for her, wanted to get her away from her family, to start a new life with her. But when he finished recovering, he found out she had been killed. Shot by her father. Klokov broke the news to him."

Pasha's mouth fell open in shock. "He shot his own daughter?"

"It was an accident. It was dark you see, and there was a lot going on. He thought he was aiming at a Breadwinner."

Pasha hung his head. "Poor Trifecta." It explained a lot. There had always been a sort of sadness surrounding him. Now he knew why. "But … if Trifecta's girlfriend died, why would he tell me I should stay with Faina?"

"Like I said, Trifecta is a romantic. But I'd listen to him if I were you. He's right. You can't spend the rest of your life alone. I certainly couldn't."

Pasha gaped at him in amazed frustration. Did no one see it his way? "It doesn't bother you that you'd be endangering the person you're in love with?"

Sergei shrugged. "I've never been that serious with anybody."

"Yeah, but you want to someday, right? You just said you could never spend the rest of your life alone. Don't you want a wife and family?"

Sergei's voice remained casual and even. "Yeah. Someday."

The calmer Sergei remained, the more Pasha became worked up. He was spitting now."But you'd be endangering them by association!"

"What am I supposed to do? Have no life? You can't worry about all that."

Pasha gaped at him. Sergei might as well have instructed him to lift his chair using his eyeballs. "How can I not worry about all that?"

"Pasha, if you don't stop overthinking everything you're gonna wind up with nobody. And I'm not just talking about Faina. I get that you're worried about everyone's safety, but you're gonna keep cutting people out and cutting people out until there's nobody left but you."

Towards the end of the night, as Pasha and Faina were preparing to leave, Dmitry pulled Pasha aside for a private word.

"I gotta hand it to you, Pasha. Faina seems really happy."

Pasha clutched his mask in his hand, his eyes darting anxiously towards the door. "Uh, yeah. She is happy." What was he doing? Was this some sort of subversive attempt at psychological intimidation? Couldn't he just leave well enough alone and butt out?

"Just so you know, there are no hard feelings. Faina is a very special girl, and I'm just glad she's found someone to take care of her."

Okay, now you're just showing off, thought Pasha. What was the point in telling him all this except to make him feel guilty? Well, it wasn't going to work.

He patted Pasha on the shoulder. "Take care of her for me, will you?"

Pasha may not have been the most animated person, but it was difficult to maintain a neutral expression at this one. *Take care of her for me?* As though the history between Faina and him predated the one she shared with Pasha. As though she were a horse Dmitry could no longer care for.

"Been doing it for six years. I'm a pro. She's safe with me."

Dmitry continued to smile, either completely unaware of Pasha's hostility or else choosing to ignore it. Fortunately, Faina reappeared at just that moment, having finished her conversation with Maimie.

"Ready to go?" She hooked her arm around Pasha's elbow.

Pasha placed his hand over hers, looking Dmitry directly in the eye. "Ready, *love*."

Chapter 47:

Locked In

Every day that passed without Staccato's correction was slow torture for Pyro and Sonata, as was Staccato's intention. Having been raised by her godfather since the age of fifteen, Sonata was well aware of his objectives, and yet such knowledge did little to abate her dread. Staccato had imposed a number of creative punishments on her as an adolescent. Such as the time she wore a pair of starfish to an aerial recital without his knowledge. Staccato had made her sew turtlenecks into all her clothing, and she hadn't been allowed to remove them for a month.

As an adult working under her godfather's leadership, however, she had never done anything to merit his correction. But that didn't mean his frequent discipline of Pyro and Skelter hadn't made a strong impression.

Would it be physical exertion? Like the time Staccato had made Skelter run a mile backwards? Or when Pyro was forced to lug a wagon wheel three miles through the mud during heavy rainfall? Once he'd made Pyro and Skelter do pushups every time they heard the word "pumpkin," which, admittedly, would have seemed a rather mild penalty were it not for the fact that they were at a pumpkin festival. Neither could lift so much as a glass of water by the end of the day.

Or would it be some unimaginably horrid chore? Like scrubbing the exterior of the caravan with their non-dominant hands? She couldn't help but remember the time Staccato had made Pyro do menial tasks in a pair of oven mitts for an entire day. Or the time Staccato dumped a bag of rice into a grassy field and made Skelter retrieve all the grains.

And then there were the just plain ridiculous: the time Pyro was having a hard time controlling his language so Staccato made him take a bite of a raw onion whenever he cursed. When Skelter had been forced to take his coffee with salt instead of sugar. When Pyro had to sleep in a cardboard box with the words "the raccoons ate my mattress and now I have to sleep here" scrawled across it. And then there was the time Staccato made Pyro sit in the driver's seat with him, and whenever a squirrel crossed in front of the caravan, Pyro had to stand up and yell "I'm sorry for my sins against nature." This was after a particularly nasty incident involving a walnut tree and a cursed nutcracker.

There was no use in trying to appeal to Staccato's better nature; he relished his reputation when it came to cruel and unusual punishments, and they usually worked … except for when Pyro was involved.

One day, a week after the incident with the barn, Staccato had Sonata go into the caravan—where Pyro happened to be repairing the radio—to fetch a dream from the loft. The two had been quiet for the past week, never arguing, but avoiding eye contact and saying as little as possible to one another. When she entered, she found Pyro sitting on his bunk with a screwdriver in his hand. Hair tousled and beard untamed, he was rather rugged today in his appearance. Dark, sleepy circles ringed his eyes. He'd hardly slept. It had been this way for several nights. Why, she did not know, but she always thought him especially handsome in this state, and couldn't keep from eyeing him longingly. Without warning, Pyro lifted his head to look at her. Sonata quickly turned and scurried up to the loft.

With a loud bang, the Dutch door slammed shut.

"Keep it open, it gets stuffy in here!" she heard Pyro call across the room. No one answered. The mattress creaked. She listened to his footsteps patter across the floor. The door handle rattled. "What did you do to the door?"

Curious, Sonata climbed down as Pyro was thumping on the wood.

"*Oi*! Staccato! Open the door!"

"I'm sorry to have to do this, Pyro," said Staccato from the other side. "But you two have left me no other choice."

"'You two?'" Pyro looked over his shoulder and, seeing Sonata, let out a dramatic groan.

Sonata's eyebrows rose in indignation. "This is our punishment?! You're locking us inside the caravan?"

"Just until you've sorted things out, and then you'll be free to exit."

Sonata ran to the side door but it, too, was locked.

"Don't bother trying the hatch," Staccato warned. "It's locked as well."

Pyro yanked on the handle. "Whatever happened to your rules about conducting ourselves with propriety and all that shrapnel? You're really going to leave us locked inside the caravan together, alone? We could get up to all sorts of trouble!"

At that moment, the gramophone in the loft began spinning out a romantic tune, and a cabinet opened revealing a host of flickering candles.

"Oh, I'm counting on it. It's far better than listening to your constant bickering! Skelter, Melodious, and I will be back to check on you in an hour, so I wouldn't misbehave too badly if I were you."

Pyro and Sonata stood there gaping at the door as the others walked away snickering.

"Suppose I could always burn the door down," Pyro finally suggested.

"You'll do no such thing! This caravan is an antique!"

Pyro shrugged. "Be honest, it's seen a lot worse in the past six years."

Sonata dropped her head between her shoulders and sighed. "We might as well admit it: he's right. We should talk."

Pyro flopped down on the bunk with his back turned. "Nope! I ain't talking about anything!"

"Why not? Don't you want to get out of here?"

"*Oi*, we've got food, we've got water, we've got shelter. We can hold out a lot longer than they can."

She sat down on the edge of the mattress. "Forget the others for a moment. Maybe we should talk more about this."

Pyro looked up at her for the first time. "Sonata, we *have* talked about it. We can learn to be civil to each other, but as far as I'm concerned we have nothing more to say." He turned over on his side and shut his eyes.

Sonata leaned against the wall and pulled her knees to her chest. When Pyro did not stir she began tracing a wrinkle in the sheets with her finger. "You're not fooling anyone, you know."

"What?"

"You can act callous, but we both know your feelings for me haven't changed."

Pyro glared at her irritably from a single open eye. Sonata shrugged and twirled a strand of hair about her finger.

"I never did understand why you took such pains to hide our relationship when you couldn't have been more obvious."

Pyro sat bolt upright. "I'm obvious?!"

Sonata said nothing, but crawled towards him. Pyro watched her with interested curiosity. Bit by bit, she lowered her head as though she were about to kiss him. His mouth fell open. Slowly, his eyes began to shut.

"You're not pushing me away," she whispered.

"Why should I?" Pyro cocked an eyebrow with an exceptionally prideful smirk. "If you wanna kiss me that's your problem."

Sonata dropped back on her haunches, her mouth hinged open in outrage. "You can be such a cad!"

Pyro threw back his head and scoffed. "What else is new?" He lay back on the pillows and reached for his cigarette case. "It's not as though you didn't already—"

Sonata seized his left wrist and pressed her lips against the soft inner skin. A mermaid kiss. Pyro's cocky mask fell at once as he was seized by the potent force of her love, his expression betraying every vulnerability and emotion buried within him. As she drew away, his head fell back in a posture of utter relaxation.

"You never do play fair."

"Don't you dare pretend like you don't love me!"

"I wasn't pretending—" He stopped, and raised his hands defensively. "I mean, I *do* love you!" His chest sank and his eyes weakened as he looked up at her. "That's what makes this so bloody hard!" He rolled up off the bed and walked to the other side of the caravan.

"Makes what so hard?"

"I don't understand why you won't say yes!" He turned, throwing his arms wide.

"I told you—"

"I know, I know! You don't want to get married until the Land Lock is broken. Really? It makes me feel like you don't want to get married at all!"

Sonata's hand flew over her chest. "What?"

"Face it, Sonata! Once the Land Lock is broken, it's back to real life for you! Back to charity balls, and ribbon-cutting ceremonies, and mummy and daddy, and everything else that comes with being a princess!"

Shocked by this revelation, it took Sonata a moment to respond. "What a horrid thing to say!"

"Is it? Think about it! It would be so much easier if you just married me now!"

Sonata rose to her feet, pinching the space between her eyebrows. "What are you talking about?"

"As long as the Land Lock is in place there's no one to stop us from being together."

"Pyro, there's never been anyone stopping us. There is no law that says I cannot marry you. My father can't even stop us."

"But he can try." His eyes, which were always so animated and full of life, now seemed to radiate a pain so strong it could have been its own entity. "He can make it harder for us. Not to mention the press, the public, the gossip, my family and their drama. If we got married now we could avoid all of that! And the fact that you won't makes me feel like it's because you don't want to. That this is just some sort of fantasy you're living out until you have to go back to real life!"

Sonata shook her head in disbelief, her voice dull. "You really think that?"

Pyro hesitated, seeing that he had hurt her. "Sometimes I think as soon as the Land Lock breaks, you'll be gone!"

Sonata sneered, his ignorance stunning her. "Do you even know me at all? Your insecurities have been a wrecking ball to this relationship from the very start! This all started with that ridiculous sleeping curse! If you want me in your life then you're going to have to get comfortable with the risks, and stop the self-sabotage!"

"It's not self-sabotage, it's the only reasonable explanation!"

"And how do you think I feel when after all these years you refuse to make our relationship public?!"

"That's to protect you!"

"And are you going to keep that up when we're married?" Her voice, even in volume up to this point, now soared above his. "You can't hide me away forever!"

Pyro froze. His mouth drew into a tense line. She seemed to have gotten through to him for once. After a long moment of silence, he sighed.

"Fine." He stepped towards her. "If you agree to marry me then we won't have to hide anymore. As soon as we're engaged we can take our relationship out into the open." He reached for her hands, his eyes seething with intensity. "Sonata, there's nothing in the world I want so much as to be with you!" He gripped her hands tighter. "We've been together for three years! I don't want to waste another blasted second not being married to you!" He slipped his hands up her delicate neck and cupped her cheeks, resting his forehead against hers. "Don't you feel the same way?"

Sonata rested her hands on his chest and closed her eyes, taking in the feeling of his warm breath on her upper lip.

"I do, love. I just … I just want my family to be there, is all. I can't imagine getting married without at least my father and mother there." She blinked her enormous eyes and stared up at him tenderly. "My whole life I've had this picture in my mind of what my wedding would be like … it was bound to happen. There's all this expectation, and ceremony, and tradition. I'd be escorted to St. Perch's Cathedral in a water chariot drawn by dolphins just like my mother, my grandmother, and all the queens who came before. The pews would be filled with marsh flowers imported from Kochab. And the reception catered by Il Decapode."

Pyro smirked. "Your favorite." He caressed her cheek. "It wouldn't be Sonata's wedding day without sea urchin."

Sonata laughed. "And of course plenty of barbecue for you." She rested her head against his chest and continued on in a dreamy voice. "You'd be waiting beneath the fountains, water up to your knees, while my father would escort me down the aisle. And when at last I was standing before the altar, I could look back and see all my family and friends there to celebrate with me."

Pyro traced his fingers over her back. "Of course you want your family there, darling. You love them." He kissed her head. "You deserve a big, royal wedding, or whatever kind of wedding you want. But these are the times we live in. Everyone has had to make sacrifices. Just look at all the families and loved ones that have been separated. Not just parents and children, but fiancés who've had to postpone weddings, students graduating, new babies that have never seen their grandparents. Not to mention elderly people who have had to die apart from their family. If we keep waiting until everything is perfect that day may never come."

Sonata sniffled, forced to face the truth of his words. "You're right."

"And we could still have a big ceremony when the Land Lock breaks, you know. Even if it winds up being ten … twelve … twenty years later!"

Sonata drew back to look him in the eye, unable to surrender her last hopes just yet.

"Can I have just one more year? One more year to see if the curse breaks?"

Pyro's countenance seemed to lift. "Yeah." His smile grew while his voice softened. "Yeah! Of course! If that's what you need. It's just nice to have a time frame."

"And then, whatever happens, Land Locked or not, I'll marry you."

Pyro grabbed her by the shoulders with an ecstatic cry. "You really mean it?"

Sonata bit back a bashful smile. "Well, of course I do!"

"Come here, gorgeous!"

Pyro lunged forward, lips puckered, but Sonata placed a hand over his mouth.

"But you have to have a ring next time in order for me to say yes."

"Darling, I'll crawl into the deepest crevice of the earth and dig you out the biggest diamond in creation with my bare hands if that's what you want!" He lifted her up in his arms and grabbed her left hand. "Now come here!" He kissed the inside of her wrist.

Sonata was overcome with his intense, ground-shaking love. It was as though the lines in her vision grew bolder. It was a dramatic, all-or-nothing, black-and-white kind of love that struck like a physical blow, and for a moment she was seeing spots.

"Woah! Woah!" Pyro lowered her gently onto the bunk. "Sonny! Are you okay?"

Sonata smiled dreamily. "More than fine."

"Sorry, I forget how intense I can be sometimes."

Sonata said nothing but stuck out her wrist for another.

Chapter 48:

Shattered Pumpkins

Pasha could hardly sleep that night, even with his mottled sweater thrown overtop his pajamas. Congested with the traffic of his woes, his mind splintered and spun. Why hadn't Trifecta told him it was his girl who had been shot? And why would he tell Pasha to stick with Faina after his own tragic experience? The way he had responded made it sound as though everything would turn out alright in the end. But that hadn't been true for Trifecta. Why would he tell Pasha differently?

Desperate for answers as well as rest, Pasha decided to go looking for Trifecta early the next morning. It was Saturday, and now that he had graduated from street fighting Trifecta was not likely to be at the Foxhole. So Pasha hunted for him on his street. He didn't even have to go to his apartment. He found Trifecta smoking in a narrow courtyard on Hester Street. Toilet paper was strewn across the laundry lines, and bits of smashed pumpkins lay already fermenting on the pavement.

Pasha stood in the opening, the pale morning sun pouring in behind him. "You didn't tell me it was your girl who was shot."

Trifecta started for a moment, but quickly composed himself, a steady stream of smoke seeping from between his lips. Judging by the dark circles beneath his eyes, one might have thought he'd been up for some time, but then Trifecta always looked as though he were running on cold coffee and a few hours' sleep.

"Would it have made a difference?"

Pasha stared at him as though he were crazy. "Of course." He plowed towards him, stepping on a bit of pumpkin in the process. "You know better than anyone the risks that come with being a Breadwinner. So why, after all that, would you tell me to stay with Faina?"

As Pasha neared he was able to fully appreciate Trifecta's disheveled state. The dry odor of spirits saturated his breath and clothes in a heavy musk. He must've been out drinking all night.

Trifecta observed him silently for several seconds before shaking his head and scoffing. "You can't think of a reason?"

Irked by his evasive answer, Pasha lowered his eyebrows. "Because you've lost your mind?"

"Because it's worth it!" He finished his cigarette and tossed the butt onto the asphalt.

Pasha blinked stupidly at him, unable to comprehend what he was saying. "It's worth it?" He couldn't believe what he was hearing. "It was worth it to you that your girlfriend died? That she never got to grow up? That you loved her and because of that she's not here anymore?" His foot collided with an empty beer bottle, sending it smashing into the bricks. "Do you hear yourself?" But Trifecta had turned his back and was now winding his watch. "Trifecta!"

Without warning, Trifecta grabbed Pasha by the collar and slung him against the brick. "Watch your mouth, kid."

Pasha eased his countenance but held onto Trifecta's wrist, stubbornly refusing to let it go. "You lied to me! You made it sound like it would all be okay, but that's not true, is it?"

"I never said it would all be okay, you just weren't listening!" He released his grip on Pasha's collar, but kept him cornered against the brick wall. "Maybe Yuri's right. Maybe you don't understand because you haven't had to struggle as long as the rest of us. So let me fill you in: we're not used to getting our own way in these parts. Happiness ain't something we expect. So when you find something special you gotta enjoy it while it lasts, because more than likely it won't. You gotta live in the present. That's all any of us can hope for. Maybe that seems selfish to you, but that's life in the Lower East Side! You can either accept your lot and live in the moment, or be miserable. It's your choice."

He started to walk away but halted in the middle of the passage. "You think I didn't love her? You think I don't blame myself for what happened?" He shook his head. "But she wouldn't want that. We both knew it was doomed from the start. But it was worth it just to have a moment with her! I'm gonna die a thug! I got no freedom, no future, no control over anything in my life! But at least I got that. So my life was worth something after all." He sniffed and wiped the corner of his eye with his sleeve.

Pasha felt his resistance crumbling away like dried mud. His head stooped forward. "I'm sorry I judged you, Trifecta."

Trifecta said nothing, but stared at the ground, his shoulders heaving. Determined to mend things, Pasha took another step forward.

"I want you to know I appreciate your advice … but I can't think like you. And maybe it is because of my upbringing. I've had privileges none of you have ever experienced. And just like you, those things have shaped me. But I don't know if I can change on this."

Trifecta took a moment before answering. "In the end you gotta do what you feel is right." He turned to leave, but Pasha quickly spoke up, his voice cracking.

"*If* I choose to let her go …" He paused as Trifecta looked back over his shoulder. "… How would I do it?"

Trifecta blinked, then shifted so they were facing each other once more. "What do you mean?"

"She would never accept it."

"No."

"And she'd know why I was doing it."

"She would."

"So what would I do?"

Trifecta shrugged and looked away. "Break her heart."

Pasha looked up at him in horror. He stepped back, crushing the already shattered remains of a beer bottle into dust. "I can't do that!"

"As long as she knows you still love her, she's gonna keep coming round. But if you break her heart, make it so that she can't stand you, then she'll move on. And you won't have to worry about her safety."

Pasha gaped and shook his head. "I can't do that to Faina. I know how she is; if she thinks she isn't loved … it'll do more harm than good."

"You know what I think you should do. Now you just have to decide." He pulled his cap down low and made for the street.

Pasha knew if he returned home, Faina would be there waiting at her window. He wasn't sure if he could face her just yet.

It's bad enough being a Breadwinner, he thought to himself. *Do I have to be alone too? Is it so wrong to keep her?*

Chapter 49:

Daydreaming

When Pasha returned to Orchard Street, Uncle Matvei was taking down Halloween decorations from the storefront. Faina was at the sitting room window, directly above. There was no way to avoid her. He'd have to pass directly in front of her just to reach the front door. Her eyes registered him from across the street. As the morning sun pressed down on her through the window, her freckles seemed to sparkle like glitter. The light teased traces of red hue in her eyes so that they glimmered like red jasper. Pasha felt the first fissure in his heart begin to form.

He strode across the street with a little wave and climbed up the fire escape to her bedroom window. It didn't take long for Faina to appear.

"Where have you been off to so early in the morning?" She helped him over the sill, her movements swift and joyful. "You couldn't have been out running errands because I saw Katya headed to the baker's with Aunt Poppy about five minutes ago."

Pasha wrapped his arms around her from behind and kissed her cheek. "Nowhere important."

Faina swatted at him playfully. "Pasha!" She wriggled around to face him. "Take it easy, I'm still trying to wake up."

"And I'm not helping?" They flopped back on the bed, Pasha holding her tight to his chest, knowing well that Uncle Matvei would murder him if they were caught like that. He wanted nothing more than to stay like this, and never think of his conversation with Trifecta again.

"Not like this, you aren't."

They stayed cuddled together for a moment or two more in silence. Pasha swallowed. He still hadn't made any final decisions yet. "You free this evening?"

She reached back and caressed his cheek.

"Maybe. What'd you have in mind?"

"Nothing special. You, me, a bottle of Coke."

Just then Mammoth came bounding around the corner and leapt atop the bed, resting his full weight on Pasha.

"And the dog," he grunted, prying Mammoth's nails out of his back and tousling his fur.

Faina sat up and laughed, affording them more room.

"Alright, Tiger. You got yourself a date." She nudged Mammoth off the bed. "Your place or mine?"

"Yours." He fingered the pillow under Faina's head, where a dark stain was ground into the material. As he sat up, he noticed several of the pillows, as well as a few spots on the bedspread bore the same blackened mark. "What happened to all your bed linens?"

Faina shrugged. "I'm not sure. I first noticed them months ago, and they keep popping up. I remember the same thing happening with all Leo's pillowcases, but we never figured out what it was."

"You don't think it could have something to do with smoking, do you? I have noticed Anya smoking near the laundry line. Maybe Leo did the same thing."

Faina rolled her eyes. "That might explain it."

Pasha rose and rubbed his hands over his face. "I'll pick up the Cokes and be over around four." He raised an eyebrow playfully, and kissed her hand. "Is that acceptable, Mademoiselle?"

Faina turned her nose up in a dramatic fashion and said in an affected voice, "I suppose so!" She smiled and threw him a wink. "You might wanna time it before the rain. This sunshine isn't supposed to last, you know."

Pasha returned to the apartment and lay back down in his bed. It wasn't long before Katya returned. He was certain she could sense his distress as the day wore on, and yet she asked no questions. In fact, she was rather quiet.

When it was nearly four, Pasha made his way down to the drugstore, picked up the Cokes, and made it to Faina's just as the sky was beginning to thunder.

"Tell me about your morning while I put away this laundry," she said, leading him through the door of her bedroom with a basket of clean clothes under her arm.

Pasha's shoulders sagged. "Like I said, there isn't much to tell."

Faina said nothing but glanced sharply at him for a moment as she set the basket down before the closet. It was obvious he was being evasive.

"I was looking for Trifecta," he admitted, wishing to avoid any conflict. "I had a question about something that happened with the Breadwinners a long time ago." He sat down on the rug in front of the bed beside Mammoth, raking his fingers through the dog's silky fur. "I'd much rather hear about your day."

Faina shrugged. "I've been doing housework. I can't really help downstairs anymore seeing as nobody wants to see the neighborhood tart at the counter. So there's not much to report." She picked up a sweater and slid it on a hanger, her enthusiasm returning. "I've been reading a lot about mastodons lately …"

Pasha was happy to hear the passion in her voice as she prattled on, and normally he would've found the subject incredibly interesting, but it seemed impossible to focus. Every time he found himself relaxing a feeling of guilt would compete for his attention, like a glare in the corner of his eye.

When she had finished putting away the laundry, she stopped and stared at him, interrupting her own thoughts.

"What's wrong?"

Pasha kept his arms folded tightly about his chest and shrugged. "Nothing is wrong."

Faina observed him a moment or two longer, her lips compressed. "Are you just saying that?"

"What makes you think something is wrong?"

"Can you answer my question before asking me one?"

Pasha closed his eyes and took a deep breath, forcing himself to relent. "Okay, yes."

Faina turned away from the closet and sat down beside him on the floor. "Go ahead. Unload. That's what I'm here for."

Pasha opened his mouth as he turned to face her, as though expecting the words to just fall out. The moment their eyes met, all resolve was lost. His chest deflated, his lips turned down, and he passed a hand over his face.

Faina jumped into action. "Baby! What is it?" She reached for his elbow, pulling him closer.

Trifecta's words were buzzing around in his head like a curse, burying themselves in his conscience, infecting his sense of self. Determined to ignore them, Pasha grabbed Faina and kissed her hard until he felt the muscles in her back go weak. He did not pull away completely but lingered with his cheek close to hers and his lips near her ear.

"You know I love you, right?"

Faina sounded confused but the smile was strong in her voice. "Yes."

Her eyelids lowered and they were drawn magnetically towards each other in another kiss. Pasha withdrew and sighed, his nose pressed to the corner of her lips, barely opening his eyes.

"If I could have anything I wanted, I would marry you right now."

The quiet shattered as Faina laughed. "We are sixteen years old!"

Pasha gave her a wry but sad smile. "And soon we'll be seventeen! Besides, that girl across the street got married at sixteen."

"Yeah, so she wouldn't have to stay behind in Italy and starve!"

Pasha shrugged. "Your uncle doesn't make what he used to."

"Sounds like a good way to make everyone think you got me pregnant."

Pasha let out a sigh and stared down at the floor. "Thanks to Anastas they think stuff like that about us anyway."

"It's still illegal."

"Feel like a trip to New Jersey?" he teased.

Faina playfully rolled her eyes. "And why is it you're wanting to race to the altar all of a sudden?"

"Because I love you." Pasha kissed the patch of freckles on her arm, exposed by her sleeve. "And so I can kiss all your freckles." His voice was just a murmur as he fought to keep his head above the waves of shyness threatening to overtake him upon such a confession.

A rapid blush spread across Faina's cheeks, but she was helpless to the grin advancing across her lips. "Well, I'm not marrying you before it's legal."

Mammoth gave a groan and batted Pasha's arm as though reprimanding him for his impropriety.

Pasha rested his forehead on Faina's shoulder and sighed. "I know. I was just daydreaming really."

Struggling to stay upright, she slipped her hand beneath his chin and forced him to look at her.

"What's all this about really?"

Pasha winced, afraid to open his eyes. "I wish I could be with you always."

She pressed her lips against his forehead and stroked the hair at his temple. "Well, nothing's stopping us from being together."

Pasha raised his head to look her in the eye. The realization settled on her face like an axe being embedded into a tree. Pasha laid a hand on hers.

"Faina …"

She jerked her hand back. "No! Pasha, do not make this about trying to do the right thing! You hear me?" Her hands curled into fists as she stood and towered over him. "I knew you were gonna do this at some point! I knew it!"

Pasha rose to his feet. "Faina, the things I've seen lately … If you only knew then you'd understand!"

"I know what being a Breadwinner entails, Pasha!"

"Do you?" He looked down at himself in shame. "Did you know that Trifecta's girlfriend was shot by the Bowery Butchers?"

"No! But what does that have to do with us?"

"It's dangerous for you to be romantically involved with me!"

Faina stared at him, her eyebrows furrowed. "You're saying they shot her because she was Trifecta's girlfriend?"

"No, they were trying to kill Trifecta. Her family was associated with the Butchers—"

"How is that anything like our situation? We're not part of rival gangs! When did this even happen?"

"Five years ago."

"So you're thinking about dumping me over something that happened five years ago?"

"That's not the only incident! There were two other fellas, foot soldiers—"

"You're not a foot soldier!"

"But I will be someday! I mean, just think about that! I'm a thug, Faina! What kinda future do you have with me?"

Faina rolled her eyes and scoffed. "Future? Pasha, I'm damaged goods! I'm the neighborhood slut! You think dating a Breadwinner is gonna drag me down? Even if it did, I don't care!" She placed a hand on his cheek. "I love you! Besides, your life's not ruined. You could end up like Leo before—you know."

Pasha took a step back and shook his head. "Klokov's not gonna put someone like me in Leo's position."

"How do you know?"

"Because I'm not the type!" He pushed his hair back, fumbling for an explanation that wouldn't reveal the truth about what had happened to Leo. "There's a certain kinda person Klokov likes to promote, and it's not me."

But Faina wouldn't have it. "What are you talking about? Before you dropped out everyone was expecting you to attend college! Klokov would be a fool to waste your intelligence!"

Pasha turned away from her, dropping to a seat on the bed. "Yeah, well, maybe it's better that way."

"How would that be better? Isn't that what you're worried about? That you're doomed to be a thug?"

"I don't wanna be Klokov's pawn! Okay?" He pinched the space between his eyebrows. He hadn't meant to shout.

Faina studied him for a moment before pressing him further. "What's that supposed to mean?"

"It means Klokov only helps guys who can help him down the road. Why else would he help a Breadwinner get on the police force? On city council? He's not doing it to fulfill some immigrant dream, he's doing it to keep himself out of hot water!"

Faina blinked and twisted a ring on her finger. "Is that what was gonna happen to Leo?"

Pasha opened his mouth to deny it but could only sigh. She grabbed hold of the bedpost and sank onto the mattress.

"Look, I don't know what Klokov's exact plans for Leo were." Pasha passed a hand over his eyes. "And I never will."

"Sounds like you know enough."

Pasha sat down beside her and bent over his knees, taking a moment to collect his thoughts.

"Trifecta said the reason Klokov wanted Leo at the *New York Daily* was so he could help keep his name out of the papers."

Faina swallowed. "So Klokov wasn't rewarding Leo … he was just using him."

Pasha nodded. Faina placed a hand over her chest and gaped at the empty space where her brother's bed had been.

"Now do you understand?" said Pasha, breaking the silence.

Faina's eyes bore into his, refusing to give in. "You're making a big deal out of nothing. All the other Breadwinners have girlfriends!"

"And they're willing to take that risk. If anything were to happen to you because of me …" he trailed off, fighting back tears. "I don't know how I could cope with that."

"Why do you always do this?" She was on her feet again, her voice rising as her lip trembled. "Why do you always have to do 'the noble thing'? That's what got you into this mess in the first place!"

"I can't help it! It's just who I am!"

"Well, you're destroying me!" She wailed as her eyes finally gave way to tears. "Don't I have any say in this?"

"Faina, you're not thinking through this clearly—"

"I don't live under a rock! I know what I signed up for! But I don't care!"

"Well, I do! You're not safe with me, Faina."

"I don't care! I want to be with you anyway! Why can't you respect my choices? Suddenly, I'm just the helpless little woman who doesn't get a say?"

"If you think this is about control then you have misunderstood me completely. You don't care if something happens to you because of your association with me, I get that. But *I* could never handle that sacrifice." His voice broke at the thought. "If something did happen to you, it would be more pain than I could endure, and I don't know how I would face it." It took him several moments before he could speak, and when he finally did he could hardly get his voice out. "We can't do this anymore."

Faina melted to the mattress, her hands tangling in her hair as she doubled over and sobbed. A shaky breath escaped Pasha's throat. He tried to swallow but choked instead as his eyes grew warm with tears. He sat down beside Faina and slid his hand towards her knee, wanting nothing more than to comfort her, but his thoughts pulled him back.

Mammoth got to his feet, poking his head between them, not sure which one to comfort first.

"You know—" He stopped to wipe the tears from his cheeks. "You know, I want nothing more than to be with you, right?" His voice was growing thick and heavy.

Faina placed her hands on both of his cheeks. "Then be with me! Please! Don't do this! Don't hurt me like this! I love you!"

Pasha's face contorted with a sob. His heart sank to his feet. They bowed their heads together, foreheads touching, tears streaming down their faces. At length, he swallowed, gently removing her hands.

"I love you too much to risk your safety. This is how it has to be."

Faina recoiled from him with such force one might have thought he had stuck a knife between her ribs. Pasha's hands shook. He couldn't take hurting her like this. Her shoulders trembled with uncontrollable sobs. Instinctively, he reached forward.

"Faina—"

"Just go."

Pasha wiped at his eye and got up to leave. Mammoth followed him to the door, staring at him as though asking where he was going.

Pasha hated himself. His heart twisted with self-disgust and loathing. Just as he was turning the handle, Faina spoke up in a shaky voice.

"You promised you would never forsake me."

He turned back to look at her. She stayed huddled over her knees, unable to make eye contact.

"Thieves' Honor. You broke your promise."

Pasha didn't know what to say. He just stood there, sniffling, and wishing his life were different. "I let you down, Faina. And I'm sorry." He turned and left the room.

***

Outside, the daylight was little more than a ghost in the midst of the thunder and black clouds. Pasha lay in his bed swathed in his quilt, his head heavy. His eyes drifted to the window, towards Faina's bedroom. He could just see her through the partially opened curtains, laid out on her bed, her body still and heavy with dreams. She must have cried herself to sleep.

The skin around Pasha's swollen eye ached with relentless tightness. He huddled down beneath the covers, but no matter which way he turned his back ached. He stared listlessly at his hand, allowing his fingers to drop open. His flesh seemed heavy and burdensome on his bones, as though his skin were made of wet flannel. His soul hungered for sleep. Every conscious thought dragged behind him like a chain.

He surrendered his ears to the sound of the rain, patiently waiting for it to absorb his senses. He slid the foot of his bent leg against the soft material of his pajamas, but the sensation did little to comfort him.

He wanted to ask someone, am I ever going to feel better? But there was no one to ask. He wouldn't involve his mother or sister. He'd resisted opening up to his friends. And now he'd cut out Faina.

Sergei's words echoed back: *You're gonna wind up with nobody.*

The moment the tears began to gather in his eyes, Pasha tore them away with frustrated violence. A sob fought its way up from his throat. Pasha clasped his hands over his head and tried to breathe normally but it was no use. Tears broke down his cheeks. There was a soft knock at the door.

"Leave me alone!" Rarely had he been so cross with his mother or sister, but after being caged for so long his escaped emotions were virtually untamable, and he struggled to control his reactions. The knock repeated.

"I said leave me alone!" But the door opened anyway.

Unable to stem his tears, he threw himself down on the mattress, and drew the covers up over his head, refusing to cry in front of them. Someone sat down on the bed. He knew from the slight weight that it was Katya. A soothing hand pressed against his trembling shoulder, while the other pulled back the covers and stroked his hair.

"It's okay to cry, Pasha. I won't laugh at you or anything."

Moved by her sweetness, Pasha did not snap at her. He did not send her away. But the urge to cry grew stronger.

"You don't have to tell me why you're crying. I think I know anyway."

Pasha sniffled and continued to lay there. "Why do you think I'm crying?"

"Your heart is broken."

Pasha squeezed his eyes shut and nodded.

"Did you and Faina break up?"

Pasha swallowed another sob, and nodded.

"I'm sorry, Pasha." She laid her head on his shoulder, hugging him close. "You don't have to say anything else."

Pasha slid his hand over hers and squeezed it, tears streaming down his face. The floor creaked as his mother entered the room. Pasha tried to harden his features but it only seemed to make the tears come faster.

"Come here, baby." She sat down at the head of the bed and stroked his hair.

"Ma, I'm fine!" But it was no use; his voice was broken with sobs.

"Katya, dear, I need to speak with your brother alone for a minute. Alright?"

"*Da*, Mama." She leaned over Pasha and kissed the side of his head. A moment later the door clicked gently behind her.

The springs of the mattress groaned as his mother peered into the wastebasket. "I see you've been hitting your stash." She was referring to the multiple Hershey bar wrappers lining the interior. Chocolate was always the first thing he reached for when he was particularly depressed. She pried his arm away from his tear-stained face. "Why are you hiding from me?"

"Because I'm not supposed to cry. Men don't cry."

Lydia's eyes glazed over, unimpressed. "Who told you that? Klokov? Well, he isn't here right now. You're home. You're safe. You're with me. You can cry all you want." She traced her fingers over his back. "Care to tell me what it is you are crying about?"

Pasha sniffed and shook his head.

"Darling, why are you hiding everything all of a sudden? You won't talk to me. You won't tell me anything. You lock yourself in your room all the time so I won't see your injuries."

"I'm just trying to protect you."

"Protect me from what? I know you're a Breadwinner. You can't just hide every time you come home with a bruise. I'd never see you again. Since when did I become so fragile? Surely, you know by now I'm made of sterner stuff."

Pasha said nothing but swallowed another sob. Lydia sighed and shook her head.

"I've had it with these archaic ideas Klokov keeps putting in your head."

"It wasn't Klokov." His voice was weak and hoarse now. "Before he died, Papa told me to take care of you and Katya."

Slowly, Lydia shut her eyes and drew a deep breath through her nose. "If your father knew just how seriously you were going to take those words, he never would have said them. Papa would never have wanted this for you, ever!"

"He said I was to be the head of the household," Pasha persisted.

Lydia stared at him for a moment, then scoffed and shook her head. "Boy, I have got news for you. You are not the head of this household. I am. So you can stop worrying about that." She leaned closer. "What kind of man was your father? Hmm? Was he macho?"

Pasha shook his head. "No."

"Was he mean?"

"No."

"Did he cry?"

Automatically, Pasha opened his mouth to answer, but stopped. He could remember his father crying the day he'd died, of course. But aside from that he wasn't sure. "I don't know, did he?"

"He did. And he wasn't ashamed of it."

Pasha gripped the quilt tighter and stared blankly at the opposite wall. "Ma, you don't understand. I get that Papa was gentle. I get that Papa was kind. I get that I'm just like him. But I'm not free to be the kind of man Papa was. I'm not free to be who I am. Don't you see? They'll kill me if I don't toughen up."

He saw his mother's jaw tighten as she swallowed. "It's one thing to put on an act," she finally replied. "It's another thing entirely to let them change who you are. When you're with the Breadwinners, do what you have to to survive. But this home is your sanctuary. Your family, your friends … those are sacred. Don't let Klokov take those away from you."

Pasha pressed his lips together as he felt another wave of tears coming on.

"You broke up with Faina, didn't you? To protect her?"

Pasha knew if he opened his mouth to answer he would start sobbing again, so he merely nodded his head. Lydia drew a long sigh.

"I knew you would at some point. I wish you wouldn't have, but I understand why you did."

Pasha watched her in silence, uncertain of what he should say.

After a moment or two, she added in a lowered voice, "Well, if you insist on keeping her out of it, then I want you to know you can depend on me. I don't want you hiding from me. I don't want to hear any nonsense about sheltering me from the pain. I'm your mother. And I'm here to support you no matter what happens."

Pasha did not much feel like saying anything more, so he simply placed his hand on her knee and closed his eyes.

Chapter 50:

Brake Lines and Corned Beef

When Pasha emerged from his window on Monday, he was shocked to find Faina standing in the courtyard waiting for him. Pasha froze with his leg halfway out the window, but Faina looked up in time to see him.

"Come on, Breadwinner! You're late!"

Pasha staggered onto the landing and straightened. "Faina … what are you doing?"

Faina threw out her hands, the baggy sleeves of her brother's coat sagging at the elbows. "What does it look like I'm doing?"

Despite her impatience, Pasha took his time making his way down the fire escape, and approached her the way someone might approach a scared alley cat.

"You wouldn't happen to be waiting to beat me up, would you?"

Faina ignored his joke and whipped around to face him. "You didn't say I couldn't help you steal."

Pasha put out his hands to steady her. "You're right, I didn't. But I didn't think you'd still want to."

Faina crossed her arms and looked away. "Well, here I am."

Pasha shoved his hands into his pockets and leaned around in an attempt to see her face.

"I see that. You know, as much as I appreciate your help, I really don't think—"

Faina twisted around, her eyes looking like candle flames as they narrowed. "Don't tell me what to do!"

"I'm not! I was just gonna suggest that maybe you take a few more days to cool off."

Faina responded with a look that could've singed steel. Pasha threw up his hands defensively.

445

"Or not! You don't … you don't have to do anything you don't wanna do."

Faina pushed her sleeves back and headed for the sidewalk. "Let's go."

Pasha hastened to keep up with her urgent stride. "Faina, don't take this the wrong way or anything, but … I'm a little confused as to why you're here. I mean, aren't you mad at me?"

Faina kept her eyes straight ahead. "Livid."

"Then why are you here?"

She stopped abruptly, nearly causing Pasha to step on her heels. She pivoted around and backed him into a basement walkout. "Because I'm not gonna let you do this to us."

Pasha was forced to grab onto the railing to keep from falling down the stairs. "What do you mean exactly?"

Faina continued to back him further down the passage. "It means that even though you completely broke my heart, took away any say I had in the matter, and completely abandoned me—"

"I didn't—"

"Shhh! It's my turn to talk now! It means even though you did all that, I still love you, and I'm never gonna stop fighting for you! Because unlike you, I don't break my promises!"

Pasha's back finally hit the wall as he reached the end of the walkout.

"You need me, Pasha. And until you realize that, I'm gonna keep showing up."

Pasha stared at her, dumbfounded. He had known she would fight it, but he hadn't expected her to bounce back so quickly.

"Besides …" She smoothed his collar, looking up at him through her lashes. "I know you still love me."

Pasha could not bring himself to protest this, but stood absolutely still as he held her gaze. It was exactly as Trifecta had predicted. As long as Faina knew Pasha loved her, she would continue to pursue him. Before he could stop her, her lips were on his, blurring out his thoughts and surroundings until there was nothing but the two of them. Without thinking, he slid his hands around her waist, then immediately withdrew.

"Woah, woah!"

Her eyes flickered with pain. Unable to stand it, Pasha said the only thing he could think of.

"Faina, why don't you go back to Dmitry? He's the better version of me anyway."

"I don't want a version of you, I want you!"

Pasha shut his eyes to hide from the agonized way she was staring up at him. "Let's not talk about it anymore. We need to get a move on." He pushed past her towards the stairs. Faina followed.

They continued on like this for the next few days. Though Faina did not try to kiss him again, she radiated love the way a candle gives off warmth, and Pasha found himself wanting nothing more than to draw physically near to her.

One evening, as they parted ways, Faina said "I love you," and Pasha, out of habit, replied "I love you too," and bent down to kiss her. Faina had been particularly pleased with herself.

By the time the weekend arrived, the pair had returned to some version of normalcy. No tears were shed, though there was no shortage of longing glances from either. They even flirted on occasion. Laughter and teasing were revived, but underneath was a feeling that at any given moment they would fall into each other's arms.

One morning, Pasha and Faina decided to hop a freight train to steal a shipment of liquor disguised as auto parts. Faina was to cause a distraction, giving them enough time to sneak into the yard and climb into a car when no one was looking. As Pasha watched Faina scramble onto the roof of the security building adjoining the freight yard, he found himself fantasizing about their future … the one they could never have. They'd go someplace rainy like Seattle, and then every day would be just like his daydream: he and Faina, snuggled together, half asleep under the quilt while rain slid down the window, and Chinese takeout boxes littered the floor.

A loud clatter brought him back to reality. He was supposed to be waiting for Faina's signal. He could hear the guards yelling back and forth to each other. Now was the time. He turned towards the chain-link fence. A shrill whistle sent him flying into the air. He jerked around in time to see the walrus-like Officer Lynch hitching up his pants and marching in Pasha's direction.

Pasha stood there with his arms out and shrugged. "What?"

Lynch reached for his handcuffs. "Hold it right there, you're under arrest!"

Pasha's eyes nearly left his head. He hadn't done anything yet. "Why?"

"Trespassing! I've told you to stay outta the damned freight yard!"

"But Officer Lynch, how do you know I was going into the freight yard? What if I was just passing in front of it?"

Officer Lynch raised an eyebrow. "Where are you headed that you need to pass in front of the freight yard?"

Pasha took one look at Faina surreptitiously poking her head out of a railcar and sighed. He thrust out his hands so that Lynch could place the cuffs on his wrists.

***

Pasha stared dully at Officer Lynch sitting across from him at his desk while he unwrapped his smelly tuna fish sandwich from the greasy paper. They were back at the precinct now, waiting on Pasha's probation officer. His left hand had been freed, but his right remained chained to Lynch's desk.

Lynch's mustache rippled from his overfull mouth as he tore off another bite of sandwich and continued to glower at Pasha.

"Betcha wish you hadn't trespassed on them damned freight yards."

Pasha tried not to glower. Over the years, he had grown somewhat desensitized to his run-ins with the police. The thought of a holding cell no longer frightened him, but getting marched back to a patrol car with his hands cuffed behind his back was no less humiliating. And Lynch loved to rub it in.

Pasha looked dismally out the window. After a moment or two of mindless staring, he noticed something odd. Something appeared to be moving beneath the patrol unit. Thinking it was a cat, Pasha leaned forward in an attempt to see better. A figure scuttled out from beneath the vehicle on his back, holding a pair of pliers, looking very much like a beetle emerging from a rock. As the figure rolled up off the pavement and stood, Pasha recognized the broad-backed silhouette and wide head. He narrowed his eyes. Anastas.

What's he doing?

Had Pasha just been released from prison, the last place anyone would have found him was outside a precinct with a pair of pliers. He supposed Anastas was stealing car parts—that seemed the obvious conclusion—and taking them from the police was his idiotic way of showing off. Pasha's eyes wandered back to Lynch.

"What do you keep staring at, boy?"

The threshold creaked behind him as another officer entered the room.

"Sullivan's left his badge in the—"

At the sound of Liebowitz's voice, Pasha turned around.

449

"Ah, kid, not again!"

Pasha smirked. "Why you gotta assume the worst? Maybe I'm thinking of joining the police academy, and dropped by to ask Officer Lynch here for some advice."

Lynch bristled at his use of humor. "You want my advice? Stay out of them damned freight yards!"

Liebowitz ignored Lynch and spoke directly to Pasha. "You were in the freight yards again?"

He shrugged. "I was standing in front of them … which is apparently just as bad."

"You know you and your girlfriend have been banned from the property."

Lynch wiped his mustache with his fist. "We're waiting for his probation officer."

"What's this?" Liebowitz stepped around Pasha's chair. "You're handcuffed to the desk?" He turned on Lynch. "What you got him cuffed to the desk for?"

"In case he tries to run."

"He's in the precinct! He ain't gonna run! You're sitting right there, aren't ya?"

Lynch gestured to the paper bag. "I was eating! He could've used that as a distraction."

While Liebowitz and Lynch continued to argue, Pasha's attention drifted back towards the window. Anastas was just leaving, his hands flexing down at his side, empty. Pasha eyed the vehicle curiously. If Anastas hadn't been stealing car parts, what was he doing?

Liebowitz pinched the space between his eyebrows. "Just un-cuff him." He opened the drawer and removed a file. "I don't have time for this right now. I gotta take these to the D.A."

Lynch begrudgingly leaned over the desk and slipped the key into the lock on Pasha's wrist. His breath wreaked of mayonnaise. "I still got my eye on you, boy."

The handcuff wrenched open. Pasha brought his hand to his chest and flexed his wrist.

Liebowitz veered towards the opposite door. "When I get back I don't wanna see any more kids cuffed to that desk, you got that? Not unless they're violent."

"Take the car."

"For a couple of blocks?"

"It needs gas."

Liebowitz waved his hand. "Fine."

Pasha glanced back out the window. There was only one car present, and it was the one Anastas had scuttled out from under. The memory of Anastas's conversation with Clyde and Steed raced to the front of his mind. It was Liebowitz who had been responsible for Anastas going to jail. Anastas had walked away empty-handed not because he was stealing car parts; he had been tampering with the car! Pasha shot out of his seat and raced to the door.

"Officer Liebowitz! Wait!"

Lynch ripped his bumbling behind from his chair, knocking it over in the process.

"I knew it!" He barreled after Pasha. "What did I say!"

Pasha flung the door open and ran onto the stoop landing. "Liebowitz!"

Liebowitz was just shutting the car door. He had not heard him. The key was in his hand, moving towards the ignition. Pasha vaulted off the landing as Lynch was reaching for his arm. The hood of the car banged beneath Pasha's body, as he landed splayed out in front of the windshield.

451

The keys flew from Liebowitz's hand, his eyes bulging at the sight of Pasha.

"Don't turn on the car!" Pasha banged his fist on the windshield. "It's been tampered with!"

A tremendous roar echoed off the brick edifice as Lynch seized Pasha by the ankles with incredible force, yanking him from the hood like a magician might pull a tablecloth out from under a table setting.

"Exactly what I said would happen!" No sooner had Pasha hit the pavement than Lynch was dragging him back up by his collar. "You thought you could pull a fast one on me!"

Liebowitz scrambled out of the car. "Hold it! Hold it! Hold it!" He wrenched Pasha out of Lynch's grasp. "What did you say about the car?"

"It's been tampered with! I saw someone getting under the car earlier."

Liebowitz shook his head. "Wait, but how do you know it's been tampered with? How do you know someone didn't just drop something under the car?"

"Because they were on their back with a pair of pliers. They were under there for a while."

"When?"

"While Officer Lynch was eating his lunch."

"Why didn't you say something then?"

Pasha's mouth went dry. He pushed his shoulders up to his ears. "Well, at first I thought he was just stealing car parts …"

Liebowitz balked at him. "And you weren't gonna say anything?"

Pasha opened his mouth to answer but quickly shut it. Lynch's stare hardened, his chin jutted out.

"I'll tell you why he didn't say anything. Because he knows the little sucker who did it. Another Breadwinner, I'd wager."

Liebowitz raised an eyebrow. "What makes you think that?"

"Because he saw him do it, but he didn't say anything until the other fella was gone. Not only that, he admitted he wasn't going to say anything when he thought the culprit was stealing. It wouldn't have been worth the risk. No thug likes a rat. The Breadwinners are no different. Isn't that right, son?"

Pasha swallowed. He could feel his face turning red. He wasn't normally a bad liar, but the threat of being labeled a rat by the Breadwinners was enough to rattle all his biological functions.

"Okay, fine. I do know this kid, and I know he has it out for Liebowitz." He shrugged."That's all I'm gonna say."

He took a step back. So they'd guessed at the truth. As long as they didn't know which Breadwinner it was, there was nothing they could do, and they couldn't force him to tell.

Lynch stared back at him with a hardened grin. "Then you've told us everything we need to know."

***

Liebowitz tossed a wrapped parcel on the desk in front of Pasha. "Here. Eat something."

Pasha peeled back the paper and thanked him, unsure of whether or not he could make himself eat.

The desk creaked as Liebowitz took a seat on the corner. "I'd be surprised if Lynch manages to catch up with Sippenhaft. But he'll have a warrant next time we run into him."

"Do you have to arrest him?" Pasha's voice cracked with desperation. "Can't you just look the other way? Just this once?"

"I can't just not do my job. He cut my brake lines. That's tampering with an auto vehicle. Look, I ordered Lynch not to tell Sippenhaft it was you."

"You really think he's gonna hold to that?"

"He has to." He picked up his own sandwich. "Revealing you as a witness would be a threat to your safety. If he doesn't follow orders then he could lose his job."

"And I could get shot."

"Trust me, it's gonna be fine."

Pasha hunched over his sandwich and sighed. What else could he do? Liebowitz took one look at Pasha's uneaten lunch and covered his full mouth.

"What? You don't like corned beef?"

"It's my favorite actually." He forced himself to take a bite.

Liebowitz laid a hand on Pasha's shoulder. "Hey, you did me a real solid today. You protected me from a dangerous situation. Trust that I'm gonna protect you."

"I've told you before, you can't protect me. Though, I appreciate the effort."

Liebowitz set down his sandwich and stared at Pasha for some time. At length, he dropped down into his chair and scooted closer.

"I know it may not seem like it now, but the Breadwinners won't be around forever. Gangs come and go all the time, even the really big ones." He leaned in closer. "You're gonna do something good with your life, Pasha Chevalsky. I can tell. You're not gonna waste it. You just wait."

Pasha looked at him funny. He didn't know what it was Liebowitz saw in him, but he wished he could see it too.

"Do me a favor." Liebowitz waved his hand. "Don't let these thugs change you. You're too good a kid." He checked the clock on the wall. "Boy, that probation officer of yours sure is taking his sweet time."

Pasha turned so that Liebowitz couldn't see and rolled his eyes. There was no telling what errand Klokov had sent Pasha's "probation officer" on. If only Liebowitz knew the truth. Before turning back around to face Liebowitz, Pasha noticed a bulletin board hanging on the wall behind the desk. Mostly it was covered in memos and newspaper clippings, but tacked in the lower right-hand corner was a missing poster. And this one was new.

Pasha's heart sank. "Another disappearance?"

Liebowitz craned his head around. "You know this kid?" He plucked the poster from the bulletin board and slid it across the desk. Pasha studied the photograph. To his surprise, he had seen the boy throughout the neighborhood off and on for the past four years, though he did not know him personally. He was a bit on the scrawny side, with a pointed chin, and his hair parted in the middle. In fact, it was just last week that Pasha had been standing behind him at the butcher's.

"I've seen him around."

"This just went out this morning. And we had another one two days ago. Myrtle Cullen. Eighteen years old."

Pasha fidgeted with the cuffs of his jacket and stared down at the floor. He wondered how much Liebowitz knew about the Butchers' involvement. There had to be a way to tip him off. Only one problem: Klokov could never find out. Even if it was to take down a common enemy, he was certain Klokov would murder him if he ever found out Pasha had tipped off the cops. And thanks to Anastas's little prank, he was already risking his boss's wrath.

Pasha was just about to open his mouth when behind them the door burst open. Lynch shoved Anastas unceremoniously through the entry, another officer bringing up the rear.

"Go on, you! We know you did it!"

Anastas's face was flushed with rage as he wrenched around and spat at his captors. Of the two, Anastas had always resembled his father, but in that moment he looked just like his mother when she'd tried to bite an officer the night she was arrested.

"Yeah? Where's your proof?"

"I told you, we have a witness!"

"You keep saying that—" Anastas's eyes caught on Pasha sitting at the desk across from Liebowitz. Pasha froze like a rabbit staring into the eyes of a cobra. The muscles in Anastas's face began to tremble and twitch like pebbles at the start of an earthquake. A vein throbbed in his forehead, pumping adrenaline into his countenance like gasoline until his complexion had gone from red to purple. Spit flung from his curling lips as he snarled. "You!"

As he lunged for Pasha, Lynch and the assisting officer seized his arms, dragging him back towards the cell.

Officer Liebowitz rose and stood protectively between them. "Lock him up until he cools down." He acknowledged Anastas with a nod. "Mr. Chevalsky is here on his own charge. He had nothing to do with it."

"Yeah, I'll bet!"

Chapter 51:

A Rat

Klokov's broad hand thrust over Pasha's head as he grabbed the back of his collar and threw him into his office.

"You ratted out another Breadwinner to the cops?"

Pasha straightened his spine only to have Klokov grab him by the scruff of the hair and force him to his knees. His nose met with a pair of dingy work boots, the laces frayed and wet from the street. Anastas loomed over him from the armchair, his eyes biting and poisonous. Pasha put a hand to his temple, feeling suddenly lightheaded. He opened his mouth to defend himself but Klokov cut him off.

"Aside from the police, you were the only other person in the precinct at the time of the incident, so don't tell me it wasn't you!" He must have obtained this information from one of his own cops.

Pasha gaped up at Klokov with helpless eyes. "I couldn't stand by and do nothing!"

A crushing pressure broke across his cheek as Klokov slammed his fist into the side of Pasha's head, knocking him off his knees. His mouth collided with the edge of Klokov's desk before he hit the floor. Blood trickled down from his gums and seeped from between his lips.

"I oughta have you dragged through the street!" Klokov thundered.

Pasha put a hand up to shield himself as he spat blood onto the ground. "A man's life was in danger."

"A cop!"

"Anastas cut his brake lines!"

Klokov seized him by the lapels, dragging Pasha towards his screaming, purple face.

"I don't care what he did!" Spit flew and arched from Klokov's mouth. "You never ever rat out a fellow member! No matter what! Ever!"

Pasha's ears were ringing from the volume. An image of Liebowitz's unit plowing through a fruit stand on Orchard Street floated past his mind. Klokov raised his fist to strike him again.

"I was obligated to do it!" Pasha exclaimed, shielding his face in anticipation of the blow. "As a Breadwinner I was obligated to say something!"

Klokov lowered his fist. For a moment, the maelstrom of god-like fury vanished, allowing room for his profound confusion. Even his voice softened.

"What are you talking about?"

He released his hold on Pasha, allowing him to stand up and make his case.

"Think for a second. The Lower East Side is one of the smallest precincts in the borough. It only covers nine blocks. In those nine blocks are countless Slavs. Orchard Street functions as an open-air market every day. Kids are constantly playing in those streets, my sister included. And Yuri's brothers and sisters, and Franklin's, and Leg Up's, and just about every other Breadwinner's family! Anastas cut the brake lines of Liebowitz's patrol unit. If he had driven that car, there's no way he wouldn't have hit someone! It would be impossible!

"As a Breadwinner, it's my job to protect our community, our people. And Anastas put them in danger. So, yeah, I stopped Liebowitz from driving the car. But it's not like I interrupted Anastas's work for you. Cutting Liebowitz's brake lines had nothing to do with the Breadwinners. It was just a revenge prank. Why do you think he did it in broad daylight? Because he wanted to humiliate the police force. A pretty bold move for someone who's been arrested six times this year. Especially when he should have been using that time to find goods for the Paddock."

By now Klokov's hairless brows had lifted to form a thoughtful knot above his nose. He glanced between them.

"Chevalsky's got a point."

Anastas rose like steam from a pot, his wrath fully present and uncloaked. "Are you serious? Even if all that's true, he still didn't have to say it was me! He didn't have to tell them I did it! All he had to do was tell Liebowitz not to drive! I've had it with you going easy on Chevalsky! We both know he's too soft to be here! He let Yuri win that fight last week, you know he did, and yet you didn't do anything! Yuri gets sent upstate because he didn't shoot some kid, but when Pasha takes a dive to spare his friend you look the other way! Now, he's ratted me out to protect a cop, and you're still letting him off easy!" He waved his hand. "I don't care if you beat me for saying it! Go ahead! I can't stand by and watch any longer!"

Pasha felt his knees start to tremble. He thought he had won with his argument about how Anastas had endangered the community. But if Klokov didn't punish Pasha now, it would look like everything Anastas had said was true.

Chapter 52:

Shards of Glass

Pasha felt the skin on the corner of his brow bone tear as his head slammed against the wall. The muscles in his knees felt like rusty springs as his legs buckled beneath him. He slid to the floor, the surface of the brick scraping his bare back and shoulders. Through bleary eyes he could just make out Klokov's bulky figure barreling towards him like a steam engine. It could have been worse, he assured himself. Klokov could have let Anastas beat him. But he had wanted to see to Pasha's punishment himself.

A record spun and scratched eerily in the distance to muffle any screams. The basement was always like this—or the Crucible, as it had come to be known. It was the place where rule breakers were punished, enemies interrogated, and new blood initiated. Pasha hadn't been here since the final stage of his own initiation four years ago, when Leo had liquored him up in an attempt to dull the sting of the lash. This was a different room with a darker purpose, though a whipping post still stood in the corner.

Thick, cold fingers dug into his skin like the knobby roots of some gnarled tree, as Klokov grabbed him by the jaw and forced his head up to look at him. Pasha pressed his lips tightly together, fearing that a whimper might escape if he didn't. Klokov raked his eye over Pasha's injuries, turning his face this way and that. They'd been at it for some time now. A satisfied growl droned somewhere beneath Klokov's collar.

"That's enough." He released Pasha's jaw and turned to the door.

Pasha scrambled to his knees, struggling to get up as his sore muscles ached. "I can go home now?"

"I meant enough with the beating. We're far from finished." He stuck his head into the hall and barked some order at an underling.

Pasha watched, slumped against the wall, as an older Breadwinner came and dumped a box of broken glass at the base of the whipping post. The shards plinked and rattled against the cement like a wind chime, a sound too sweet for such a horrifying place. Pasha threw Klokov a questioning look as he gestured for him to stand.

"Take off your shoes, socks, and trousers."

Pasha's eyes went blank with confusion. He was already shirtless. Why would Klokov want him stripped down to his underwear? He glanced back at the pile of glass, trying to make sense of it all. Fearful of trying Klokov's patience, he quickly did as told, neatly folding his clothes and setting them aside. The floor was icy against his feet. He stood there shivering in his wool drawers, hugging his bare arms close to his chest. Klokov snapped his fingers in the direction of the whipping post.

"Kneel down."

Pasha's mouth fell open at the command. The glass sparkled like a wicked smile in the dim light.

"I said kneel!"

Klokov pinched him by the scruff of the neck and forced Pasha down. His knees were accosted with the unbearable stinging grate of infinite rough-edged motes biting into his flesh until blood leaked from his skin. The shock of the sadistic burn drove him to cry out in misery, his hands clawing instinctively at the pillar before him to relieve the weight off his knees. Flakes of rust fluttered to the floor as Klokov shut the iron vices over his wrists, locking him into place.

"You're to stay here the rest of the night."

Pasha met his superior's icy glare with dilated eyes and a gaping mouth, his shoulders already trembling from the torment. Would anyone tell his mother where he was? Could he freeze to death naked in this torture chamber? But he was too frightened to ask questions.

Klokov took a step back and shook his head. He had the look of a man being forced to shoot his dog because it had become rabid.

"Rogue's right. I've been too easy on you. You ratted out your brother, and now you have to pay the consequences." He turned to leave.

"Why?" The question flew from Pasha's mouth in a moment of panic. "Why have you gone easy on me?"

Klokov halted in the doorway, and for a moment Pasha was uncertain if he would even answer. In the bottomless silence, Pasha realized the record was still playing. And he wondered how it had yet to come to an end. Before he could ponder on it further, Klokov finally turned to face him.

"Of all the bucks I got working for me you're one of the only ones who truly gets it. I didn't take you in because of your size or strength. Hell, if that were the case I'd never have given you a second glance. It was your principles. Plenty of boys want to protect their mas and put bread on the table. Most men are protective. But you … you're something else. Something more. Selfless. Where others have to strive to let go of their pride, for you it comes naturally. But maybe that's the problem. You're not tough enough. Maybe you can't have it both ways."

And with that, he turned and shut the door, leaving Pasha to freeze in the dark.

Chapter 53:

A Moment of Weakness

The moist, hot breath from Pasha's open mouth warmed a patch of chapped skin on his hand as he drifted in and out of consciousness. His mind waded through shallow dreams, heavy and wretched with despair. Every now and then he would try to bend his fingers, but the joints felt stiff and brittle like a starfish bleached by the sun. The first hour had been the worst, with his body freshly denuded to the cold and the abrasive scourge of the glass against his knees.

Despite his recent efforts to deaden his emotions, the very first thing Pasha did when Klokov shut the door was break down into tears. Shame tore at his insides the way glass was tearing at his legs. It seemed that what came naturally to other men was hopelessly beyond him. And yet if Pasha didn't find a way to access the grit Klokov so valued he would surely be killed.

He was soon grateful for the cold as it helped to numb him from the pain in his legs and feet. When he found he could no longer bear the weight on his knees, he dropped down to his side, exposing parts of his thigh and hip to the spiny particles.

In the beginning, he could still hear a faint anthem of savage applause from upstairs, and the vibrating hum of the bell as the other boys battled for their bread and pay. But after several hours the routine drone grew fainter and thinner as bit by bit the men drifted away, their bellies bubbling with beer, foam clinging to their mustaches like spume on a gnarled sea cliff. And Pasha was left behind with the eerily bright echoes of that infernal record, wondering who was turning it over.

"God …" His prayer bounced off the soft, moldering wood and warmed his nose and mouth. "Please, God … I don't want to be a Breadwinner. I only did this to protect my mother, because I thought it's what my father would have wanted." He stopped as tears leaked from his eyes, the heat sweet on his frozen cheeks. "If I stay here, I will be killed. And maybe I deserve that. I'm a criminal, after all. But my family needs me. Faina needs me. Once you join the Breadwinners you can't leave. There is nowhere I can go, nowhere I can run to. Only you can get me out! Please, God, please! I can't do this anymore! *Vo imya Khristos Iisusa!*"

It was by sheer exhaustion that he fell asleep at all, though it was not a deep sleep, and certainly not a comfortable one. When the door flung open the next morning, the steel hammering the brick with an audible clamor, Pasha scrambled to his knees, terrified for Klokov to catch him leaning on his side where the glass was less painful. Klokov said nothing, but wrenched open the rusty vices. Pasha couldn't help but notice he was wearing gloves, and his thick, fur coat. He didn't have a chance to drag himself out of the refuse. Klokov seized him by the back of the neck, and threw him out of the pile. Pasha was cast to the frozen floor, his arms too weak to catch himself.

"Alright, boy," Klokov shoved him forward with his foot. "Get dressed and get on out of here." His clothes landed in a heap at his elbow. "You're free to go."

Eager for the warm relief of his clothes, Pasha scuttled clumsily on the ground to pull his pants on. He watched Klokov's frame disappear out the door from the corner of his eye. His shadow was still clinging to the threshold when a new figure pushed into the room.

"Pasha!"

Pasha lifted his head and squinted into the stinging light. "Faina?"

Faina flew down to his side, her stockings snagging on the concrete.

"*Blin!*" Her gloved hands climbed up his bare shoulders and cradled his bruised cheeks. "What did they do to you?"

Pasha hesitated, not wishing to upset her with the truth, but it was impossible not to notice the cuts and bruises.

465

"They beat you?" she pressed.

"Klokov did."

Faina's mouth hinged open in horror as she removed her gloves to examine the wounds more closely.

"Does that hurt?" she asked, grazing the inflamed skin on his cheek with her finger.

Pasha winced. "A bit."

Her eyes must have struggled to adjust to the dim light, for she was just now taking in the heavy bruises along his torso. Pasha flinched as her warm hand brushed across the bluish mark marring his chest. It was almost worth the pain to have his skin prickle beneath her touch. She walked her fingers down his ribs, lingering at a tender bruise.

"Your skin is freezing." She slipped her arms around his waist and flattened her palms against his back, rubbing the chill from his body. Pasha could hardly breathe as she pressed her cheek to his sternum, her hair tickling his neck and chin. Without a second thought, he hugged her closer, his arms still weak and trembling. They froze as their eyes briefly met. Faina glanced shyly at the shirt lying on the floor.

"We should probably get you dressed."

Pasha let go, heat rising to his cheeks. "Yeah. I guess so."

He turned away from her, and lifted his undershirt over his head.

"So they just left you in here without a shirt all night?" Before he could answer, she saw the post. "You were chained up?" She rose and approached the pillory.

Pasha winced as glass crunched beneath her shoes.

"What's all this?" She kicked at the bloody shards and looked questioningly at him. She took in his bare feet and unbuttoned pants. There was a sharp intake of breath as her pupils swelled with horror. Pasha said nothing when she laid a hand on his shoulder and lowered herself down beside him. He didn't stop her when she rolled up his pant leg and saw his skin. She put a hand to her lips.

"*Patulya …*"

He pulled away as she ran a finger across the cuts. "It stings."

She nodded, continuing to stare. "I bet it does."

Pasha fumbled with the buttons of his shirt, wincing at the pain in his wrists, which were stained brown from the rust.

"What is it?"

Pasha massaged his forearm. "Just sore from being strapped to the pillar."

"I bet some camphor would help that." She reached for the unfinished buttons of his shirt. "Let me help."

Too fatigued to protest, Pasha allowed her to finish. Her hands tenderly smoothed his collar.

"Let's get you home, *Pavlushka*."

They made their way upstairs, Faina never letting go of his hand. With every bend of his knees, the open cuts sizzled and seared like hot slag stuck in his flesh. When Faina held the door open, Pasha winced in anticipation of the brightness, but it appeared the sun had yet to finish its climb into the sky. The clouds were red and raw as though they had been scrubbed with a brush, inflamed with a glowing, scarlet nimbus. Pasha checked his watch. It was only six thirty in the morning.

"How did you know to come get me?" he asked.

"When you didn't return home I went down to the Foxhole to find out if you were still at the police station. Moneyrider told me you had gotten in trouble, and that Klokov was having you stay in the Crucible overnight. I told your mother you wouldn't be home until morning." She led him onto the sidewalk.

"Did you tell her why?"

She shook her head. "I didn't think you'd want me to."

467

Halfway up Delancey, Pasha spotted a uniformed Liebowitz emerging from a bakery, a cup of coffee steaming in his gloved hand. At the sight of Pasha, Liebowitz did a double-take, surprised to see him out so early in the morning.

"Hey, kid!" He stretched his arm over his head to wave, but the moment Pasha looked up, Liebowitz's friendly smile slid from his mouth like rain on a tarp. They slowed to a stop, Faina shifting uncomfortably between them. Pasha could barely hold his head up. Liebowitz's shock was cold and fresh like a bucket of ice water on his already frozen skin, and Pasha could hardly bear the chill.

"Kid, what …" his voice trailed off. And then it hit him. Pity and regret gushed into his countenance like water through cracked stone. His lips faltered for some comforting word, some promise of safety. But Pasha knew there was nothing he could give, nothing he could say to change his circumstances.

Hopeless and ashamed, Pasha hid his face and hurried away, towing Faina alongside him.

"Why did they do this to you?" Faina asked when they reached the tenement building.

Pasha closed his eyes and took a deep breath.

"We don't have to talk about it now." She opened the front door. "You can tell me after we've cleaned you up."

Once they were inside Pasha's tenement, Faina had him take a shower to remove any stray bits of glass and prevent any infection. She had already sent Katya downstairs to keep Uncle Matvei company, sheltering her from everything Pasha had been through. When he finished his shower, he put on his baggiest pair of pajama pants and his favorite sweater, and returned to his bedroom. Faina was waiting for him with a magnifying glass and a pair of tweezers.

"Lay down, toots."

Pasha took one look at the tweezers and groaned, but did as told.

"We don't want any shards left in your skin." She gestured to his left. "Food's on the nightstand."

Pasha sat up and turned. There, on the table, was a plate of eggs and toast along with an entire mug of coffee. He hadn't even noticed the smell of breakfast cooking.

"You need to eat." She pushed his pant leg above his knee.

"Thank you, *Fay*—Ah!" Pasha threw his head back and winced.

Faina held up a large splinter of glass with the tweezers. "Did you know this was in your foot?"

Pasha's eyes bulged. "That thing was in my foot?"

"You didn't feel it? It wasn't hurting?"

"Everything is hurting."

Faina shook her head and held the magnifying glass over his ankle. "This may take a while."

Pasha covered his eyes, and flopped back down on the mattress.

It took an entire hour to remove all the remaining glass from his legs and sides, and when it was all over Pasha lay there completely exhausted.

"Let's take care of your wrists," said Faina, rummaging through the first-aid kit. "You're almost out of bandages, by the way." She uncorked a bottle of camphor.

"Doesn't surprise me."

Terpenoids shone on her palms as she gently lifted his arm. The tips of her fingers sank into his flesh and eased down the length of his forearm. Pasha's chest deflated with a sigh, savoring the gentle relief. She paused and met his gaze from beneath her lashes.

"Is it helping?"

Pasha nodded with a feeble smirk, and watched her rake her fingers down his right arm, resisting the urge to pine over her.

"You never said why they did this to you."

Pasha let his head fall to the side, pausing to consider his explanation. "It doesn't matter what I did."

Faina ceased massaging his arms and flashed him a look. "Just tell me."

But Pasha remained silent and stared at his knees.

"Was it because you got arrested?"

When he still didn't answer, she let his hand drop to his lap, and rose to return the camphor to the box.

"It has nothing to do with you, Faina. I just … I don't wanna talk about it."

"Don't want to, or are afraid to?"

He dared to look at her, then quickly swallowed, shutting his eyes against the pain of keeping it all in. But it wasn't going to stay down. His heart seemed to push the words up into his mouth until his throat felt heavy and swollen from fighting it. Tears sprang from his eyes. His hardened expression melted and drained like a spirit flushed away with holy water, and his eyes became soft and sweet once more. He crumpled forward into his hands, as though to physically push back the tears. Faina's hand lighted on his back like a dove. Pasha reached his arms out and hugged her waist, burying his face in her abdomen like a frightened child.

"I can't do it anymore, Faina! I can't!"

Faina stroked the back of his head and held him close. "Tell me what happened, love."

"But I can't! That's the problem! Don't you see? I have to do this on my own, Faina! A real man would do this on his own. He wouldn't go crying to his former girlfriend!"

Faina stiffened. Her fingers slowed. The words tasted vinegary and toxic in his mouth. Pasha swallowed, regretting having referred to her as his former girlfriend. When she spoke again, her voice was soft.

"Well, you know my thoughts on that sentiment."

"I have to change or they're gonna kill me!"

Even in sorrow the passion in her eyes burned like young stars, fueled by a sad longing to comfort him and to love him. And Pasha wanted so badly to let her.

"Keeping everything bottled up will also kill you." She dropped her arms and sat down beside him. "And so will isolating yourself from everyone you love."

Pasha sighed and shut his eyes. His nerves warmed as her fingers traced a faint line from his temple to his jaw.

"It wasn't long ago that you pulled me out of a dark place."

He opened his eyes. She was inches from his face.

"Let me do the same for you." She pressed her palm into his, winding their fingers together. "Let me love you." She brought his hand to her lips, kissing his knuckles. "I can make you feel better if you just let me in. Talk to me. You need me. I need you. We need each other." Though the sensation was somewhat dulled due to his condition, the image of her brushing her lips against his skin was more than he could bear. It pained him to pull his hand away.

"Faina, we can't." He bit his lip, reconsidering Trifecta's advice. Faina had said it herself. As long as she knew Pasha still loved her, she would never stop trying. Pasha swallowed.

"Maybe—maybe I don't feel the way you think." He couldn't bring himself to say the actual words, even if it was for her own good.

Faina stiffened. Pasha knew it sounded silly, but even her freckles appeared to sharpen at the edges. "What do you mean?"

471

"Just … maybe … I've been doing some thinking …" He trailed off, unable to say more.

Faina did not soften, and yet there was something tender and sacred in her hardness. And then Pasha realized it wasn't hostility steeling her eyes, it was her passion, her relentless devotion to him.

She brought her face close to his. "Say you don't love me, I dare you."

Pasha hesitated. He'd tried his best to cut away all his ties, pruning each and every presence from his existence in a desperate attempt to survive. But Faina was the vine that refused to let go. She had anchored her stem into the bedrock on which he stood, tangling her roots with his until they grew as one. Faina would stand by him even when there was no ground to stand upon. And he loved her for it. He loved her relentless love.

He opened his mouth, but could only sigh.

"Say it." She swayed against him, brushing her nose against his cheek. Her breath warmed his skin.

"I—can't." Pasha wove his arms around her waist, dragging her against him, and pressing his mouth to hers. Like two magnets finally coming together, the tension, the aching pull of their attraction was alleviated upon contact.

"I love you," she breathed into his ear.

Pasha rubbed the space between her shoulder blades. "I love you, *Faya*." As their lips touched once more, Pasha's conscience was struck with a wave of guilt. He pulled away. "What am I doing?"

She kissed him again, as though trying to silence the inevitable, but Pasha cupped her cheeks and held her at length.

"Faina, we can't! I shouldn't be doing this! I shouldn't have kissed you!"

"*Nyet*, don't say that!" She traced his cheek with her fingers and forced a lighthearted smile. "Someone's gotta kiss those bruises!"

"Faina—"

"You can't do this on your own, you know you can't!" He felt her frame crumpling against his. "Pasha, don't do this to me again! I can't take it!"

Pasha stroked her hair. "Faina, listen. As long as I'm a Breadwinner we can't be together. But there's something I need you to understand. I love you! I might not be able to kiss you, or hold you, or take you out on dates, but I love you so much it hurts. And that's gonna have to be enough. Unless by some miracle Klokov lets me go, that's all I can give you."

Faina's lip trembled. "But you need me!"

Pasha squeezed her hand and held it to his chest. "I do need you."

"You need someone to hold you, to support you, to love you. Don't you feel better now that we're together?"

"I do feel better, *Radnaya*. I'm not asking you to not be a part of my life. I'm asking you to be a part of my life in a way that's gonna keep you safe. And I need you to accept that."

Faina stared at him for a long time, her cheeks wet with tears. "I understand." She sat up and sniffed. "You'll find a way out someday. I know it. And when you do, I'll be waiting."

Chapter 54:

A Russian Lullaby

When the day came for Faina to perform at the Foxhole, three months had passed since the incident with the photograph. Things had improved somewhat. No one shouted names at her in the street anymore, but her reputation on the whole had been destroyed. She couldn't work in the storefront, and could hardly run errands for Uncle Matvei, as some of their neighbors refused to acknowledge her.

In the meantime, she received plenty of help constructing her routine not only from Uncle Matvei, but from Mama Lydia, and the outspoken Aunt Poppy. Day after day, she had practiced and rehearsed before the looking glass until it felt as though the routine had become embedded in her bones.

As for the beautiful, pearl-colored dress, the wine stain could unfortunately not be removed. Ever Faina's fairy-godmother, Aunt Poppy had paid to have the dress dyed. Now, instead of a vernal alabaster, the gown was the spellbinding shade of the witching hour: a sophisticated midnight blue, no longer shimmering with subtle shades of lavender and blush, but rippling with faint traces of smoky silver and elegant indigo.

Though visually striking, the color was no longer what gave the dress its magic. No, it was the sterling-hued constellations Aunt Poppy had embroidered into the fabric. The vast entirety of the ecliptic band girded her waist, from the horns of Aries to the cord of Pisces. The belt of Orion, the seven stars of the Pleiades, the scales of Libra, were all stitched into her skirt in shining calligraphy.

Inspired by the story her mother had told her as a girl, Aunt Poppy had then taken her jar of "dreams" and braided them into Faina's abundance of dense, black hair. A host of silver flickered in the swirling twists of raven helixes and blue-black parabolas of her waves. At first glimpse, one could have easily mistaken her hair for a veil of sky, a chunk of firmament chiseled from the stratosphere, streaked with a shower of sparkling meteors.

When Faina first saw her reflection, she was all at once struck with a disoriented revelation. It was as though she had been reaching for the shoulder of an old friend in a busy crowd, only to see them turn and realize she had mistaken them for someone else. She took in her appearance, dissecting her image piece by piece. Her skin remained youthful, her cheeks were still full, her freckles as constant as the stars. She couldn't quite put her finger on it, but something about her had aged.

And then she saw it … or maybe she felt it. It was so subtle she wasn't quite sure. Buried in her eyes were truths she hadn't been ready to know. Wisdom she wasn't ready to confront but had been forced to learn. And for a brief moment she was tempted to grieve. But then she remembered Aunt Poppy's story. The girl in the white dress hadn't vanished, merely transformed. Transformed into a young woman swathed in silver asterisms. True, she had known more sorrow, but she was stronger than before.

Rather than change behind the curtain again, Faina entered the restaurant in full regalia.

The doors were held aloft and a spotlight wandered down the aisles of tables and patrons until it found her silhouette. Faina felt her nerves simmering at the bottom of her stomach but she hid them beneath her most dazzling smile. With every step she radiated a dignity so graceful not a single harsh stare could extinguish it. Class dripped from her bearing like a string of pearls.

She soared above the whispers and made her way to the stage while the audience applauded.

"Thank you," she said into the microphone.

The lights were hot and warm, but she could see Anya and Pasha at the table directly in front of her, dressed with encouraging smiles. Anya may have sworn off Breadwinners, but she wasn't above popping into the restaurant now and again, especially to support her cousin. If Faina squinted she could just make out Mama Lydia and Uncle Matvei standing against the wall in back. Uncle Matvei kept his fingers steepled over his lips as though trying to hold in all his emotions. She had entered a world of white tablecloths and piano keys, of silver microphones and smoky vocals. She savored the way the stage creaked beneath her feet, and the hot smell of the spotlight. Even the blinding spots of color invading her vision were cherished.

"I can't begin to tell you how happy I am to be here tonight. Of course, I'm here a lot these days. But if you haven't seen me, I'm sure many of you have seen my picture up around town."

The drummer played a percussive sting. A few members of the audience gave an awkward chuckle, but otherwise did not appear to know how to react. Faina swallowed and pasted on a comedic grin.

"Show us your bubs!" shouted Stan from a table in the back.

"Shut your mouth, Stan," snapped Sergei.

Faina waved her hands as though it were nothing. "Eh, that's old news. Hey, I got a better idea! Why don't you come up here and show us yours?" She stepped aside as though making room for him. "What do you folks think? Who wants to see Stan get up here and bare it all? Clap your hands!"

The audience hooted and hollered with laughter, supplying a hearty round of applause while the band played a slinky jazz tune fit for a striptease. Faina beckoned him forward.

"Look out Josephine Baker, Stan the Man's about to show us the goods!"

Angry and embarrassed, Stan got up and left with a nasty scowl. The audience gave a disappointed "aww."

"Ah, well." Faina threw up her shoulders. "Guess he's a little shy, folks. Not everyone has what it takes to flash their goods to all of lower Manhattan. But I can tell you from experience, it takes a little something extra. To put it plainly, it takes a couple of morons with a Kodak."

Several of the girls burst out with laughter.

"If you ask my uncle, he'll tell you I was the victim of an elaborate conspiracy!" She snorted. "Apparently, it takes brains to be a peeping tom!"

She went on for some time, and soon the audience began to warm up to her jokes about what had taken place. What's more, they seemed to thoroughly enjoy her comedy.

"I'd like to sing you one of my favorite songs, and I wouldn't be surprised if a few of you recognized it. It's by one of my favorite composers, Irving Berlin. Like most everyone here tonight, I wasn't born in this country. I was born in Russia, and I came to America with my brother after our parents were shot and killed by the Bolsheviks. We were no longer safe in our own home. We were forced to leave our country, the place we were born, by an oppressive government. There are many still who wish they could leave Russia. Many who are desperate to escape its reach." She paused. Her gaze swept out over the audience. "So I'm dedicating my song to them."

The lights dimmed gradually. Faina cleared her throat and waited for the music to begin.

"Where the dreamy Volga flows
There's a lonely Russian rose
Gazing tenderly
Down upon her knee
Where a baby's brown eyes glisten

Listen ..."

The room was absolutely silent. Amused smiles faded into pensive stares. Faina could feel a sort of euphoria building in her chest as each note unfolded with dreamy ambience.

"Every night you'll hear her croon
A Russian lullaby
Just a little plaintive tune
When baby starts to cry
Rock-a-bye my baby
Somewhere there may be
A land that's free for you and me
And a Russian lullaby."

By the time she had finished, her knees were shaking from the exhilaration. People rose from their seats to applaud her. Her friends cheered and whistled. Pasha and Anya, who had brought a bouquet of flowers, took turns throwing roses at her feet. At the back of the room, Uncle Matvei had tears in his eyes. Faina had never seen him looking at her with such pride.

***

When the show was over, Faina changed back into her street clothes and headed downstairs to meet up with her family outside. To avoid the cold as much as possible, she took the back exit that led out to the garage. A large male figure was leaned up against the outside wall of the loading bay.

He turned his head. Their eyes met. It was Anastas.

"Well, if it isn't the Sheba herself." He threw back his head and exhaled a smoky cloud. "I'd beat it if I were you. I ain't exactly the type you wanna run into in an empty loading bay at night." He flashed her a cruel grin. "But you already know that, don't you?"

Rather than run, or tremble, or gasp, Faina stared dully back at him.

"I'm not afraid of you, Anastas."

"No?" He strode towards her with slow, predatory movements, until at last they were standing toe to toe. "You should be." He blew a puff of smoke in her face.

Faina coughed and waved it away, unimpressed. "You gonna do something?"

"Maybe."

"Then go ahead, try it, I dare you."

He stood there rocking back on his heels, sizing her up.

"I'm not running," she added. "Now's your chance."

The first traces of vulnerability were materializing in his demeanor like faint blue stars in the summer twilight. He took out his cigarette and spat.

"It ain't like you think, you know. There's too much going on. No one will be able to hear you calling for help. And it will be my word against yours."

"Then do it."

Anastas lowered his head with a scowl. He was a mad dog on a chain, snapping and snarling, but completely powerless. She shook her head.

"It must eat you up inside."

"What?"

"That you have no control over me. You have gone out of your way to destroy me. You have lied to me, manipulated me, violated me, and hurt me. But that's all over now, because I realize just how small you are. You're dying for power because you know you're weak. You are so desperate for attention that you have to trick and manipulate people to get it. In the end, you're just a noise. So go ahead. Try to hurt me. Try to scare me. It won't work anymore."

She pushed past him with proud, angry steps, leaving him to stand and stare after her, a powerless expression on his face.

Epilogue

Sleep often came to Staccato when he was least prepared for it. As Pyro had once pointed out, he had a way of constantly fluctuating between insomnia and narcolepsy. So much so that when his lack of sleep finally did catch up with him, he was borderline comatose. And that is precisely how he came to be lying undisturbed in the loft of the caravan at present, still clutching the documents approving his grandson's admission into Voiler.

With so little time left before their departure to New York, Staccato had striven to make sure everything was in order for Pasha's return. It had taken nearly nine months to prove his grandson's Voilerian roots to the V.I.P.A., but somehow he had managed to pull it off. Meanwhile, the company had stayed in Aquarius, arranging a new circus routine to perform in Grand Central Station.

The plan was far from simple. To hear Sonata tell it, Staccato was making things unnecessarily complicated. Prior to their meeting, Staccato would plant dreams in Pasha's head about his heritage. He would send him visions of things he couldn't explain, so that when they finally did meet, Pasha would be open-minded about the existence of magic. Sonata was not in the least bit pleased by the idea, calling it manipulative, conniving, and scheming, and would have much preferred for Staccato to go to Lydia first and tell her he was alive.

The caravan was completely quiet save for the wind groaning against the exterior. It had taken only moments after shutting his eyes for Staccato to begin dreaming.

The pavement was wet and moldering beneath his feet, and the light was so dim he could scarcely see the outline of his hand. He appeared to be in some sort of tunnel. He took a step forward. Water splashed the toes of his shoes. A familiar voice, faint and feminine, danced down the ribs of the passage.

"Pasha … Pasha?"

It sounded like Matvei's niece. Staccato continued forward, straining to see through the heavy shadows.

"I have nothing," said the voice of Pasha. "*Nichono*, nothing! He's gonna flog me!"

"Pasha!" At the sound of his grandson's declaration, Staccato could not help but cry out, and ran blindly into the nothingness. A seam of light appeared suddenly, revealing the top steps of a rusty staircase. This was a subway tunnel. He could just barely make out the figures of Pasha and Faina huddled on the floor.

"Did you hear that?"

Staccato froze and took a step back. They were staring in his direction. He had yet to recall he was in a prophetic dream when suddenly a blazing fireball fizzled down the length of the subway tunnel, briefly illuminating the graffitied stone walls, and blasting Staccato with a breeze so hot it made him wince. It tore up the stairs and out into the city, Pasha and Faina following after.

Staccato raced up the stairs just in time to see the legendary Firebird circling around the pair, jewels spitting from her fiery stream like embers from a bonfire. With a trill whistle she spiraled back into the sky, shrinking until she had disappeared amongst the stars.

***

Staccato's eyes snapped open, and he was once again staring at the ceiling of the caravan.

"Pasha's the other competitor!"

The End

Keep reading for a preview of The Acolyte!

Outside, the morning air was fresh and invigorating. The strange lights had gradually faded from the foliage, but one or two had stuck around for a late evening, and were winking dreamily. The woods glimmered with romantic solitude. Unable to resist, Pasha hurried out of the tent. The pegasi were enjoying an extended breakfast of ripe, dewy clover and didn't bother to lift their noses when they heard Pasha approaching.

Pasha ran a hand from the tip of Harpagos's crest to the broad place between his shoulder blades.

"Hey, buddy," he whispered, "what would you say to an early morning ride, huh?"

Harpagos shivered his silvery head and, snorting, took a step or two forward to get at some especially good-looking bluegrass. Pasha hesitated for a moment, then stroked along Harpagos's slate-colored mane.

"Aw, come on, Harpagos, can't you snack later? The grass will still be here when we get back."

Harpagos threw a hasty look at the other pegasi, some of which were very large, and walked away with his snout still pinned to the earth. Pasha rolled his eyes and let his hands drop down by his sides.

"Alright then, fine." He gave a short whistle. "Come on, Mammoth."

Mammoth bounded across the stream in three strides, and together they made off down the path. With the lavender fog hanging about the trees it looked as though the dawn were leaking from a hole in the sky and flooding the earth. As Pasha mounted a tall rock overlooking the hillside he let out a long exhale just for the satisfaction of watching his breath cloud at the end of his nose.

They hadn't gone very far when Pasha's hands began to sting with cold. He glanced back at the mounting sun spinning onto the horizon.

Specks of pollen floated amongst the platinum rays of light pooling through the trees. He thrust his hands into the sunlight, but no warmth penetrated his skin. It was as though the light were an illusion. He shrugged it off. Perhaps it was colder than he'd realized. Shoving his hands in his pockets, he made his way uphill.

As the land began to level, Pasha came upon a twisted live oak. He stopped and gazed up at the labyrinth of convoluted branches. Suddenly his fingers were longing for the feel of rough, scratchy bark. His arms wanted to stretch, his legs wanted to push. It'd been so long since he'd done something as simple as climb a tree. He grabbed a hold of the lower branch and swung himself into the leaves. Below him, Mammoth barked and scratched at the trunk.

"Stay, Mammoth. I'll be down in a minute."

Hoisting himself onto his feet, Pasha reached for the next branch, and the next branch, until finally he was twenty-five feet from the ground. He sighed and straddled a sturdy limb. He leaned back against the tree and surveyed the woodland scenery.

From his vantage point he could see down into the clearing where the tents were set up. As far as he could tell everyone was still asleep, or at least inside their tents. The horses were still grazing, and the sun continued to rise. Further off was Alfbern Hall, and the Sea of Karkinos, and all the way out into the offing was Alveare.

Once he'd had his fill, he turned northwards to everything that lay ahead. Suddenly Pasha's eyes widened. He was surprised he hadn't noticed it before. Beyond the tree was a beautiful meadow with more flowers than he could name. As the breeze wound its way through the thicket, Pasha was overcome with the fragrance of honey and lavender. He scooted closer, eager for a better look. Just as he was bending forward, something white and pearly glimmered through the heather. Pasha's heart stopped. It was a unicorn.

Slowly, she brought her head up. The sun shimmered down the whorl of her horn. She saw Pasha in the tree, and blinked her enormous sapphire eyes. Pasha wasn't sure how to react. He decided it was best to keep still. But the unicorn pawed the ground and gamboled about jovially. She rolled through the flowers. She skipped. She whinnied. Every now and then she looked back at Pasha to see if he was watching. It seemed as though she wanted to play. When Pasha was a young boy his mother used to tell him stories about the unicorns in Lake Baikal. They were friendly, affectionate creatures, and the young were quite outgoing. He decided he would try to approach her.

Pasha was down the tree in a matter of minutes. As soon as his feet hit the ground, Mammoth was trotting around him and whimpering.

"Shhh, Mammoth!" He drew near to the blackthorn hedge dividing him from the meadow. "You don't want to scare her away."

She was closer now, only a few yards away. At the sight of Pasha drawing closer, she threw her head back and nickered. Pasha chuckled and waded through the blackthorn. The unicorn whipped her tail and whinnied.

Pasha didn't realize it, but he was running towards her now, the wind combing his hair back. Briars tore at his clothes. Thorns hooked into his hands and neck, wrenching long, bloody scratches into his flesh, but he never felt them. He was so eager to reach her he wasn't paying attention to his surroundings, and the next thing he knew his shoe shoved up under a root. Pasha sailed forward in a long, sickening arc, landing on his face.

The ground felt parched and frigid beneath him. Dust filled his nostrils and seeped into the stinging cuts where the shrubbery had scratched him. Pasha looked down at his hands and was shocked to see blood dripping down between his fingers. He had run straight through the blackthorn, but he'd never felt a thing.

He lifted his head up. Stone pillars blanketed in moss surrounded him on all sides. His fingers brushed across a relief of serpentine patterns

485

carved into the ground. He was laying in the middle of an old ruin. The unicorn was gone, or more likely, had never been there. He scrambled to an upright position. Dried blood stained the broken flagstones. It was far from fresh, but Pasha could smell the iron.

The bushes rumbled behind him. Mammoth came crashing through the brush. His ears lay back on his head as he sniffed the ground, and nudged Pasha in the opposite direction. But Pasha didn't move.

"Hang on, Mammoth."

He took a couple of steps forward. Dry foliage crunched beneath his boots. Outside the ruins, the fallen leaves littering the path still had color to them, but here they were ashen and brown, as though they had died a long time ago. Frost clung to the stones like the dew of a cold sweat. Pasha shivered and turned around. What he saw made him draw back in horror. Where moments ago stood nothing, a life-sized monument appeared. It was a statue of a man with the head and horns of a bull. Pasha's breath caught in his throat. He began to pant. Mammoth was outright barking now, jumping in place, and snarling at the statue. Pasha licked his chapped lips.

"Something tells me this is the altar no one's been able to find."

He wanted to leave, wanted to run far away. But if this really was the altar they'd been looking for, then he needed to investigate. He drew closer to the statue. The iron exterior had rusted considerably, and the smell of tarnish was nearly as strong as the blood. The idol's arms were bent at the elbow and thrust forward, almost as though he were expecting to have something laid in his arms. Pasha's heart was racing now. It was important that he remember the location of the altar and be able to describe it when he returned to camp, but he could hardly bear to linger a second longer.

He fumbled backwards, but the ground seemed to have disappeared beneath him. Before he knew it he was falling down a flight of stone steps. His head struck the floor. A flood of foul-smelling damp seeped towards the back of his scalp as he rolled over and realized he was lying in a pile of moist, rotting leaves. He groaned and rubbed the back of his head. Above him, Mammoth was trying desperately to claw his way inside, but the hole was narrow and Mammoth was enormous.

As Pasha was about to get up, there came an odd sliding sound of twigs snapping, and dead fronds flattening beneath the drag of long, heavy muscle. Four shrewd eyes the color of sapphires slithered towards him in the darkness. A shimmering onyx serpent with two diamond-shaped heads passed out of the shadow, staring at Pasha and sizing him up.

Pasha instinctively edged backwards. It was hardly a large snake, being only a little over two feet. But the moment Pasha met eyes with the serpent he could think of only one word to describe it: demonic. At the sight of the creature, Mammoth snapped and growled.

The snake tensed, and reared into the air. The two necks stretched outwards in a broad mantle. The lips butterflied and flared, exposing inky black gums. The venom-coated fangs were like opal scimitars, waxing orange and lavender when they caught the light. The crescent-shaped sheaths were fat, veiny, and wet. The slick blue tongues were like separate creatures in a burrow, projecting from a curved tube in the bottom of the mouth.

The creature slid in front of the stairs, cutting Pasha off from the exit. He glanced over his shoulder. The space behind him was closed off by a heavy wooden door.

Pasha jumped to his feet. He inched towards the entrance, thinking if he moved away the snake would feel less threatened. Maybe it would crawl back to wherever it'd come from. Instead it followed him, cutting a winding path through the slime. Pasha pressed down on the handle and flew inside, slamming the door behind him.

The light was completely gone now. So overwhelming was the darkness that Pasha felt he could've bounced a ball off of it. Anything could've lurked in the nothingness, maybe even more snakes. He couldn't stay here long. He stepped forward. Something hard and calcified crunched beneath him. He narrowed his eyes, trying to make out the shapes in the dark, but it was impossible.

Something slipped against his boots. He could hear the debris shifting. He dodged away. The snake was slipping itself under the crack of the door. Pasha scuffled blindly through the room. A stray object caught around his leg, and he pitched forward. His hands groped the air and happened to latch around a rusty lever. Orange light blistered his eyes as a fire sprang up in front of him, chasing away the darkness.

As Pasha's eyes adjusted and absorbed his new surroundings, his heart sank. Now he knew what he had stepped on. Animal bones littered the ground, festering with pulpy, yellowing mold. Pasha's stomach twisted. He slammed a hand over his mouth as tears leaked from the corners of his eyes. That was when four blades enclosed around his calf like a bear trap. The serpent had struck. Pasha whipped his leg forward, throwing off the snake. It soared into the air and ricocheted off the opposite wall. Pasha crumpled forward and ground his teeth together. His veins were throbbing. It felt as though the tendons in his legs had been severed. He was struggling to stay upright.

Much to his surprise the snake bounced back almost immediately. It swiveled towards him with such speed it looked as though it were swimming. Thick, sour-smelling liquid sapped from its fangs in fat, inky drops. Its tail snapped like the tapering black wick of a candle. Pasha's eyes darted across the floor in search of a weapon. He zoned in on an old spear hanging above an archway. Pasha tore the javelin from its brackets and jammed it warningly towards the serpent. It arched its head back with an electrified hiss.

The pike felt cold and stiff in his hands. He limped backwards, still pointing it at the beast.

"Staccato," he hollered. "Pyro! Javaid! Help! Please!"

The muscles in his fingers grew airy and cold. The serpent lowered its heads and propelled itself towards Pasha in a heedful drag. Pasha backed up against the door. They locked eyes. His breath felt frosted and heavy on his upper lip. He watched the sinews contract in the serpent's abdomen. It coiled back. Pasha filled his lungs with moldy, humid oxygen. As the snake sprang into the air Pasha lifted his arm and swept the spear in a perfect arc. He expected the blow to force the snake across the room like a baseball bat. Much to his surprise the two heads severed from the body. In midair the detached skulls threw open their mouths and clamped down on Pasha's opposite wrist.

Pasha cried out in pain. The lance fell from his grasp as the fangs drove into the tender flesh. Pasha contorted into himself. He slammed against the door. The barrier gave way, and he tumbled to the ground.

"Help," he shouted until the inside of his throat felt scratched. The teeth were still embedded in his skin. He would have to pry them off. But when he reached for the heads, they were still blinking. Adrenaline washed through his chest in a cold rinse. His arm reflexed and beat against the ground in a panic to throw them off. The two sets of eyes narrowed into spiteful slits as the heads bit down harder. Pasha's lungs forced a hoarse cry of distress through his windpipe. His right hand clawed around the snake heads as he ripped the teeth from his veins and flung them into the wall.

With one hand he dragged himself up the stairs. Clumps of rancid, pithy dirt fell upon the stairwell as Mammoth continued to try and force his way in. Between growls, he whimpered. Pasha's elbows twitched as he fought to pull himself along. But his strength was gone. He could see the tips of his fingers fading to gray. Defeated, he rolled onto his back and stared up at Mammoth with tired, unfocused eyes. He couldn't fight anymore. This was it. He was going to die.

Want more content from The Breadwinner Series? Head to <u>morgantrueblum.com</u> for illustration galleries, deleted chapters, concept art, and more!